DOPE

Rita Irvin is in a panic. She must see Kazmah immediately! She's become hooked on the drugs that Kazmah supplies, and frantically enlists the aid of her old friend Sir Lucien to secure an appointment. But the meeting does not go well. There is a murder… a kidnapping… and now Chief Inspector Red Kerry is involved. But what can he do? There is a body, but no clues. Kazmah's house has been picked clean. Rita's husband is beside himself—Rita has completely disappeared. And as each hour, each day, goes by, Kerry begins to lose hope that they will find her alive, if at all. For behind Kazmah lurks the devious opium merchant Sin Sin Wa and his cunning wife, Mrs. Sin, who stop at nothing to hide their tracks!

YELLOW SHADOWS

Bernard Hope is returning to London by train when a frantic young woman boards at a stop and asks for his aid. He gives her his ticket and watches her quickly depart. But when he tries to depart the station himself, the police stop him. There has been a murder in Chinatown. Burma Chang, a very important man in the area, has been found dead in his home. And Hope can't account for himself! Then Superintendent Red Kerry gets involved, and discovers a larger mystery than that of the hapless Hope. Chang has been cleverly poisoned in a house full of secret passageways. And it begins to look like Hope's girlfriend Yvette is involved. What was Yvette doing at Burma Chang's … and who was the mysterious woman on the train?

DOPE
— — —
YELLOW SHADOWS

SAX ROHMER

INTRODUCTION BY
WILLIAM PATRICK MAYNARD

Stark House Press • Eureka California

DOPE / YELLOW SHADOWS

Published by Stark House Press
1315 H Street
Eureka, CA 95501, USA
griffinskye3@sbcglobal.net
www.starkhousepress.com

DOPE
First published in hardback by Robert M. McBride & Co., New
York, and Cassell, London, copyright © 1919.

YELLOW SHADOWS
First published in hardback by Doubleday, Doran & Company,
New York, copyright © 1926. and Cassell, London, copyright ©
1925.

"Ripped from the Pages of the Yellow Press" copyright © 2025 by
William Patrick Maynard

All rights reserved under International and Pan-American
Copyright Conventions. Copyright © 2025 Stark House Press.

ISBN: 979-8-88601-155-5

Book and cover design by Mark Shepard, shepgraphics.com.

PUBLISHER'S NOTE:
This is a work of fiction. Names, characters, places and incidents
are either the products of the author's imagination or used
fictionally, and any resemblance to actual persons, living or dead,
events or locales, is entirely coincidental.
Without limiting the rights under copyright reserved above, no
part of this publication may be reproduced, stored, or introduced
into a retrieval system or transmitted in any form or by any
means (electronic, mechanical, photocopying, recording or
otherwise) without the prior written permission of both the
copyright owner and the above publisher of the book.

First Stark House Press Edition: July 2025

TABLE OF CONTENTS

INTRODUCTION: RIPPED FROM THE PAGES OF THE YELLOW PRESS

by William Patrick Maynard

British author Arthur Henry Ward found fame over a century ago, under the exotic pseudonym of Sax Rohmer, by chronicling the exploits of the diabolical Dr. Fu-Manchu, the "Yellow Peril" incarnate in one man. Early on, Rohmer strayed from his winning formula with a more realistic Limehouse crime thriller, *The Yellow Claw* (1915). The resulting novel was an international bestseller. Rohmer quickly sold movie rights to the book that, in 1920, became the first of his works to reach the silver screen.

However, the public's fascination with his weird thrillers had not abated. Rohmer was happy enough to continue the Devil Doctor's exploits so long as the public was buying, but he also broadened his portfolio by introducing multiple series concerning an English consulting detective (Paul Harley), a dapper French detective (Gaston Max), an unsettling occult detective (Morris Klaw), and a hardboiled Irish detective who investigates crime in Limehouse.

Rohmer turned for inspiration to the recently retired Inspector Yeo of the C.I.D.'s K. Division (Limehouse). Inspector Yeo had proved an invaluable contact for the young author to have made in the early days of his writing career. Years later, Rohmer alleged it was through Inspector Yeo that he caught a fleeting glimpse of the Chinese crime lord who controlled Limehouse gambling, prostitution, and drug trade. Rohmer alleged it was this shadowy figure who inspired so much of his bestselling fiction. It is impossible to determine how much of Rohmer's accounts were real since he was fond of spinning yarns to gullible reporters as a means of promoting his latest work. Rohmer played fast and loose with dates, combining incidents that occurred nearly a decade apart, if it suited whatever narrative he wanted the public to accept as fact.

What is undeniable was that Rohmer's newest series detective, Chief Inspector Daniel Kerry (better known as "Red" Kerry due to his ginger hair, ruddy complexion, and fiery Irish temper) was based on the real-life Inspector Yeo, as the prefatory note in the character's first appearance in Rohmer's 1919 novel, *Dope* made explicit. Kerry not only shares his author's Irish heritage and Roman Catholic upbringing, but Kerry and his wife live in Herne Hill, the South London district where Rohmer and his wife lived at the time he created the character.

Dope first appeared as a serial in the UK in the pages of *The New Magazine* beginning in March 1919. Later, it appeared in the US in the pages of *Detective Story Magazine* from July to September 1919. Book publication followed in the UK under the title, *Dope: A Story of Chinatown and the Drug Traffic* and as *Dope: A Tale of the Drug Traffic* in the US. The lurid subtitles were a reflection on the real-life scandal that helped inspire the novel and certainly bolstered the book's commercial appeal.

Billie Carleton was a rising star of the West End theater district who was preparing to make her film debut when the Armistice was signed, effectively bringing an end to the Great War in 1918. Like so many young people in London, Miss Carleton went dancing at the Royal Albert Hall's Victory Ball held in celebration of Britain's hard-won peace. Shortly thereafter, the 22-year-old star of the legitimate stage died of a drug overdose in her hotel room. The resulting scandal shocked the nation, sold countless newspapers, and led to a sensational courtroom trial involving the arrest of several shady Limehouse denizens.

The scandal sheets had a field day alluding to the fact that the actress' best friend and theatrical costume designer was a cross-dressing bisexual who was also her coke dealer. They were thrilled to lay bare Miss Carleton's shocking past as a child born out of wedlock whose own mother did not know the identity of her father. They reveled in the fact that the actress was the kept woman of a much older and outwardly respectable man and that her closest confidante and opium supplier was a Scotswoman married to a Chinese immigrant who ran a notorious Limehouse opium den.

The press' moral outrage overflowed with contempt for criminal foreigners and the sordid drug use and libertine sexual exploits of those degenerates in show business. The coroner's inquest revealed Billie Carleton had succumbed to a combination of cocaine and barbiturates. It seemed that the entire nation was enraptured by the awful secrets the press betrayed each day. The Yellow Journalism of the day made it clear they were immersing their readers in such tawdry scandals only to protect respectable Englishmen and women from corruption.

The timing could not have been better for Rohmer. Whatever Limehouse thriller he had been plotting for "Red" Kerry's debut was quickly superseded by the sensationalism generated by the Billie Carleton case. Even as Rohmer borrowed wholesale facts from the real-life scandal for his book, altering some aspects to prevent legal action, the press picked up on the fact that the celebrated chronicler of Limehouse thrillers was now at work on the Billie Carleton scandal. Months before the book was published, Rohmer was compelled to clarify matters with a carefully worded response to *The London Opinion* dated 22 January 1919:

"Thanks for your paragraph about the 'Dope' book, but actually it was on the stocks long before the Carleton case brought the matter so prominently before the public. The increasing drug habit has had my attention for some time past & knowing of the link between certain purveyors frequenting the night clubs & like resorts & Limehouse, I saw an opportunity for a dramatic & strongly contrasted novel. Some further inquiries have brought to light very odd facts respecting this traffic, the increase in which I ascribe to the spirit restrictions."

The "Red" Kerry series marked Rohmer's only foray into hardboiled detective fiction, but it proved to be a successful one. Chief Inspector Kerry subsequently appeared in a pair of short stories, "The Daughter of Huang Chow" (1921) and "Kerry's Kid" (1922). Both stories are featured in Rohmer's collection, *Tales of Chinatown* (1922). The caustic, tightly wound Irish detective with his incessant gum chewing betraying his barely restrained emotions is also devoted to his wife, Mary, despite the occasional strain felt by their interfaith marriage. When their teenage son, Daniel, Jr., is abducted in "Kerry's Kid," the Irishman promises the criminal that he will kick him to death before all is said and done. While far from Race Williams' extremes, violence is never far from the surface in the "Red" Kerry stories as Rohmer's Chief Inspector on the job in Limehouse is more than willing to serve as judge and executioner when he deems it necessary. The emphasis on gritty violence, tong wars, and drug dealing stand in sharp contrast to Rohmer's Fu-Manchu stories.

No sooner was *Tales of Chinatown*, with its more realistic exploits of Paul Harley and "Red" Kerry, on the bestseller lists than Britain found itself captivated by yet another Limehouse scandal. A 21-year-old taxi dancer named Freda Kempton had died of a cocaine overdose in her apartment in March 1922. Miss Kempton was "kept" woman of (and pimped by) the notorious Brilliant Chang, a suave Chinese womanizer who made his fortune from illegal gambling, prostitution, and drug trade in Limehouse. Chang "kept" a sizable stable of willing English women and was known to flash his money around freely in posh London night clubs (some of which he also owned). Despite the overwhelming evidence that should have brought the blackguard to justice, Miss Kempton's overdose was inexplicably ruled a suicide by the court and Brilliant Chang walked away a free man surrounded by his adoring conquests.

However, the public appetite for Brilliant Chang's sordid exploits ensured he continued to be splashed all over the press. For his part, Chang reveled in his new-found celebrity. Meantime, the C.I.D. determined to bring Chang and his empire down. His clubs and opium dens were regularly raided. The following year, an up-and-coming stage actress called Violet Payne was arrested for using and trafficking cocaine. She confirmed under police interrogation that Brilliant Chang was both her supplier and lover. This time, there was no walking away free for Chang. He served a prison sentence and was then deported in 1925. He went on to become the "Dope King of Europe" brazenly operating opium dens in France, Belgium, and Switzerland. By the early 1930s, the media had given up interest in him and no more is known about his remaining years.

The press attention to Brilliant Chang's lurid sex life, which included orgies with chorus girls and flagrantly promoting prostitution and drugs all the while living the high life as a handsome, charismatic, smartly dressed Chinese businessman in London was not lost on Rohmer. Brilliant Chang inspired his creation of the villainous Burma Chang in his second "Red" Kerry novel, *Yellow Shadows*. The novel was first serialized in the UK in the *London Daily Graphic* from May 25 to July 7, 1925, prior to its publication in book form. US readers thrilled to the novel in the pages of *Short Stories* from March 10 to April 25, 1926, prior to the book's publication in the States.

As was his practice, Rohmer allowed his characters to age in real time. Daniel Kerry and his wife have moved to a bigger home (as had Rohmer and his wife) and Kerry has been promoted to Police Superintendent in the three years since "Kerry's Kid" was published. Rohmer incorporated his own real-life experiences with Fong-Wah, the Limehouse shopkeeper, and his residence on Three Colt Street in 1911 as part of the novel bringing the book still another added level of realism.

Both "Red" Kerry novels benefit from Rohmer's familiarity with Limehouse, though he exaggerates the atmosphere for dramatic purposes. The Kerry stories present the classic riverfront establishment that became a staple of mysteries and thrillers for decades to come. Any low-income urban area peopled with questionable characters (foreign and domestic) would require a tough, uncompromising detective to keep the district in order. "Red" Kerry more than adequately fit the bill. Apart from the setting, there is nothing to make one recall the Fu-Manchu stories despite the uninformed opinion of countless lazy critics and journalists over the years who conclude Rohmer did little more than malign the reputation of Chinese immigrants. Yes, the attitudes portrayed in the "Red" Kerry stories are more racist and intolerant than his Fu-Manchu weird thrillers, but they reflect the prevailing attitudes of the public and the media during these same years. Sordid tales of crime amid squalor call for a tough, unforgiving knight errant to carry out justice. Viewed in context, it becomes clear that "Red" Kerry represents the link between Rohmer and the hardboiled American school of pulp fiction that did so much to color escapist fiction throughout the last century.

—April 2025

William Patrick Maynard was born and raised in Cleveland, Ohio. He was licensed by the Sax Rohmer Literary Estate to continue the Fu Manchu thrillers beginning with *The Terror of Fu Manchu* (2009; Black Coat Press) and *The Destiny of Fu Manchu* (2012; Black Coat Press). As for a third Fu Manchu title, the Devil Doctor himself promised that "the world shall hear from me again…"

DOPE

— ＊ —

SAX ROHMER

PART FIRST

KAZMAH THE DREAM-READER

CHAPTER I

A MESSAGE FOR IRVIN

Monte Irvin, alderman of the city and prospective Lord Mayor of London, paced restlessly from end to end of the well-appointed library of his house in Prince's Gate. Between his teeth he gripped the stump of a burnt-out cigar. A tiny spaniel lay beside the fire, his beady black eyes following the nervous movements of the master of the house.

At the age of forty-five Monte Irvin was not ill-looking, and, indeed, was sometimes spoken of as handsome. His figure was full without being corpulent; his well-groomed black hair and moustache and fresh if rather coarse complexion, together with the dignity of his upright carriage, lent him something of a military air. This he assiduously cultivated as befitting an ex-Territorial officer, although as he had seen no active service he modestly refrained from using any title of rank.

Some quality in his brilliant smile, an oriental expressiveness of the dark eyes beneath their drooping lids, hinted a Semitic strain; but it was otherwise not marked in his appearance, which was free from vulgarity, whilst essentially that of a successful man of affairs.

In fact, Monte Irvin had made a success of every affair in life with the lamentable exception of his marriage. Of late his forehead had grown lined, and those business friends who had known him for a man of abstemious habits had observed in the City chophouse at which he lunched almost daily that whereas formerly he had been a noted trencherman, he now ate little but drank much.

Suddenly the spaniel leapt up with that feverish, spider-like activity of the toy species and began to bark.

Monte Irvin paused in his restless patrol and listened.

"Lie down!" he said. "Be quiet."

The spaniel ran to the door, sniffing eagerly. A muffled sound of voices became audible, and Irvin, following a moment of hesitation, crossed and opened the door. The dog ran out, yapping in his irritating staccato fashion, and an expression of hope faded from Irvin's face as he saw a tall fair girl standing in the hallway talking to Hinkes, the butler. She wore soiled Burberry, high-legged tan boots, and a peaked cap of distinctly military appearance. Irvin would have retired again, but the girl glanced up and saw him where he stood by the library door. He summoned up a smile and advanced.

"Good evening, Miss Halley," he said, striving to speak genially—for of all of his wife's friends he liked Margaret Halley the best. "Were you expecting to find Rita at home?"

The girl's expression was vaguely troubled. She had the clear complexion and bright eyes of perfect health, but to-night her eyes seemed over-bright, whilst her face was slightly pale.

"Yes," she replied; "that is, I hoped she might be at home."

"I am afraid I cannot tell you when she is likely to return. But please come in, and I will make inquiries."

"Oh, no, I would rather you did not trouble and I won't stay, thank you nevertheless. I expect she will ring me up when she comes in."

"Is there any message I can give her?"

"Well"—she hesitated for an instant—"you might tell her, if you would, that I only returned home at eight o'clock, so that I could not come around any earlier." She glanced rapidly at Irvin, biting her lip. "I wish I could have seen her," she added in a low voice.

"She wishes to see you particularly?"

"Yes. She left a note this afternoon." Again she glanced at him in a troubled way. "Well, I suppose it cannot be helped," she added and smilingly extended her hand. "Good night, Mr. Irvin. Don't bother to come to the door."

But Irvin passed Hinkes and walked out under the porch with Margaret Halley. Humid yellow mist floated past the street lamps, and seemed to have gathered in a moving reef around the little runabout car which was standing outside the house, its motor chattering tremulously.

"Phew! a beastly night!" he said. "Foggy and wet."

"It's a brute isn't it?" said the girl laughingly, and turned on the steps so that the light shining out of the hallway gleamed on her white teeth and upraised eyes. She was pulling on big, ugly, furred gloves, and Monte Irvin mentally contrasted her fresh, athletic type of beauty with the delicate, exotic charm of his wife.

She opened the door of the little car, got in and drove off, waving one hugely gloved hand to Irvin as he stood in the porch looking after her. When the red tail-light had vanished in the mist he returned to the house and re-entered the library. If only all his wife's friends were like Margaret Halley, he mused, he might have been spared the insupportable misgivings which were goading him to madness. His mind filled with poisonous suspicions, he resumed his pacing of the library, awaiting and dreading that which should confirm his blackest theories. He was unaware of the fact that throughout the interview he had held the stump of cigar between his teeth. He held it there yet, pacing, pacing up and down the long room.

Then came the expected summons. The telephone bell rang. Monte Irvin clenched his hands and inhaled deeply. His color changed in a manner that would have aroused a physician's interest. Regaining his self-possession by a visible effort, he crossed to a small side-table upon which the instrument rested. Rolling the cigar stump into the left corner of his mouth, he took up the receiver.

"Hallo!" he said.

"Someone named Brisley, sir, wishes—"

"Put him through to me here."

"Very good, sir."

A short interval, then:

"Yes?" said Monte Irvin.

"My name is Brisley. I have a message for Mr. Monte Irvin."

"Monte Irvin speaking. Anything to report, Brisley?"

Irvin's deep, rich voice was not entirely under control.

"Yes, sir. The lady drove by taxicab from Prince's Gate to Albemarle Street."

"Ah!"

"Went up to chambers of Sir Lucien Pyne and was admitted."

"Well?"

"Twenty minutes later came out. Lady was with Sir Lucien. Both walked around to old Bond Street. The Honorable Quentin Gray—"

"Ah!" breathed Irvin.

"—Overtook them there. He got out of a cab. He joined them. All three up to apartments of a professional crystal-gazer styling himself Kazmah 'the dream-reader.'"

A puzzled expression began to steal over the face of Monte Irvin. At the sound of the telephone bell he had paled somewhat. Now he began to recover his habitual florid coloring.

"Go on," he directed, for the speaker had paused.

"Seven to ten minutes later," resumed the nasal voice, "Mr. Gray came down. He hailed a passing cab, but man refused to stop. Mr. Gray seemed to be very irritable."

The fact that the invisible speaker was reading from a notebook he betrayed by his monotonous intonation and abbreviated sentences, which resembled those of a constable giving evidence in a police court.

"He walked off rapidly in direction of Piccadilly. Colleague followed. Near the Ritz he obtained a cab. He returned in same to old Bond Street. He ran upstairs and was gone from four-and-a-half to five minutes. He then came down again. He was very pale and agitated. He discharged cab and walked away. Colleague followed. He saw Mr. Gray enter Prince's Restaurant. In the hall Mr. Gray met a gent unknown by sight to colleague. Following some conversation both gents went in to dinner. They are there now. Speaking from Dover Street Tube."

"Yes, yes. But the lady?"

"A native, possibly Egyptian, apparently servant of Kazmah, came out a few minutes after Mr. Gray had gone for cab, and went away. Sir Lucien Pyne and lady are still in Kazmah's rooms."

"What!" cried Irvin, pulling out his watch and glancing at the disk. "But it's after eight o'clock!"

"Yes, sir. The place is all shut up, and other offices in block closed at six. Door of Kazmah's is locked. I knocked and got no reply."

"Damn it! You're talking nonsense! There must be another exit."

"No, sir. Colleague has just relieved me. Left two gents over their wine at Prince's."

Monte Irvin's color began to fade slowly.

"Then it's Pyne!" he whispered. The hand which held the receiver shook. "Brisley—meet me at the Piccadilly end of Bond Street. I am coming now."

He put down the telephone, crossed to the wall and pressed a button. The cigar stump held firmly between his teeth, he stood on the rug before the hearth, facing the door. Presently it opened and Hinkes came in.

"The car is ready, Hinkes?"

"Yes, sir, as you ordered. Shall Pattison come round to the door?"

"At once."

"Very good, sir."

He withdrew, closing the door quietly, and Monte Irvin stood staring across the library at the full-length portrait in oils of his wife in the pierrot dress which she had worn in the third act of *The Maid of the Masque.*

The clock in the hall struck half-past eight.

CHAPTER II

THE APARTMENTS OF KAZMAH

It was rather less than two hours earlier on the same evening that Quentin Gray came out of the confectioner's shop in old Bond Street carrying a neat parcel. Yellow dusk was closing down upon this bazaar of the New Babylon, and many of the dealers in precious gems, vendors of rich stuffs, and makers of modes had already deserted their shops. Smartly dressed show-girls, saleswomen, girl clerks and others crowded the pavements, which at high noon had been thronged with ladies of fashion. Here a tailor's staff, there a hatter's lingered awhile as iron shutters and gratings were secured, and bidding one another good night, separated and made off towards Tube and bus. The working day was ended. Society was dressing for dinner.

Gray was about to enter the cab which awaited him, and his fresh-colored, boyish face wore an expression of eager expectancy, which must have betrayed the fact to an experienced beholder that he was hurrying to keep an agreeable appointment. Then, his hand resting on the handle of the cab-door, this expression suddenly changed to one of alert suspicion.

A tall, dark man, accompanied by a woman muffled in grey furs and wearing a silk scarf over her hair, had passed on foot along the opposite side of the street. Gray had seen them through the cab windows.

His smooth brow wrinkled and his mouth tightened to a thin straight line beneath the fair "regulation" moustache. He fumbled under his overcoat for loose silver, drew out a handful and paid off the taximan.

Sometimes walking in the gutter in order to avoid the throngs upon the pavement, regardless of the fact that his glossy dress-boots were becoming spattered with mud, Gray hurried off in pursuit of the pair. Twenty yards ahead he overtook them, as they were on the point of passing a picture dealer's window, from which yellow light streamed forth into the humid dusk. They were walking slowly, and Gray stopped in front of them.

"Hello, you two!" he cried. "Where are you off to? I was on my way to call for you, Rita."

Flushed and boyish he stood before them, and his annoyance was increased by their failure to conceal the fact that his appearance was embarrassing if not unwelcome. Mrs. Monte Irvin was a petite, pretty woman, although some of the more wonderful bronzed tints of her hair suggested the employment of henna, and her naturally lovely complexion was delicately and artistically enhanced by art. Nevertheless, the flower-like face peeping out from the folds of a gauzy scarf, like a rose from a mist, whilst her soft little chin nestled into the fur, might have explained even in the case of an older man the infatuation which Quentin Gray was at no pains to hide.

She glanced up at her companion, Sir Lucien Pyne, a swarthy, cynical type of aristocrat, imperturbably. Then: "I had left a note for you, Quentin," she said hurriedly. She seemed to be in a dangerously high-strung condition.

"But I have booked a table and a box," cried Gray, with a hint of juvenile petulance.

"My dear Gray," said Sir Lucien coolly, "we are men of the world—and we do not look for consistency in womenfolk. Mrs. Irvin has decided to consult a palmist or a hypnotist or some such occult authority before dining with you this evening. Doubtless she seeks to learn if the play to which you propose to take her is an amusing one."

His smile of sardonic amusement Gray found to be almost insupportable, and although Sir Lucien refrained from looking at Mrs. Irvin whilst he spoke, it was evident enough that his words held some covert significance, for:

"You know perfectly well that I have a particular reason for seeing him," she said.

"A woman's particular reason is a man's feeble excuse," murmured Sir Lucien rudely. "At least, according to a learned Arabian philosopher."

"I was going to meet you at Prince's," said Mrs. Irvin hurriedly, and again glancing at Gray. There was a pathetic hesitancy in her manner, the hesitancy of a weak woman who adheres to a purpose only by supreme effort.

"Might I ask," said Gray, "the name of the pervert you are going to consult?"

Again she hesitated and glanced rapidly at Sir Lucien, but he was staring coolly in another direction.

"Kazmah," she replied in a low voice.

"Kazmah!" cried Gray. "The man who sells perfume and pretends to read dreams? What an extraordinary notion. Wouldn't tomorrow do? He will surely have shut up shop!"

"I have been at pains to ascertain," replied Sir Lucien, "at Mrs. Irvin's express desire, that the man of mystery is still in session and will receive her."

Beneath the mask of nonchalance which he wore it might have been possible to detect excitement repressed with difficulty; and had Gray been more composed and not obsessed with the idea that Sir Lucien had deliberately intruded upon his plans for the evening, he could not have failed to perceive that Mrs. Monte Irvin was feverishly preoccupied with matters having no relation to dinner and the theatre. But his private suspicions grew only the more acute.

"Then if the dinner is not off," he said, "may I come along and wait for you?"

"At Kazmah's?" asked Mrs. Irvin. "Certainly." She turned to Sir Lucien. "Shall you wait? It isn't much use as I'm dining with Quentin."

"If I do not intrude," replied the baronet, "I will accompany you as far as the cave of the oracle, and then bid you good night."

The trio proceeded along old Bond Street. Quentin Gray regarded the story of Kazmah as a very poor lie devised on the spur of the moment. If he had been less infatuated, his natural sense of dignity must have dictated an offer to release Mrs. Irvin from her engagement. But jealousy stimulates the worst instincts and destroys the best. He was determined to attach himself as closely as the old Man of the Sea attached himself to Es-Sindibad, in order that the lie might be unmasked. Mrs. Irvin's palpable embarrassment and nervousness he ascribed to her perception of his design.

A group of shop girls and others waiting for buses rendered it impossible for the three to keep abreast, and Gray, falling to the rear, stepped upon the foot of a little man who was walking close behind them.

"Sorry, sir," said the man, suppressing an exclamation of pain—for the fault had been Gray's.

Gray muttered an ungenerous acknowledgment, all anxiety to regain the side of Mrs. Irvin; for she seemed to be speaking rapidly and excitedly to Sir Lucien.

He recovered his place as the two turned in at a lighted doorway. Upon the wall was a bronze plate bearing the inscription:

KAZMAH
Second Floor

Gray fully expected Mrs. Irvin to suggest that he should return later. But without a word she began to ascend the stairs. Gray followed, Sir Lucien standing aside to give him precedence. On the second floor was a door painted in Oriental fashion. It possessed neither bell nor knocker, but as one stepped upon the threshold this door opened noiselessly as if dumbly inviting the visitor to enter the square apartment discovered. This apartment was richly furnished in the Arab manner, and lighted by a fine brass lamp swung upon chains from the painted ceiling. The intricate perforations of the lamp were inset with colored glass, and the result was a subdued and warm illumination. Odd-looking oriental vessels, long-necked jars, jugs with tenuous spouts and squat bowls possessing engraved and figured covers emerged from the shadows of niches. A low divan with gaily colored mattresses extended from the door around one corner of the room where it terminated beside a kind of *mushrabîyeh* cabinet or cupboard. Beyond this cabinet was a long, low counter laden with statuettes of Nile gods, amulets, mummy-beads and little stoppered flasks of blue enamel ware. There were two glass cases filled with other strange-looking antiquities. A faint perfume was perceptible.

Sir Lucien entering last of the party, the door closed behind him, and from the cabinet on the right of the divan a young Egyptian stepped out. He wore the customary white robe, red sash and red slippers, and a *tarbûsh*, the little scarlet cap commonly called a fez, was set upon his head. He walked to a door on the left of the counter, and slid it noiselessly open. Bowing gravely, "The Sheikh el Kazmah awaits," he said, speaking with the soft intonation of a native of Upper Egypt.

It now became evident, even to the infatuated Gray, that Mrs. Irvin was laboring under the influence of tremendous excitement. She turned to him quickly, and he thought that her face looked almost haggard, whilst her eyes seemed to have changed color—become lighter, although he could not be certain that this latter effect was not due to the peculiar illumination of the room. But when she spoke her voice was unsteady.

"Will you see if you can find a cab," she said. "It is so difficult at night, and my shoes will get frightfully muddy crossing Piccadilly. I shall not be more than a few minutes." She walked through the doorway, the Egyptian standing aside as she passed. He followed her, but came out again almost immediately, reclosed the door, and retired into the cabinet, which was evidently his private cubicle.

Silence claimed the apartment. Sir Lucien threw himself nonchalantly upon the divan, and took out his cigarette-case.

"Will you have a cigarette, Gray?" he asked.

"No thanks," replied the other, in tones of smothered hostility. He was ill at ease, and paced the apartment nervously. Pyne lighted a cigarette, and tossed the extinguished match into a brass bowl.

"I think," said Gray jerkily, "I shall go for a cab. Are you remaining?"

"I am dining at the club," answered Pyne, "but I can wait until you return."

"As you wish," jerked Gray. "I don't expect to be long."

He walked rapidly to the outer door, which opened at his approach and closed noiselessly behind him as he made his exit.

CHAPTER III

KAZMAH

Mrs. Monte Irvin entered the inner room. The air was heavy with the perfume of frankincense which smouldered in a brass vessel set upon a tray. This was the audience chamber of Kazmah. In marked contrast to the overcrowded appointments, divans and cupboards of the first room, it was sparsely furnished. The floor was thickly carpeted, but save for an ornate inlaid table upon which stood the tray and incense-burner, and a long, low-cushioned seat placed immediately beneath a hanging lamp burning dimly in a globular green shade, it was devoid of decoration. The walls were draped with green curtains, so that except for the presence of the painted door, the four sides of the apartment appeared to be uniform.

Having conducted Mrs. Irvin to the seat, the Egyptian bowed and retired again through the doorway by which they had entered. The visitor found herself alone.

She moved nervously, staring across at the blank wall before her. With her little satin shoe she tapped the carpet, biting her under lip and seeming to be listening. Nothing stirred. Not even an echo of busy Bond Street penetrated to the place. Mrs. Irvin unfastened her cloak and allowed it to fall back upon the settee. Her bare shoulders looked waxen and unnatural in the weird light which shone down upon them. She was breathing rapidly.

The minutes passed by in unbroken silence. So still was the room that Mrs. Irvin could hear the faint crackling sound made by the burning charcoal in the brass vessel near her. Wisps of blue-grey smoke arose through the perforated lid and she began to watch them fascinatedly, so lithe they seemed, like wraiths of serpents creeping up the green draperies.

So she was seated, her foot still restlessly tapping, but her gaze arrested by the hypnotic movements of the smoke, when at last a sound from the outer world, penetrated to the room. A church clock struck the hour of seven, its clangor intruding upon the silence only as a muffled boom. Almost coincident with the last stroke came the sweeter note of a silver gong from somewhere close at hand.

Mrs. Irvin started, and her eyes turned instantly in the direction of the greenly draped wall before her. Her pupils had grown suddenly dilated, and she clenched her hands tightly.

The light above her head went out.

Now that the moment was come to which she had looked forward with mingled hope and terror, long pent-up emotion threatened to overcome her, and she trembled wildly.

Out of the darkness dawned a vague light and in it a shape seemed to take form. As the light increased the effect was as though part of the wall had become transparent so as to reveal the interior of an inner room where a figure was seated in a massive ebony chair. The figure was that of an oriental, richly robed and wearing a white turban. His long slim hands, of the color of old ivory, rested upon the arms of the chair, and on the first finger of the right hand gleamed a big talismanic ring. The face of the seated man was lowered, but from under heavy brows his abnormally large eyes regarded her fixedly.

So dim the light remained that it was impossible to discern the details with anything like clearness, but that the clean-shaven face of the man with those wonderful eyes was strikingly and intellectually handsome there could be no doubt.

This was Kazmah, "the dream reader," and although Mrs. Irvin had seen him before, his statuesque repose and the weirdness of his unfaltering gaze thrilled her uncannily.

Kazmah slightly raised his hand in greeting: the big ring glittered in the subdued light.

"Tell me your dream," came a curious mocking voice; "and I will read its portent."

Such was the set formula with which Kazmah opened all interviews. He spoke with a slight and not unmusical accent. He lowered his hand again. The gaze of those brilliant eyes remained fixed upon the woman's face. Moistening her lips, Mrs. Irvin spoke.

"Dreams! What I have to say does not belong to dreams, but to reality!" She laughed unmirthfully. "You know well enough why I am here."

She paused.

"Why are you here?"

"You know! You know!" Suddenly into her voice had come the unmistakable note of hysteria. "Your theatrical tricks do not impress me. I know what you are! A spy—an eavesdropper who watches— watches, and listens! But you may go too far! I am nearly desperate— do you understand?—nearly desperate. Speak! Move! Answer me!"

But Kazmah preserved his uncanny repose.

"You are distracted," he said. "I am sorry for you. But why do you come to *me* with your stories of desperation? You have insisted upon seeing me. I am here."

"And you play with me—taunt me!"

"The remedy is in your hands."

"For the last time, I tell you I will never do it! Never, never, never!"

"Then why do you complain? If you cannot afford to pay for your amusements, and you refuse to compromise in a simple manner, why do you approach *me?*"

"Oh, my God!" She moaned and swayed dizzily—"have pity on me! Who are you, what are you, that you can bring ruin on a woman because—" She uttered a choking sound, but continued hoarsely, "Raise your head. Let me see your face. As heaven is my witness, I am ruined—ruined!"

"Tomorrow—"

"I cannot wait for tomorrow—"

That quivering, hoarse cry betrayed a condition of desperate febrile excitement. Mrs. Irvin was capable of proceeding to the wildest extremities. Clearly the mysterious Egyptian recognized this to be the case, for slowly raising his hand:

"I will communicate with you," he said, and the words were spoken almost hurriedly. "Depart in peace—"; a formula wherewith he terminated every seance. He lowered his hand.

The silver gong sounded again—and the dim light began to fade.

Thereupon the unhappy woman acted; the long suppressed outburst came at last. Stepping rapidly to the green transparent veil behind which Kazmah was seated, she wrenched it asunder and leapt toward the figure in the black chair.

"You shall not trick me!" she panted. "Hear me out or I go straight to the police—now—*now!*"

She grasped the hands of Kazmah as they rested motionless, on the chair-arms.

Complete darkness came.

Out of it rose a husky, terrified cry—a second, louder cry; and then a long, wailing scream ... horror-laden as that of one who has touched some slumbering reptile....

CHAPTER IV

THE CLOSED DOOR

Rather less than five minutes later a taxicab drew up in old Bond Street, and from it Quentin Gray leapt out impetuously and ran in at the doorway leading to Kazmah's stairs. So hurried was his progress that he collided violently with a little man who, carrying himself with a pronounced stoop, was slinking furtively out.

The little man reeled at the impact and almost fell, but:

"Hang it all!" cried Gray irritably. "Why the devil don't you look where you're going!"

He glared angrily into the face of the other. It was a peculiar and rememberable face, notable because of a long, sharp, hooked nose and very little, foxy, brown eyes; a sly face to which a small, fair moustache only added insignificance. It was crowned by a wide-brimmed bowler hat which the man wore pressed down upon his ears like a Jew pedlar.

"Why!" cried Gray, "this is the second time tonight you have jostled me!"

He thought he had recognized the man for the same who had been following himself, Mrs. Irvin and Sir Lucien Pyne along old Bond Street.

A smile, intended to be propitiatory, appeared upon the pale face.

"No, sir, excuse me, sir—"

"Don't deny it!" said Gray angrily. "If I had the time I should give you in charge as a suspicious loiterer."

Calling to the cabman to wait, he ran up the stairs to the second floor landing. Before the painted door bearing the name of Kazmah he halted, and as the door did not open, stamped impatiently, but with no better result.

At that, since there was neither bell nor knocker, he raised his fist and banged loudly.

No one responded to the summons.

"Hi, there!" he shouted. "Open the door! Pyne! Rita!"

Again he banged—and yet again. Then he paused, listening, his ear pressed to the panel.

He could detect no sound of movement within. Fists clenched, he stood staring at the closed door, and his fresh color slowly deserted him and left him pale.

"Damn him!" he muttered savagely. "Damn him! he has fooled me!"

Passionate and self-willed, he was shaken by a storm of murderous anger. That Pyne had planned this trick, with Rita Irvin's consent, he did not doubt, and his passive dislike of the man became active hatred of the woman he dared not think. He had for long looked upon Sir Lucien in the light of a rival, and the irregularity of his own infatuation for another's wife in no degree lessened his resentment.

Again he pressed his ear to the door, and listened intently. Perhaps they were hiding within. Perhaps this charlatan, Kazmah, was an accomplice in the pay of Sir Lucien. Perhaps this was a secret place of rendezvous.

To the manifest absurdity of such a conjecture he was blind in his anger. But that he was helpless, befooled, he recognized; and with a final muttered imprecation he turned and slowly descended the stair. A lingering hope was dispelled when, looking right and left along Bond Street, he failed to perceive the missing pair.

The cabman glanced at him interrogatively. "I shall not require you," said Gray, and gave the man half-a-crown.

Busy with his poisonous conjectures, he remained all unaware of the presence of a furtive, stooping figure which lurked behind the railings of the arcade at this point linking old Bond Street to Albemarle Street. Nor had the stooping stranger any wish to attract Gray's attention. Most of the shops in the narrow lane were already closed, although the florist's at the corner remained open, but of the shadow which lay along the greater part of the arcade this alert watcher took every advantage. From the recess formed by a shop door he peered out at Gray, where the light of a street lamp fell upon him, studying his face, his movements, with unrelaxing vigilance.

Gray, following some moments of indecision, strode off towards Piccadilly. The little man came out cautiously from his hiding-place and looked after him. Out of a dark porch, ten paces along Bond Street, appeared a burly figure to fall into step a few yards behind Gray. The little man licked his lips appreciatively and returned to the doorway below the premises of Kazmah.

Reaching Piccadilly, Gray stood for a time on the corner, indifferent to the jostling of passers-by. Finally he crossed, walked along to the Prince's Restaurant, and entered the lobby. He glanced at his wrist-watch. It registered the hour of seven-twenty-five.

He cancelled his order for a table and was standing staring moodily towards the entrance when the doors swung open and a man entered who stepped straight up to him, hand extended, and:

"Glad to see you, Gray," he said. "What's the trouble?"

Quentin Gray stared as if incredulous at the speaker, and it was with an unmistakable note of welcome in his voice that he replied:

"Seton! Seton Pasha!"

The frown disappeared from Gray's forehead, and he gripped the other's hand in hearty greeting. But:

"Stick to plain Seton!" said the new-comer, glancing rapidly about him. "Ottoman titles are not fashionable."

The speaker was a man of arresting personality. Above medium height, well but leanly built, the face of Seton "Pasha" was burned to a deeper shade than England's wintry sun is capable of producing. He wore a close-trimmed beard and moustache, and the bronze on his cheeks enhanced the brightness of his grey eyes and rendered very noticeable a slight frosting of the dark hair above his temples. He had the indescribable air of a "sure" man, a sound man to have beside one in a tight place; and looking into the rather grim face, Quentin Gray felt suddenly ashamed of himself. From Seton Pasha he knew that he could keep nothing back. He knew that presently he should find himself telling this quiet, brown-skinned man the whole story of his humiliation—and he knew that Seton would not spare his feelings.

"My dear fellow," he said, "you must pardon me if I sometimes fail to respect your wishes in this matter. When I left the East the name of Seton Pasha was on everybody's tongue. But are you alone?"

"I am. I only arrived in London tonight and in England this morning."

"Were you thinking of dining here?"

"No; I saw you through the doorway as I was passing. But this will do as well as another place. I gather that you are disengaged. Perhaps you will dine with me?"

"Splendid!" cried Gray. "Wait a moment. Perhaps my table hasn't gone!"

He ran off in his boyish, impetuous fashion, and Seton watched him, smiling quietly.

The table proved to be available, and ere long the two were discussing an excellent dinner. Gray lost much of his irritability and began to talk coherently upon topics of general interest. Presently, following an interval during which he had been covertly watching his companion:

"Do you know, Seton," he said, "you are the one man in London whose company I could have tolerated tonight."

"My arrival was peculiarly opportune."

"Your arrivals are always peculiarly opportune." Gray stared at Seton with an expression of puzzled admiration. "I don't think I shall ever understand your turning up immediately before the Senussi raid in Egypt. Do you remember? I was with the armored cars."

"I remember perfectly."

"Then you vanished in the same mysterious fashion, and the C. O. was a sphinx on the subject. I next saw you strolling out of the gate at Baghdad. How the devil you'd got to Baghdad, considering that you didn't come with us and that you weren't with the cavalry, heaven only knows!"

"No," said Seton judicially, gazing through his uplifted wine-glass; "when one comes to consider the matter without prejudice it is certainly odd. But do I know the lady to whose non-appearance I owe the pleasure of your company tonight?"

Quentin Gray stared at him blankly.

"Really, Seton, you amaze me. Did I say that I had an appointment with a lady?"

"My dear Gray, when I see a man standing biting his nails and glaring out into Piccadilly from a restaurant entrance I ask myself a question. When I learn that he has just cancelled an order for a table for two I answer it."

Gray laughed. "You always make me feel so infernally young, Seton."

"Good!"

"Yes, it's good to feel young, but bad to feel a young fool; and that's what I feel—and what I am. Listen!"

Leaning across the table so that the light of the shaded lamp fell fully upon his flushed, eager face, Gray, not without embarrassment, told his companion of the "dirty trick"—so he phrased it—which Sir Lucien Pyne had played upon him. In conclusion:

"What would you do, Seton?" he asked.

Seton sat regarding him in silence with a cool, calculating stare which some men had termed insolent, absently tapping his teeth with the gold rim of a monocle which he carried but apparently never used for any other purpose; and it was at about this time that a long low car passed near the door of the restaurant, crossing the traffic stream of Piccadilly to draw up at the corner of old Bond Street.

From the car Monte Irvin alighted and, telling the man to wait, set out on foot. Ten paces along Bond Street he encountered a small, stooping figure which became detached from the shadows of a shop door. The light of a street lamp shone down upon the sharp, hooked nose and into the cunning little brown eyes of Brisley, of Spinker's Detective Agency. Monte Irvin started.

"Ah, Brisley!" he said, "I was looking for you. Are they still there?"

"Probably, sir." Brisley licked his lips. "My colleague, Gunn, reports no one came out whilst I was away 'phoning."

"But the whole thing seems preposterous. Are there no other offices in the block where they might be?"

"I personally saw Mr. Gray, Sir Lucien Pyne and the lady go into Kazmah's. At that time—roughly, ten to seven—all the other offices had been closed, approximately, one hour."

"There is absolutely no possibility that they might have come out unseen by you?"

"None, sir. I should not have troubled a client if in doubt. Here's Gunn."

Old Bond Street now was darkened and deserted; the yellow mist had turned to fine rain, and Gunn, his hands thrust in his pockets, was sheltering under the porch of the arcade. Gunn possessed a purple complexion which attained to full vigor of coloring in the nasal region. His moustache of dirty grey was stained brown in the centre as if by frequent potations of stout, and his bulky figure was artificially enlarged by the presence of two overcoats, the outer of which was a waterproof and the inner a blue garment appreciably longer both in sleeve and skirt than the former. The effect produced was one of great novelty. Gunn touched the brim of his soft felt hat, which he wore turned down all round apparently in imitation of a flower-pot.

"All snug, sir," he said, hoarsely and confidentially, bending forward and breathing the words into Irvin's ear. "Snug as a bee in a hive. You're as good as a bachelor again."

Monte Irvin mentally recoiled.

"Lead the way to the door of this place," he said tersely.

"Yes, sir, this way, sir. Be careful of the step there. You may remark that the outer door is not yet closed. I am informed upon reliable authority as the last to go locks the door. Hence we perceive that the last has not yet gone. It is likewise opened by the first to come of a mornin'. Here we are, sir; door on the right."

The landing was in darkness, but as Gunn spoke he directed the ray of a pocket lamp upon a bronze plate bearing the name "Kazmah." He rested one hand upon his hip.

"All snug," he repeated; "as snug as a eel in mud. The *decree nisi* is yours, sir. As an alderman of the City of London and a Justice of the Peace you are entitled to call a police officer—"

"Hold your tongue!" rapped Irvin. "You've been drinking: and I place no reliance whatever in your evidence. I do not believe that my wife or any one else but ourselves is upon these premises."

The watery eyes of the insulted man protruded unnaturally. "Drinkin'!" he whispered, "drink—"

But indignation now deprived Gunn of speech and:

"Excuse me, sir," interrupted the nasal voice of Brisley, "but I can absolutely answer for Gunn. Reputation of the Agency at stake. Worked with us for three years. Parties undoubtedly on the premises as reported."

"Drink—" whispered Gunn.

"I shall be glad," said Monte Irvin, and his voice shook emotionally, "if you will lend me your pocket lamp. I am naturally upset. Will you kindly both go downstairs. I will call if I want you."

The two men obeyed, Gunn muttering hoarsely to Brisley; and Monte Irvin was left standing on the landing, the lamp in his hand. He waited until he knew from the sound of their footsteps that the pair had regained the street, then, resting his arm against the closed door, and pressing his forehead to the damp sleeve of his coat, he stood awhile, the lamp, which he held limply, shining down upon the floor.

His lips moved, and almost inaudibly he murmured his wife's name.

CHAPTER V

THE DOOR IS OPENED

Quentin Gray and Seton strolled out of Prince's and both paused whilst Seton lighted a long black cheroot.

"It seems a pity to waste that box," said Gray. "Suppose we look in at the Gaiety for an hour?"

His humor was vastly improved, and he watched the passing throngs with an expression more suited to his boyish good looks than that of anger and mortification which had rested upon him an hour earlier.

Seton Pasha tossed a match into the road.

"My official business is finished for the day," he replied. "I place myself unreservedly in your hands."

"Well, then," began Gray—and paused.

A long, low car, the chauffeur temporarily detained by the stoppage of a motorbus ahead, had slowed up within three yards of the spot where they were standing. Gray seized Seton's arm in a fierce grip.

"Seton," he said, his voice betraying intense excitement, "Look! There is Monte Irvin!"

"In the car?"

"Yes, yes! But—he has two *police* with him! Seton, what can it mean?"

The car moved away, swinging to the right across the traffic stream and clearly heading for old Bond Street. Quentin Gray's mercurial color deserted him, and he turned to Seton a face grown suddenly pale.

"Good God," he whispered, "something has happened to Rita!"

Neglectful of his personal safety, he plunged out into the traffic, dodging this way and that, and making after Monte Irvin's car. Of the fact that his friend was close beside him he remained unaware until, on the corner of old Bond Street, a firm grip settled upon his shoulder. Gray turned angrily. But the grip was immovable, and he found himself staring into the unemotional face of Seton Pasha.

"Seton, for God's sake, don't detain me! I must learn what's wrong."

"Pull up, Gray."

Quentin Gray clenched his teeth.

"Listen to me, Seton. This is no time for interference. I—"

"You are about to become involved in some very unsavory business; and I repeat—pull up. In a moment we shall learn all there is to be learned. But are you determined openly to thrust yourself into the family affairs of Mr. Monte Irvin?"

"If anything has happened to Rita I'll kill that damned cur Pyne!"

"You are determined to intrude upon this man in your present frame of mind at a time of evident trouble?"

But Gray was deaf to the promptings of prudence and good taste alike.

"I'm going to see the thing through," he said hoarsely.

"Quite so. Rely upon me. But endeavor to behave more like a man of the world and less like a dangerous lunatic, or we shall quarrel atrociously."

Quentin Gray audibly gnashed his teeth, but the cool stare of the other's eyes was quelling, and now as their glances met and clashed, a sympathetic smile softened the lines of Seton's grim mouth, and:

"I quite understand, old chap," he said, linking his arm in Gray's. "But can't you see how important it is, for everybody's sake, that we should tackle the thing coolly?"

"Seton"—Gray's voice broke—"I'm sorry. I know I'm mad; but I was with her only an hour ago, and now—"

"And now 'her' husband appears on the scene accompanied by a police inspector and a sergeant. What are your relations with Mr. Monte Irvin?"

They were walking rapidly again along Bond Street.

"What do you mean, Seton?" asked Gray.

"I mean does he approve of your friendship with his wife, or is it a clandestine affair?"

"Clandestine?—certainly not. I was on my way to call at the house when I met her with Pyne this evening."

"That is what I wanted to know. Very well; since you intend to follow the thing up, it simplifies matters somewhat. Here is the car."

"At Kazmah's door! What in heaven's name does it mean?"

"It means that we shall get a very poor reception if we intrude. Question the chauffeur."

But Gray had already approached the man, who touched his cap in recognition.

"What's the trouble, Pattison?" he demanded breathlessly. "I saw police in the car a moment ago."

"Yes, sir. I don't rightly know, sir, what's happened. But Mr. Irvin drove from home to the corner of old Bond Street a quarter of an hour ago and told me to wait, then came back again and drove round to Vine Street to fetch the police. They're inside now."

Even as he spoke, with excitement ill-concealed, a police-sergeant came out of the doorway, and:

"Move on, there," he said to Seton and Gray. "You mustn't hang about this door."

"Excuse me, Sergeant," cried Gray, "but if the matter concerns Mrs. Monte Irvin I can probably supply information."

The Sergeant stared at him hard, saw that both he and his friend wore evening dress, and grew proportionately respectful.

"What is your name, sir?" he asked. "I'll mention it to the officer in charge."

"Quentin Gray. Inform Mr. Monte Irvin that I wish to speak to him."

"Very good, sir." He turned to the chauffeur. "Hand me out the bag I gave you at Vine Street." Pattison leaned over the door at the front of the car, and brought out a big leather grip. With this in hand the police-sergeant returned into the doorway.

"We're in for it now," said Seton grimly, "whatever it is."

Gray returned no answer, moving restlessly up and down before the door in a fever of excitement and dread. Presently the Sergeant reappeared.

"Step this way, please," he said.

Followed by Seton and Gray he led the way up to the landing before Kazmah's apartments. It was vaguely lighted by two police-lanterns. Four men were standing there, and four pairs of eyes were focussed upon the stair-head.

Monte Irvin, his features a distressing ashen color, spoke.

"That you, Gray?" Quentin Gray would not have recognized the voice. "Thanks for offering your help. God knows I need all I can get. You were with Rita tonight. What happened? Where is she?"

"Heaven knows where she is!" cried Gray. "I left her here with Pyne shortly after seven o'clock."

He paused, fixing his gaze upon the face of Brisley, whose shifty eyes avoided him and who was licking his lips in the manner of a dog who has seen the whip.

"Why," said Gray, "I believe you are the fellow who has been following me all night for some reason."

He stepped toward the foxy little man but:

"Never mind, Gray," interrupted Irvin. "*I* was to blame. But he was following my wife, not you. Tell me quickly: Why did she come here?"

Gray raised his hand to his brow with a gesture of bewilderment.

"To consult this man, Kazmah. I actually saw her enter the inner room, I went to get a cab, and when I returned the door was locked."

"You knocked?"

"Of course. I made no end of a row. But I could get no reply and went away."

Monte Irvin turned, a pathetic figure, to the Inspector who stood beside him.

"We may as well proceed, Inspector Whiteleaf," he said. "Mr. Gray's evidence throws no light on the matter at all."

"Very well, sir," was the reply; "we have the warrant, and have given the usual notice to whoever may be hiding inside. Burton!"

The Sergeant stepped forward, placed the leather bag on the floor, and stooping, opened it, revealing a number of burglarious-looking instruments.

"Shall I try to cut through the panel?" he asked.

"No, no!" cried Monte Irvin. "Waste no time. You have a crowbar there. Force the door from its hinges. Hurry, man!"

"It doesn't work on hinges!" Gray interrupted excitedly. "It slides to the right by means of some arrangement concealed under the mat."

"Pass that lantern," directed Burton, glancing over his shoulder to Gunn.

Setting it beside him, the Sergeant knelt and examined the threshold of the door.

"A metal plate," he said. "The weight moves a lever, I suppose, which opens the door if it isn't locked. The lock will be on the left of the door as it opens to the right. Let's see what we can do."

He stood up, crowbar in hand, and inserted the chisel blade of the implement between the edge of the door and the doorcase.

"Hold steady!" said the Inspector, standing at his elbow.

The dull metallic sound of hammer blows on steel echoed queerly around the well of the staircase. Brisley and Gunn, standing very close together on the bottom step of the stair to the third floor, watched the police furtively. Irvin and Gray found a common fascination in the door itself, and Seton, cheroot in mouth, looked from group to group with quiet interest.

"Right!" cried the Sergeant.

The blows ceased.

Firmly grasping the bar, Burton brought all his weight to bear upon it. There was a dull, cracking sound and a sort of rasping. The door moved slightly.

"There's where it locks!" said the Inspector, directing the light of a lantern upon the crevice created. "Three inches lower. But it may be bolted as well."

"We'll soon get at the bolts," replied Burton, the lust of destruction now strong upon him.

Wrenching the crowbar from its place he attacked the lower panel of the door, and amid a loud splintering and crashing created a hole big enough to allow of the passage of a hand and arm.

The Inspector reached in, groped about, and then uttered an exclamation of triumph.

"I've unfastened the bolt," he said. "If there isn't another at the top you ought to be able to force the door now, Burton."

The jimmy was thrust back into position, and:

"Stand clear!" cried Burton.

Again he threw his weight upon the bar—and again.

"Drive it further in!" said Monte Irvin; and snatching up the heavy hammer, he rained blows upon the steel butt. "Now try."

Burton exerted himself to the utmost.

"Take hold up here, someone!" he panted. "Two of us can pull."

Gray leapt forward, and the pair of them bent to the task.

There came a dull report of parting mechanism, more sounds of splintering wood ... and the door rolled open!

A moment of tense silence, then:

"Is anyone inside there?" cried the Inspector loudly.

Not a sound came from the dark interior.

"The lantern!" whispered Monte Irvin.

He stumbled into the room, from which a heavy smell of perfume swept out upon the landing. Quentin Gray, snatching the lantern from the floor, where it had been replaced, was the next to enter.

"Look for the switch, and turn the lights on!" called the Inspector, following.

Even as he spoke, Gray had found the switch, and the apartment of Kazmah became flooded with subdued light.

A glance showed it to be unoccupied.

Gray ran across to the *mushrabîyeh* cabinet and jerked the curtains aside. There was no one in the cabinet. It contained a chair and a table. Upon the latter was a telephone and some papers and books.

"This way!" he cried, his voice high pitched and unnatural.

He burst through the doorway into the inner room which he had seen Mrs. Irvin enter. The air was laden with the smell of frankincense.

"A lantern!" he called. "I left one on the divan."

But Monte Irvin had caught it up and was already at his elbow. His hand was shaking so that the light danced wildly now upon the carpet, now upon the green walls. This room also was deserted. A black gap in the curtain showed where the material had been roughly torn. Suddenly:

"My God, look!" muttered the Inspector, who, with the others, now stood in the curious draped apartment.

A thin stream of blood was trickling out from beneath the torn hangings!

Monte Irvin staggered and fell back against the Inspector, clutching at him for support. But Sergeant Burton, who carried the second lantern, crossed the room and wrenched the green draperies bodily from their fastenings.

They had masked a wooden partition or stout screen, having an aperture in the centre which could be closed by means of another of the sliding doors. A space some five feet deep was thus walled off from this second room. It contained a massive ebony chair. Behind the chair, and dividing the second room into yet a third section, extended another wooden partition in one end of which was an ordinary office door; and immediately at the back of the chair appeared a little opening or window, some three feet up from the floor. The sound of a groan, followed by that of a dull thud, came from the outer room.

"Hullo!" cried Inspector Whiteleaf. "Mr. Irvin has fainted. Lend a hand."

"I am here," replied the quiet voice of Seton Pasha.

"My God!" whispered Gray. "Seton! Seton!"

"Touch nothing," cried the Inspector from outside, "until I come!"

And now the narrow apartment became filled with all the awe-stricken company, only excepting Monte Irvin, and Brisley, who was attending to the swooning man.

Flat upon the floor, between the door and the ebony chair, arms extended and eyes staring upward at the ceiling, lay Sir Lucien Pyne, his white shirt front redly dyed. In the hush which had fallen, the footsteps of Inspector Whiteleaf sounded loudly as he opened the final door, and swept the interior of an inner room with the rays of the lantern.

The room was barely furnished as an office. There was another half-glazed door opening on to a narrow corridor. This door was locked.

"*Pyne!*" whispered Gray, pale now to the lips. "Do you understand, Seton? It's Pyne! Look! He has been stabbed!"

Sergeant Burton knelt down and gingerly laid his hand upon the stained linen over the breast of Sir Lucien.

"Dead?" asked the Inspector, speaking from the inner doorway.

"Yes."

"You say, sir," turning to Quentin Gray, "that this is Sir Lucien Pyne?"

"Yes."

Inspector Whiteleaf rather clumsily removed his cap. The odor of Seton's cheroot announced itself above the oriental perfume with which the place was laden.

"Burton!"

"Yes?"

"See if this telephone in the office is in order. It appears to be an extension from the outer room."

While the others stood grouped about that still figure on the floor, Sergeant Burton entered the little office.

"Hello!" he cried. "Yes?" A momentary interval, then: "It's all right, sir. What number?"

"Gentlemen," said the Inspector, firmly and authoritatively, "I am about to telephone to Vine Street for instructions. No one will leave the premises."

Amid an intense hush:

"Regent 201," called Sergeant Burton.

CHAPTER VI

RED KERRY

Chief Inspector Kerry, of the Criminal Investigation Department, stood before the empty grate of his cheerless office in New Scotland Yard, one hand thrust into the pocket of his blue reefer jacket and the other twirling a malacca cane, which was heavily silver-mounted and which must have excited the envy of every sergeant-major beholding it. Chief Inspector Kerry wore a very narrow-brimmed bowler hat, having two ventilation holes conspicuously placed immediately above the band. He wore this hat tilted forward and to the right.

"Red Kerry" wholly merited his sobriquet, for the man was as red as fire. His hair, which he wore cropped close as a pugilist's, was brilliantly red, and so was his short, wiry, aggressive moustache. His complexion was red, and from beneath his straight red eyebrows he surveyed the world with a pair of unblinking, intolerant steel-blue eyes. He never smoked in public, as his taste inclined towards Irish twist and a short clay pipe; but he was addicted to the use of chewing-gum, and as he chewed—and he chewed incessantly—he revealed a perfect row of large, white, and positively savage-looking teeth. High cheek bones and prominent maxillary muscles enhanced the truculence indicated by his chin.

But, next to this truculence, which was the first and most alarming trait to intrude itself upon the observer's attention, the outstanding characteristic of Chief Inspector Kerry was his compact neatness. Of no more than medium height but with shoulders like an acrobat, he had slim, straight legs and the feet of a dancing master. His attire, from the square-pointed collar down to the neat black brogues, was spotless. His reefer jacket fitted him faultlessly, but his trousers were cut so unfashionably narrow that the protuberant thigh muscles and the line of a highly developed calf could quite easily be discerned. The hand twirling the cane was small but also muscular, freckled and covered with light down. Red Kerry was built on the lines of a whippet, but carried the equipment of an Irish terrier.

The telephone bell rang. Inspector Kerry moved his square shoulders in a manner oddly suggestive of a wrestler, laid the malacca cane on the mantleshelf, and crossed to the table. Taking up the telephone:

"Yes?" he said, and his voice was high-pitched and imperious.

He listened for a moment.

"Very good, sir."

He replaced the receiver, took up a wet oilskin overall from the back of a chair and the cane from the mantleshelf. Then rolling chewing-gum from one corner of his mouth into the other, he snapped off the electric light and walked from the room.

Along the corridor he went with a lithe, silent step, moving from the hips and swinging his shoulders. Before a door marked "Private" he paused. From his waistcoat pocket he took a little silver convex mirror and surveyed himself critically therein. He adjusted his neat tie, replaced the mirror, knocked at the door and entered the room of the Assistant Commissioner.

This important official was a man constructed on huge principles, a man of military bearing, having tired eyes and a bewildered manner. He conveyed the impression that the collection of documents, books, telephones, and other paraphernalia bestrewing his table had reduced him to a state of stupor. He looked up wearily and met the fierce gaze of the chief inspector with a glance almost apologetic.

"Ah, Chief Inspector Kerry?" he said, with vague surprise. "Yes. I told you to come. Really, I ought to have been at home hours ago. It's most unfortunate. I have to do the work of three men. This is your department, is it not, Chief Inspector?"

He handed Kerry a slip of paper, at which the Chief Inspector stared fiercely.

"Murder!" rapped Kerry. "Sir Lucien Pyne. Yes, sir, I am still on duty."

His speech, in moments of interest, must have suggested to one overhearing him from an adjoining room, for instance, the operation of a telegraphic instrument. He gave to every syllable the value of a rap and certain words he terminated with an audible snap of his teeth.

"Ah," murmured the Assistant Commissioner. "Yes. Divisional Inspector—Somebody (I cannot read the name) has detained all the parties. But you had better report at Vine Street. It appears to be a big case."

He sighed wearily.

"Very good, sir. With your permission I will glance at Sir Lucien's pedigree."

"Certainly—certainly," said the Assistant Commissioner, waving one large hand in the direction of a bookshelf.

Kerry crossed the room, laid his oilskin and cane upon a chair, and from the shelf where it reposed took a squat volume. The Assistant Commissioner, hand pressed to brow, began to study a document which lay before him.

"Here we are," said Kerry, *sotto voce*. "Pyne, Sir Lucien St. Aubyn, fourth baronet, son of General Sir Christian Pyne, K.C.B. H'm! Born Malta.... Oriel College; first in classics.... H'm. Blue.... India, Burma.... Contested Wigan.... attached British Legation.... H'm!..."

He returned the book to its place, took up his overall and cane, and:

"Very good, sir," he said. "I will proceed to Vine Street."

"Certainly—certainly," murmured the Assistant Commissioner, glancing up absently. "Good night."

"Good night, sir."

"Oh, Chief Inspector!"

Kerry turned, his hand on the door-knob.

"Sir?"

"I—er—what was I going to say? Oh, yes! The social importance of the murdered man raises the case from the—er—you follow me? Public interest will become acute, no doubt. I have therefore selected you for your well known discretion. I met Sir Lucien once. Very sad. Good night."

"Good night, sir."

Kerry passed out into the corridor, closing the door quietly. The Assistant Commissioner was a man for whom he entertained the highest respect. Despite the bewildered air and wandering manner, he knew this big, tired-looking soldier for an administrator of infinite capacity and inexhaustive energy.

Proceeding to a room further along the corridor, Chief Inspector Kerry opened the door and looked in.

"Detective-Sergeant Coombes." he snapped, and rolled chewing-gum from side to side of his mouth.

Detective-Sergeant Coombes, a plump, short man having lank black hair and a smile of sly contentment perpetually adorning his round face, rose hurriedly from the chair upon which he had been seated. Another man who was in the room rose also, as if galvanized by the glare of the fierce blue eyes.

"I'm going to Vine Street," said Kerry succinctly; "you're coming with me," turned, and went on his way.

Two taxicabs were standing in the yard, and into the first of these Inspector Kerry stepped, followed by Coombes, the latter breathing heavily and carrying his hat in his hand, since he had not yet found time to put it on.

"Vine Street," shouted Kerry. "Brisk."

He leaned back in the cab, chewing industriously. Coombes, having somewhat recovered his breath, essayed speech.

"Is it something big?" he asked.

"Sure," snapped Kerry. "Do they send *me* to stop dog-fights?"

Knowing the man and recognizing the mood, Coombes became silent, and this silence he did not break all the way to Vine Street. At the station:

"Wait," said Chief Inspector Kerry, and went swinging in, carrying his overall and having the malacca cane tucked under his arm.

A few minutes later he came out again and reentered the cab.

"Piccadilly corner of Old Bond Street," he directed the man.

"Is it burglary?" asked Detective-Sergeant Coombes with interest.

"No," said Kerry. "It's murder; and there seems to be stacks of evidence. Sharpen your pencil."

"Oh!" murmured Coombes.

They were almost immediately at their destination, and Chief Inspector Kerry, dismissing the cabman, set off along Bond Street with his lithe, swinging gait, looking all about him intently. Rain had ceased, but the air was damp and chilly, and few pedestrians were to be seen.

A car was standing before Kazmah's premises, the chauffeur walking up and down on the pavement and flapping his hands across his chest in order to restore circulation. The Chief Inspector stopped, "Hi, my man!" he said.

The chauffeur stood still.

"Whose car?"

"Mr. Monte Irvin's."

Kerry turned on his heel and stepped to the office door. It was ajar, and Kerry, taking an electric torch from his overall pocket, flashed the light upon the name-plate. He stood for a moment, chewing and looking up the darkened stairs. Then, torch in hand, he ascended.

Kazmah's door was closed, and the Chief Inspector rapped loudly. It was opened at once by Sergeant Burton, and Kerry entered, followed by Coombes.

The room at first sight seemed to be extremely crowded. Monte Irvin, very pale and haggard, sat upon the divan beside Quentin Gray. Seton was standing near the cabinet, smoking. These three had evidently been conversing at the time of the detective's arrival with an alert-looking, clean-shaven man whose bag, umbrella, and silk hat stood upon one of the little inlaid tables. Just inside the second door were Brisley and Gunn, both palpably ill at ease, and glancing at Inspector Whiteleaf, who had been interrogating them.

Kerry chewed silently for a moment, bestowing a fierce stare upon each face in turn, then:

"Who's in charge?" he snapped.

"I am," replied Whiteleaf.

"Why is the lower door open?"

"I thought—"

"Don't think. Shut the door. Post your Sergeant inside. No one is to go out. Grab anybody who comes in. Where's the body?"

"This way," said Inspector Whiteleaf hurriedly; then, over his shoulder: "Go down to the door, Burton."

He led Kerry towards the inner room, Coombes at his heels. Brisley and Gunn stood aside to give them passage; Gray and Monte Irvin prepared to follow. At the doorway Kerry turned.

"You will all be good enough to stay where you are," he said. He directed the aggressive stare in Seton's direction. "And if the gentleman smoking a cheroot is not satisfied that he has quite destroyed any clue perceptible by the sense of smell I should be glad to send out for some fireworks."

He tossed his oilskin and his cane on the divan and went into the room of seance, savagely biting at a piece of apparently indestructible chewing-gum.

The torn green curtain had been laid aside and the electric lights turned on in the inside rooms. Pallid, Sir Lucien Pyne lay by the ebony chair glaring horribly upward.

Always with the keen eyes glancing this way and that, Inspector Kerry crossed the little audience room and entered the enclosure contained between the two screens. By the side of the dead man he stood, looking down silently. Then he dropped upon one knee and peered closely into the white face. He looked up.

"He has not been moved?"

"No."

Kerry bent yet lower, staring closely at a discolored abrasion on Sir Lucien's forehead. His glance wandered from thence to the carved ebony chair. Still kneeling, he drew from his waistcoat pocket a powerful lens contained in a washleather bag. He began to examine the back and sides of the chair. Once he laid his finger lightly on a protruding point of the carving, and then scrutinised his finger through the glass. He examined the dead man's hands, his nails, his garments. Then he crawled about, peering closely at the carpet.

He stood up suddenly. "The doctor," he snapped.

Inspector Whiteleaf retired, but returned immediately with the clean-shaven man to whom Monte Irvin had been talking when Kerry arrived.

"Good evening, doctor," said Kerry. "Do I know your name? Start your notes, Coombes."

"My name is Dr. Wilbur Weston, and I live in Albemarle Street."

"Who called you?"

"Inspector Whiteleaf telephoned to me about half an hour ago."

"You examined the dead man?"

"I did."

"You avoided moving him?"

"It was unnecessary to move him. He was dead, and the wound was in the left shoulder. I pulled his coat open and unbuttoned his shirt. That was all."

"How long dead?"

"I should say he had been dead not more than an hour when I saw him."

"What had caused death?"

"The stab of some long, narrow-bladed weapon, such as a stiletto."

"Why a stiletto?" Kerry's fierce eyes challenged him. "Did you ever see a wound made by a stiletto?"

"Several—in Italy, and one at Saffron Hill. They are characterised by very little external bleeding."

"Right, doctor. It had reached his heart?"

"Yes. The blow was delivered from behind."

"How do you know?"

"The direction of the wound is forward. I have seen an almost identical wound in the case of an Italian woman stabbed by a jealous rival."

"He would fall on his back."

"Oh, no. He would fall on his face, almost certainly."

"But he lies on his back."

"In my opinion he had been moved."

"Right. I know he had. Good night, doctor. See him out, Inspector."

Dr. Weston seemed rather startled by this abrupt dismissal, but the steel-blue eyes of Inspector Kerry were already bent again upon the dead man, and, murmuring "good night," the doctor took his departure, followed by Whiteleaf.

"Shut this door," snapped Kerry after the Inspector. "I will call when I want you. You stay, Coombes. Got it all down?"

Sergeant Coombes scratched his head with the end of a pencil, and:

"Yes," he said, with hesitancy. "That is, except the word after 'narrow-bladed weapon such as a' I've got what looks like 'steelhatto.'"

Kerry glared.

"Try taking the cotton-wool out of your ears," he suggested. "The word was stiletto, s-t-i-l-e-t-t-o—stiletto."

"Oh," said Coombes, "thanks."

Silence fell between the two men from Scotland Yard. Kerry stood awhile, chewing and staring at the ghastly face of Sir Lucien. Then:

"Go through all pockets," he directed.

Sergeant Coombes placed his notebook and pencil upon the seat of the chair and set to work. Kerry entered the inside room or office. It contained a writing-table (upon which was a telephone and a pile of old newspapers), a cabinet, and two chairs. Upon one of the chairs lay a crush-hat, a cane, and an overcoat. He glanced at some of the newspapers, then opened the drawers of the writing-table. They were empty. The cabinet proved to be locked, and a door which he saw must open upon a narrow passage running beside the suite of rooms was locked also. There was nothing in the pockets of the overcoat, but inside the hat he found pasted the initials L. P. He rolled chewing-gum, stared reflectively at the little window immediately above the table, through which a glimpse might be obtained of the ebony chair, and went out again.

"Nothing," reported Coombes.

"What do you mean—nothing?"

"His pockets are empty!"

"All of them?"

"Every one."

"Good," said Kerry. "Make a note of it. He wears a real pearl stud and a good signet ring; also a gold wrist watch, face broken and hands stopped at seven-fifteen. That was the time he died. He was stabbed from behind as he stood where I'm standing now, fell forward, struck his head on the leg of the chair, and lay face downwards."

"I've got that," muttered Coombes. "What stopped the watch?"

"Broken as he fell. There are tiny fragments of glass stuck in the carpet, showing the exact position in which his body originally lay; and for God's sake stop smiling."

Kerry threw open the door.

"Who first found the body?" he demanded of the silent company.

"I did," cried Quentin Gray, coming forward. "I and Seton Pasha."

"Seton Pasha!" Kerry's teeth snapped together, so that he seemed to bite off the words. "I don't see a Turk present."

Seton smiled quietly.

"My friend uses a title which was conferred upon me some years ago by the ex-Khedive," he said. "My name is Greville Seton."

Inspector Kerry glanced back across his shoulder.

"Notes," he said. "Unlock your ears, Coombes." He looked at Gray. "What is your name?"

"Quentin Gray."

"Who are you, and in what way are you concerned in this case?"

"I am the son of Lord Wrexborough, and I—"

He paused, glancing helplessly at Seton. He had recognized that the first mention of Rita Irvin's name in the police evidence must be made by himself.

"Speak up, sir," snapped Kerry. "Sergeant Coombes is deaf."

Gray's face flushed, and his eyes gleamed angrily.

"I should be glad, Inspector," he said, "if you would remember that the dead man was a personal acquaintance and that other friends are concerned in this ghastly affair."

"Coombes will remember it," replied Kerry frigidly. "He's taking notes."

"Look here—" began Gray.

Seton laid his hand upon the angry man's shoulder.

"Pull up, Gray," he said quietly. "Pull up, old chap." He turned his cool regard upon Chief Inspector Kerry, twirling the cord of his monocle about one finger. "I may remark, Inspector Kerry—for I understand this to be your name—that your conduct of the inquiry is not always characterised by the best possible taste."

Kerry rolled chewing-gum, meeting Seton's gaze with a stare intolerant and aggressive. He imparted that odd writhing movement to his shoulders.

"For my conduct I am responsible to the Commissioner," he replied. "And if he's not satisfied the Commissioner can have my written resignation at any hour in the twenty-four that he's short of a pipe-lighter. If it would not inconvenience you to keep quiet for two minutes I will continue my examination of this witness."

CHAPTER VII

FURTHER EVIDENCE

The examination of Quentin Gray was three times interrupted by telephone messages from Vine Street; and to the unsatisfactory character of these the growing irascibility of Chief Inspector Kerry bore testimony. Then the divisional surgeon arrived, and Burton incurred the wrath of the Chief Inspector by deserting his post to show the doctor upstairs.

"If inspired idiocy can help the law," shouted Kerry, "the man who did this job is as good as dead!" He turned his fierce gaze in Gray's direction. "Thank you, sir. I need trouble you no further."

"Do you wish me to remain?"

"No. Inspector Whiteleaf, see these two gentlemen past the Sergeant on duty."

"But damn it all!" cried Gray, his pent-up emotions at last demanding an outlet, "I won't submit to your infernal dragooning! Do you realize that while you're standing here, doing nothing—absolutely nothing—an unhappy woman is—"

"I realize," snapped Kerry, showing his teeth in canine fashion, "that if you're not outside in ten seconds there's going to be a cloud of dust on the stairs!"

White with passion, Gray was on the point of uttering other angry and provocative words when Seton took his arm in a firm grip. "Gray!" he said sharply. "You leave with me now or I leave alone."

The two walked from the room, followed by Whiteleaf. As they disappeared:

"Read out all the *times* mentioned in the last witness's evidence," directed Kerry, undisturbed by the rencontre.

Sergeant Coombes smiled rather uneasily, consulting his notebook.

"'At about half-past six I drove to Bond Street,'" he began.

"I said the *times*," rapped Kerry. "I know to what they refer. Just give me the times as mentioned."

"Oh," murmured Coombes, "Yes. 'About half-past six.'" He ran his finger down the page. "'A quarter to seven.' 'Seven o'clock.' 'Twenty-five minutes past seven.' 'Eight o'clock.'"

"Stop!" said Kerry. "That's enough." He fixed a baleful glance upon Gunn, who from a point of the room discreetly distant from the terrible red man was watching with watery eyes. "Who's the smart in all the overcoats?" he demanded.

"My name is James Gunn," replied this greatly insulted man in a husky voice.

"Who are you? What are you? What are you doing here?"

"I'm employed by Spinker's Agency, and—"

"Oh!" shouted Kerry, moving his shoulders. He approached the speaker and glared menacingly into his purple face. "Ho, ho! So you're one of the queer birds out of that roost, are you? Spinker's Agency! Ah, yes!" He fixed his gaze now upon the pale features of Brisley. "I've seen you before, haven't I?"

"Yes, Chief Inspector," said Brisley, licking his lips. "Hayward's Heath. We have been retained by—"

"*You* have been retained!" shouted Kerry. "*You* have!"

He twisted round upon his heel, facing Monte Irvin. Angry words trembled on his tongue. But at sight of the broken man who sat there alone, haggard, a subtle change of expression crept into his fierce eyes, and when he spoke again the high-pitched voice was almost gentle. "You had employed these men, sir, to watch—"

He paused, glancing towards Whiteleaf, who had just entered again, and then in the direction of the inner room where the divisional surgeon was at work.

"To watch my wife, Inspector. Thank you, but all the world will know tomorrow. I might as well get used to it."

Monte Irvin's pallor grew positively alarming. He swayed suddenly and extended his hands in a significant groping fashion. Kerry sprang forward and supported him.

"All right, Inspector—all right," muttered Irvin. "Thank you. It has been a great shock. At first I feared—"

"You thought your wife had been attacked, I understand? Well—it's not so bad as that, sir. I am going to walk downstairs to the car with you."

"But there is so much you will want to know—"

"It can keep until tomorrow. I've enough work in this peep-show here to have me busy all night. Come along. Lean on my arm."

Monte Irvin rose unsteadily. He knew that there was cardiac trouble in his family, but he had never realized before the meaning of his heritage. He felt physically ill.

"Inspector"—his voice was a mere whisper—"have you any theory to explain—"

"Mrs. Irvin's disappearance? Don't worry, sir. Without exactly having a theory I think I may say that in my opinion she will turn up presently."

"God bless you," murmured Irvin, as Kerry assisted him out on to the landing.

Inspector Whiteleaf held back the sliding door, the mechanism of which had been broken so that the door now automatically remained half closed.

"Funny, isn't it," said Gunn, as the two disappeared and Inspector Whiteleaf re-entered, "that a man should be so upset about the disappearance of a woman he was going to divorce?"

"Damn funny!" said Whiteleaf, whose temper was badly frayed by contact with Kerry. "I should have a good laugh if I were you."

He crossed the room, going in to where the surgeon was examining the victim of this mysterious crime. Gunn stared after him dismally.

"A person doesn't get much sympathy from the police, Brisley," he declared. "That one's almost as bad as *him*," jerking his thumb in the direction of the landing.

Brisley smiled in a somewhat sickly manner.

"Red Kerry is a holy terror," he agreed, *sotto voce*, glancing aside to where Coombes was checking his notes. "Look out! Here he comes."

"Now," cried Kerry, swinging into the room, "what's the game? Plotting to defeat the ends of justice?"

He stood with hands thrust in reefer pockets, feet wide apart, glancing fiercely from Brisley to Gunn, and from Gunn back again to Brisley. Neither of the representatives of Spinker's Agency ventured any remark, and:

"How long have you been watching Mrs. Monte Irvin?" demanded Kerry.

"Nearly a fortnight," replied Brisley.

"Got your evidence in writing?"

"Yes."

"Up to tonight?"

"Yes."

"Dictate to Sergeant Coombes."

He turned on his heel and crossed to the divan upon which his oilskin overall was lying. Rapidly he removed his reefer and his waistcoat, folded them, and placed them neatly beside his overall. He retained his bowler at its jaunty angle.

A cud of presumably flavorless chewing-gum he deposited in a brass bowl, and from a little packet which he had taken out of his jacket pocket he drew a fresh piece, redolent of mint. This he put into his mouth, and returned the packet to its resting-place. A slim, trim figure, he stood looking round him reflectively.

"Now," he muttered, "what about it?"

CHAPTER VIII.

KERRY CONSULTS THE ORACLE

The clock of Brixton Town Hall was striking the hour of 1 a.m. as Chief Inspector Kerry inserted his key in the lock of the door of his house in Spenser Road.

A light was burning in the hallway, and from the little dining-room on the left the reflection of a cheerful fire danced upon the white paint of the half-open door. Kerry deposited his hat, cane, and overall upon the rack, and moving very quietly entered the room and turned on the light. A modestly furnished and scrupulously neat apartment was revealed. On the sheepskin rug before the fire a Manx cat was dozing beside a pair of carpet slippers. On the table some kind of cold repast was laid, the viands concealed under china covers. At a large bottle of Guinness's Extra Stout Kerry looked with particular appreciation.

He heaved a long sigh of contentment, and opened the bottle of stout. Having poured out a glass of the black and foaming liquid and satisfied an evidently urgent thirst, he explored beneath the covers, and presently was seated before a spread of ham and tongue, tomatoes, and bread and butter.

A door opened somewhere upstairs, and:

"Is that yoursel', Dan?" inquired a deep but musical female voice.

"Sure it is," replied Kerry; and no one who had heard the high official tones of the imperious Chief Inspector would have supposed that they could be so softened and modulated. "You should have been asleep hours ago, Mary."

"Have ye to go out again?"

"I have, bad luck; but don't trouble to come down. I've all I want and more."

"If 'tis a new case I'll come down."

"It's the devil's own case; but you'll get your death of cold."

Sounds of movement in the room above followed, and presently footsteps on the stairs. Mrs. Kerry, enveloped in a woollen dressing-gown, which obviously belonged to the Inspector, came into the room.

Upon her Kerry directed a look from which all fierceness had been effaced, and which expressed only an undying admiration. And, indeed, Mary Kerry was in many respects a remarkable character. Half an inch taller than Kerry, she fully merited the compliment designed by that trite apothegm, "a fine woman." Large-boned but shapely, as she came in with her long dark hair neatly plaited, it seemed to her husband—who had remained her lover—that he saw before him the rosy-cheeked lass whom ten years before he had met and claimed on the chilly shores of Loch Broom. By all her neighbors Mrs. Kerry was looked upon as a proud, reserved person, who had held herself much aloof since her husband had become Chief Inspector; and the reputation enjoyed by Red Kerry was that of an aggressive and uncompanionable man. Now here was a lover's meeting, not lacking the shy, downward glance of dark eyes as steel-blue eyes flashed frank admiration.

Kerry, who quarrelled with everybody except the Assistant Commissioner, had only found one cause of quarrel with Mary. He was a devout Roman Catholic, and for five years he had clung with the bull-dog tenacity which was his to the belief that he could convert his wife to the faith of Rome. She remained true to the Scottish Free Church, in whose precepts she had been reared, and at the end of the five years Kerry gave it up and admired her all the more for her Caledonian strength of mind. Many and heated were the debates he had held with worthy Father O'Callaghan respecting the validity of a marriage not solemnized by a priest, but of late years he had grown reconciled to the parting of the ways on Sunday morning; and as the early mass was over before the Scottish service he was regularly to be seen outside a certain Presbyterian chapel waiting for his heretical spouse.

He pulled her down on to his knee and kissed her.

"It's twelve hours since I saw you," he said.

She rested her arm on the back of the saddle-back chair, and her dark head close beside Kerry's fiery red one.

"I kenned ye had a new case on," she said, "when it grew so late. How long can ye stay?"

"An hour. No more. There's a lot to do before the papers come out in the morning. By breakfast time all England, including the murderer, will know I'm in charge of the case. I wish I could muzzle the Press."

"'Tis a murder, then? The Lord gi'e us grace. Ye'll be wishin' to tell me?"

"Yes. I'm stumped!"

"Ye've time for a rest an' a smoke. Put ye're slippers on."

"I've no time for that, Mary."

She stood up and took the slippers from the hearth.

"Put ye're slippers on," she repeated firmly.

Kerry stooped without another word and began to unlace his brogues. Meanwhile from a side-table his wife brought a silver tobacco-box and a stumpy Irish clay. The slippers substituted for his shoes, Kerry lovingly filled the cracked and blackened bowl with strong Irish twist, which he first teased carefully in his palm. The bowl rested almost under his nostrils when he put the pipe in his mouth, and how he contrived to light it without burning his moustache was not readily apparent. He succeeded, however, and soon was puffing clouds of pungent smoke into the air with the utmost contentment.

"Now," said his wife, seating herself upon the arm of the chair, "tell me, Dan."

Thereupon began a procedure identical to that which had characterized the outset of every successful case of the Chief Inspector. He rapidly outlined the complexities of the affair in old Bond Street, and Mary Kerry surveyed the problem with a curious and almost fey detachment of mind, which enabled her to see light where all was darkness to the man on the spot. With the clarity of a trained observer Kerry described the apartments of Kazmah, the exact place where the murdered man had been found, and the construction of the rooms. He gave the essential points from the evidence of the several witnesses, quoting the exact times at which various episodes had taken place. Mary Kerry, looking straightly before her with unseeing eyes, listened in silence until he ceased speaking; then:

"There are really but twa rooms," she said, in a faraway voice, "but the second o' these is parteetioned into three parts?"

"That's it."

"A door free the landing opens upon the fairst room, a door free a passage opens upon the second. Where does yon passage lead?"

"From the main stair along beside Kazmah's rooms to a small back stair. This back stair goes from top to bottom of the building, from the end of the same hallway as the main stair."

"There is na either way out but by the front door?"

"No."

"Then if the evidence o' the Spinker man is above suspeecion, Mrs. Irvin and this Kazmah were still on the premises when ye arrived?"

"Exactly. I gathered that much at Vine Street before I went on to Bond Street. The whole block was surrounded five minutes after my arrival, and it still is."

"What ither offices are in this passage?"

"None. It's a blank wall on the left, and one door on the right—the one opening into the Kazmah office. There are other premises on the same floor, but they are across the landing."

"What premises?"

"A solicitor and a commission agent."

"The floor below?"

"It's all occupied by a modiste, Renan."

"The top floor?"

"Cubanis Cigarette Company, a servants' and an electrician."

"Nae more?"

"No more."

"Where does yon back stair open on the topmaist floor?"

"In a corridor similar to that alongside Kazmah's. It has two windows on the right overlooking a narrow roof and the top of the arcade, and on the left is the Cubanis Cigarette Company. The other offices are across the landing."

Mary Kerry stared into space awhile.

"Kazmah and Mrs. Irvin could ha' come down to the fairst floor, or gane up to the thaird floor unseen by the Spinker man," she said dreamily.

"But they couldn't have reached the street, my dear!" cried Kerry.

"No—they couldn'a ha' gained the street."

She became silent again, her husband watching her expectantly. Then:

"If puir Sir Lucien Pyne was killed at a quarter after seven—the time his watch was broken—the native sairvent did no' kill him. Frae the Spinker's evidence the black man went awe' before then," she said. "Mrs. Irvin?"

Kerry shook his head.

"From all accounts a slip of a woman," he replied. "It was a strong hand that struck the blow."

"Kazmah?"

"Probably."

"Mr. Quentin Gray came back wi' a cab and went upstairs, free the Spinker's evidence, at aboot a quarter after seven, and came doon five meenites later sair pale an' fretful."

Kerry surrounded himself and the speaker with wreaths of stifling smoke.

"We have only the bare word of Mr. Gray that he didn't go in again, Mary; but I believe him. He's a hot-headed fool, but square."

"Then 'twas yon Kazmah," announced Mrs. Kerry. "Who is Kazmah?"

Her husband laughed shortly.

"That's the point at which I got stumped," he replied. "We've heard of him at the Yard, of course, and we know that under the cloak of a dealer in Eastern perfumes he carried on a fortune-telling business. He managed to avoid prosecution, though. It took me over an hour tonight to explore the thought-reading mechanism; it's a sort of Maskelyne's Mysteries worked from the inside room. But who Kazmah is or what's his nationality I know no more than the man in the moon."

"Pairfume?" queried the far-away voice.

"Yes, Mary. The first room is a sort of miniature scent bazaar. There are funny little imitation antique flasks of Kazmah preparations, creams, perfumes and incense, also small square wooden boxes of a kind of Turkish delight, and a stock of Egyptian mummy-beads, statuettes, and the like, which may be genuine for all I know."

"Nae books or letters?"

"Not a thing, except his own advertisements, a telephone directory, and so on."

"The inside office bureau?"

"Empty as Mother Hubbard's cupboard!"

"The place was ransacked by the same folk that emptied the dead man's pockets so as tee leave nae clue," pronounced the sibyl-like voice. "Mr. Gray said he had choc'lates wi' him. Where did he leave them?"

"Mary, you're a wonder!" exclaimed the admiring Kerry. "The box was lying on the divan in the first room where he said he had left it on going out for a cab."

"Does nane o' the evidence show if Mrs. Irvin had been to Kazmah's before?"

"Yes. She went there fairly regularly to buy perfume."

"No' for the fortune-tellin'?"

"No. According to Mr. Gray, to buy perfume."

"Had Mr. Gray been there wi' her before?"

"No. Sir Lucien Pyne seems to have been her pretty constant companion."

"Do ye suspect she was his lady-love?"

"I believe Mr. Gray suspects something of the kind."

"And Mr. Gray?"

"He is not such an old friend as Sir Lucien was. But I fancy nevertheless it was Mr. Gray that her husband doubted."

"Do ye suspect the puir soul had cause, Dan?"

"No," replied Kerry promptly; "I don't. The boy is mad about her, but I fancy she just liked his company. He's the heir of Lord Wrexborough, and Mrs. Irvin used to be a stage beauty. It's a usual state of affairs, and more often than not means nothing."

"I dinna ken sich folk," declared Mary Kerry. "They a'most desairve all they get. They are bound tee come tee nae guid end. Where did ye say Sir Lucien lived?"

"Albemarle Street; just round the corner."

"Ye told me that he only kepit twa sairvents: a cook, hoosekeper, who lived awe', an' a man—a foreigner?"

"A kind of half-baked Dago, named Juan Mareno. A citizen of the United States according to his own account."

"Ye dinna like Juan Mareno?"

"He's a hateful swine!" flashed Kerry, with sudden venom. "I'm watching Mareno very closely. Coombes is at work upon Sir Lucien's papers. His life was a bit of a mystery. He seems to have had no relations living, and I can't find that he even employed a solicitor."

"Ye'll be sairchin' for yon Egyptian?"

"The servant? Yes. We'll have him by the morning, and then we shall know who Kazmah is. Meanwhile, in which of the offices is Kazmah hiding?"

Mary Kerry was silent for so long that her husband repeated the question:

"In which of the offices is Kazmah hiding?"

"In nane," she said dreamily. "Ye surrounded the buildings too late, I ken."

"Eh!" cried Kerry, turning his head excitedly. "But the man Brisley was at the door all night!"

"It doesna' matter. They have escapit."

Kerry scratched his close-cropped head in angry perplexity.

"You're always right, Mary," he said. "But hang me if—Never mind! When we get the servant we'll soon get Kazmah."

"Aye," murmured his wife. "If ye hae na' got Kazmah the now."

"But—Mary! This isn't helping me! It's mystifying me deeper than ever!"

"It's no' clear eno', Dan. But for sure behind this mystery o' the death o' Sir Lucien there's a darker mystery still; sair dark. 'Tis the biggest case ye ever had. Dinna look for Kazmah. Look tee find why the woman went tee him; and try tee find the meanin' o' the sma' window behind the big chair.... Yes"—she seemed to be staring at some distant visible object—"watch the man Mareno—"

"But—Mrs. Irvin—"

"Is in God's guid keepin'—"

"You don't think she's dead!"

"She is wairse than dead. Her sins have found her out." The fey light suddenly left her eyes, and they became filled with tears. She turned impulsively to her husband. "Oh, Dan! Ye must find her! Ye must find her! Puir weak hairt—dinna ye ken how she is suffering!"

"My dear," he said, putting his arms around her, "What is it? What is it?"

She brushed the tears from her eyes and tried to smile. "'Tis something like the second sight, Dan," she answered simply. "And it's escapit me again. I a'most had the clue to it a' oh, there's some horrible wickedness in it, an' cruelty an' shame."

The clock on the mantel shelf began to peal. Kerry was watching his wife's rosy face with a mixture of loving admiration and wonder. She looked so very bonny and placid and capable that he was puzzled anew at the strange gift which she seemingly inherited from her mother, who had been equally shrewd, equally comely and similarly endowed.

"God bless us all!" he said, kissed her heartily, and stood up. "Back to bed you go, my dear. I must be off. There's Mr. Irvin to see in the morning, too."

A few minutes later he was swinging through the deserted streets, his mind wholly occupied with lover-like reflections to the exclusion of those professional matters which properly should have been engaging his attention. As he passed the end of a narrow court near the railway station, the gleam of his silver mounted malacca attracted the attention of a couple of loafers who were leaning one on either side of an iron pillar in the shadow of the unsavory alley. Not another pedestrian was in sight, and only the remote night-sounds of London broke the silence.

Twenty paces beyond, the footpads silently closed in upon their prey. The taller of the pair reached him first, only to receive a back-handed blow full in his face which sent him reeling a couple of yards.

Round leapt the assaulted man to face his second assailant.

"If you two smarts really want handling," he rapped ferociously, "say the word, and I'll bash you flat."

As he turned, the light of a neighboring lamp shone down upon the savage face, and a smothered yell came from the shorter ruffian:

"Blimey, Bill! It's *Red Kerry!*"

Whereupon, as men pursued by devils, the pair made off like the wind!

Kerry glared after the retreating figures for a moment, and a grin of fierce satisfaction revealed his gleaming teeth. He turned again and swung on his way toward the main road. The incident had done him good. It had banished domestic matters from his mind, and he was become again the highly trained champion of justice, standing, an unseen buckler, between society and the criminal.

CHAPTER IX

A PACKET OF CIGARETTES

Following their dismissal by Chief Inspector Kerry, Seton and Gray walked around to the latter's chambers in Piccadilly. They proceeded in silence, Gray too angry for speech, and Seton busy with reflections. As the man admitted them:

"Has anyone 'phoned, Willis?" asked Gray.

"No one, sir."

They entered a large room which combined the characteristics of a library with those of a military gymnasium. Gray went to a side table and mixed drinks. Placing a glass before Seton, he emptied his own at a draught.

"If you'll excuse me for a moment," he said, "I should like to ring up and see if by any possible chance there's news of Rita."

He walked out to the telephone, and Seton heard him making a call. Then:

"Hullo! Is that you, Hinkes?" he asked.... "Yes, speaking. Is Mrs. Irvin at home?"

A few moments of silence followed, and:

"Thanks! Good-bye," said Gray.

He rejoined his friend.

"Nothing," he reported, and made a gesture of angry resignation. "Evidently Hinkes is still unaware of what has happened. Irvin hasn't returned yet. Seton, this business is driving me mad."

He refilled his glass, and having looked in his cigarette-case, began to ransack a small cupboard.

"Damn it all!" he exclaimed. "I haven't got a cigarette in the place!"

"I don't smoke them myself," said Seton, "but I can offer you a cheroot."

"Thanks. They are a trifle too strong. Hullo! here are some."

From the back of a shelf he produced a small, plain brown packet, and took out of it a cigarette at which he stared oddly. Seton, smoking one of the inevitable cheroots, watched him, tapping his teeth with the rim of his eyeglass.

"Poor old Pyne!" muttered Gray, and, looking up, met the inquiring glance. "Pyne left these here only the other day," he explained awkwardly. "I don't know where he got them, but they are something very special. I suppose I might as well."

He lighted one, and, uttering a weary sigh, threw himself into a deep leather-covered arm-chair. Almost immediately he was up again. The telephone bell had rung. His eyes alight with hope, he ran out, leaving the door open so that his conversation was again audible to the visitor.

"Yes, yes, speaking. What?" His tone changed "Oh, it's you, Margaret. What?... Certainly, delighted. No, there's nobody here but old Seton Pasha. What? You've heard the fellows talk about him who were out East.... Yes, that's the chap.... Come right along."

"You don't propose to lionise me, I hope, Gray?" said Seton, as Gray returned to his seat.

The other laughed.

"I forgot you could hear me," he admitted. "It's my cousin, Margaret Halley. You'll like her. She's a tip-top girl, but eccentric. Goes in for pilling."

"Pilling?" inquired Seton gravely.

"Doctoring. She's an M.R.C.S., and only about twenty-four or so. Fearfully clever kid; makes me feel an infant."

"Flat heels, spectacles, and a judicial manner?"

"Flat heels, yes. But not the other. She's awfully pretty, and used to look simply terrific in khaki. She was an M.O. in Serbia, you know, and afterwards at some nurses' hospital in Kent. She's started in practice for herself now round in Dover Street. I wonder what she wants."

Silence fell between them; for, although prompted by different reasons, both were undesirous of discussing the tragedy; and this silence prevailed until the ringing of the doorbell announced the arrival of the girl. Willis opening the door, she entered composedly, and Gray introduced Seton.

"I am so glad to have met you at last, Mr. Seton," she said laughingly. "From Quentin's many accounts I had formed the opinion that you were a kind of *Arabian Nights* myth."

"I am glad to disappoint you," replied Seton, finding something very refreshing in the company of this pretty girl, who wore a creased Burberry, and stray locks of whose abundant bright hair floated about her face in the most careless fashion imaginable.

She turned to her cousin, frowning in a rather puzzled way.

"Whatever have you been burning here?" she asked. "There is such a curious smell in the room."

Gray laughed more heartily than he had laughed that night, glancing in Seton's direction.

"So much for your taste in cigars!" he cried

"Oh!" said Margaret, "I'm sure it's not Mr. Seton's cigar. It isn't a smell of tobacco."

"I don't believe they're *made* of tobacco!" cried Gray, laughing louder yet, although his merriment was forced.

Seton smiled good-naturedly at the joke, but he had perceived at the moment of Margaret's entrance the fact that her gaiety also was assumed. Serious business had dictated her visit, and he wondered the more to note how deeply this odor, real or fancied, seemed to intrigue her.

She sat down in the chair which Gray placed by the fireside, and her cousin unceremoniously slid the brown packet of cigarettes across the little table in her direction.

"Try one of these, Margaret," he said. "They are great, and will quite drown the unpleasant odor of which you complain."

Whereupon the observant Seton saw a quick change take place in the girl's expression. She had the same clear coloring as her cousin, and now this freshness deserted her cheeks, and her pretty face became quite pale. She was staring at the brown packet. "Where did you get them?" she asked quietly.

A smile faded from Gray's lips. Those five words had translated him in spirit to that green-draped room in which Sir Lucien Pyne was lying dead. He glanced at Seton in the appealing way which sometimes made him appear so boyish.

"Er—from Pyne," he replied. "I must tell you, Margaret—"

"Sir Lucien Pyne?" she interrupted.

"Yes."

"Not from Rita Irvin?"

Quentin Gray started upright in his chair.

"No! But why do you mention her?"

Margaret bit her lip in sudden perplexity.

"Oh, I don't know." She glanced apologetically toward Seton. He rose immediately.

"My dear Miss Halley," he said, "I perceive, indeed I had perceived all along, that you have something of a private nature to communicate to your cousin."

But Gray stood up, and:

"Seton! ... Margaret!" he said, looking from one to the other. "I mean to say, Margaret, if you've anything to tell me about Rita ... Have you? Have you?"

He fixed his gaze eagerly upon her.

"I have—yes."

Seton prepared to take his leave, but Gray impetuously thrust him back, immediately turning again to his cousin.

"Perhaps you haven't heard, Margaret," he began.

"I have heard what has happened tonight—to Sir Lucien."

Both men stared at her silently for a moment.

"Seton has been with me all the time," said Gray. "If he will consent to stay, with your permission, Margaret, I should like him to do so."

"Why, certainly," agreed the girl. "In fact, I shall be glad of his advice."

Seton inclined his head, and without another word resumed his seat. Gray was too excited to sit down again. He stood on the tiger-skin rug before the fender, watching his cousin and smoking furiously.

"Firstly, then," continued Margaret, "please throw that cigarette in the fire, Quentin."

Gray removed the cigarette from between his lips, and stared at it dazedly. He looked at the girl, and the clear grey eyes were watching him with an inscrutable expression.

"Right-o!" he said awkwardly, and tossed the cigarette in the fire. "You used to smoke like a furnace, Margaret. Is this some new 'cult'?"

"I still smoke a great deal more than is good for me," she confessed, "but I don't smoke opium."

The effect of these words upon the two men who listened was curious. Gray turned an angry glance upon the brown packet lying on the table, and "Faugh!" he exclaimed, and drawing a handkerchief from his sleeve began disgustedly to wipe his lips. Seton stared hard at the speaker, tossed his cheroot into the fire, and taking up the packet withdrew a cigarette and sniffed at it critically. Margaret watched him.

He tore the wrapping off, and tasted a strand of the tobacco.

"Good heavens!" he whispered. "Gray, these things are doped!"

CHAPTER X

SIR LUCIEN'S STUDY WINDOW

Old Bond Street presented a gloomy and deserted prospect to Chief Inspector Kerry as he turned out of Piccadilly and swung along toward the premises of Kazmah. He glanced at the names on some of the shop windows as he passed, and wondered if the furriers, jewelers and other merchants dealing in costly wares properly appreciated the services of the Metropolitan Police Force. He thought of the peacefully slumbering tradesmen in their suburban homes, the safety of their stocks wholly dependent upon the vigilance of that Unsleeping Eye—for to an unsleeping eye he mentally compared the service of which he was a member.

A constable stood on duty before the door of the block. Red Kerry was known by sight and reputation to every member of the force, and the constable saluted as the celebrated Chief Inspector appeared.

"Anything to report, constable?"

"Yes, sir."

"What?"

"The ambulance has been for the body, and another gentleman has been."

Kerry stared at the man.

"Another gentleman? Who the devil's the other gentleman?"

"I don't know, sir. He came with Inspector Whiteleaf, and was inside for nearly an hour."

"Inspector Whiteleaf is off duty. What time was this?"

"Twelve-thirty, sir."

Kerry chewed reflectively ere nodding to the man and passing on.

"Another gentleman!" he muttered, entering the hallway. "Why didn't Inspector Warley report this? Who the devil—" Deep in thought he walked upstairs, finding his way by the light of the pocket torch which he carried. A second constable was on duty at Kazmah's door. He saluted.

"Anything to report?" rapped Kerry.

"Yes, sir. The body has been removed, and the gentleman with Inspector—"

"Damn that for a tale! Describe this gentleman."

"Rather tall, pale, dark, clean-shaven. Wore a fur-collared overcoat, collar turned up. He was accompanied by Inspector Whiteleaf."

"H'm. Anything else?"

"Yes. About an hour ago I heard a noise on the next floor—"

"Eh!" snapped Kerry, and shone the light suddenly into the man's face so that he blinked furiously.

"Eh? What kind of noise?"

"Very slight. Like something moving."

"Like *something!* Like *what* thing? A cat or an elephant?"

"More like, say, a box or a piece of furniture."

"And you did—what?"

"I went up to the top landing and listened."

"What did you hear?"

"Nothing at all."

Chief Inspector Kerry chewed audibly.

"All quiet?" he snapped.

"Absolutely. But I'm certain I heard something all the same."

"How long had Inspector Whiteleaf and this dark horse in the fur coat been gone at the time you heard the noise?"

"About half an hour, sir."

"Do you think the noise came from the landing or from one of the offices above?"

"An office I should say. It was very dim."

Chief Inspector Kerry pushed upon the broken door, and walked into the rooms of Kazmah. Flashing the ray of his torch on the wall, he found the switch and snapped up the lights. He removed his overall and tossed it on a divan with his cane. Then, tilting his bowler further forward, he thrust his hands into his reefer pockets, and stood staring toward the door, beyond which lay the room of the murder, in darkness.

"Who is he?" he muttered. "What's it mean?"

Taking up the torch, he walked through and turned on the lights in the inner rooms. For a long time he stood staring at the little square window low down behind the ebony chair, striving to imagine uses for it as his wife had urged him to do. The globular green lamp in the second apartment was worked by three switches situated in the inside room, and he had discovered that in this way the visitor who came to consult Kazmah was treated to the illusion of a gradually falling darkness. Then, the door in the first partition being opened, whoever sat in the ebony chair would become visible by the gradual uncovering of a light situated above the chair. On this light being covered again the figure would apparently fade away.

It was ingenious, and, so far, quite clear. But two things badly puzzled the inquirer; the little window down behind the chair, and the fact that all the arrangements for raising and lowering the lights were situated not in the narrow chamber in which Kazmah's chair stood, and in which Sir Lucien had been found, but in the room behind it— the room with which the little window communicated.

The table upon which the telephone rested was set immediately under this mysterious window, the window was provided with a green blind, and the switchboard controlling the complicated lighting scheme was also within reach of anyone seated at the table.

Kerry rolled mint gum from side to side of his mouth, and absently tried the handle of the door opening out from this interior room— evidently the office of the establishment—into the corridor. He knew it to be locked. Turning, he walked through the suite and out on to the landing, passing the constable and going upstairs to the top floor, torch in hand.

From the main landing he walked along the narrow corridor until he stood at the head of the back stairs. The door nearest to him bore the name: "Cubanis Cigarette Company." He tried the handle. The door was locked, as he had anticipated. Kneeling down, he peered into the keyhole, holding the electric torch close beside his face and chewing industriously.

Ere long he stood up, descended again, but by the back stair, and stood staring reflectively at the door communicating with Kazmah's inner room. Then walking along the corridor to where the man stood on the landing, he went in again to the mysterious apartments, but only to get his cane and his overall and to turn out the lights.

Five minutes later he was ringing the late Sir Lucien's door-bell.

A constable admitted him, and he walked straight through into the study where Coombes, looking very tired but smiling undauntedly, sat at a littered table studying piles of documents.

"Anything to report?" rapped Kerry.

"The man, Mareno, has gone to bed, and the expert from the Home Office has been—"

Inspector Kerry brought his cane down with a crash upon the table, whereat Coombes started nervously.

"So that's it!" he shouted furiously, "an 'expert from the Home Office'! So that's the dark horse in the fur coat. Coombes! I'm fed up to the back teeth with this gun from the Home Office! If I'm not to have entire charge of the case I'll throw it up. I'll stand for no blasted overseer checking my work! Wait till I see the Assistant Commissioner! What the devil has the job to do with the Home Office!"

"Can't say," murmured Coombes. "But he's evidently a big bug from the way Whiteleaf treated him. He instructed me to stay in the kitchen and keep an eye on Mareno while he prowled about in here."

"Instructed you!" cried Kerry, his teeth gleaming and his steel-blue eyes creating upon Coombes' mind an impression that they were emitting sparks. "*Instructed* you! I'll ask you a question, Detective-Sergeant Coombes: Who is in charge of this case?"

"Well, I thought you were."

"You *thought* I was?"

"Well, you are."

"I am? Very well—you were saying—?"

"I was saying that I went into the kitchen—"

"Before that! Something about 'instructed.'"

Poor Coombes smiled pathetically.

"Look here," he said, bravely meeting the ferocious glare of his superior, "as man to man. What could I do?"

"You could stop smiling!" snapped Kerry. "Hell!" He paced several times up and down the room. "Go ahead, Coombes."

"Well, there's nothing much to report. I stayed in the kitchen, and the man from the Home Office was in here alone for about half an hour."

"Alone?"

"Inspector Whiteleaf stayed in the dining-room."

"Had he been 'instructed' too?"

"I expect so. I think he just came along as a sort of guide."

"Ah!" muttered Kerry savagely, "a sort of guide! Any idea what the bogey man did in here?"

"He opened the window. I heard him."

"That's funny. It's exactly what I'm going to do! This smart from Whitehall hasn't got a corner in notions yet, Coombes."

The room was a large and lofty one, and had been used by a former tenant as a studio. The toplights had been roofed over by Sir Lucien, however, but the raised platform, approached by two steps, which had probably been used as a model's throne, was a permanent fixture of the apartment. It was backed now by bookcases, except where a blue plush curtain was draped before a French window.

Kerry drew the curtain back, and threw open the folding leaves of the window. He found himself looking out upon the leads of Albemarle Street. No stars and no moon showed through the grey clouds draping the wintry sky, but a dim and ghostly half-light nevertheless rendered the ugly expanse visible from where he stood.

On one side loomed a huge tank, to the brink of which a rickety wooden ladder invited the explorer to ascend. Beyond it were a series of iron gangways and ladders forming part of the fire emergency arrangements of the neighboring institution. Straight ahead a section of building jutted up and revealed two small windows, which seemed to regard him like watching eyes.

He walked out on to the roof, looking all about him. Beyond the tank opened a frowning gully—the Arcade connecting Albemarle Street with old Bond Street; on the other hand, the scheme of fire gangways was continued. He began to cross the leads, going in the direction of Bond Street. Coombes watched him from the study. When he came to the more northerly of the two windows which had attracted his attention, he knelt down and flashed the ray of his torch through the glass.

A kind of small warehouse was revealed, containing stacks of packages. Immediately inside the window was a rough wooden table, and on this table lay a number of smaller packages, apparently containing cigarettes.

Kerry turned his attention to the fastening of the window. A glance showed him that it was unlocked. Resting the torch on the leads, he grasped the sash and gently raised the window, noting that it opened almost noiselessly. Then, taking up the torch again, he stooped and stepped in on to the table below.

It moved slightly beneath his weight. One of the legs was shorter than its fellows. But he reached the floor as quietly as possible, and instantly snapped off the light of the torch.

A heavy step sounded from outside—someone was mounting the stairs—and a disk of light suddenly appeared upon the ground-glass panel of the door.

Kerry stood quite still, chewing steadily.

"Who's there?" came the voice of the constable posted on Kazmah's landing.

The inspector made no reply.

"Is there anyone here?" cried the man.

The disk of light disappeared, and the alert constable could be heard moving along the corridor to inspect the other offices. But the ray had shone upon the frosted glass long enough to enable Kerry to read the words painted there in square black letters. They had appeared reversed, of course, and had read thus:

.OƆ ƎTTƎЯAƆIƆ ƨINAꟖUƆ

CHAPTER XI

THE DRUG SYNDICATE

At six-thirty that morning Margaret Halley was aroused by her maid—the latter but half awake—and sitting up in bed and switching on the lamp, she looked at the card which the servant had brought to her, and read the following:

CHIEF INSPECTOR KERRY,
C.I.D.
New Scotland Yard, S.W.I.

"Oh, dear," she said sleepily, "what an appallingly early visitor. Is the bath ready yet, Janet?"

"I'm afraid not," replied the maid, a plain, elderly woman of the old-fashioned useful servant type. "Shall I take a kettle into the bathroom?"

"Yes—that will have to do. Tell Inspector Kerry that I shall not be long."

Five minutes later Margaret entered her little consulting-room, where

Kerry, having adjusted his tie, was standing before the mirror in the overmantle, staring at a large photograph of the charming lady doctor in military uniform. Kerry's fierce eyes sparkled appreciatively as his glance rested on the tall figure arrayed in a woollen dressing-gown, the masculine style of which by no means disguised the beauty of Margaret's athletic figure. She had hastily arranged her bright hair with deliberate neglect of all affectation. She belonged to that ultra-modern school which scorns to sue masculine admiration, but which cannot dispense with it nevertheless. She aspired to be assessed upon an intellectual basis, an ambition which her unfortunate good looks rendered difficult of achievement.

"Good morning, Inspector," she said composedly. "I was expecting you."

"Really, miss?" Kerry stared curiously. "Then you know what I've come about?"

"I think so. Won't you sit down? I am afraid the room is rather cold. Is it about—Sir Lucien Pyne?"

"Well," replied Kerry, "it concerns him certainly. I've been in communication by telephone with Hinkes, Mr. Monte Irvin's butler, and from him I learned that you were professionally attending Mrs. Irvin."

"I was not her regular medical adviser, but—"

Margaret hesitated, glancing rapidly at the Inspector, and then down at the writing-table before which she was seated. She began to tap the blotting-pad with an ivory paper-knife. Kerry was watching her intently.

"Upon your evidence, Miss Halley," he said rapidly, "may depend the life of the missing woman."

"Oh!" cried Margaret, "whatever can have happened to her? I rang up as late as two o'clock this morning; after that I abandoned hope."

"There's something underlying the case that I don't understand, miss. I look to you to put me wise."

She turned to him impulsively.

"I will tell you all I know, Inspector," she said. "I will be perfectly frank with you."

"Good!" rapped Kerry. "Now—you have known Mrs. Monte Irvin for some time?"

"For about two years."

"You didn't know her when she was on the stage?"

"No. I met her at a Red Cross concert at which she sang."

"Do you think she loved her husband?"

"I know she did."

"Was there any—prior attachment?"

"Not that I know of."

"Mr. Quentin Gray?"

Margaret smiled, rather mirthlessly.

"He is my cousin, Inspector, and it was I who introduced him to Rita Irvin. I sincerely wish I had never done so. He lost his head completely."

"There was nothing in Mrs. Irvin's attitude towards him to justify her husband's jealousy?"

"She was always frightfully indiscreet, Inspector, but nothing more. You see, she is greatly admired, and is used to the company of silly, adoring men. Her husband doesn't really understand the ways of these Bohemian folks. I knew it would lead to trouble sooner or later."

"Ah!"

Chief Inspector Kerry thrust his hands into the pockets of his jacket. "Now—Sir Lucien?"

Margaret tapped more rapidly with the paper-knife.

"Sir Lucien belonged to a set of which Rita had been a member during her stage career. I think—he admired her; in fact, I believe he had offered her marriage. But she did not care for him in the least—in that way."

"Then in what way did she care for him?" rapped Kerry.

"Well—now we are coming to the point." Momentarily she hesitated, then: "They were both addicted—"

"Yes?"

"—to drugs."

"Eh?" Kerry's eyes grew hard and fierce in a moment. "What drugs?"

"All sorts of drugs. Shortly after I became acquainted with Rita Irvin I learned that she was a victim of the drug habit, and I tried to cure her. I regret to say that I failed. At that time she had acquired a taste for opium."

Kerry said not a word, and Margaret raised her head and looked at him pathetically.

"I can see that you have no pity for the victims of this ghastly vice, Inspector Kerry," she said.

"I haven't!" he snapped fiercely. "I admit I haven't, miss. It's bad enough in the heathens, but for an Englishwoman to dope herself is downright unchristian and beastly."

"Yet I have come across so many of these cases, during the war and since, that I have begun to understand how easy, how dreadfully easy it is, for a woman especially, to fall into the fatal habit. Bereavement or that most frightful of all mental agonies, suspense, will too often lead the poor victim into the path that promises forgetfulness. Rita Irvin's case is less excusable. I think she must have begun drug-taking because of the mental and nervous exhaustion resulting from late hours and over-much gaiety. The demands of her profession proved too great for her impaired nervous energy, and she sought some stimulant which would enable her to appear bright on the stage when actually she should have been recuperating, in sleep, that loss of vital force which can be recuperated in no other way."

"But *opium!*" snapped Kerry.

"I am afraid her other drug habits had impaired her will, and shaken her self-control. She was tempted to try opium by its promise of a new and novel excitement."

"Her husband, I take it, was ignorant of all this?"

"I believe he was. Quentin—Mr. Gray—had no idea of it either."

"Then it was Sir Lucien Pyne who was in her confidence in the matter?"

Margaret nodded slowly, still tapping the blotting-pad.

"He used to accompany her to places where drugs could be obtained, and on several occasions—I cannot say how many—I believe he went with her to some den in Chinatown. It may have been due to Mr. Irvin's discovery that his wife could not satisfactorily account for some of these absences from home which led him to suspect her fidelity."

"Ah!" said Kerry hardly, "I shouldn't wonder. And now"—he thrust out a pointing finger—"where did she get these drugs?"

Margaret met the fierce stare composedly.

"I have said that I shall be quite frank," she replied. "In my opinion she obtained them from Kazmah."

"Kazmah!" shouted Kerry. "Excuse me, miss, but I see I've been wearing blinkers without knowing it! Kazmah's was a dope-shop?"

"That has been my belief for a long time, Inspector. I may add that I have never been able to obtain a shred of evidence to prove it. I am so keenly interested in seeing the people who pander to this horrible vice unmasked and dealt with as they merit, that I have tried many times to find out if my suspicion was correct."

Inspector Kerry was writhing his shoulders excitedly. "Did you ever visit Kazmah?" he asked.

"Yes. I asked Rita Irvin to take me, but she refused, and I could see that the request embarrassed her. So I went alone."

"Describe exactly what took place."

Margaret Halley stared reflectively at the blotting-pad for a moment, and then described a typical seance at Kazmah's. In conclusion:

"As I came away," she said, "I bought a bottle of every kind of perfume on sale, some of the incense, and also a box of sweetmeat; but they all proved to be perfectly harmless. I analyzed them."

Kerry's eyes glistened with admiration.

"We could do with you at the Yard, miss," he said. "Excuse me for saying so."

Margaret smiled rather wanly.

"Now—this man Kazmah," resumed the Chief Inspector. "Did you ever see him again?"

"Never. I have been trying for months and months to find out who he is."

Kerry's face became very grim.

"About ten trained men are trying to find that out at the present moment!" he rapped. "Do you think he wore a make-up?"

"He may have done so," Margaret admitted. "But his features were obviously undisguised, and his eyes one would recognize anywhere. They were larger than any human eyes I have ever seen."

"He couldn't have been the Egyptian who looked after the shop, for instance?"

"Impossible! He did not remotely resemble him. Besides, the man to whom you refer remained outside to receive other visitors. Oh, that's out of the question, Inspector."

"The light was very dim?"

"Very dim indeed, and Kazmah never once raised his head. Indeed, except for a dignified gesture of greeting and one of dismissal, he never moved. His immobility was rather uncanny."

Kerry began to pace up and down the narrow room, and:

"He bore no resemblance to the late Sir Lucien Pyne, for instance?" he rapped.

Margaret laughed outright and her laughter was so inoffensive and so musical that the Chief Inspector laughed also.

"That's more hopeless than ever!" she said. "Poor Sir Lucien had strong, harsh features and rather small eyes. He wore a moustache, too. But Sir Lucien, I feel sure, was one of Kazmah's clients."

"Ah!" said Kerry. "And what leads you to suppose Miss Halley, that this Kazmah dealt in drugs?"

"Well, you see, Rita Irvin was always going there to buy perfumes, and she frequently sent her maid as well."

"But"—Kerry stared—"you say that the perfume was harmless."

"That which was sold to casual visitors was harmless, Inspector. But I strongly suspect that regular clients were supplied with something quite different. You see, I know no fewer than thirty unfortunate women in the West End of London alone who are simply helpless slaves to various drugs, and I think it more than a coincidence that upon their dressing-tables I have almost invariably found one or more of Kazmah's peculiar antique flasks."

Chief Inspector Kerry's jaw muscles protruded conspicuously.

"You speak of patients?" he asked.

Margaret nodded her head.

"When a woman becomes addicted to the drug habit," she explained, "she sometimes shuns her regular medical adviser. I have many patients who came to me originally simply because they dared not face their family doctor. In fact, since I gave up Army work, my little practice has threatened to develop into that of a drug-habit specialist."

"Have you taxed any of these people with obtaining drugs from Kazmah?"

"Not directly. It would have been undiplomatic. But I have tried to surprise them into telling me. Unfortunately, these poor people are as cunning as any other kind of maniac, for, of course, it becomes a form of mania. They recognize that confession might lead to a stoppage of supplies—the eventuality they most dread."

"Did you examine the contents of any of these flasks found on dressing-tables?"

"I rarely had an opportunity; but when I did they proved to contain perfume when they contained anything."

"H'm," mused Kerry, and although in deference to Margaret, he had denied himself chewing-gum, his jaws worked automatically. "I gather that Mrs. Monte Irvin had expressed a wish to see you last night?"

"Yes. Apparently she was threatened with a shortage of cocaine."

"Cocaine was her drug?"

"One of them. She had tried them all, poor, silly girl! You must understand that for a habitual drug-taker suddenly to be deprived of drugs would lead to complete collapse, perhaps death. And during the last few days I had noticed a peculiar nervous symptom in Rita Irvin which had interested me. Finally, the day before yesterday, she confessed that her usual source of supply had been closed to her. Her words were very vague, but I gathered that some form of coercion was being employed."

"With what object?"

"I have no idea. But she used the words, 'They will drive me mad,' and seemed to be in a dangerously nervous condition. She said that she was going to make a final attempt to obtain a supply of the poison which had become indispensable to her. 'I cannot do without it!' she said. 'But if they refuse, will you give me some?'"

"What did you say?"

"I begged of her, as I had done on many previous occasions, to place herself in my hands. But she evaded a direct answer, as is the way of one addicted to this vice. 'If I cannot get some by tomorrow,' she said, 'I shall go mad, or dead. Can I rely on you?'"

"I told her that I would prescribe cocaine for her on the distinct understanding that from the first dose she was to place herself under my care for a cure."

"She agreed?"

"She agreed. Yesterday afternoon, while I was away at an important case, she came here. Poor Rita!" Margaret's soft voice trembled. "Look— she left this note."

From a letter-rack she took a square sheet of paper and handed it to the Chief Inspector. He bent his fierce eyes upon the writing—large, irregular and shaky.

"'Dear Margaret,'" he read aloud. "'Why aren't you at home? I am wild with pain, and feel I am going mad. Come to me *directly* you return, and bring enough to keep me alive. I—', Hullo! there's no finish!"

He glanced up from the page. Margaret Halley's eyes were dim.

"She despaired of my coming and went to Kazmah," she said. "Can you doubt that that was what she went for?"

"No!" snapped Kerry savagely, "I can't. But do you mean to tell me, Miss Halley, that Mrs. Irvin couldn't get cocaine anywhere else? I know for a fact that it's smuggled in regularly, and there's more than one receiver."

Margaret looked at him strangely.

"I know it, too, Inspector," she said quietly. "Owing to the lack of enterprise on the part of our British drug-houses, even reputable chemists are sometimes dependent upon illicit stock from Japan and America. But do you know that the price of these smuggled drugs has latterly become so high as to be prohibitive in many cases?"

"I don't. What are you driving at, miss?"

"At this: Somebody had made a corner in contraband drugs. The most wicked syndicate that ever was formed has got control of the lives of, it may be, thousands of drug-slaves!"

Kerry's teeth closed with a sharp snap.

"At last," he said, "I see where the smart from the Home Office comes in."

"The Secretary of State has appointed a special independent commissioner to inquire into this hellish traffic," replied Margaret quietly. "I am glad to say that I have helped in getting this done by the representations which I have made to my uncle, Lord Wrexborough. But I give you my word, Inspector Kerry, that I have withheld nothing from you any more than from him."

"Him!" snapped Kerry, eyes fiercely ablaze.

"From the Home Office representative—before whom I have already given evidence."

Chief Inspector Kerry took up his hat, cane and overall from the chair upon which he had placed them and, his face a savage red mask, bowed with a fine courtesy. He burned to learn particulars; he disdained to obtain them from a woman.

"Good morning, Miss Halley," he said. "I am greatly indebted to you."

He walked stiffly from the room and out of the flat without waiting for a servant to open the door.

PART SECOND

MRS. SIN

CHAPTER XII

THE MAID OF THE MASQUE

The past life of Mrs. Monte Irvin, in which at this time three distinct groups of investigators became interested—namely, those of Whitehall, Scotland Yard, and Fleet Street—was of a character to have horrified the prudish, but to have excited the compassion of the wise.

Daughter of a struggling suburban solicitor, Rita Esden, at the age of seventeen, from a delicate and rather commonplace child began to develop into a singularly pretty girl of an elusive and fascinating type of beauty, almost ethereal in her dainty coloring, and possessed of large and remarkably fine eyes, together with a wealth of copper-red hair, a crown which seemed too heavy for her slender neck to support. Her father viewed her increasing charms and ever-growing list of admirers with the gloomy apprehension of a disappointed man who had come to look upon each gift of the gods as a new sorrow cunningly disguised. Her mother, on the contrary, fanned the girl's natural vanity and ambition with a success which rarely attended the enterprises of this foolish old woman, and Rita proving to be endowed with a moderately good voice, a stage career was determined upon without reference to the contrary wishes of Mr. Esden.

Following the usual brief "training" which is counted sufficient for an aspirant to musical comedy honors, Rita, by the prefixing of two letters to her name, set out to conquer the play-going world as Rita Dresden.

Two years of hard work and disappointment served to dispel the girl's illusions. She learned to appreciate at its true value that masculine admiration which, in an unusual degree, she had the power to excite. Those of her admirers who were in a position to assist her professionally were only prepared to use their influence upon terms which she was unprepared to accept. Those whose intentions were strictly creditable, by some malignancy of fate, possessed no influence whatever. She came to regard herself as a peculiarly unlucky girl, being ignorant of the fact that Fortune, an impish hierophant, imposes identical tests upon every candidate who aspires to the throne of a limelight princess.

Matters stood thus when a new suitor appeared in the person of Sir Lucien Pyne. When his card was brought up to Rita, her heart leaped because of a mingled emotion of triumph and fear which the sight of the baronet's name had occasioned. He was a director of the syndicate in whose production she was playing—a man referred to with awe by every girl in the company as having it in his power to make or mar a professional reputation. Not that he took any active part in the affairs of the concern; on the contrary, he was an aristocrat who held himself aloof from all matters smacking of commerce, but at the same time one who invested his money shrewdly. Sir Lucien's protegée of today was London's idol of tomorrow, and even before Rita had spoken to him she had fought and won a spiritual battle between her true self and that vain, admiration-loving Rita Dresden who favored capitulation.

She knew that Sir Lucien's card represented a signpost at the crossroads where many a girl, pretty but not exceptionally talented, had hesitated with beating heart. It was no longer a question of remaining a member of the chorus (and understudy for a small part) or of accepting promotion to "lead" in a new production; it was that of accepting whatever Sir Lucien chose to offer—or of retiring from the profession so far as this powerful syndicate was concerned.

Such was the reputation enjoyed at this time by Sir Lucien Pyne among those who had every opportunity of forming an accurate opinion.

Nevertheless, Rita was determined not to succumb without a struggle. She did not count herself untalented nor a girl to be lightly valued, and Sir Lucien might prove to be less black than rumor had painted him. As presently appeared, both in her judgment of herself and in that of Sir Lucien, she was at least partially correct. He was very courteous, very respectful, and highly attentive.

Her less favored companions smiled significantly when the familiar Rolls-Royce appeared at the stage door night after night, never doubting that Rita Dresden was chosen to "star" in the forthcoming production, but, with rare exceptions, frankly envying her this good fortune.

Rita made no attempt to disillusion them, recognizing that it must fail. She was resigned to being misjudged. If she could achieve success at that price, success would have been purchased cheaply.

That Sir Lucien was deeply infatuated she was not slow to discover, and with an address perfected by experience and a determination to avoid the easy path inherited from a father whose scrupulous honesty had ruined his professional prospects, she set to work to win esteem as well as admiration.

Sir Lucien was first surprised, then piqued, and finally interested by such unusual tactics. The second phase was the dangerous one for Rita, and during a certain luncheon at Romanos her fate hung in the balance. Sir Lucien realized that he was in peril of losing his head over this tantalizingly pretty girl who gracefully kept him at a distance, fencing with an adroitness which was baffling, and Sir Lucien Pyne had set out with no intention of doing anything so preposterous as falling in love. Keenly intuitive, Rita scented danger and made a bold move. Carelessly rolling a bread-crumb along the cloth:

"I am giving up the stage when the run finishes," she said.

"Indeed," replied Sir Lucien imperturbably. "Why?"

"I am tired of stage life. I have been invited to go and live with my uncle in New York and have decided to accept. You see"—she bestowed upon him a swift glance of her brilliant eyes—"men in the theatrical world are not all like you. Real friends, I mean. It isn't very nice, sometimes."

Sir Lucien deliberately lighted a cigarette. If Rita was bluffing, he mused, she had the pluck to make good her bluff. And if she did so? He dropped the extinguished match upon a plate. Did he care? He glanced at the girl, who was smiling at an acquaintance on the other side of the room. Fortune's wheel spins upon a needle point. By an artistic performance occupying less than two minutes, but suggesting that Rita possessed qualities which one day might spell success, she had decided her fate. Her heart was beating like a hammer in her breast, but she preserved an attitude of easy indifference. Without for a moment believing in the American uncle, Sir Lucien did believe, correctly, that Rita Dresden was about to elude him. He realized, too, that he was infinitely more interested than he had ever been hitherto, and more interested than he had intended to become.

This seemingly trivial conversation was a turning point, and twelve months later Rita Dresden was playing the title role in *The Maid of the Masque*. Sir Lucien had discovered himself to be really in love with her, and he might quite possibly have offered her marriage even if a dangerous rival had not appeared to goad him to that desperate leap— for so he regarded it. Monte Irvin, although considerably Rita's senior, had much to commend him in the eyes of the girl—and in the eyes of her mother, who still retained a curious influence over her daughter. He was much more wealthy than Pyne, and although the latter was a baronet, Irvin was certain to be knighted ere long, so that Rita would secure the appendage of "Lady" in either case. Also, his reputation promised a more reliable husband than Sir Lucien could be expected to make. Moreover, Rita liked him, whereas she had never sincerely liked and trusted Sir Lucien. And there was a final reason—of which

Mrs. Esden knew nothing.

On the first night that Rita had been entrusted with a part of any consequence—and this was shortly after the conversation at Romanos—she had discovered herself to be in a state of hopeless panic. All her scheming and fencing would have availed her nothing if she were to break down at the critical moment. It was an eventuality which Sir Lucien had foreseen, and he seized the opportunity at once of securing a new hold upon the girl and of rendering her more pliable than he had hitherto found her to be. At this time the idea of marriage had not presented itself to Sir Lucien.

Some hours before the performance he detected her condition of abject fright ... and from his waistcoat pocket he took a little gold snuff-box.

At first the girl declined to follow advice which instinctively she distrusted, and Sir Lucien was too clever to urge it upon her. But he glanced casually at his wrist-watch—and poor Rita shuddered. The gold box was hidden again in the baronet's pocket.

To analyze the process which thereupon took place in Rita's mind would be a barren task, since its result was a foregone conclusion. Daring ambition rather than any merely abstract virtue was the keynote of her character. She had rebuffed the advances of Sir Lucien as she had rebuffed others, primarily because her aim in life was set higher than mere success in light comedy. This she counted but a means to a more desirable end—a wealthy marriage. To the achievement of such an alliance the presence of an accepted lover would be an obstacle; and true love Rita Dresden had never known. Yet, short of this final sacrifice which some women so lightly made, there were few scruples which she was not prepared to discard in furtherance of her designs. Her morality, then, was diplomatic, for the vice of ambition may sometimes make for virtue.

Rita's vivacious beauty and perfect self-possession on the fateful night earned her a permanent place in stageland: Rita Dresden became a "star." She had won a long and hard-fought battle; but in avoiding one master she had abandoned herself to another.

The triumph of her debut left her strangely exhausted. She dreaded the coming of the second night almost as keenly as she had dreaded the ordeal of the first. She struggled, poor victim, and only increased her terrors. Not until the clock showed her that in twenty minutes she must make her first entrance did she succumb. But Sir Lucien's gold snuff-box lay upon her dressing-table—and she was trembling. When at last she heard the sustained note of the oboe in the orchestra giving the pitch to the answering violins, she raised the jewelled lid of the box.

So she entered upon the path which leads down to destruction, and since to conjure with the drug which pharmacists know as methylbenzoyl ecgonine is to raise the demon Insomnia, ere long she found herself exploring strange by-paths in quest of sleep.

By the time that she was entrusted with the leading part in *The Maid of the Masque*, she herself did not recognize how tenacious was the hold which this fatal habit had secured upon her. In the company of Sir Lucien Pyne she met other devotees, and for a time came to regard her unnatural mode of existence as something inseparable from the Bohemian life. To the horrible side of it she was blind.

It was her meeting with Monte Irvin during the run of this successful play which first awakened a dawning comprehension; not because she ascribed his admiration to her artificial vivacity, but because she realized the strength of the link subsisting between herself and Sir Lucien. She liked and respected Irvin, and as a result began to view her conduct from a new standpoint. His life was so entirely open and free from reproach while part of her own was dark and secret. She conceived a desire to be done with that dark and secret life.

This was a shadow-land over which Sir Lucien Pyne presided, and which must be kept hidden from Monte Irvin; and it was not until she thus contemplated cutting herself adrift from it all that she perceived the Gordian knot which bound her to the drug coterie. How far, yet how smoothly, by all but imperceptible stages she had glided down the stream since that night when the gold box had lain upon her dressing-table! Kazmah's drug store in Bond Street had few secrets for her; or so she believed. She knew that the establishment of the strange, immobile Egyptian was a source from which drugs could always be obtained; she knew that the dream-reading business served some double purpose; but she did not know the identity of Kazmah.

Two of the most insidious drugs familiar to modern pharmacy were wooing her to slavery, and there was no strong hand to hold her back. Even the presence of her mother might have offered some slight deterrent at this stage of Rita's descent, but the girl had quitted her suburban home as soon as her salary had rendered her sufficiently independent to do so, and had established herself in a small but elegant flat situated in the heart of theatreland.

But if she had walked blindly into the clutches of cocaine and veronal, her subsequent experiments with *chandu* were prompted by indefensible curiosity, and a false vanity which urged her to do everything that was "done" by the ultra-smart and vicious set of which she had become a member.

Her first introduction to opium-smoking was made under the auspices of an American comedian then appearing in London, an old devotee of the poppy, and it took place shortly after Sir Lucien Pyne had proposed marriage to Rita. This proposal she had not rejected outright; she had pleaded time for consideration. Monte Irvin was away, and Rita secretly hoped that on his return he would declare himself. Meanwhile she indulged in every new craze which became fashionable among her associates. A *chandu* party took place at the American's flat in Duke Street, and Rita, who had been invited, and who had consented to go with Sir Lucien Pyne, met there for the first time the woman variously known as "Lola" and "Mrs. Sin."

CHAPTER XIII

A CHANDU PARTY

From the restaurant at which she had had supper with Sir Lucien, Rita proceeded to Duke Street. Alighting from Pyne's car at the door, they went up to the flat of the organizer of the opium party—Mr. Cyrus Kilfane. One other guest was already present—a slender, fair woman, who was introduced by the American as Mollie Gretna, but whose weakly pretty face Rita recognized as that of a notorious society divorcee, foremost in the van of every new craze, a past-mistress of the smartest vices.

Kilfane had sallow, expressionless features and drooping, light-colored eyes. His straw-hued hair, brushed back from a sloping brow, hung lankly down upon his coat-collar. Long familiarity with China's ruling vice and contact with those who practiced it had brought about that mysterious physical alteration—apparently reflecting a mental change—so often to be seen in one who has consorted with Chinamen. Even the light eyes seemed to have grown slightly oblique; the voice, the unimpassioned greeting, were those of a son of Cathay. He carried himself with a stoop and had a queer, shuffling gait.

"Ah, my dear daughter," he murmured in a solemnly facetious manner, "how glad I am to welcome you to our poppy circle."

He slowly turned his half-closed eyes in Pyne's direction, and slowly turned them back again.

"Do you seek forgetfulness of old joys?" he asked. "This is my own case and Pyne's. Or do you, as Mollie does, seek new joys—youth's eternal quest?"

Rita laughed with a careless abandon which belonged to that part of her character veiled from the outer world.

"I think I agree with Miss Gretna," she said lightly. "There is not so much happiness in life that I want to forget the little I have had."

"Happiness," murmured Kilfane. "There is no real happiness. Happiness is smoke. Let us smoke."

"I am curious, but half afraid," declared Rita. "I have heard that opium sometimes has no other effect than to make one frightfully ill."

"Oh, my dear!" cried Miss Gretna, with a foolish giggling laugh, "you will love it! Such fascinating dreams! Such delightful adventures!"

"Other drugs," drawled Sir Lucien, "merely stimulate one's normal mental activities. *Chandu* is a key to another life. Cocaine, for instance enhances our capacity for work. It is only a heretic like De Quincey who prostitutes the magic gum to such base purposes. *Chandu* is misunderstood in Europe; in Asia it is the companion of the aesthete's leisure."

"But surely," said Rita, "one pipe of opium will not produce all these wonders."

"Some people never experience them at all," interrupted Miss Gretna. "The great idea is to get into a comfortable position, and just resign yourself—let yourself go. Oh, it's heavenly!"

Cyrus Kilfane turned his dull eyes in Rita's direction.

"A question of temperament and adaptability," he murmured. "De Quincey, Pyne"—slowly turning towards the baronet—"is didactic, of course; but his *Confessions* may be true, nevertheless. He forgets, you see, that he possessed an unusual constitution, and the temperament of a Norwegian herring. He forgets, too, that he was a laudanum drinker, not an opium smoker. Now you, my daughter"—the lustreless eyes again sought Rita's flushed face—"are vivid—intensely vital. If you can succeed in resigning yourself to the hypnosis induced your experiences will be delightful. Trust your Uncle Cy."

Leaving Rita chatting with Miss Gretna, Kilfane took Pyne aside, offering him a cigarette from an ornate, jewelled case.

"Hello," said the baronet, "can you still get these?"

"With the utmost difficulty," murmured Kilfane, returning the case to his pocket. "Lola charges me five guineas a hundred for them, and only supplies them as a favor. I shall be glad to get back home, Pyne. The right stuff is the wrong price in London."

Sir Lucien laughed sardonically, lighting Kilfane's cigarette and then his own.

"I find it so myself," he said. "Everything except opium is to be had at Kazmah's, and nothing except opium interests me."

"He supplies me with cocaine," murmured the comedian. "His figure works out, as nearly as I can estimate it, at 10s. 7½d. a grain. I saw him about it yesterday afternoon, pointing out to the brown guy that as the wholesale price is roughly 2¼d., I regarded his margin of profit as somewhat broad."

"Indeed!"

"The first time I had ever seen him, Pyne. I brought an introduction from Dr. Silver, of New York, and Kazmah supplied me without question—at a price."

"You always saw Rashid?"

"Yes. If there were other visitors I waited. But yesterday I made a personal appointment with Kazmah. He pretended to think I had come to have a dream interpreted. He is clever, Pyne. He never moved a muscle throughout the interview. But finally he assured me that all the receivers in England had amalgamated, and that the price he charged represented a very narrow margin of profit. Of course he is a liar. He is making a fortune. Do you know him personally?"

"No," replied Sir Lucien, "outside his Bond Street home of mystery he is unknown. A clever man, as you say. You obtain your opium from Lola?"

"Yes. Kazmah sent her to me. She keeps me on ridiculously low rations, and if I had not brought my own outfit I don't think she would have sold me one. Of course, her game is beating up clients for the Limehouse dive."

"You have visited 'The House of a Hundred Raptures'?"

"Many times, at week-ends. Opium, like wine, is better enjoyed in company."

"Does she post you the opium?"

"Oh, no; my man goes to Limehouse for it. Ah! here she is."

A woman came in, carrying a brown leather attaché case. She had left her hat and coat in the hall, and wore a smart blue serge skirt and a white blouse. She was not tall, but she possessed a remarkably beautiful figure which the cut of her garments was not intended to disguise, and her height was appreciably increased by a pair of suede shoes having the most wonderful heels which Rita ever remembered to have seen worn on or off the stage. They seemed to make her small feet appear smaller, and lent to her slender ankles an exaggerated frontal curve.

Her hair was of that true, glossy black which suggests the blue sheen of raven's plumage, and her thickly fringed eyes were dark and southern as her hair. She had full, voluptuous lips, and a bold self-assurance. In the swift, calculating glance which she cast about the room there was something greedy and evil; and when it rested upon Rita Dresden's dainty beauty to the evil greed was added cruelty.

"Another little sister, dear Lola," murmured Kilfane. "Of course, you know who it is? This, my daughter," turning the sleepy glance towards Rita, "is our officiating priestess, Mrs. Sin."

The woman so strangely named revealed her gleaming teeth in a swift, unpleasant smile, then her nostrils dilated and she glanced about her suspiciously.

"Someone smokes the *chandu* cigarettes," she said, speaking in a low tone which, nevertheless, failed to disguise her harsh voice, and with a very marked accent.

"I am the offender, dear Lola," said Kilfane, dreamily waving his cigarette towards her. "I have managed to make the last hundred spin out. You have brought me a new supply?"

"Oh no, indeed," replied Mrs. Sin, tossing her head in a manner oddly reminiscent of a once famous Spanish dancer. "Next Tuesday you get some more. Ah! it is no good! You talk and talk and it cannot alter anything. Until they come I cannot give them to you."

"But it appears to me," murmured Kilfane, "that the supply is always growing less."

"Of course. The best goes all to Edinburgh now. I have only three sticks of Yezd left of all my stock."

"But the cigarettes—"

"Are from Buenos Ayres? Yes. But Buenos Ayres must get the opium before we get the cigarettes, eh? Five cases come to London on Tuesday, Cy. Be of good courage, my dear."

She patted the sallow cheek of the American with her jewelled fingers, and turned aside, glancing about her.

"Yes," murmured Kilfane. "We are all present, Lola. I have had the room prepared. Come, my children, let us enter the poppy portico."

He opened a door and stood aside, waving one thin yellow hand between the first two fingers of which smouldered the drugged cigarette. Led by Mrs. Sin the company filed into an apartment evidently intended for a drawing-room, but which had been hastily transformed into an opium divan.

Tables, chairs, and other items of furniture had been stacked against one of the walls and the floor spread with rugs, skins, and numerous silk cushions. A gas fire was alight, but before it had been placed an ornate Japanese screen whereon birds of dazzling plumage hovered amid the leaves of gilded palm trees. In the centre of the room stood a small card-table, and upon it were a large brass tray and an ivory pedestal exquisitely carved in the form of a nude figure having one arm upraised. The figure supported a lamp, the light of which was subdued by a barrel-shaped shade of Chinese workmanship.

Mollie Gretna giggled hysterically.

"Make yourself comfortable, dear," she cried to Rita, dropping down upon a heap of cushions stacked in a recess beside the fireplace. "I am going to take off my shoes. The last time, Cyrus, when I woke up my feet were quite numb."

"You should come down to my place," said Mrs. Sin, setting the leather case on the little card-table beside the lamp. "You have there your own little room and silken sheets to lie in, and it is quiet—so quiet."

"Oh!" cried Mollie Gretna, "I must come! But I daren't go alone. Will you come with me, dear?" turning to Rita.

"I don't know," was the reply. "I may not like opium."

"But if you do—and I know you will?"

"Why," said Rita, glancing rapidly at Pyne, "I suppose it would be a novel experience."

"Let me arrange it for you," came the harsh voice of Mrs. Sin. "Lucy will drive you both down—won't you, my dear?" The shadowed eyes glanced aside at Sir Lucien Pyne.

"Certainly," he replied. "I am always at the ladies' service."

Rita Dresden settled herself luxuriously into a nest of silk and fur in another corner of the room, regarding the baronet coquettishly through her half-lowered lashes.

"I won't go unless it is my party, Lucy," she said. "You must let me pay."

"A detail," murmured Pyne, crossing and standing beside her.

Interest now became centred upon the preparations being made by Mrs. Sin. From the attaché case she took out a lacquered box, silken-lined like a jewel-casket. It contained four singular-looking pipes, the parts of which she began to fit together. The first and largest of these had a thick bamboo stem, an amber mouthpiece, and a tiny, disproportionate bowl of brass. The second was much smaller and was of some dark, highly-polished wood, mounted with silver conceived in an ornate Chinese design representing a long-tailed lizard. The mouthpiece was of jade. The third and fourth pipes were yet smaller, a perfectly matched pair in figured ivory of exquisite workmanship, delicately gold-mounted.

"These for the ladies," said Mrs. Sin, holding up the pair. "You"—glancing at Kilfane—"have got your own pipe, I know."

She laid them upon the tray, and now took out of the case a little copper lamp, a smaller lacquered box and a silver spatula, her jewelled fingers handling the queer implements with a familiarity bred of habit.

"What a strange woman!" whispered Rita to Pyne. "Is she an oriental?"

"Cuban-Jewess," he replied in a low voice.

Mrs. Sin carefully lighted the lamp, which burned with a short, bluish flame, and, opening the lacquered box, she dipped the spatula into the thick gummy substance which it contained and twisted the little instrument round and round between her fingers, presently withdrawing it with a globule of *chandu*, about the size of a bean, adhering to the end. She glanced aside at Kilfane.

"Chinese way, eh?" she said.

She began to twirl the prepared opium above the flame of the lamp. From it a slight, sickly smelling vapor arose. No one spoke, but all watched her closely; and Rita was conscious of a growing, pleasurable excitement. When by evaporation the *chandu* had become reduced to the size of a small pea, and a vague spirituous blue flame began to dance round the end of the spatula, Mrs. Sin pressed it adroitly into the tiny bowl of one of the ivory pipes, having first held the bowl inverted for a moment over the lamp. She turned to Rita.

"The guest of the evening," she said. "Do not be afraid. Inhale—oh, so gentle—and blow the smoke from the nostrils. You know how to smoke?"

"The same as a cigarette?" asked Rita excitedly, as Mrs. Sin bent over her.

"The same, but very, very gentle."

Rita took the pipe and raised the mouthpiece to the lips.

CHAPTER XIV

IN THE SHADE OF THE LONELY PALM

Persian opium of good quality contains from ten to fifteen percent morphine, and *chandu* made from opium of Yezd would contain perhaps twenty-five per cent of this potent drug; but because in the act of smoking distillation occurs, nothing like this quantity of morphine reaches the smoker. To the distilling process, also, may be due the different symptoms resulting from smoking *chandu* and injecting morphia—or drinking tincture of opium, as De Quincey did.

Rita found the flavor of the preparation to be not entirely unpleasant. Having overcome an initial aversion, caused by its marked medicinal tang, she grew reconciled to it and finished her first smoke without experiencing any other effect than a sensation of placid contentment. Deftly, Mrs. Sin renewed the pipe. Silence had fallen upon the party.

The second "pill" was no more than half consumed when a growing feeling of nausea seized upon the novice, becoming so marked that she dropped the ivory pipe weakly and uttered a faint moan.

Instantly, silently, Mrs. Sin was beside her.

"Lean forward—so," she whispered, softly, as if fearful of intruding her voice upon these sacred rites. "In a moment you will be better. Then, if you feel faint, lie back. It is the sleep. Do not fight against it."

The influence of the stronger will prevailed. Self-control and judgment are qualities among the first to succumb to opium. Rita ceased to think longingly of the clean, fresh air, of escape from these sickly fumes which seemed now to fill the room with a moving vacuum. She bent forward, her chin resting upon her breast, and gradually the deathly sickness passed. Mentally, she underwent a change, too. From an active state of resistance the ego traversed a descending curve ending in absolute passivity. The floor had seemingly begun to revolve and was moving insidiously, so that the pattern of the carpet formed a series of concentric rings. She found this imaginary phenomenon to be soothing rather than otherwise, and resigned herself almost eagerly to the delusion.

Mrs. Sin allowed her to fall back upon the cushions—so gently and so slowly that the operation appeared to occupy several minutes and to resemble that of sinking into innumerable layers of swansdown. The sinuous figure bending over her grew taller with the passage of each minute, until the dark eyes of Mrs. Sin were looking down at Rita from a dizzy elevation. As often occurs in the case of a neurotic subject, delusion as to time and space had followed the depression of the sensory cells.

But surely, she mused, this could not be Mrs. Sin who towered so loftily above her. Of course, how absurd to imagine that a woman could remain motionless for so many hours. And Rita thought, now, that she had been lying for several hours beneath the shadow of that tall, graceful, and protective shape.

Why—it was a slender palm-tree, which stretched its fanlike foliage over her! Far, far above her head the long, dusty green fronds projected from the mast-like trunk. The sun, a ball of fiery brass, burned directly in the zenith, so that the shadow of the foliage lay like a carpet about her feet. That which she had mistaken for the ever-receding eyes of Mrs. Sin, wondering with a delightful vagueness why they seemed constantly to change color, proved to be a pair of brilliantly plumaged parrakeets perched upon a lofty branch of the palm.

This was an equatorial noon, and even if she had not found herself to be under the influence of a delicious abstraction Rita would not have moved; for, excepting the friendly palm, not another vestige of vegetation was visible right away to the horizon; nothing but an ocean of sand whereon no living thing moved. She and the parrakeets were alone in the heart of the Great Sahara.

But stay! Many, many miles away, a speck on the dusty carpet of the desert, something moved! Hours must elapse before that tiny figure, provided it were approaching, could reach the solitary palm. Delightedly, Rita contemplated the infinity of time. Even if the figure moved ever so slowly, she should be waiting there beneath the palm to witness its arrival. Already, she had been there for a period which she was far too indolent to strive to compute—a week, perhaps. She turned her attention to the parrakeets. One of them was moving, and she noted with delight that it had perceived her far below and was endeavoring to draw the attention of its less observant companion to her presence. For many hours she lay watching it and wondering why, since the one bird was so singularly intelligent, its companion was equally dull. When she lowered her eyes and looked out again across the sands, the figure had approached so close as to be recognizable.

It was that of Mrs. Sin. Rita appreciated the fitness of her presence, and experienced no surprise, only a mild curiosity. This curiosity was not concerned with Mrs. Sin herself, but with the nature of the burden which she bore upon her head.

She was dressed in a manner which Rita dreamily thought would have been inadequate in England, or even in Cuba, but which was appropriate in the Great Sahara. How exquisitely she carried herself, mused the dreamer; no doubt this fine carriage was due in part to her wearing golden shoes with heels like stilts, and in part to her having been trained to bear heavy burdens upon her head. Rita remembered that Sir Lucien had once described to her the elegant deportment of the Arab women, ascribing it to their custom of carrying water-jars in that way.

The appearance of the speck on the horizon had marked the height of her trance. Her recognition of Mrs. Sin had signalized the decline of the *chandu* influence. Now, the intrusion of a definite, uncontorted memory was evidence of returning cerebral activity.

Rita had no recollection of the sunset; indeed, she had failed to perceive any change in the form and position of the shadow cast by the foliage. It had spread, an ebony patch, equally about the bole of the tree, so that the sun must have been immediately overhead. But, of course, she had lain watching the parrakeets for several hours, and now night had fallen. The desert mounds were touched with silver, the sky was a nest of diamonds, and the moon cast a shadow of the palm like a bar of ebony right across the prospect to the rim of the sky dome.

Mrs. Sin stood before her, one half of her lithe body concealed by this strange black shadow and the other half gleaming in the moonlight so that she resembled a beautiful ivory statue which some iconoclast had cut in two.

Placing her burden upon the ground, Mrs. Sin knelt down before Rita and reverently kissed her hand, whispering: "I am your slave, my poppy queen."

She spoke in a strange language, no doubt some African tongue, but one which Rita understood perfectly. Then she laid one hand upon the object which she had carried on her head, and which now proved to be a large lacquered casket covered with Chinese figures and bound by three hoops of gold. It had a very curious shape.

"Do you command that the chest be opened?" she asked.

"Yes," answered Rita languidly.

Mrs. Sin threw up the lid, and from the interior of the casket which, because of the glare of the moon light, seemed every moment to assume a new form, drew out a bronze lamp.

"The sacred lamp," she whispered, and placed it on the sand. "Do you command that it be lighted?"

Rita inclined her head.

The lamp became lighted; in what manner she did not observe, nor was she curious to learn. Next from the large casket Mrs. Sin took another smaller casket and a very long, tapering silver bodkin. The first casket had perceptibly increased in size. It was certainly much larger than Rita had supposed; for now out from its shadowy interior Mrs. Sin began to take pipes—long pipes and short pipes, pipes of gold and pipes of silver, pipes of ivory and pipes of jade. Some were carved to represent the heads of demons, some had the bodies of serpents wreathed about them; others were encrusted with precious gems, and filled the night with the venomous sheen of emeralds, the blood-rays of rubies and golden glow of topaz, while the spear-points of diamonds flashed a challenge to the stars.

"Do you command that the pipes be lighted?" asked the harsh voice.

Rita desired to answer, "No," but heard herself saying, "Yes."

Thereupon, from a thousand bowls, linking that lonely palm to the remote horizon, a thousand elfin fires arose—blue-tongued and spirituous. Grey pencilings of smoke stole straightly upward to the sky, so that look where she would Rita could discern nothing but these countless thin, faintly wavering, vertical lines of vapor.

The dimensions of the lacquered casket had increased so vastly as to conceal the kneeling figure of Mrs. Sin, and staring at it wonderingly, Rita suddenly perceived that it was not an ordinary casket. She knew at last why its shape had struck her as being unusual.

It was a Chinese coffin.

The smell of the burning opium was stifling her. Those remorseless threads of smoke were closing in, twining themselves about her throat. It was becoming cold, too, and the moonlight was growing dim. The position of the moon had changed, of course, as the night had stolen on towards morning, and now it hung dimly before her. The smoke obscured it.

But was this smoke obscuring the moon? Rita moved her hands for the first time since she had found herself under the palm tree, weakly fending off those vaporous tentacles which were seeking to entwine themselves about her throat. Of course, it was not smoke obscuring the moon, she decided; it was a lamp, upheld by an ivory figure—a lamp with a Chinese shade.

A subdued roaring sound became audible; and this was occasioned by the gas fire, burning behind the Japanese screen on which gaily plumaged birds sported in the branches of golden palms. Rita raised her hands to her eyes. Mist obscured her sight. Swiftly, now, reality was asserting itself and banishing the phantasmagoria conjured up by *chandu*.

In her dim, cushioned corner Mollie Gretna lay back against the wall, her face pale and her weak mouth foolishly agape. Cyrus Kilfane was indistinguishable from the pile of rugs amid which he sprawled by the table, and of Sir Lucien Pyne nothing was to be seen but the outstretched legs and feet which projected grotesquely from a recess. Seated, oriental fashion, upon an improvised divan near the grand piano and propped up by a number of garish cushions, Rita beheld Mrs. Sin. The long bamboo pipe had fallen from her listless fingers. Her face wore an expression of mystic rapture like that characterizing the features of some Chinese Buddhas.

Fear, unaccountable but uncontrollable, suddenly seized upon Rita. She felt weak and dizzy, but she struggled partly upright.

"Lucy!" she whispered.

Her voice was not under control, and once more she strove to call to Pyne.

"Lucy!" came the hoarse whisper again.

The fire continued its muted roaring, but no other sound answered to the appeal. A horror of the companionship in which she found herself thereupon took possession of the girl. She must escape from these sleepers, whose spirits had been expelled by the potent necromancer, opium, from these empty tenements whose occupants had fled. The idea of the cool night air in the open streets was delicious.

She staggered to her feet, swaying drunkenly, but determined to reach the door. She shuddered, because of a feeling of internal chill which assailed her, but step by step crept across the room, opened the door, and tottered out into the hallway. There was no sound in the flat. Presumably Kilfane's man had retired, or perhaps he, too, was a devotee.

Rita's fur coat hung upon the rack, and although her fingers appeared to have lost all their strength and her arm to have become weak as that of an infant, she succeeded in detaching the coat from the hook. Not pausing to put it on, she opened the door and stumbled out on to the darkened landing. Whereas her first impulse had been to awaken someone, preferably Sir Lucien, now her sole desire was to escape undetected.

She began to feel less dizzy, and having paused for a moment on the landing, she succeeded in getting her coat on. Then she closed the door as quietly as possible, and clutching the handrail began to grope her way downstairs. There was only one flight, she remembered, and a short passage leading to the street door. She reached the passage without mishap, and saw a faint light ahead.

The fastenings gave her some trouble, but finally her efforts were successful, and she found herself standing in deserted Duke Street. There was no moon, but the sky was cloudless. She had no idea of the time, but because of the stillness of the surrounding streets she knew that it must be very late. She set out for her flat, walking slowly and wondering what explanation she should offer if a constable observed her.

Oxford Street showed deserted as far as the eye could reach, and her light footsteps seemed to awaken a hundred echoes. Having proceeded for some distance without meeting anyone, she observed—and experienced a childish alarm—the head-lights of an approaching car. Instantly the idea of hiding presented itself to her, but so rapidly did the big automobile speed along the empty thoroughfare that Rita was just passing a street lamp as the car raced by, and she must therefore have been clearly visible to the occupants.

Never for a moment glancing aside, Rita pressed on as quickly as she could. Then her vague alarm became actual terror. She heard the brakes being applied to the car, and heard the gritty sound of the tires upon the roadway as the vehicle's headlong progress was suddenly checked. She had been seen—perhaps recognized, and whoever was in the car proposed to return to speak to her.

If her strength had allowed she would have run, but now it threatened to desert her altogether and she tottered weakly. A pattering of footsteps came from behind. Someone was running back to overtake her.

Recognizing escape to be impossible, Rita turned just as the runner came up with her.

"Rita!" he cried, rather breathlessly. "Miss Dresden!"

She stood very still, looking at the speaker.

It was Monte Irvin.

CHAPTER XV

METAMORPHOSIS

As Irvin seized her hands and looked at her eagerly, half-fearfully, Rita achieved sufficient composure to speak.

"Oh, Mr. Irvin," she said, and found that her voice was not entirely normal, "what must you think—"

He continued to hold her hands, and:

"I think you are very indiscreet to be out alone at three o'clock in the morning," he answered gently. "I was recalled to London by urgent business, and returned by road—fortunately, since I have met you."

"How can I explain—"

"I don't ask you to explain—Miss Dresden. I have no right and no desire to ask. But I wish I had the right to advise you."

"How good you are," she began, "and I—"

Her voice failed her completely, and her sensitive lips began to tremble. Monte Irvin drew her arm under his own and led her back to meet the car, which the chauffeur had turned and which was now approaching.

"I will drive you home," he said, "and if I may call in the morning I should like to do so."

Rita nodded. She could not trust herself to speak again. And having placed her in the car, Monte Irvin sat beside her, reclaiming her hand and grasping it reassuringly and sympathetically throughout the short drive. They parted at her door.

"Good night," said Irvin, speaking very deliberately because of an almost uncontrollable desire which possessed him to take Rita in his arms, to hold her fast, to protect her from her own pathetic self and from those influences, dimly perceived about her, but which intuitively he knew to be evil.

"If I call at eleven will that be too early?"

"No," she whispered. "Please come early. There is a matinee tomorrow."

"You mean today," he corrected. "Poor little girl, how tired you will be. Good night."

"Good night," she said, almost inaudibly.

She entered, and, having closed the door, stood leaning against it for several minutes. Bleakness and nausea threatened to overcome her anew, and she felt that if she essayed another step she must collapse upon the floor. Her maid was in bed, and had not been awakened by Rita's entrance. After a time she managed to grope her way to her bedroom, where, turning up the light, she sank down helplessly upon the bed.

Her mental state was peculiar, and her thoughts revolved about the journey from Oxford Street homeward. A thousand times she mentally repeated the journey, speaking the same words over and over again, and hearing Monte Irvin's replies.

In those few minutes during which they had been together her sentiments in regard to him had undergone a change. She had always respected Irvin, but this respect had been curiously compounded of the personal and the mercenary; his well-ordered establishment at Prince's Gate had loomed behind the figure of the man forming a pleasing background to the portrait. Without being showy he was a splendid "match" for any woman. His wife would have access to good society, and would enjoy every luxury that wealth could procure. This was the picture lovingly painted and constantly retouched by Rita's mother.

Now it had vanished. The background was gone, and only the man remained; the strong, reserved man whose deep voice had spoken so gently, whose devotion was so true and unselfish that he only sought to shield and protect her from follies the nature of which he did not even seek to learn. She was stripped of her vanity, and felt loathsome and unworthy of such a love.

"Oh," she moaned, rocking to and fro. "I hate myself—I hate myself!"

Now that the victory so long desired seemed at last about to be won, she hesitated to grasp the prize. One solacing reflection she had. She would put the errors of the past behind her. Many times of late she had found herself longing to be done with the feverish life of the stage. Envied by those who had been her companions in the old chorus days, and any one of whom would have counted ambition crowned could she have played *The Maid of the Masque*, Rita thought otherwise. The ducal mansions and rose-bowered Riviera hotels through which she moved nightly had no charm for her; she sighed for reality, and had wearied long ago of the canvas palaces and the artificial Southern moonlight. In fact, stage life had never truly appealed to her—save as a means to an end.

Again and yet again her weary brain reviewed the episodes of the night since she had left Cyrus Kilfane's flat, so that nearly an hour had elapsed before she felt capable of the operation of undressing. Finally, however, she undressed, shuddering although the room was warmed by an electric radiator. The weakness and sickness had left her, but she was quite wide awake, although her brain demanded rest from that incessant review of the events of the evening.

She put on a warm wrap and seated herself at the dressing-table, studying her face critically. She saw that she was somewhat pale and that she had an indefinable air of dishevelment. Also she detected shadows beneath her eyes, the pupils of which were curiously contracted. Automatically, as a result of habit, she unlocked her jewel-case and took out a tiny phial containing minute cachets. She shook several out on to the palm of her hand, and then paused, staring at her reflection in the mirror.

For fully half a minute she hesitated, then:

"I shall never close my eyes all night if I don't!" she whispered, as if in reply to a spoken protest, "and I should be a wreck in the morning."

Thus, in the very apogee of her resolve to reform, did she drive one more rivet into the manacles which held her captive to Kazmah and Company.

Upon a little spirit-stove stood a covered vessel containing milk, which was placed there nightly by Rita's maid. She lighted the burner and warmed the milk. Then, swallowing three of the cachets from the phial, she drank the milk. Each cachet contained three decigrams of malourea, the insidious drug notorious under its trade name of Veronal.

She slept deeply, and was not awakened until ten o'clock. Her breakfast consisted of a cup of strong coffee; but when Monte Irvin arrived at eleven Rita exhibited no sign of nerve exhaustion. She looked bright and charming, and Irvin's heart leapt hotly in his breast at sight of her.

Following some desultory and unnatural conversation:

"May I speak quite frankly to you?" he said, drawing his chair nearer to the settee upon which Rita was seated.

She glanced at him swiftly. "Of course," she replied. "Is it—about my late hours?"

He shook his head, smiling rather sadly.

"That is only one phase of your rather feverish life, little girl," he said. "I don't mean that I want to lecture you or reproach you. I only want to ask you if you are satisfied?"

"Satisfied?" echoed Rita, twirling a tassel that hung from a cushion beside her.

"Yes. You have achieved success in your profession." He strove in vain to banish bitterness from his voice. "You are a 'star,' and your photograph is to be seen frequently in the smartest illustrated papers. You are clever and beautiful and have hosts of admirers. But—are you satisfied?"

She stared absently at the silk tassel, twirling it about her white fingers more and more rapidly. Then:

"No," she answered softly.

Monte Irvin hesitated for a moment ere bending forward and grasping her hands.

"I am glad you are not satisfied," he whispered. "I always knew you had a soul for something higher—better."

She avoided his ardent gaze, but he moved to the settee beside her and looked into the bewitching face.

"Would it be a great sacrifice to give it all up?" he whispered in a yet lower tone.

Rita shook her head, persistently staring at the tassel.

"For me?"

She gave him a swift, half-frightened glance, pressing her hands against his breast and leaning back.

"Oh, you don't know me—you don't know me!" she said, the good that was in her touched to life by the man's sincerity. "I—don't deserve it."

"Rita!" he murmured. "I won't hear you say that!"

"You know nothing about my friends—about my life—"

"I know that I want you for my wife, so that I can protect you from those 'friends.'" He took her in his arms, and she surrendered her lips to him.

"My sweet little girl," he whispered. "I cannot believe it—yet."

But the die was cast, and when Rita went to the theatre to dress for the afternoon performance she was pledged to sever her connection with the stage on the termination of her contract. She had luncheon with Monte Irvin, and had listened almost dazedly to his plans for the future. His wealth was even greater than her mother had estimated it to be, and Rita's most cherished dreams were dwarfed by the prospects which Monte Irvin opened up before her. It almost seemed as though he knew and shared her dearest ambitions. She was to winter beneath real Southern palms and to possess a cruising yacht, not one of boards and canvas like that which figured in *The Maid of the Masque*.

Real Southern palms, she mused guiltily, not those conjured up by opium. That he was solicitous for her health the nature of his schemes revealed. They were to visit Switzerland, and proceed thence to a villa which he owned in Italy. Christmas they would spend in Cairo, explore the Nile to Assouan in a private *dahabiyeh*, and return home via the

Riviera in time to greet the English spring. Rita's delicate, swiftly changing color, her almost ethereal figure, her intense nervous energy he ascribed to a delicate constitution.

She wondered if she would ever dare to tell him the truth; if she ought to tell him.

Pyne came to her dressing-room just before the performance began. He had telephoned at an early hour in the morning, and had learned from her maid that Rita had come home safely and was asleep. Rita had expected him; but the influence of Monte Irvin, from whom she had parted at the stage-door, had prevailed until she actually heard Sir Lucien's voice in the corridor. She had resolutely refrained from looking at the little jewelled casket, engraved "From Lucy to Rita," which lay in her make-up box upon the table. But the imminence of an ordeal which she dreaded intensely weakened her resolution. She swiftly dipped a little nail-file into the white powder which the box contained, and when Pyne came in she turned to him composedly.

"I am so sorry if I gave you a scare last night, Lucy," she said. "But I woke up feeling sick, and I had to go out into the fresh air."

"I was certainly alarmed," drawled Pyne, whose swarthy face looked more than usually worn in the hard light created by the competition between the dressing-room lamps and the grey wintry daylight which crept through the windows. "Do you feel quite fit again?"

"Quite, thanks." Rita glanced at a ring which she had not possessed three hours before. "Oh, Lucy—I don't know how to tell you—"

She turned in her chair, looking up wistfully at Pyne, who was standing behind her. His jaw hardened, and his glance sought the white hand upon which the costly gems glittered. He coughed nervously.

"Perhaps"—his drawling manner of speech temporarily deserted him; he spoke jerkily—"perhaps—I can guess."

She watched him in a pathetic way, and there was a threat of tears in her beautiful eyes; for whatever his earlier intentions may have been, Sir Lucien had proved a staunch friend and, according to his own peculiar code, an honorable lover.

"Is it—Irvin?" he asked jerkily.

Rita nodded, and a tear glistened upon her darkened lashes.

Sir Lucien cleared his throat again, then coolly extended his hand, once more master of his emotions.

"Congratulations, Rita," he said. "The better man wins. I hope you will be very happy."

He turned and walked quietly out of the dressing-room.

CHAPTER XVI

LIMEHOUSE

It was on the following Tuesday evening that Mrs. Sin came to the theatre, accompanied by Mollie Gretna. Rita instructed that she should be shown up to the dressing-room. The personality of this singular woman interested her keenly. Mrs. Sin was well known in certain Bohemian quarters, but was always spoken of as one speaks of a pet vice. Not to know Mrs. Sin was to be outside the magic circle which embraced the exclusively smart people who practiced the latest absurdities.

The so-called artistic temperament is compounded of great strength and great weakness; its virtues are whiter than those of ordinary people and its vices blacker. For such a personality Mrs. Sin embodied the idea of secret pleasure. Her bold good looks repelled Rita, but the knowledge in her dark eyes was alluring.

"I arrange for you for Saturday night," she said. "Cy Kilfane is coming with Mollie, and you bring—"

"Oh," replied Rita hesitatingly, "I am sorry you have gone to so much trouble."

"No trouble, my dear," Mrs. Sin assured her. "Just a little matter of business, and you can pay the bill when it suits you."

"I am frightfully excited!" cried Mollie Gretna. "It is so nice of you to have asked me to join your party. Of course Cy goes practically every week, but I have always wanted another girl to go with. Oh, I shall be in a perfectly delicious panic when I find myself all among funny Chinamen and things! I think there is something so magnificently wicked-looking about a pigtail—and the very name of Limehouse thrills me to the soul!"

That fixity of purpose which had enabled Rita to avoid the cunning snares set for her feet and to snatch triumph from the very cauldron of shame without burning her fingers availed her not at all in dealing with Mrs. Sin. The image of Monte receded before this appeal to the secret pleasure-loving woman, of insatiable curiosity, primitive and unmoral, who dwells, according to a modern cynic philosopher, within every daughter of Eve touched by the fire of genius.

She accepted the arrangement for Saturday, and before her visitors had left the dressing-room her mind was busy with plausible deceits to cover the sojourn in Chinatown. Something of Mollie Gretna's foolish enthusiasm had communicated itself to Rita.

Later in the evening Sir Lucien called, and on hearing of the scheme grew silent. Rita glancing at his reflection in the mirror, detected a black and angry look upon his face. She turned to him.

"Why, Lucy," she said, "don't you want me to go?"

He smiled in his sardonic fashion.

"Your wishes are mine, Rita," he replied.

She was watching him closely.

"But you don't seem keen," she persisted. "Are you angry with me?"

"Angry?"

"We are still friends, aren't we?"

"Of course. Do you doubt my friendship?"

Rita's maid came in to assist her in changing for the third act, and Pyne went out of the room. But, in spite of his assurances, Rita could not forget that fierce, almost savage expression which had appeared upon his face when she had told him of Mrs. Sin's visit.

Later she taxed him on the point, but he suffered her inquiry with imperturbable sangfroid, and she found herself no wiser respecting the cause of his annoyance. Painful twinges of conscience came during the ensuing days, when she found herself in her fiancé's company, but she never once seriously contemplated dropping the acquaintance of Mrs. Sin.

She thought, vaguely, as she had many times thought before, of cutting adrift from the entire clique, but there was no return of that sincere emotional desire to reform which she had experienced on the day that Monte Irvin had taken her hand, in blind trust, and had asked her to be his wife. Had she analyzed, or been capable of analyzing, her intentions with regard to the future, she would have learned that daily they inclined more and more towards compromise. The drug habit was sapping will and weakening morale, insidiously, imperceptibly. She was caught in a current of that "sacred river" seen in an opium-trance by Coleridge, and which ran—

> *"Through caverns measureless to man*
> *Down to a sunless sea."*

Pyne's big car was at the stage-door on the fateful Saturday night, for Rita had brought her dressing-case to the theatre, and having called for Kilfane and Mollie Gretna they were to proceed direct to Limehouse.

Rita, as she entered the car, noticed that Juan Mareno, Sir Lucien's man, and not the chauffeur with whom she was acquainted, sat at the wheel. As they drove off:

"Why is Mareno driving tonight, Lucy?" she asked.

Sir Lucien glanced aside at her.

"He is in my confidence," he replied. "Fraser is not."

"Oh, I see. You don't want Fraser to know about the Limehouse journey?"

"Naturally I don't. He would talk to all the men at the garage, and from South Audley Street the tit-bit of scandal would percolate through every stratum of society."

Rita was silent for a few moments, then:

"Were you thinking about Monte?" she asked diffidently.

Pyne laughed.

"He would scarcely approve, would he?"

"No," replied Rita. "Was that why you were angry when I told you I was going?"

"This 'anger,' to which you constantly revert, had no existence outside your own imagination, Rita. But"—he hesitated—"you will have to consider your position, dear, now that you are the future Mrs. Monte."

Rita felt her cheeks flush, and she did not reply immediately.

"I don't understand you, Lucy," she declared at last. "How odd you are."

"Am I? Well, never mind. We will talk about my eccentricity later. Here is Cyrus."

Kilfane was standing in the entrance to the stage door of the theatre at which he was playing. As the car drew up he lifted two leather grips on to the step, and Mareno, descending, took charge of them.

"Come along, Mollie," said Kilfane, looking back.

Miss Gretna, very excited, ran out and got into the car beside Rita. Pyne lowered two of the collapsible seats for Kilfane and himself, and the party set out for Limehouse.

"Oh!" cried the fair-haired Mollie, grasping Rita's hand, "my heart began palpitating with excitement the moment I woke up this morning! How calm you are, dear."

"I am only calm outside," laughed Rita.

The *joie de vivre* and apparently unimpaired vitality, of this woman, for whom (if half that which rumor whispered were true) vice had no secrets, astonished Rita. Her physical resources were unusual, no doubt, because the demand made upon them by her mental activities was slight.

As the car sped along the Strand, where theatre-goers might still be seen making for tube, omnibus, and tramcar, and entered Fleet Street, where the car and taxicab traffic was less, a mutual silence fell upon the party. Two at least of the travellers were watching the lighted windows of the great newspaper offices with a vague sense of foreboding, and thinking how, bound upon a secret purpose, they were passing along the avenue of publicity. It is well that man lacks prescience. Neither Rita nor Sir Lucien could divine that a day was shortly to come when the hidden presses which throbbed about them that night should be busy with the story of the murder of one and disappearance of the other.

Around St. Paul's Churchyard whirled the car, its engine running strongly and almost noiselessly. The great bell of St. Paul's boomed out the half-hour.

"Oh!" cried Mollie Gretna, "how that made me jump! What a beautifully gloomy sound!"

Kilfane murmured some inaudible reply, but neither Pyne nor Rita spoke.

Cornhill and Leadenhall Street, along which presently their route lay, offered a prospect of lamp-lighted emptiness, but at Aldgate they found themselves amid East End throngs which afforded a marked contrast to those crowding theatreland; and from thence through Whitechapel and the seemingly endless Commercial Road it was a different world into which they had penetrated.

Rita hitherto had never seen the East End on a Saturday night, and the spectacle afforded by these busy marts, lighted by naphtha flames, in whose smoky glare Jews and Jewesses, Poles, Swedes, Easterns, dagoes, and halfcastes moved feverishly, was a fascinating one. She thought how utterly alien they were, the men and women of a world unknown to that society upon whose borders she dwelled; she wondered how they lived, where they lived, why they lived. The wet pavements were crowded with nondescript humanity, the night was filled with the unmusical voices of Hebrew hucksters, and the air laden with the smoky odor of their lamps. Tramcars and motorbuses were packed unwholesomely with these children of shadowland drawn together from the seven seas by the magnet of London.

She glanced at Pyne, but he was seemingly lost in abstraction, and Kilfane appeared to be asleep. Mollie Gretna was staring eagerly out on the opposite side of the car at a group of three dago sailors, whom Mareno had nearly run down, but she turned at that moment and caught Rita's glance.

"Don't you simply love it!" she cried. "Some of those men were really handsome, dear. If they would only wash I am sure I could adore them!"

"Even such charms as yours can be bought at too high a price," drawled Sir Lucien. "They would gladly do murder for you, but never wash."

Crossing Limehouse Canal, the car swung to the right into West India Dock Road. The uproar of the commercial thoroughfare was left far behind. Dark, narrow streets and sinister-looking alleys lay right and left of them, and into one of the narrowest and least inviting of all Mareno turned the car.

In the dimly-lighted doorway of a corner house the figure of a Chinaman showed as a motionless silhouette.

"Oh!" sighed Mollie Gretna rapturously, "a Chinaman! I begin to feel deliciously sinful!"

The car came to a standstill.

"We get out here and walk," said Sir Lucien. "It would not be wise to drive further. Mareno will deliver our baggage by hand presently."

"But we shall all be murdered," cried Mollie, "murdered in cold blood! I am dreadfully frightened!"

"Something of the kind is quite likely," drawled Sir Lucien, "if you draw attention to our presence in the neighborhood so deliberately. Walk ahead, Kilfane, with Mollie. Rita and I will follow at a discreet distance. Leave the door ajar."

Temporarily subdued by Pyne's icy manner, Miss Gretna became silent, and went on ahead with Cyrus Kilfane, who had preserved an almost unbroken silence throughout the journey. Rita and Sir Lucien followed slowly.

"What a creepy neighborhood," whispered Rita. "Look! Someone is standing in that doorway over there, watching us."

"Take no notice," he replied. "A cat could not pass along this street unobserved by the Chinese, but they will not interfere with us provided we do not interfere with them."

Kilfane had turned to the right into a narrow court, at the entrance to which stood an iron pillar. As he and his companion passed under the lamp in a rusty bracket which projected from the wall, they vanished into a place of shadows. There was a ceaseless chorus of distant machinery, and above it rose the grinding and rattling solo of a steam winch. Once a siren hooted apparently quite near them, and looking upward at a tangled, indeterminable mass which overhung the street at this point, Rita suddenly recognized it for a ship's bow-sprit.

"Why," she said, "we are right on the bank of the river!"

"Not quite," answered Pyne. "We are skirting a dock basin. We are nearly at our destination."

Passing in turn under the lamp, they entered the narrow court, and from a doorway immediately on the left a faint light shone out upon the wet pavement. Pyne pushed the door fully open and held it for

Rita to enter. As she did so:

"Hello! hello!" croaked a harsh voice. "Number one p'lice chop, lo! Sin Sin Wa!"

The uncanny cracked voice proceeded to give an excellent imitation of a police whistle, and concluded with that of the clicking of castanets.

"Shut the door, Lucy," came the murmurous tones of Kilfane from the gloom of the stuffy little room, in the centre of which stood a stove wherefrom had proceeded the dim light shining out upon the pavement. "Light up, Sin Sin."

"Sin Sin Wa! Sin Sin Wa!" shrieked the voice, and again came the rattling of imaginary castanets. "Smartest leg in Buenos Ayres—Buenos Ayres—p'lice chop—p'lice chop, lo!"

"Oh," whispered Mollie Gretna, in the darkness, "I believe I am going to scream!"

Pyne closed the door, and a dimly discernible figure on the opposite side of the room stooped and opened a little cupboard in which was a lighted ship's lantern. The lantern being lifted out and set upon a rough table near the stove, it became possible to view the apartment and its occupants.

It was a small, low-ceiled place, having two doors, one opening upon the street and the other upon a narrow, uncarpeted passage. The window was boarded up. The ceiling had once been whitewashed and a few limp, dark fragments of paper still adhering to the walls proved that some forgotten decorator had exercised his art upon them in the past. A piece of well-worn matting lay upon the floor, and there were two chairs, a table, and a number of empty tea-chests in the room.

Upon one of the tea-chests placed beside the cupboard which had contained the lantern a Chinaman was seated. His skin was of so light a yellow color as to approximate to dirty white, and his face was pock-marked from neck to crown. He wore long, snake-like moustaches, which hung down below his chin. They grew from the extreme outer edges of his upper lip, the centre of which, usually the most hirsute, was hairless as the lip of an infant. He possessed the longest and thickest pigtail which could possibly grow upon a human scalp, and his left eye was permanently closed, so that a smile which adorned his extraordinary countenance seemed to lack the sympathy of his surviving eye, which, oblique, beady, held no mirth in its glittering depths.

The garments of the one-eyed Chinaman, who sat complacently smiling at the visitors, consisted of a loose blouse, blue trousers tucked into grey socks, and a pair of those native, thick-soled slippers which suggest to a Western critic the acme of discomfort. A raven, black as a bird of ebony, perched upon the Chinaman's shoulder, head a-tilt, surveying the newcomers with a beady, glittering left eye which strangely resembled the beady, glittering right eye of the Chinaman. For, singular, uncanny circumstance, this was a one-eyed raven which sat upon the shoulder of his one-eyed master!

Mollie Gretna uttered a stifled cry. "Oh!" she whispered. "I knew I was going to scream!"

The eye of Sin Sin Wa turned momentarily in her direction, but otherwise he did not stir a muscle.

"Are you ready for us, Sin?" asked Sir Lucien.

"All ready. Lola hab gotchee topside loom leady," replied the Chinaman in a soft, crooning voice.

"Go ahead, Kilfane," directed Sir Lucien.

He glanced at Rita, who was standing very near him, surveying the evil little room and its owner with ill-concealed disgust.

"This is merely the foyer, Rita," he said, smiling slightly. "The state apartments are upstairs and in the adjoining house."

"Oh," she murmured—and no more.

Kilfane and Mollie Gretna were passing through the inner doorway, and Mollie turned.

"Isn't it loathsomely delightful?" she cried.

"Smartest leg in Buenos Ayres!" shrieked the raven. "Sin Sin, Sin Sin!"

Uttering a frightened exclamation, Mollie disappeared along the passage. Sir Lucien indicated to Rita that she was to follow; and he, passing through last of the party, closed the door behind him.

Sin Sin Wa never moved, and the raven, settling down upon the Chinaman's shoulder, closed his serviceable eye.

CHAPTER XVII

THE BLACK SMOKE

Up an uncarpeted stair Cyrus Kilfane led the party, and into a kind of lumber-room lighted by a tin oil lamp and filled to overflowing with heterogeneous and unsavory rubbish. Here were garments, male and female, no less than five dilapidated bowler hats, more tea-chests, broken lamps, tattered fragments of cocoanut-matting, steel bed-laths and straw mattresses, ruins of chairs—the whole diffusing an indescribably unpleasant odor.

Opening a cupboard door, Kilfane revealed a number of pendent, ragged garments, and two more bowler hats. Holding the garments aside, he banged upon the back of the cupboard—three blows, a pause, and then two blows.

Following a brief interval, during which even Mollie Gretna was held silent by the strangeness of the proceedings.

"Who is it?" inquired a muffled voice.

"Cy and the crowd," answered Kilfane.

Thereupon ensued a grating noise, and hats and garments swung suddenly backward, revealing a doorway in which Mrs. Sin stood framed. She wore a Japanese kimona of embroidered green silk and a pair of green and gold brocaded slippers which possessed higher heels than Rita remembered to have seen even Mrs. Sin mounted upon before. Her ankles were bare, and it was impossible to determine in what manner she was clad beneath the kimona. Undoubtedly she had a certain dark beauty, of a bold, abandoned type.

"Come right in," she directed. "Mind your head, Lucy."

The quartette filed through into a carpeted corridor, and Mrs. Sin reclosed the false back of the cupboard, which, viewed from the other side, proved to be a door fitted into a recess in the corridor of the adjoining house. This recess ceased to exist when a second and heavier door was closed upon the first.

"You know," murmured Kilfane, "old Sin Sin has his uses, Lola. Those doors are perfectly made."

"Pooh!" scoffed the woman, with a flash of her dark eyes; "he is half a ship's carpenter and half an ape!"

She moved along the passage, her arm linked in that of Sir Lucien. The others followed, and:

"Is she truly *married* to that dreadful Chinaman?" whispered Mollie Gretna.

"Yes, I believe so," murmured Kilfane. "She is known as Mrs. Sin Sin Wa."

"Oh!" Mollie's eyes opened widely. "I almost envy her! I have read that Chinamen tie their wives to beams in the roof and lash them with leather thongs until they swoon. I could die for a man who lashed me with leather thongs. Englishmen are so ridiculously gentle to women."

Opening a door on the left of the corridor, Mrs. Sin displayed a room screened off into three sections. One shaded lamp high up near the ceiling served to light all the cubicles, which were heated by small charcoal stoves. These cubicles were identical in shape and appointment, each being draped with quaint Chinese tapestry and containing rugs, a silken divan, an armchair, and a low, Eastern table.

"Choose for yourself," said Mrs. Sin, turning to Rita and Mollie Gretna.

"Nobody else come tonight. You two in this room, eh? Next door each other for company."

She withdrew, leaving the two girls together. Mollie clasped her hands ecstatically.

"Oh, my dear!" she said. "What do you think of it all?"

"Well," confessed Rita, looking about her, "personally I feel rather nervous."

"My dear!" cried Mollie. "*I* am simply quivering with delicious terror!"

Rita became silent again, looking about her, and listening. The harsh voice of the Cuban-Jewess could be heard from a neighboring room, but otherwise a perfect stillness reigned in the house of Sin Sin Wa. She remembered that Mrs. Sin had said, "It is quiet—so quiet."

"The idea of undressing and reclining on these divans in real oriental fashion," declared Mollie, giggling, "makes me feel that I am an odalisque already. I have dreamed that I was an odalisque, dear— after smoking, you know. It was heavenly. At least, I don't know that 'heavenly' is quite the right word."

And now that evil spirit of abandonment came to Rita—communicated to her, possibly, by her companion. Dread, together with a certain sense of moral reluctance, departed, and she began to enjoy the adventure at last. It was as though something in the faintly perfumed atmosphere of the place had entered into her blood, driving out reserve and stifling conscience.

When Sir Lucien reappeared she ran to him excitedly, her charming face flushed and her eyes sparkling.

"Oh, Lucy," she cried, "how long will our things be? I'm keen to smoke!"

His jaw hardened, and when he spoke it was with a drawl more marked than usual.

"Mareno will be here almost immediately," he answered.

The tone constituted a rebuff, and Rita's coquetry deserted her, leaving her mortified and piqued. She stared at Pyne, biting her lip.

"You don't like me tonight," she declared. "If I look ugly, it's your fault; you told me to wear this horrid old costume!"

He laughed in a forced, unnatural way.

"You are quite well aware that you could never look otherwise than maddeningly beautiful," he said harshly. "Do you want me to recall the fact to you again that you are shortly to be Monte Irvin's wife—or should you prefer me to remind you that you have declined to be mine?"

Turning slowly, he walked away, but:

"Oh, Lucy!" whispered Rita.

He paused, looking back.

"I know now why you didn't want me to come," she said. "I—I'm sorry."

The hard look left Sir Lucien's face immediately and was replaced by a curious, indefinable expression, an expression which rarely appeared there.

"You only know half the reason," he replied softly.

At that moment Mrs. Sin came in, followed by Mareno carrying two dressing-cases. Mollie Gretna had run off to Kilfane, and could be heard talking loudly in another room; but, called by Mrs. Sin, she now returned, wide-eyed with excitement.

Mrs. Sin cast a lightning glance at Sir Lucien, and then addressed Rita.

"Which of these three rooms you choose?" she asked, revealing her teeth in one of those rapid smiles which were mirthless as the eternal smile of Sin Sin Wa.

"Oh," said Rita hurriedly, "I don't know. Which do you want, Mollie?"

"I love this end one!" cried Mollie. "It has cushions which simply reek of oriental voluptuousness and cruelty. It reminds me of a delicious book I have been reading called *Musk, Hashish, and Blood.*"

"Hashish!" said Mrs. Sin, and laughed harshly. "One night you shall eat the hashish, and then—"

She snapped her fingers, glancing from Rita to Pyne.

"Oh, really? Is that a promise?" asked Mollie eagerly.

"No, no!" answered Mrs. Sin. "It is a threat!"

Something in the tone of her voice as she uttered the last four words in mock dramatic fashion caused Mollie and Rita to stare at one another questioningly. That suddenly altered tone had awakened an elusive memory, but neither of them could succeed in identifying it.

Mareno, a lean, swarthy fellow, his foreign cast of countenance accentuated by close-cut side-whiskers, deposited Miss Gretna's case in the cubicle which she had selected and, Rita pointing to that adjoining it, he disposed the second case beside the divan and departed silently. As the sound of a closing door reached them:

"You notice how quiet it is?" asked Mrs. Sin.

"Yes," replied Rita. "It is extraordinarily quiet."

"This an empty house—'To let,'" explained Mrs. Sin. "We watch it stay so. Sin the landlord, see? Windows all boarded up and everything padded. No sound outside, no sound inside. Sin call it the 'House of a Hundred Raptures,' after the one he have in Buenos Ayres."

The voice of Cyrus Kilfane came, querulous, from a neighboring room.

"Lola, my dear, I am almost ready."

"Ho!" Mrs. Sin uttered a deep-toned laugh. "He is a glutton for *chandu!*

I am coming, Cy."

She turned and went out. Sir Lucien paused for a moment, permitting her to pass, and:

"Good night, Rita," he said in a low voice. "Happy dreams!"

He moved away.

"Lucy!" called Rita softly.

"Yes?"

"Is it—is it really safe here?"

Pyne glanced over his shoulder towards the retreating figure of Mrs. Sin, then:

"I shall be awake," he replied. "I would rather you had not come, but since you are here you must go through with it." He glanced again along the narrow passage created by the presence of the partitions, and spoke in a voice lower yet. "You have never really trusted me, Rita. You were wise. But you can trust me now. Good night, dear."

He walked out of the room and along the carpeted corridor to a little apartment at the back of the house, furnished comfortably but in execrably bad taste. A cheerful fire was burning in the grate, the flue of which had been ingeniously diverted by Sin Sin Wa so that the smoke issued from a chimney of the adjoining premises. On the mantelshelf, which was garishly draped, were a number of photographs of Mrs. Sin in Spanish dancing costume.

Pyne seated himself in an armchair and lighted a cigarette. Except for the ticking of a clock the room was silent as a padded cell. Upon a little Moorish table beside a deep, low settee lay a complete opium-smoking outfit.

Lolling back in the chair and crossing his legs, Sir Lucien became lost in abstraction, and he was thus seated when, some ten minutes later, Mrs. Sin came in.

"Ah!" she said, her harsh voice softened to a whisper. "I wondered. So you wait to smoke with me?" Pyne slowly turned his head, staring at her as she stood in the doorway, one hand resting on her hip and her shapely figure boldly outlined by the kimono.

"No," he replied. "I don't want to smoke. Are they all provided for?"

Mrs. Sin shook her head.

"Not Cy," she said. "Two pipes are nothing to him. He will need two more—perhaps three. But you are not going to smoke?"

"Not tonight, Lola."

She frowned, and was about to speak, when:

"Lola, my dear," came a distant, querulous murmur. "Give me another pipe."

Sin tossed her head, turned, and went out again. Sir Lucien lighted another cigarette. When finally the woman came back, Cyrus Kilfane had presumably attained the opium-smoker's paradise, for Lola closed the door and seated herself upon the arm of Sir Lucien's chair. She bent down, resting her dusky cheek against his.

"You smoke with me?" she whispered coaxingly.

"No, Lola, not tonight," he said, patting her jewel-laden hand and looking aside into the dark eyes which were watching him intently.

Mrs. Sin became silent for a few moments.

"Something has changed in you," she said at last. "You are different—lately."

"Indeed!" drawled Sir Lucien. "Possibly you are right. Others have said the same thing."

"You have lots of money now. Your investments have been good. You want to become respectable, eh?"

Pyne smiled sardonically.

"Respectability is a question of appearance," he replied. "The change to which you refer would seem to go deeper."

"Very likely," murmured Mrs. Sin. "I know why you don't smoke. You have promised your pretty little friend that you will stay awake and see that nobody tries to cut her sweet white throat."

Sir Lucien listened imperturbably.

"She is certainly nervous," he admitted coolly. "I may add that I am sorry I brought her here."

"Oh," said Mrs. Sin, her voice rising half a note. "Then why do you bring her to the House?"

"She made the arrangement herself, and I took the easier path. I am considering your interests as much as my own, Lola. She is about to marry Monte Irvin, and if his suspicions were aroused he is quite capable of digging down to the 'Hundred Raptures.'"

"You brought her to Kazmah's."

"She was not at that time engaged to Irvin."

"Ah, I see. And now everybody says you are changed. Yes, she is a charming friend."

Pyne looked up into the half-veiled dark eyes.

"She never has been and never can be any more to me, Lola," he said.

At those words, designed to placate, the fire which smouldered in Lola's breast burst into sudden flame. She leapt to her feet, confronting Sir Lucien.

"I know! I know!" she cried harshly. "Do you think I am blind? If she had been like any of the others, do you suppose it would have mattered to *me?* But you *respect* her—you *respect* her!"

Eyes blazing and hands clenched, she stood before him, a woman mad with jealousy, not of a successful rival but of a respected one. She quivered with passion, and Pyne, perceiving his mistake too late, only preserved his wonted composure by dint of a great effort. He grasped Lola and drew her down on to the arm of the chair by sheer force, for she resisted savagely. His ready wit had been at work, and:

"What a little spitfire you are," he said, firmly grasping her arms, which felt rigid to the touch. "Surely you can understand? Rita amused me, at first. Then, when I found she was going to marry Monte Irvin I didn't bother about her any more. In fact, because I like and admire Irvin, I tried to keep her away from the dope. We don't want trouble with a man of that type, who has all sorts of influence. Besides, Monte Irvin is a good fellow."

Gradually, as he spoke, the rigid arms relaxed and the lithe body ceased to quiver. Finally, Lola sank back against his shoulder, sighing.

"I don't believe you," she whispered. "You are telling me lies. But you have always told me lies; one more does not matter, I suppose. How strong you are. You have hurt my wrists. You will smoke with me now?"

For a moment Pyne hesitated, then:

"Very well," he said. "Go and lie down. I will roast the *chandu*."

CHAPTER XVIII

THE DREAM OF SIN SIN WA

For a habitual opium-smoker to abstain when the fumes of *chandu* actually reach his nostrils is a feat of will-power difficult adequately to appraise. An ordinary tobacco smoker cannot remain for long among those who are enjoying the fragrant weed without catching the infection and beginning to smoke also. Twice to redouble the lure of my lady Nicotine would be but loosely to estimate the seductiveness of the Spirit of the Poppy; yet Sir Lucien Pyne smoked one pipe with Mrs. Sin, and perceiving her to be already in a state of dreamy abstraction, loaded a second, but in his own case with a fragment of cigarette stump which smouldered in a tray upon the table. His was that rare type of character whose possessor remains master of his vices.

Following the fourth pipe—Pyne, after the second, had ceased to trouble to repeat his feat of legerdemain, "The sleep" claimed Mrs. Sin. Her languorous eyes closed, and her face assumed that rapt expression of Buddha-like beatitude which Rita had observed at Kilfane's flat. According to some scientific works on the subject, sleep is not invariably induced in the case of Europeans by the use of *chandu*. Loosely, this is true. But this type of European never becomes an habitué; the habitué always sleeps. That dream-world to which opium alone holds the key becomes the real world "for the delights of which the smoker gladly resigns all mundane interests." The exiled Chinaman returns again to the sampan of his boyhood, floating joyously on the waters of some willow-lined canal; the Malay hears once more the mystic whispering in the mangrove swamps, or scents the fragrance of nutmeg and cinnamon in the far-off golden Chersonese. Mrs. Sin doubtless lived anew the triumphs of earlier days in Buenos Ayres, when she had been La Belle Lola, the greatly beloved, and before she had met and married Sin Sin Wa. *Chandu* gives much, but claims all, and he who would open the poppy-gates must close the door of ambition and bid farewell to manhood.

Sir Lucien stood looking at the woman, and although one pipe had affected him but slightly, his imagination momentarily ran riot and a pageant of his life swept before him, so that his jaw grew hard and grim and he clenched his hands convulsively. An unbroken stillness prevailed in the opium-house of Sin Sin Wa.

Recovering from his fit of abstraction, Pyne, casting a final keen glance at the sleeper, walked out of the room. He looked along the carpeted corridor in the direction of the cubicles, paused, and then opened the heavy door masking the recess behind the cupboard. Next opening the false back of the cupboard, he passed through to the lumber-room beyond, and partly closed the second door.

He descended the stair and went along the passage; but ere he reached the door of the room on the ground floor:

"Hello! hello! Sin Sin! Sin Sin Wa!" croaked the raven. "Number one p'lice chop, lo!" The note of a police whistle followed, rendered with uncanny fidelity.

Pyne entered the room. It presented the same aspect as when he had left it. The ship's lantern stood upon the table, and Sin Sin Wa sat upon the tea-chest, the great black bird perched on his shoulder. The fire in the stove had burned lower, and its downcast glow revealed less mercilessly the dirty condition of the floor. Otherwise no one, nothing, seemed to have been disturbed. Pyne leaned against the doorpost, taking out and lighting a cigarette. The eye of Sin Sin Wa glanced sideways at him.

"Well, Sin Sin," said Sir Lucien, dropping a match and extinguishing it under his foot, "you see I am not smoking tonight."

"No smokee," murmured the Chinaman. "Velly good stuff."

"Yes, the stuff is all right, Sin."

"Number one proper," crooned Sin Sin Wa, and relapsed into smiling silence.

"Number one p'lice," croaked the raven sleepily. "Smartest—" He even attempted the castanets imitation, but was overcome by drowsiness.

For a while Sir Lucien stood watching the singular pair and smiling in his ironical fashion. The motive which had prompted him to leave the neighboring house and to seek the companionship of Sin Sin Wa was so obscure and belonged so peculiarly to the superdelicacies of chivalry, that already he was laughing at himself. But, nevertheless, in this house and not in its secret annex of a Hundred Raptures he designed to spend the night. Presently:

"Hon'lable p'lice patrol come 'long plenty soon," murmured Sin Sin Wa.

"Indeed?" said Sir Lucien, glancing at his wristwatch. "The door is open above."

Sin Sin Wa raised one yellow forefinger, without moving either hand from the knee upon which it rested, and shook it slightly to and fro.

"Allee lightee," he murmured. "No bhobbery. Allee peaceful fellers."

"Will they want to come in?"

"Wantchee dlink," replied Sin Sin Wa.

"Oh, I see. If I go out into the passage it will be all right?"

"Allee lightee."

Even as he softly crooned the words came a heavy squelch of rubbers upon the wet pavement outside, followed by a rapping on the door. Sin Sin Wa glanced aside at Sir Lucien, and the latter immediately withdrew, partly closing the door. The Chinaman shuffled across and admitted two constables. The raven, remaining perched upon his shoulder, shrieked, "Smartest leg in Buenos Ayres," and, fully awakened, rattled invisible castanets.

The police strode into the stuffy little room without ceremony, a pair of burly fellows, fresh-complexioned, and genial as men are wont to be who have reached a welcome resting-place on a damp and cheerless night. They stood by the stove, warming their hands; and one of them stooped, took up the little poker, and stirred the embers to a brighter glow.

"Been havin' a pipe, Sin?" he asked, winking at his companion. "I can smell something like opium!"

"No smokee opium," murmured Sin Sin Wa complacently. "Smokee Woodbine."

"Ho, ho!" laughed the other constable. "I *don't* think."

"You likee tly one piecee pipee one time?" inquired the Chinaman.

"Gotchee fliend makee smokee."

The man who had poked the fire slapped his companion on the back.

"Now's your chance, Jim!" he cried. "You always said you'd like to have a cut at it."

"H'm!" muttered the other. "A 'double' o' that fifteen over-proof Jamaica of yours, Sin, would hit me in a tender spot tonight."

"Lum?" murmured Sin Sin blandly. "No hab got."

He resumed his seat on the tea-chest, and the raven muttered sleepily, "Sin Sin—Sin."

"H'm!" repeated the constable.

He raised the skirt of his heavy top-coat, and from his trouser-pocket drew out a leather purse. The eye of Sin Sin Wa remained fixed upon a distant corner of the room. From the purse the constable took a shilling, ringing it loudly upon the table.

"Double rum, miss, please!" he said, facetiously. "There's no treason allowed nowadays, so my pal's payin' for his own!"

"I stood *yours* last night Jim, anyway!" cried the other, grinning. "Go on, stump up!"

Jim rang a second shilling on the table.

"*Two* double rums!" he called.

Sin Sin Wa reached a long arm into the little cupboard beside him and withdrew a bottle and a glass. Leaning forward he placed bottle and glass on the table, and adroitly swept the coins into his yellow palm.

"Number one p'lice chop," croaked the raven.

"You're right, old bird!" said Jim, pouring out a stiff peg of the spirit and disposing of it at a draught. "We should freeze to death on this blasted riverside beat if it wasn't for Sin Sin."

He measured out a second portion for his companion, and the latter drank the raw spirit off as though it had been ale, replaced the glass on the table, and having adjusted his belt and lantern in that characteristic way which belongs exclusively to members of the Metropolitan Police Force, turned and departed.

"Good night, Sin," he said, opening the door.

"So-long," murmured the Chinaman.

"Good night, old bird," cried Jim, following his colleague.

"So-long."

The door closed, and Sin Sin Wa, shuffling across, rebolted it. As Sir Lucien came out from his hiding-place Sin Sin Wa returned to his seat on the tea-chest, first putting the glass, unwashed, and the rum bottle back in the cupboard.

To the ordinary observer the Chinaman presents an inscrutable mystery. His seemingly unemotional character and his racial inability to express his thoughts intelligibly in any European tongue stamp him as a creature apart, and one whom many are prone erroneously to classify very low in the human scale and not far above the ape. Sir Lucien usually spoke to Sin Sin Wa in English, and the other replied in that weird jargon known as "pidgin." But the silly Sin Wa who murmured gibberish and the Sin Sin Wa who could converse upon many and curious subjects in his own language were two different beings—as Sir Lucien was aware. Now, as the one-eyed Chinaman resumed his seat and the one-eyed raven sank into slumber, Pyne suddenly spoke in Chinese, a tongue which he understood as it is understood by few Englishmen; that strange, sibilant speech which is alien from all Western conceptions of oral intercourse as the Chinese institutions and ideals are alien from those of the rest of the civilized world.

"So you make a profit on your rum, Sin Sin Wa," he said ironically, "at the same time that you keep in the good graces of the police?"

Sin Sin Wa's expression underwent a subtle change at the sound of his native language. He moved his hands and became slightly animated.

"A great people of the West, most honorable sir," he replied in the pure mandarin dialect, "claim credit for having said that 'business is business.' Yet he who thus expressed himself was a Chinaman."

"You surprise me."

"The wise man must often find occasion for surprise most honorable sir."

Sir Lucien lighted a cigarette.

"I sometimes wonder, Sin Sin Wa," he said slowly, "what your aim in life can be. Your father was neither a ship's carpenter nor a shopkeeper. This I know. Your age I do not know and cannot guess, but you are no longer young. You covet wealth. For what purpose, Sin Sin Wa?"

Standing behind the Chinaman, Sir Lucien's dark face, since he made no effort to hide his feelings, revealed the fact that he attached to this seemingly abstract discussion a greater importance than his tone of voice might have led one to suppose. Sin Sin Wa remained silent for some time, then:

"Most honorable sir," he replied, "when I have smoked the opium, before my eyes—for in dreams I have two—a certain picture arises. It is that of a farm in the province of Ho-Nan. Beyond the farm stretch paddy-fields as far as one can see. Men and women and boys and girls move about the farm, happy in their labors, and far, far away dwell the mountain gods, who send the great Yellow River sweeping down through the valleys where the poppy is in bloom. It is to possess that farm, most honorable sir, and those paddy-fields that I covet wealth."

"And in spite of the opium which you consume, you have never lost sight of this ideal?"

"Never."

"But—your wife?"

Sin Sin Wa performed a curious shrugging movement, peculiarly racial.

"A man may not always have the same wife," he replied cryptically. "The honorable wife who now attends to my requirements, laboring unselfishly in my miserable house and scorning the love of other men as she has always done—and as an honorable and upright woman is expected to do—may one day be gathered to her ancestors. A man never knows. Or she may leave me. I am not a good husband. It may be that some little maiden of Ho-Nan, mild-eyed like the musk-deer and modest and tender, will consent to minister to my old age. Who knows?"

Sir Lucien blew a thick cloud of tobacco smoke into the room, and:

"She will never love you, Sin Sin Wa," he said, almost sadly. "She will come to your house only to cheat you."

Sin Sin Wa repeated the eloquent shrug.

"We have a saying in Ho-Nan, most honorable sir," he answered, "and it is this: 'He who has tasted the poppy-cup has nothing to ask of love.' She will cook for me, this little one, and stroke my brow when I am weary, and light my pipe. My eye will rest upon her with pleasure. It is all I ask."

There came a soft rapping on the outer door—three raps, a pause, and then two raps. The raven opened his beady eye.

"Sin Sin Wa," he croaked, "number one p'lice chop, lo!"

Sin Sin Wa glanced aside at Sir Lucien.

"The traffic. A consignment of opium," he said. "Sam Tûk calls."

Sir Lucien consulted his watch, and:

"I should like to go with you, Sin Sin Wa," he said. "Would it be safe to leave the house—with the upper door unlocked?"

Sin Sin Wa glanced at him again.

"All are sleeping, most honorable sir?"

"All."

"I will lock the room above and the outer door. It is safe."

He raised a yellow hand, and the raven stepped sedately from his shoulder on to his wrist.

"Come, Tling-a-Ling," crooned Sin Sin Wa, "you go to bed, my little black friend, and one day you, too, shall see the paddy-fields of Ho-Nan."

Opening the useful cupboard, he stooped, and in hopped the raven. Sin Sin Wa closed the cupboard, and stepped out into the passage.

"I will bring you a coat and a cap and scarf," he said. "Your magnificent apparel would be out of place among the low pigs who wait in my other disgusting cellar to rob me. Forgive my improper absence for one moment, most honorable sir."

CHAPTER XIX

THE TRAFFIC

Sir Lucien came out into the alley wearing a greasy cloth cap pulled down over his eyes and an old overall, the collar turned up about a red woollen muffler which enveloped the lower part of his face. The odor of the outfit was disgusting, but this man's double life had brought him so frequently in contact with all forms of uncleanness, including that of the Far East, compared with which the dirt of the West is hygienic, that he suffered it without complaint.

A Chinese "boy" of indeterminable age, wearing a slop-shop suit and a cap, was waiting outside the door, and when Sin Sin Wa appeared, carefully locking up, he muttered something rapidly in his own sibilant language.

Sin Sin Wa made no reply. To his indoor attire he had added a pea-jacket and a bowler hat; and the oddly assorted trio set off westward, following the bank of the Thames in the direction of Limehouse Basin. The narrow, ill-lighted streets were quite deserted, but from the river and the riverside arose that ceaseless jangle of industry which belongs to the great port of London. On the Surrey shore whistles shrieked, and endless moving chains sent up their monstrous clangor into the night. Human voices sometimes rose above the din of machinery.

In silence the three pursued their way, crossing inlets and circling around basins dimly divined, turning to the right into a lane flanked by high, eyeless walls, and again to the left, finally to emerge nearly opposite a dilapidated gateway giving access to a small wharf, on the rickety gates bills were posted announcing, "This Wharf to Let." The annexed building appeared to be a mere shell. To the right again they turned, and once more to the left, halting before a two-story brick house which had apparently been converted into a barber's shop. In one of the grimy windows were some loose packets of cigarettes, a soapmaker's advertisement, and a card:

SAM TÛK
BARBER

Opening the door with a key which he carried, the boy admitted Sir Lucien and Sin Sin Wa to the dimly-lighted interior of a room the pretensions of which to be regarded as a shaving saloon were supported by the presence of two chairs, a filthy towel, and a broken mug. Sin Sin Wa shuffled across to another door, and, followed by Sir Lucien, descended a stone stair to a little cellar apparently intended for storing coal. A tin lamp stood upon the bottom step.

Removing the lamp from the step, Sin Sin Wa set it on the cellar floor, which was black with coal dust, then closed and bolted the door. A heap of nondescript litter lay piled in a corner of the cellar. This Sin Sin Wa disturbed sufficiently to reveal a movable slab in the roughly paved floor. It was so ingeniously concealed by coal dust that one who had sought it unaided must have experienced great difficulty in detecting it. Furthermore, it could only be raised in the following manner:

A piece of strong iron wire, which lay among the other litter, was inserted in a narrow slot, apparently a crack in the stone. About an inch of the end of the wire being bent outward to form a right angle, when the seemingly useless piece of scrap-iron had been thrust through the slab and turned, it formed a handle by means of which the trap could be raised.

Again Sin Sin Wa took up the lamp, placing it at the brink of the opening revealed. A pair of wooden steps rested below, and Sir Lucien, who evidently was no stranger to the establishment, descended awkwardly, since there was barely room for a big man to pass. He found himself in the mouth of a low passage, unpaved and shored up with rough timbers in the manner of a mine-working. Sin Sin Wa followed with the lamp, drawing the slab down into its place behind him.

Stooping forward and bending his knees, Sir Lucien made his way along the passage, the Chinaman following. It was of considerable length, and terminated before a strong door bearing a massive lock. Sin Sin Wa reached over the stooping figure of Sir Lucien and unfastened the lock. The two emerged in a kind of dug-out. Part of it had evidently been in existence before the ingenious Sin Sin Wa had exercised his skill upon it, and was of solid brickwork and stone-paved; palpably a storage vault. But it had been altered to suit the Chinaman's purpose, and one end—that in which the passage came out—was timbered. It contained a long counter and many shelves; also a large oil-stove and a number of pots, pans, and queer-looking jars. On the counter stood a ship's lantern. The shelves were laden with packages and bottles. Behind the counter sat a venerable and perfectly bald Chinaman. The only trace of hair upon his countenance grew on the shrunken upper lip—mere wisps of white down. His skin was shrivelled like that of a preserved fig, and he wore big horn-rimmed spectacles. He never once exhibited the slightest evidence of life, and his head and face, and the horn-rimmed spectacles, might quite easily have passed for those of an unwrapped mummy. This was Sam Tûk.

Bending over a box upon which rested a canvas-bound package was a burly seaman engaged in unknotting the twine with which the canvas was kept in place. As Sin Sin Wa and Sir Lucien came in he looked up, revealing a red-bearded, ugly face, very puffy under the eyes.

"Wotcher, Sin Sin!" he said gruffly. "Who's your long pal?"

"Friend," murmured Sin Sin Wa complacently. "You gotchee *pukka* stuff thisee time, George?"

"I allus brings the *pukka* stuff!" roared the seaman, ceasing to fumble with the knots and glaring at Sin Sin Wa. "Wotcher mean—*pukka* stuff?"

"Gotchee no use for bran," murmured Sin Sin Wa. "Gotchee no use for tin-tack. Gotchee no use for glue."

"Bran!" roared the man, his glance and pose very menacing. "Tin-tacks and glue! Who the flamin' 'ell ever tried to sell you glue?"

"Me only wantchee lemindee you," said Sin Sin Wa. "No pidgin."

"George" glared for a moment, breathing heavily; then he stooped and resumed his task, Sin Sin Wa and Sir Lucien watching him in silence. A sound of lapping water was faintly audible.

Opening the canvas wrappings, the man began to take out and place upon the counter a number of reddish balls of "leaf" opium, varying in weight from about eight ounces to a pound or more.

"H'm!" murmured Sin Sin Wa. "Smyrna stuff."

From a pocket of his pea-jacket he drew a long bodkin, and taking up one of the largest balls he thrust the bodkin in and then withdrew it, the steel stained a coffee color. Sin Sin Wa smelled and tasted the substance adhering to the bodkin, weighed the ball reflectively in his yellow palm, and then set it aside. He took up a second, whereupon:

"'Alf a mo', guvnor!" cried the seaman furiously. "D'you think I'm going to wait 'ere while you prods about in all the blasted lot? It's damn near high tide—I shan't get out. 'Alf time! Savvy? Shove it on the scales!"

Sin Sin Wa shook his head.

"Too muchee slick. Too muchee bhobbery," he murmured. "Sin Sin Wa gotchee sabby what him catchee buy or no pidgin."

"What's the game?" inquired George menacingly. "Don't you know a cake o' Smyrna when you smells it?"

"No sabby lead chop till ploddem withee dipper," explained the Chinaman, imperturbably.

"Lead!" shouted the man. "There ain't no bloody lead in 'em!"

"H'm," murmured Sin Sin Wa smilingly. "So fashion, eh? All velly proper."

He calmly inserted the bodkin in the second cake; seemed to meet with some obstruction, and laid the ball down upon the counter. From beneath his jacket he took out a clasp-knife attached to a steel chain. Undeterred by a savage roar from the purveyor, he cut the sticky mass in half, and digging his long nails into one of the halves, brought out two lead shots. He directed a glance of his beady eye upon the man.

"Bloody liar," he murmured sweetly. "Lobber."

"Who's a robber?" shouted George, his face flushing darkly, and apparently not resenting the earlier innuendo; "Who's a robber?"

"One sarcee Smyrna feller packee stuff so fashion," murmured Sin Sin Wa. "Thief-feller lobbee poor sailorman."

George jerked his peaked cap from his head, revealing a tangle of unkempt red hair. He scratched his skull with savage vigor.

"Blimey!" he said pathetically. "'Ere's a go! I been done brown, guv'nor."

"Lough luck," murmured Sin Sin Wa, and resumed his examination of the cakes of opium.

The man watched him now in silence, only broken by exclamations of "Blimey" and "Flaming hell" when more shot was discovered. The tests concluded:

"Gotchee some more?" asked Sin Sin Wa.

From the canvas wrapping George took out and tossed on the counter a square packet wrapped in grease-paper.

"H'm," murmured Sin Sin Wa, "Patna. Where you catchee?"

"Off of a lascar," growled the man.

The cake of Indian opium was submitted to the same careful scrutiny as that which the balls of Turkish had already undergone, but the Patna opium proved to be unadulterated. Reaching over the counter Sin Sin Wa produced a pair of scales, and, watched keenly by George, weighed the leaf and then the cake.

"Ten-six Smyrna; one 'leben Patna," muttered Sin Sin Wa. "You catchee eighty jimmies."

"Eh?" roared George. "Eighty quid! Eighty quid! Flamin' blind o'

Riley! D'you think I'm up the pole? Eighty quid? You're barmy!"

"Eighty-ten," murmured Sin Sin Wa. "Eighty jimmies opium; ten bob lead."

"I give more'n that for it!" cried the seaman. "An' I damn near hit a police boat comin' in, too!"

Sir Lucien spoke a few words rapidly in Chinese. Sin Sin Wa performed his curious oriental shrug, and taking a fat leather wallet from his hip-pocket, counted out the sum of eighty-five pounds upon the counter.

"You catchee eighty-five," he murmured. "Too muchee price."

The man grabbed the money and pocketed it without a word of acknowledgment. He turned and strode along the room, his heavy, iron-clamped boots ringing on the paved floor.

"Fetch a grim, Sin Sin," he cried. "I'll never get out if I don't jump to it."

Sin Sin Wa took the lantern from the counter and followed. Opening a door at the further end of the place, he set the lantern at the head of three descending wooden steps discovered. With the opening of the door the sound of lapping water had grown perceptibly louder. George clattered down the steps, which led to a second but much stouter door. Sin Sin Wa followed, nearly closing the first door, so that only a faint streak of light crept down to them.

The second door was opened, and the clangor of the Surrey shore suddenly proclaimed itself. Cold, damp air touched them, and the faint light of the lantern above cast their shadows over unctuous gliding water, which lapped the step upon which they stood. Slimy shapes uprose dim and ghostly from its darkly moving surface.

A boat was swinging from a ring beside the door, and into it George tumbled. He unhitched the lashings, and strongly thrust the boat out upon the water. Coming to the first of the dim shapes, he grasped it and thereby propelled the skiff to another beyond. These indistinct shapes were the piles supporting the structure of a wharf.

"Good night, guv'nor!" he cried hoarsely

"So-long," muttered Sin Sin Wa.

He waited until the boat was swallowed in the deeper shadows, then reclosed the water-gate and ascended to the room where Sir Lucien awaited. Such was the receiving office of Sin Sin Wa. While the wharf remained untenanted it was not likely to be discovered by the authorities, for even at low tide the river-door was invisible from passing craft. Prospective lessees who had taken the trouble to inquire about the rental had learned that it was so high as to be prohibitive.

Sin Sin Wa paid fair prices and paid cash. This was no more than a commercial necessity. For those who have opium, cocaine, veronal, or heroin to sell can always find a ready market in London and elsewhere. But one sufficiently curious and clever enough to have solved the riddle of the vacant wharf would have discovered that the mysterious owner who showed himself so loath to accept reasonable offers for the property could well afford to be thus independent. Those who control "the traffic" control El Dorado—a city of gold which, unlike the fabled Manoa, actually exists and yields its riches to the unscrupulous adventurer.

Smiling his mirthless, eternal smile, Sin Sin Wa placed the newly purchased stock upon a shelf immediately behind Sam Tûk; and Sam Tûk exhibited the first evidence of animation which had escaped him throughout the progress of the "deal." He slowly nodded his hairless head.

CHAPTER XX

KAZMAH'S METHODS

Rita Dresden married Monte Irvin in the spring and bade farewell to the stage. The goal long held in view was attained at last. But another farewell which at one time she had contemplated eagerly no longer appeared desirable or even possible. To cocamania had been added a tolerance for opium, and at the last *chandu* party given by Cyrus Kilfane she had learned that she could smoke nearly as much opium as the American habitué.

The altered attitude of Sir Lucien surprised and annoyed her. He, who had first introduced her to the spirit of the coca leaf and to the goddess of the poppy, seemed suddenly to have determined to convince her of the folly of these communions. He only succeeded in losing her confidence. She twice visited the "House of a Hundred Raptures" with Mollie Gretna, and once with Mollie and Kilfane, unknown to Sir Lucien.

Urgent affairs of some kind necessitated his leaving England a few weeks before the date fixed for Rita's wedding, and as Kilfane had already returned to America, Rita recognized with a certain dismay that she would be left to her own resources—handicapped by the presence of a watchful husband. This subtle change in her view of Monte Irvin she was incapable of appreciating, for Rita was no psychologist. But the effect of the drug habit was pointedly illustrated by the fact that in a period of little more than six months, from regarding Monte Irvin as a rock of refuge—a chance of salvation—she had come to regard him in the light of an obstacle to her indulgence. Not that her respect had diminished. She really loved at last, and so well that the idea of discovery by this man whose wholesomeness was the trait of character which most potently attracted her, was too appalling to be contemplated. The chance of discovery would be enhanced, she recognized, by the absence of her friends and accomplices.

Of course she was acquainted with many other devotees. In fact, she met so many of them that she had grown reconciled to her habits, believing them to be common to all "smart" people—a part of the Bohemian life. The truth of the matter was that she had become a prominent member of a coterie closely knit and associated by a bond of mutual vice—a kind of masonry whereof Kazmah of Bond Street was Grand Master and Mrs. Sin Grand Mistress.

The relations existing between Kazmah and his clients were of a most peculiar nature, too, and must have piqued the curiosity of anyone but a drug-slave. Having seen him once, in his oracular cave, Rita had been accepted as one of the initiated. Thereafter she had had no occasion to interview the strange, immobile Egyptian, nor had she experienced any desire to do so. The method of obtaining drugs was a simple one. She had merely to present herself at the establishment in Bond Street and to purchase either a flask of perfume or a box of sweetmeats. There were several varieties of perfume, and each corresponded to a particular drug. The sweetmeats corresponded to morphine. Rashid, the attendant, knew all Kazmah's clients, and with the box or flask he gave them a quantity of the required drug. This scheme was precautionary. For if a visitor should chance to be challenged on leaving the place, there was the legitimate purchase to show in evidence of the purpose of the visit.

No conversation was necessary, merely the selection of a scent and the exchange of a sum of money. Rashid retired to wrap up the purchase, and with it a second and smaller package was slipped into the customer's hand. That the prices charged were excessive—nay, ridiculous—did not concern Rita, for, in common with the rest of her kind, she was careless of expenditure.

Chandu, alone, Kazmah did not sell. He sold morphine, tincture of opium, and other preparations; but those who sought the solace of the pipe were compelled to deal with Mrs. Sin. She would arrange *chandu* parties, or would prepare the "Hundred Raptures" in Limehouse for visitors; but, except in the form of opiated cigarettes, she could rarely be induced to part with any of the precious gum. Thus she cleverly kept a firm hold upon the devotees of the poppy.

Drug-takers form a kind of brotherhood, and outside the charmed circle they are secretive as members of the Mafia, the Camorra, or the Catouse-Menegant. In this secrecy, which, indeed, is a recognized symptom of drug mania, lay Kazmah's security. Rita experienced no desire to peer behind the veil which, literally and metaphorically, he had placed between himself and the world. At first she had been vaguely curious, and had questioned Sir Lucien and others, but nobody seemed to know the real identity of Kazmah, and nobody seemed to care provided that he continued to supply drugs. They all led secret, veiled lives, these slaves of the laboratory, and that Kazmah should do likewise did not surprise them. He had excellent reasons.

During this early stage of faint curiosity she had suggested to Sir Lucien that for Kazmah to conduct a dream-reading business seemed to be to add to the likelihood of police interference.

The baronet had smiled sardonically.

"It is an additional safeguard," he had assured her. "It corresponds to the method of a notorious Paris assassin who was very generally regarded by the police as a cunning pickpocket. Kazmah's business of 'dream-reading' does not actually come within the Act. He is clever enough for that. Remember, he does not profess to tell fortunes. It also enables him to balk idle curiosity."

At the time of her marriage Rita was hopelessly in the toils, and had been really panic-stricken at the prospect—once so golden—of a protracted sojourn abroad. The war, which rendered travel impossible, she regarded rather in the light of a heaven-sent boon. Irvin, though personally favoring a quiet ceremony, recognized that Rita cherished a desire to quit theatreland in a chariot of fire, and accordingly the wedding was on a scale of magnificence which outshone that of any other celebrated during the season. Even the lugubrious Mr. Esden, who gave his daughter away, was seen to smile twice. Mrs. Esden moved in a rarified atmosphere of gratified ambition and parental pride, which no doubt closely resembled that which the angels breathe.

It was during the early days of her married life, and while Sir Lucien was still abroad, that Rita began to experience difficulty in obtaining the drugs which she required. She had lost touch to a certain extent with her former associates; but she had retained her maid, Nina, and the girl regularly went to Kazmah's and returned with the little flasks of perfume. When an accredited representative was sent upon such a mission, Kazmah dispatched the drugs disguised in a scent flask; but on each successive occasion that Nina went to him the prices increased, and finally became so exorbitant that even Rita grew astonished and dismayed.

She mentioned the matter to another habitué, a lady of title addicted to the use of the hypodermic syringe, and learned that she (Rita) was being charged nearly twice as much as her friend.

"I should bring the man to his senses, dear," said her ladyship. "I know a doctor who will be only too glad to supply you. When I say a doctor, he is no longer recognized by the B.M.A., but he's none the less clever and kind for all that."

To the clever and kind medical man Rita repaired on the following day, bearing a written introduction from her friend. The discredited physician supplied her for a short time, charging only moderate fees. Then, suddenly, this second source of supply was closed. The man declared that he was being watched by the police, and that he dared not continue to supply her with cocaine and veronal. His shifty eyes gave the lie to his words, but he was firm in his resolution, whatever may have led him to it, and Rita was driven back to Kazmah. His charges had become more exorbitant than ever, but her need was imperative. Nevertheless, she endeavored to find another drug dealer, and after a time was again successful.

At a certain supper club she was introduced to a suave little man, quite palpably an uninterned alien, who smilingly offered to provide her with any drug to be found in the British Pharmacopeia, at most moderate charges. With this little German-Jew villain she made a pact, reflecting that, provided that his wares were of good quality, she had triumphed over Kazmah.

The craving for *chandu* seized her sometimes and refused to be exorcised by morphia, laudanum, or any other form of opium; but she had not dared to spend a night at the "House of a Hundred Raptures" since her marriage. Her new German friend volunteered to supply the necessary gum, outfit, and to provide an apartment where she might safely indulge in smoking. She declined—at first. But finally, on Mollie Gretna's return from France, where she had been acting as a nurse, Rita and Mollie accepted the suave alien's invitation to spend an evening in his private opium divan.

Many thousands of careers were wrecked by the war, and to the war and the consequent absence of her husband Rita undoubtedly owed her relapse into opium-smoking. That she would have continued secretly to employ cocaine, veronal, and possibly morphine was probable enough; but the constant society of Monte Irvin must have made it extremely difficult for her to indulge the craving for *chandu*. She began to regret the gaiety of her old life. Loneliness and monotony plunged her into a state of suicidal depression, and she grasped eagerly at every promise of excitement.

It was at about this time that she met Margaret Halley, and between the two, so contrary in disposition, a close friendship arose. The girl doctor ere long discovered Rita's secret, of course, and the discovery was hastened by an event which occurred shortly after they had become acquainted.

The suave alien gentleman disappeared.

That was the entire story in five words—or all of the story that Rita ever learned. His apartments were labelled "To Let," and the night clubs knew him no more. Rita for a time was deprived of drugs, and the nervous collapse which resulted revealed to Margaret Halley's trained perceptions the truth respecting her friend.

Kazmah's terms proved to be more outrageous than ever, but Rita found herself again compelled to resort to the Egyptian. She went personally to the rooms in old Bond Street and arranged with Rashid to see Kazmah on the following day, Friday, for Kazmah only received visitors by appointment. As it chanced, Sir Lucien Pyne returned to England on Thursday night and called upon Rita at Prince's Gate. She welcomed him as a friend in need, unfolding the pitiful story, to the truth of which her nervous condition bore eloquent testimony.

Sir Lucien began to pace up and down the charming little room in which Rita had received him. She watched him, haggard-eyed. Presently:

"Leave Kazmah to me," he said. "If you visit him he will merely shield himself behind the mystical business, or assure you that he is making no profit on his sales. Kilfane had similar trouble with him."

"Then *you* will see him?" asked Rita.

"I will make a point of interviewing him in the morning. Meanwhile, if you will send Nina around to Albemarle Street in about an hour I will see what can be done."

"Oh, Lucy," whispered Rita, "what a pal you are."

Sir Lucien smiled in his cold fashion.

"I try to be," he said enigmatically; "but I don't always succeed." He turned to her. "Have you ever thought of giving up this doping?" he asked. "Have you ever realized that with increasing tolerance the quantities must increase as well, and that a day is sure to come when—"

Rita repressed a nervous shudder.

"You are trying to frighten me," she replied. "You have tried before; I don't know why. But it's no good, Lucy. You know I cannot give it up."

"You can try."

"I don't want to try!" she cried irritably. "It will be time enough when Monte is back again, and we can really 'live.' This wretched existence, with everything restricted and rationed, and all one's friends in Flanders or Mesopotamia or somewhere, drives me mad! I tell you I should die,

Lucy, if I tried to do without it now."

The hollow presence of reform contemplated in a hazy future did not deceive Sir Lucien. He suppressed a sigh, and changed the topic of conversation.

CHAPTER XXI

THE CIGARETTES FROM BUENOS AYRES

Sir Lucien's intervention proved successful. Kazmah's charges became more modest, and Rita no longer found it necessary to deprive herself of hats and dresses in order to obtain drugs. But, nevertheless, these were not the halcyon days of old. She was now surrounded by spies. It was necessary to resort to all kinds of subterfuge in order to cover her expenditures at the establishment in old Bond Street. Her husband never questioned her outlay, but on the other hand it was expedient to be armed against the possibility of his doing so, and Rita's debts were accumulating formidably.

Then there was Margaret Halley to consider. Rita had never hitherto given her confidence to anyone who was not addicted to the same practices as herself, and she frequently experienced embarrassment beneath the grave scrutiny of Margaret's watchful eyes. In another this attitude of gentle disapproval would have been irritating, but Rita loved and admired Margaret, and suffered accordingly.

As for Sir Lucien, she had ceased to understand him. An impalpable barrier seemed to have arisen between them. The inner man had became inaccessible. Her mind was not subtle enough to grasp the real explanation of this change in her old lover. Being based upon wrong premises, her inferences were necessarily wide of the truth, and she believed that Sir Lucien was jealous of Margaret's cousin, Quentin Gray.

Gray met Rita at Margaret Halley's flat shortly after he had returned home from service in the East, and he immediately conceived a violent infatuation for this pretty friend of his cousin's. In this respect his conduct was in no way peculiar. Few men were proof against the seductive Mrs. Monte Irvin, not because she designedly encouraged admiration, but because she was one of those fortunately rare characters who inspire it without conscious effort. Her appeal to men was sweetly feminine and quite lacking in that self-assertive and masculine "take me or leave me" attitude which characterizes some of the beauties of today. There was nothing abstract about her delicate loveliness, yet her charm was not wholly physical. Many women disliked her.

At dance, theatre, and concert Quentin Gray played the doting cavalier; and Rita, who was used to at least one such adoring attendant, accepted his homage without demur. Monte Irvin returned to civil life, but Rita showed no disposition to dispense with her new admirer. Both Gray and Sir Lucien had become frequent visitors at Prince's Gate, and Irvin, who understood his wife's character up to a point, made them his friends.

Shortly after Monte Irvin's return Sir Lucien taxed Rita again with her increasing subjection to drugs. She was in a particularly gay humor, as the supplies from Kazmah had been regular, and she laughingly fenced with him when he reminded her of her declared intention to reform when her husband should return.

"You are really as bad as Margaret," she declared. "There is nothing the matter with me. You talk of 'curing' me as though I were ill. Physician, heal thyself."

The sardonic smile momentarily showed upon Pyne's face, and:

"I know when and where to pull up, Rita," he said. "A woman never knows this. If I were deprived of opium tomorrow I could get along without it."

"I have given up opium," replied Rita. "It's too much trouble, and the last time Mollie and I went—"

She paused, glancing quickly at Sir Lucien.

"Go on," he said grimly. "I know you have been to Sin Sin Wa's. What happened the last time?"

"Well," continued Rita hurriedly, "Monte seemed to be vaguely suspicious. Besides, Mrs. Sin charged me most preposterously. I really cannot afford it, Lucy."

"I am glad you cannot. But what I was about to say was this: Suppose *you* were to be deprived, not of *chandu*, but of cocaine and veronal, do you know what would happen to you?"

"Oh!" whispered Rita, "why *will* you persist in trying to frighten me! I am not going to be deprived of them."

"I persist, dear, because I want you to try, gradually, to depend less upon drugs, so that if the worst should happen you would have a chance."

Rita stood up and faced him, biting her lip.

"Lucy," she said, "do you mean that Kazmah—"

"I mean that anything might happen, Rita. After all, we do possess a police service in London, and one day there might be an accident. Kazmah has certain influence, but it may be withdrawn. Rita, won't you try?"

She was watching him closely, and now the pupils of her beautiful eyes became dilated.

"You know something," she said slowly, "which you are keeping from me."

He laughed and turned aside.

"I know that I am compelled to leave England again, Rita, for a time; and I should be a happier man if I knew that you were not so utterly dependent upon Kazmah."

"Oh, Lucy, are you going away again?"

"I must. But I shall not be absent long, I hope."

Rita sank down upon the settee from which she had risen, and was silent for some time; then:

"I *will* try, Lucy," she promised. "I will go to Margaret Halley, as she is always asking me to do."

"Good girl," said Pyne quietly. "It is just a question of making the effort, Rita. You will succeed, with Margaret's help."

A short time later Sir Lucien left England, but throughout the last week that he remained in London Rita spent a great part of every day in his company. She had latterly begun to experience an odd kind of remorse for her treatment of the inscrutably reserved baronet. His earlier intentions she had not forgotten, but she had long ago forgiven them, and now she often felt sorry for this man whom she had deliberately used as a stepping-stone to fortune.

Gray was quite unable to conceal his jealousy. He seemed to think that he had a proprietary right to Mrs. Monte Irvin's society, and during the week preceding Sir Lucien's departure Gray came perilously near to making himself ridiculous on more than one occasion.

One night, on leaving a theatre, Rita suggested to Pyne that they should proceed to a supper club for an hour. "It will be like old times," she said.

"But your husband is expecting you," protested Sir Lucien.

"Let's ring him up and ask him to join us. He won't, but he cannot very well object then."

As a result they presently found themselves descending a broad carpeted stairway. From the rooms below arose the strains of an American melody. Dancing was in progress, or, rather, one of those orgiastic ceremonies which passed for dancing during this pagan period. Just by the foot of the stairs they paused and surveyed the scene.

"Why," said Rita, "there is Quentin—glaring insanely, silly boy."

"Do you see whom he is with?" asked Sir Lucien.

"Mollie Gretna."

"But I mean the woman sitting down."

Rita stood on tiptoe, trying to obtain a view, and suddenly:

"Oh!" she exclaimed, "Mrs. Sin!"

The dance at that moment concluding, they crossed the floor and joined the party. Mrs. Sin greeted them with one of her rapid, mirthless smiles. She was wearing a gown noticeable, but not for quantity, even in that semi-draped assembly. Mollie Gretna giggled rapturously. But Gray's swiftly changing color betrayed a mood which he tried in vain to conceal by his manner. Having exchanged a few words with the new arrivals, he evidently realized that he could not trust himself to remain longer, and:

"Now I must be off," he said awkwardly. "I have an appointment—important business. Good night, everybody."

He turned away and hurried from the room. Rita flushed slightly and exchanged a glance with Sir Lucien. Mrs. Sin, who had been watching the three intently, did not fail to perceive this glance. Mollie Gretna characteristically said a silly thing.

"Oh!" she cried. "I wonder whatever is the matter with him! He looks as though he had gone mad!"

"It is perhaps his heart," said Mrs. Sin harshly, and she raised her bold dark eyes to Sir Lucien's face.

"Oh, please don't talk about hearts," cried Rita, willfully misunderstanding. "Monte has a weak heart, and it frightens me."

"So?" murmured Mrs. Sin. "Poor fellow."

"*I* think a weak heart is most romantic," declared Mollie Gretna.

But Gray's behavior had cast a shadow upon the party which even Mollie's empty light-hearted chatter was powerless to dispel, and when, shortly after midnight, Sir Lucien drove Rita home to Prince's Gate, they were very silent throughout the journey. Just before the car reached the house:

"Where does Mrs. Sin live?" asked Rita, although it was not of Mrs. Sin that she had been thinking.

"In Limehouse, I believe," replied Sir Lucien; "at The House. But I fancy she has rooms somewhere in town also."

He stayed only a few minutes at Prince's Gate, and as the car returned along Piccadilly, Sir Lucien, glancing upward towards the windows of a tall block of chambers facing the Green Park, observed a light in one of them. Acting upon a sudden impulse, he raised the speaking-tube.

"Pull up, Fraser," he directed.

The chauffeur stopped the car and Sir Lucien alighted, glancing at the clock inside as he did so, and smiling at his own quixotic behavior. He entered an imposing doorway and rang one of the bells. There was an interval of two minutes or so, when the door opened and a man looked out.

"Is that you, Willis?" asked Pyne.

"Oh, I beg pardon, Sir Lucien. I didn't know you in the dark."

"Has Mr. Gray retired yet?"

"Not yet. Will you please follow me, Sir Lucien. The stairway lights are off."

A few moments later Sir Lucien was shown into the apartment of Gray's which oddly combined the atmosphere of a gymnasium with that of a study. Gray, wearing a dressing-gown and having a pipe in his mouth, was standing up to receive his visitor, his face rather pale and the expression of his lips at variance with that in his eyes. But:

"Hello, Pyne," he said quietly. "Anything wrong—or have you just looked in for a smoke?"

Sir Lucien smiled a trifle sadly.

"I wanted a chat, Gray," he replied. "I'm leaving town tomorrow, or I should not have intruded at such an unearthly hour."

"No intrusion," muttered Gray; "try the armchair, no, the big one. It's more comfortable." He raised his voice: "Willis, bring some fluid!"

Sir Lucien sat down, and from the pocket of his dinner jacket took out a plain brown packet of cigarettes and selected one.

"Here," said Gray, "have a cigar!"

"No, thanks," replied Pyne. "I rarely smoke anything but these."

"Never seen that kind of packet before," declared Gray. "What brand are they?"

"No particular brand. They are imported from Buenos Ayres, I believe."

Willis having brought in a tray of refreshments and departed again, Sir Lucien came at once to the point.

"I really called, Gray," he said, "to clear up any misunderstanding there may be in regard to Rita Irvin."

Quentin Gray looked up suddenly when he heard Rita's name, and:

"What misunderstanding?" he asked.

"Regarding the nature of my friendship with her," answered Sir Lucien coolly. "Now, I am going to speak quite bluntly, Gray, because I like Rita and I respect her. I also like and respect Monte Irvin; and I don't want you, or anybody else, to think that Rita and I are, or ever have been, anything more than pals. I have known her long enough to have learned that she sails straight, and has always sailed straight. Now—listen, Gray, please. You embarrassed me tonight, old chap, and you embarrassed Rita. It was unnecessary." He paused, and then added slowly: "She is as sacred to me, Gray, as she is to you—and we are both friends of Monte Irvin."

For a moment Quentin Gray's fiery temper flickered up, as his heightened color showed, but the coolness of the older and cleverer man prevailed. Gray laughed, stood up, and held out his hand.

"You're right, Pyne!" he said. "But she's damn pretty!" He uttered a loud sigh. "If only she were not married!"

Sir Lucien gripped the outstretched hand, but his answering smile had much pathos in it.

"If only she were not, Gray," he echoed.

He took his departure shortly afterwards, absently leaving a brown packet of cigarettes upon the table. It was an accident. Yet there were few, when the truth respecting Sir Lucien Pyne became known, who did not believe it to have been a deliberate act, designed to lure Quentin Gray into the path of the poppy.

CHAPTER XXII

THE STRANGLE-HOLD

Less than a month later Rita was in a state of desperation again. Kazmah's prices had soared above anything that he had hitherto extorted. Her bank account, as usual, was greatly overdrawn, and creditors of all kinds were beginning to press for payment. Then, crowning catastrophe, Monte Irvin, for the first time during their married life, began to take an interest in Rita's reckless expenditure. By a combination of adverse circumstances, she, the wife of one of the wealthiest aldermen of the City of London, awakened to the fact that literally she had no money.

She pawned as much of her jewellery as she could safely dispose of, and temporarily silenced the more threatening tradespeople; but Kazmah declined to give credit, and cheques had never been acceptable at the establishment in old Bond Street.

Rita feverishly renewed her old quest, seeking in all directions for some less extortionate purveyor. But none was to be found. The selfishness and secretiveness of the drug slave made it difficult for her to learn on what terms others obtained Kazmah's precious goods; but although his prices undoubtedly varied, she was convinced that no one of all his clients was so cruelly victimized as she.

Mollie Gretna endeavored to obtain an extra supply to help Rita, but Kazmah evidently saw through the device, and the endeavor proved a failure.

She demanded to see Kazmah, but Rashid, the Egyptian, blandly assured her that "the Sheikh-el-Kazmah" was away. She cast discretion to the winds and wrote to him, protesting that it was utterly impossible for her to raise so much ready money as he demanded, and begging him to grant her a small supply or to accept the letter as a promissory note to be redeemed in three months. No answer was received, but when Rita again called at old Bond Street, Rashid proposed one of the few compromises which the frenzied woman found herself unwilling to accept.

"The Sheikh-el-Kazmah say, my lady, your friend Mr. Gray never come to him. If you bring him it will be all right."

Rita found herself stricken dumb by this cool proposal. The degradation which awaits the drug slave had never been more succinctly expounded to her. She was to employ Gray's foolish devotion for the commercial advantage of Kazmah. Of course Gray might any day become one of the three wealthiest peers in the realm. She divined the meaning of Kazmah's hitherto incomprehensible harshness (or believed that she did); she saw what was expected of her. "My God!" she whispered. "I have not come to that yet."

Rashid she knew to be incorruptible or powerless, and she turned away, trembling, and left the place, whose faint perfume of frankincense had latterly become hateful to her.

She was at this time bordering upon a state of collapse. Insomnia, which latterly had defied dangerously increased doses of veronal, was telling upon nerve and brain. Now, her head aching so that she often wondered how long she could retain sanity, she found herself deprived not only of cocaine, but also of malourea. Margaret Halley was her last hope, and to Margaret she hastened on the day before the tragedy which was destined to bring to light the sinister operations of the Kazmah group.

Although, perhaps mercifully, she was unaware of the fact, representatives of Spinker's Agency had been following her during the whole of the preceding fortnight. That Rita was in desperate trouble of some kind her husband had not failed to perceive, and her reticence had quite naturally led him to a certain conclusion. He had sought to win her confidence by every conceivable means and had failed. At last had come doubt—and the hateful interview with Spinker.

As Rita turned in at the doorway below Margaret's flat, then, Brisley was lighting a cigarette in the shelter of a porch nearly opposite, and Gunn was not far away.

Margaret immediately perceived that her friend's condition was alarming. But she realized that whatever the cause to which it might be due, it gave her the opportunity for which she had been waiting. She wrote a prescription containing one grain of cocaine, but declined firmly to issue others unless Rita authorized her, in writing, to undertake a cure of the drug habit.

Rita's disjointed statements pointed to a conspiracy of some kind on the part of those who had been supplying her with drugs, but Margaret knew from experience that to exhibit curiosity in regard to the matter would be merely to provoke evasions.

A hopeless day and a pain-racked, sleepless night found Kazmah's unhappy victim in the mood for any measure, however desperate, which should promise even temporary relief. Monte Irvin went out very early, and at about eleven o'clock Rita rang up Kazmah's, but only to be informed by Rashid, who replied, that Kazmah was still away. "This evening he tell me that he see your friend if he come, my lady." As if the Fates sought to test her endurance to the utmost, Quentin Gray called shortly afterwards and invited her to dine with him and go to a theatre that evening.

For five age-long seconds Rita hesitated. If no plan offered itself by nightfall she knew that her last scruple would be conquered. "After all," whispered a voice within her brain, "Quentin is a man. Even if I took him to Kazmah's and he was in some way induced to try opium, or even cocaine, he would probably never become addicted to drug-taking. But I should have done my part—"

"Very well, Quentin," she heard herself saying aloud. "Will you call for me?"

But when he had gone Rita sat for more than half an hour, quite still, her hands clenched and her face a tragic mask. (Gunn, of Spinker's Agency, reported telephonically to Monte Irvin in the City that the Hon. Quentin Gray had called and had remained about twenty-five minutes; that he had proceeded to the Prince's Restaurant, and from there to Mudie's, where he had booked a box at the Gaiety Theatre.)

Towards the fall of dusk the more dreadful symptoms which attend upon a sudden cessation of the use of cocaine by a victim of cocainophagia began to assert themselves again. Rita searched wildly in the lining of her jewel-case to discover if even a milligram of the drug had by chance fallen there from the little gold box. But the quest was in vain.

As a final resort she determined to go to Margaret Halley again.

She hurried to Dover Street, and her last hope was shattered. Margaret was out, and Janet had no idea when she was likely to return. Rita had much ado to prevent herself from bursting into tears. She scribbled a few lines, without quite knowing what she was writing, sealed the paper in an envelope, and left it on Margaret's table.

Of returning to Prince's Gate and dressing for the evening she had only a hazy impression. The hammer-beats in her head were depriving her of reasoning power, and she felt cold, numbed, although a big fire blazed in her room. Then as she sat before her mirror, drearily wondering if her face really looked as drawn and haggard as the image in the glass, or if definite delusions were beginning, Nina came in and spoke to her. Some moments elapsed before Rita could grasp the meaning of the girl's words.

"Sir Lucien Pyne has rung up, Madam, and wishes to speak to you."

Sir Lucien! Sir Lucien had come back? Rita experienced a swift return of feverish energy. Half dressed as she was, and without pausing to take a wrap, she ran out to the telephone.

Never had a man's voice sounded so sweet as that of Sir Lucien when he spoke across the wires. He was at Albemarle Street, and Rita, wasting no time in explanations, begged him to await her there. In another ten minutes she had completed her toilette and had sent Nina to 'phone for a cab. (One of the minor details of his wife's behavior which latterly had aroused Irvin's distrust was her frequent employment of public vehicles in preference to either of the cars.)

Quentin Gray she had quite forgotten, until, as she was about to leave:

"Is there any message for Mr. Gray, Madam?" inquired Nina naively.

"Oh!" cried Rita. "Of course! Quick! Give me some paper and a pencil."

She wrote a hasty note, merely asking Gray to proceed to the restaurant, where she promised to join him, left it in charge of the maid, and hurried off to Albemarle Street.

Mareno, the silent, yellow-faced servant who had driven the car on the night of Rita's first visit to Limehouse, admitted her. He showed her immediately into the lofty study, where Sir Lucien awaited.

"Oh, Lucy—Lucy!" she cried, almost before the door had closed behind Mareno. "I am desperate—desperate!"

Sir Lucien placed a chair for her. His face looked very drawn and grim. But Rita was in too highly strung a condition to observe this fact, or indeed to observe anything.

"Tell me," he said gently.

And in a torrent of disconnected, barely coherent language, the tortured woman told him of Kazmah's attempt to force her to lure Quentin Gray into the drug coterie. Sir Lucien stood behind her chair, and the icy reserve which habitually rendered his face an impenetrable mask deserted him as the story of Rita's treatment at the hands of the Egyptian of Bond Street was unfolded in all its sordid hideousness. Rita's soft, musical voice, for which of old she had been famous, shook and wavered; her pose, her twitching gestures, all told of a nervous agony bordering on prostration or worse. Finally:

"He dare not refuse *you!*" she cried. "Ring him up and insist upon him seeing me tonight!"

"*I* will see him, Rita."

She turned to him, wild-eyed.

"You shall not! You shall not!" she said. "I am going to speak to that man face to face, and if he is human he must listen to me. Oh! I have realized the hold he has upon me, Lucy! I know what it means, this disappearance of all the others who used to sell what Kazmah sells. If I am to suffer, *he* shall not escape! I swear it. Either he listens to me tonight or I go straight to the police!"

"Be calm, little girl," whispered Sir Lucien, and he laid his hand upon her shoulder.

But she leapt up, her pupils suddenly dilating and her delicate nostrils twitching in a manner which unmistakably pointed to the impossibility of thwarting her if sanity were to be retained.

"Ring him up, Lucy," she repeated in a low voice. "He is there. Now that I have someone behind me I see my way at last!"

"There may, nevertheless, be a better way," said Sir Lucien; but he added quickly: "Very well, dear, I will do as you wish. I have a little cocaine, which I will give you."

He went out to the telephone, carefully closing the study door.

That he had counted upon the influence of the drug to reduce Rita to a more reasonable frame of mind was undoubtedly the fact, for presently as they proceeded on foot towards old Bond Street he reverted to something like his old ironical manner. But Rita's determination was curiously fixed. Unmoved by every kind of appeal, she proceeded to the appointment which Sir Lucien had made—ignorant of that which Fate held in store for her—and Sir Lucien, also humanly blind, walked on to meet his death.

PART THIRD

THE MAN FROM WHITEHALL

CHAPTER XXIII

CHIEF INSPECTOR KERRY RESIGNS

"Come in," said the Assistant Commissioner. The door opened and Chief Inspector Kerry entered. His face was as fresh-looking, his attire as spruce and his eyes were as bright, as though he had slept well, enjoyed his bath and partaken of an excellent breakfast. Whereas he had not been to bed during the preceding twenty-four hours, had breakfasted upon biscuits and coffee, and had spent the night and early morning in ceaseless toil. Nevertheless he had found time to visit a hairdressing saloon, for he prided himself upon the nicety of his personal appearance.

He laid his hat, cane and overall upon a chair, and from a pocket of his reefer jacket took out a big notebook.

"Good morning, sir," he said.

"Good morning, Chief Inspector," replied the Assistant Commissioner. "Pray be seated. No doubt"—he suppressed a weary sigh—"you have a long report to make. I observe that some of the papers have the news of Sir Lucien Pyne's death."

Chief Inspector Kerry smiled savagely.

"Twenty pressmen are sitting downstairs," he said "waiting for particulars. One of them got into my room." He opened his notebook. "He didn't stay long."

The Assistant Commissioner gazed wearily at his blotting-pad, striking imaginary chords upon the table-edge with his large widely extended fingers. He cleared his throat.

"Er—Chief Inspector," he said, "I fully recognize the difficulties which—you follow me? But the Press is the Press. Neither you nor I could hope to battle against such an institution even if we desired to do so. Where active resistance is useless, a little tact—you quite understand?"

"Quite, sir. Rely upon me," replied Kerry. "But I didn't mean to open my mouth until I had reported to you. Now, sir, here is a précis of evidence, nearly complete, written out clearly by Sergeant Coombes.

You would probably prefer to read it?"

"Yes, yes, I will read it. But has Sergeant Coombes been on duty all night?"

"He has, sir, and so have I. Sergeant Coombes went home an hour ago."

"Ah," murmured the Assistant Commissioner

He took the notebook from Kerry, and resting his head upon his hand began to read. Kerry sat very upright in his chair, chewing slowly and watching the profile of the reader with his unwavering steel-blue eyes. The reading was twice punctuated by telephone messages, but the Assistant Commissioner apparently possessed the Napoleonic faculty of doing two things at once, for his gaze travelled uninterruptedly along the lines of the report throughout the time that he issued telephonic instructions.

When he had arrived at the final page of Coombes' neat, schoolboy writing, he did not look up for a minute or more, continuing to rest his head in the palm of his hand. Then:

"So far you have not succeeded in establishing the identity of the missing man, Kazmah?" he said.

"Not so far, sir," replied Kerry, enunciating the words with characteristic swift precision, each syllable distinct as the rap of a typewriter. "Inspector Whiteleaf, of Vine Street, has questioned all constables in the Piccadilly area, and we have seen members of the staffs of many shops and offices in the neighborhood, but no one is familiar with the appearance of the missing man."

"Ah—now, the Egyptian servant?"

Inspector Kerry moved his shoulders restlessly.

"Rashid is his name. Many of the people in the neighborhood knew him by sight, and at five o'clock this morning one of my assistants had the good luck to find out, from an Arab coffee-house keeper named Abdulla, where Rashid lived. He paid a visit to the place—it's off the West India Dock Road—half an hour later. But Rashid had gone. I regret to report that all traces of him have been lost."

"Ah—considering this circumstance side by side with the facts that no scrap of evidence has come to light in the Kazmah premises and that the late Sir Lucien's private books and papers cannot be found, what do you deduce, Chief Inspector?"

"My report indicates what I deduce, sir! An accomplice of Kazmah's must have been in Sir Lucien's household! Kazmah and Mrs. Irvin can only have left the premises by going up to the roof and across the leads to Sir Lucien's flat in Albemarle Street. I shall charge the man Juan Mareno."

"What has he to say?" murmured the Assistant Commissioner, absently turning over the pages of the notebook. "Ah, yes. 'Claims to be a citizen of the United States but has produced no papers. Engaged by Sir Lucien Pyne in San Francisco. Professes to have no evidence to offer. Admitted Mrs. Monte Irvin to Sir Lucien's flat on night of murder. Sir Lucien and Mrs. Irvin went out together shortly afterwards, and Sir Lucien ordered him (Mareno) to go for the car to garage in South Audley Street and drive to club, where Sir Lucien proposed to dine. Mareno claims to have followed instructions. After waiting near club for an hour, learned from hall porter that Sir Lucien had not been there that evening. Drove car back to garage and returned to Albemarle Street shortly after eight o'clock.' H'm. Is this confirmed in any way?"

Kerry's teeth snapped together viciously.

"Up to a point it is, sir. The club porter remembers Mareno inquiring about Sir Lucien, and the people at the garage testify that he took out the car and returned it as stated."

"No one has come forward who actually saw him waiting outside the club?"

"No one. But unfortunately it was a dark, misty night, and cars waiting for club members stand in a narrow side turning. Mareno is a surly brute, and he might have waited an hour without speaking to a soul. Unless another chauffeur happened to notice and recognize the car nobody would be any wiser."

The Assistant Commissioner sighed, glancing up for the first time.

"You don't think he waited outside the club at all?" he said.

"I don't, sir!" rapped Kerry.

The Assistant Commissioner rested his head upon his hand again.

"It doesn't seem to be germane to your case, Chief Inspector, in any event. There is no question of an alibi. Sir Lucien's wrist-watch was broken at seven-fifteen—evidently at the time of his death; and this man Mareno does not claim to have left the flat until after that hour."

"I know it, sir," said Kerry. "He took out the car at half-past seven. What I want to know is where he went to!"

The Assistant Commissioner glanced rapidly into the speaker's fierce eyes.

"From what you have gathered respecting the appearance of Kazmah, does it seem possible that Mareno may be Kazmah?"

"It does not, sir. Kazmah has been described to me, at first hand and at second hand. All descriptions tally in one respect: Kazmah has remarkably large eyes. In Miss Halley's evidence you will note that she refers to them as 'larger than any human eyes I have ever seen.' Now, Mareno has eyes like a pig!"

"Then I take it you are charging him as accessory?"

"Exactly, sir. Somebody got Kazmah and Mrs. Irvin away, and it can only have been Mareno. Sir Lucien had no other resident servant; he was a man who lived almost entirely at restaurants and clubs. Again, somebody cleaned up his papers, and it was somebody who knew where to look for them."

"Quite so—quite so," murmured the Assistant Commissioner. "Of course, we shall learn today something of his affairs from his banker. He must have banked *somewhere*. But surely, Chief Inspector, there is a safe or private bureau in his flat?"

"There is, sir," said Kerry grimly; "a safe. I had it opened at six o'clock this morning. It had been hastily cleaned out; not a doubt of it. I expect Sir Lucien carried the keys on his person. You will remember, sir, that his pockets had been emptied?"

"H'm," mused the Assistant Commissioner. "This Cubanis Cigarette Company, Chief Inspector?"

"Dummy goods!" rapped Kerry. "A blind. Just a back entrance to Kazmah's office. Premises were leased on behalf of an agent. This agent—a reputable man of business—paid the rent quarterly. I've seen him."

"And who was his client?" asked the Assistant Commissioner, displaying a faint trace of interest.

"A certain Mr. Isaacs!"

"Who can be traced?"

"Who can't be traced!"

"His checks?"

Chief Inspector Kerry smiled, so that his large white teeth gleamed savagely.

"Mr. Isaacs represented himself as a dealer in Covent Garden who was leasing the office for a lady friend, and who desired, for domestic reasons, to cover his tracks. As ready money in large amounts changes hands in the market, Mr. Isaacs paid ready money to the agent. Beyond doubt the real source of the ready money was Kazmah's."

"But his address?"

"A hotel in Covent Garden."

"Where he lives?"

"Where he is known to the booking-clerk, a girl who allowed him to have letters addressed there. A man of smoke, sir, acting on behalf of someone in the background."

"Ah! and these Bond Street premises have been occupied by Kazmah for the past eight years?"

"So I am told. I have yet to see representatives of the landlord. I may add that Sir Lucien Pyne had lived in Albemarle Street for about the same time."

Wearily raising his head:

"The point is certainly significant," said the Assistant Commissioner. "Now we come to the drug traffic, Chief Inspector. You have found no trace of drugs on the premises?"

"Not a grain, sir!"

"In the office of the cigarette firm?"

"No."

"By the way, was there no staff attached to the latter concern?"

Kerry chewed viciously.

"No business of any kind seems to have been done there," he replied. "An office-boy employed by the solicitor on the same floor as Kazmah has seen a man and also a woman, go up to the third floor on several occasions, and he seems to think they went to the Cubanis office. But he's not sure, and he can give no useful description of the parties, anyway. Nobody in the building has ever seen the door open before this morning."

The Assistant Commissioner sighed yet more wearily.

"Apart from the suspicions of Miss Margaret Halley, you have no sound basis for supposing that Kazmah dealt in prohibited drugs?" he inquired.

"The evidence of Miss Halley, the letter left for her by Mrs. Irvin, and the fact that Mrs. Irvin said, in the presence of Mr. Quentin Gray, that she had 'a particular reason' for seeing Kazmah, point to it unmistakably, sir. Then, I have seen Mrs. Irvin's maid. (Mr. Monte Irvin is still too unwell to be interrogated.) The girl was very frightened, but she admitted outright that she had been in the habit of going regularly to Kazmah for certain perfumes. She wouldn't admit that she knew the flasks contained cocaine or veronal, but she did admit that her mistress had been addicted to the drug habit for several years. It began when she was on the stage."

"Ah, yes," murmured the Assistant Commissioner; "she was Rita Dresden, was she not—*The Maid of the Masque*' A very pretty and talented actress. A pity—a great pity. So the girl, characteristically, is trying to save herself?"

"She is," said Kerry grimly. "But it cuts no ice. There is another point. After this report was made out, a message reached me from Miss Halley, as a result of which I visited Mr. Quentin Gray early this morning."

"Dear, dear," sighed the Assistant Commissioner, "your intense zeal and activity are admirable, Chief Inspector, but appalling. And what did you learn?"

From an inside pocket Chief Inspector Kerry took out a plain brown paper packet containing several cigarettes and laid the packet on the table.

"I got these, sir," he said grimly. "They were left at Mr. Gray's some weeks ago by the late Sir Lucien. They are doped."

The Assistant Commissioner, his head resting upon his hand, gazed abstractedly at the packet. "If only you could trace the source of supply," he murmured.

"That brings me to my last point, sir. From Mrs. Irvin's maid I learned that her mistress was acquainted with a certain Mrs. Sin."

"Mrs. Sin? Incredible name."

"She's a woman reputed to be married to a Chinaman. Inspector Whiteleaf, of Vine Street, knows her by sight as one of the night-club birds—a sort of mysterious fungus, sir, flowering in the dark and fattening on gilded fools. Unless I'm greatly mistaken, Mrs. Sin is the link between the doped cigarettes and the missing Kazmah."

"Does anyone know where she lives?"

"Lots of 'em know!" snapped Kerry. "But it's making them speak."

"To whom do you more particularly refer, Chief Inspector?"

"To the moneyed asses and the brainless women belonging to a certain West End set, sir," said Kerry savagely. "They go in for every monstrosity from Buenos Ayres, Port Said and Pekin. They get up dances that would make a wooden horse blush. They eat *hashish* and they smoke opium. They inject morphine, and they would have their hair dyed blue if they heard it was 'being done.'"

"Ah," sighed the Assistant Commissioner, "a very delicate and complex case, Chief Inspector. The agony of mind which Mr. Irvin must be suffering is too horrible for one to contemplate. An admirable man, too; honorable and generous. I can conceive no theory to account for the disappearance of Mrs. Irvin other than that she was a party to the murder."

"No, sir," said Kerry guardedly. "But we have the dope clue to work on. That the Chinese receive stuff in the East End and that it's sold in the West End every constable in the force is well aware. Leman Street is getting busy, and every shady case in the Piccadilly area will be beaten up within the next twenty-four hours, too. It's purely departmental, sir, from now onwards, and merely a question of time. Therefore I don't doubt the issue."

Kerry paused, cleared his throat, and produced a foolscap envelope which he laid upon the table before the Assistant Commissioner.

"With very deep regret, sir," he said, "after a long and agreeable association with the Criminal Investigation Department, I have to tender you this."

The Assistant Commissioner took up the envelope and stared at it vaguely.

"Ah, yes, Chief Inspector," he murmured. "Perhaps I fail entirely to follow you; I am somewhat over-worked, as you know. What does this envelope contain?"

"My resignation, sir," replied Kerry.

CHAPTER XXIV

TO INTRODUCE 719

Some moments of silence followed. Sounds of traffic from the Embankment penetrated dimly to the room of the Assistant Commissioner; ringing of tram bells and that vague sustained noise which is created by the whirring of countless wheels along hard pavements. Finally:

"You have selected a curious moment to retire, Chief Inspector," said the Assistant Commissioner. "Your prospects were never better. No doubt you have considered the question of your pension?"

"I know what I'm giving up, sir," replied Kerry.

The Assistant Commissioner slowly revolved in his chair and gazed sadly at the speaker. Chief Inspector Kerry met his glance with that fearless, unflinching stare which lent him so formidable an appearance.

"You might care to favor me with some explanation which I can lay before the Chief Commissioner?"

Kerry snapped his white teeth together viciously.

"May I take it, sir, that you accept my resignation?"

"Certainly not. I will place it before the responsible authority. I can do no more."

"Without disrespect, sir, I want to speak to you as man to man. As a private citizen I could do it. As your subordinate I can't."

The Assistant Commissioner sighed, stroking his neatly brushed hair with one large hand.

"Equally without disrespect, Chief Inspector," he murmured, "it is news for me to learn that you have ever refrained from speaking your mind either in my presence or in the presence of any man."

Kerry smiled, unable wholly to conceal a sense of gratified vanity.

"Well, sir," he said, "you have my resignation before you, and I'm prepared to abide by the consequences. What I want to say is this: I'm a man that has worked hard all his life to earn the respect and the trust of his employers. I am supposed to be Chief Inspector of this department, and as Chief Inspector I'll kow-tow to nothing on two legs once I've been put in charge of a case. I work right in the sunshine. There's no grafting about me. I draw my salary every week, and any man that says I earn sixpence in the dark is at liberty to walk right in here and deposit his funeral expenses. If I'm supposed to be under a cloud—there's my reply. But I demand a public inquiry."

At ever increasing speed, succinctly, viciously he rapped out the words. His red face grew more red, and his steel-blue eyes more fierce. The Assistant Commissioner exhibited bewilderment. As the high tones ceased:

"Really, Chief Inspector," he said, "you pain and surprise me. I do not profess to be ignorant of the cause of your—annoyance. But perhaps if I acquaint you with the facts of my own position in the matter you will be open to reconsider your decision."

Kerry cleared his throat loudly.

"I won't work in the dark, sir," he declared truculently. "I'd rather be a pavement artist and my own master than Chief Inspector with an unknown spy following me about."

"Quite so—quite so." The Assistant Commissioner was wonderfully patient. "Very well, Chief Inspector. It cannot enhance my personal dignity to admit the fact, but I'm nearly as much in the dark as yourself."

"What's that, sir?" Kerry sat bolt upright, staring at the speaker.

"At a late hour last night the Secretary of State communicated in person with the Chief Commissioner—at the latter's town residence. He instructed him to offer every facility to a newly appointed agent of the Home Office who was empowered to conduct an official inquiry into the drug traffic. As a result Vine Street was advised that the Home Office investigator would proceed at once to Kazmah's premises, and from thence wherever available clues might lead him. For some reason which has not yet been explained to me, this investigator chooses to preserve a strict anonymity."

Traces of irritation became perceptible in the weary voice. Kerry staring, in silence, the Assistant Commissioner continued:

"I have been advised that this nameless agent is in a position to establish his bona fides at any time, as he bears a number of these cards. You see, Chief Inspector, I am frank with you."

From a table drawer the Assistant Commissioner took a visiting-card, which he handed to Kerry. The latter stared at it as one stares at a rare specimen. It was the card of Lord Wrexborough, His Majesty's

Principal Secretary of State for the Home Department, and in the cramped caligraphy of his lordship it bore a brief note, initialled, thus:

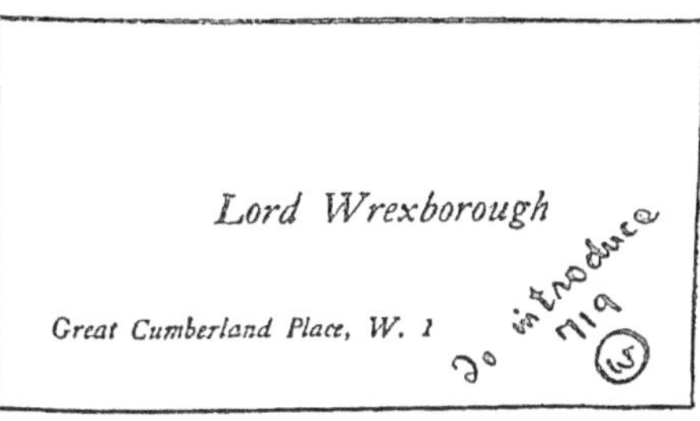

Some moments of silence followed; then:

"Seven-one-nine," said Kerry in a high, strained voice. "Why seven-one-nine? And why all this hocus-pocus? Am I to understand, sir, that not only myself but all the Criminal Investigation Department is under a cloud?"

The Assistant Commissioner stroked his hair.

"You are to understand, Chief Inspector, that for the first time throughout my period of office I find myself out of touch with the Chief Commissioner. It is not departmental for me to say so, but I believe the Chief Commissioner finds himself similarly out of touch with the Secretary of State. Apparently very powerful influences are at work, and the line of conduct taken up by the Home Office suggests to my mind that collusion between the receivers and distributors of drugs and the police is suspected by someone. That being so, possibly out of a sense of fairness to all officially concerned, the committee which I understand has been appointed to inquire into the traffic has decided to treat us all alike, from myself down to the rawest constable. It's highly irritating and preposterous, of course, but I cannot disguise from you or from myself that we are on trial, Chief Inspector!"

Kerry stood up and slowly moved his square shoulders in the manner of an athlete about to attempt a feat of weight-lifting. From the Assistant Commissioner's table he took the envelope which contained his resignation, and tore it into several portions. These he deposited in a waste-paper basket.

"That's that!" he said. "I am very deeply indebted to you, sir. I know now what to tell the Press."

The Assistant Commissioner glanced up.

"Not a word about 719," he said, "of course, you understand this?"

"If we don't exist as far as 719 is concerned, sir," said Kerry in his most snappy tones, "719 means nothing to me!"

"Quite so—quite so. Of course, I may be wrong in the motives which I ascribe to this Whitehall agent, but misunderstanding is certain to arise out of a system of such deliberate mystification, which can only be compared to that employed by the Russian police under the Tsars."

Half an hour later Chief Inspector Kerry came out of New Scotland Yard, and, walking down on to the Embankment, boarded a Norwood tramcar. The weather remained damp and gloomy, but upon the red face of Chief Inspector Kerry, as he mounted to the upper deck of the car, rested an expression which might have been described as one of cheery truculence. Where other passengers, coat collars upturned, gazed gloomily from the windows at the yellow murk overhanging the river, Kerry looked briskly about him, smiling pleasurably.

He was homeward bound, and when he presently alighted and went swinging along Spenser Road towards his house, he was still smiling. He regarded the case as having developed into a competition between himself and the man appointed by Whitehall. And it was just such a position, disconcerting to one of less aggressive temperament, which stimulated Chief Inspector Kerry and put him in high good humor.

Mrs. Kerry, arrayed in a serviceable rain-coat, and wearing a plain felt hat, was standing by the dining-room door as Kerry entered. She had a basket on her arm. "I was waiting for ye, Dan," she said simply.

He kissed her affectionately, put his arm about her waist, and the two entered the cosy little room. By no ordinary human means was it possible that Mary Kerry should have known that her husband would come home at that time, but he was so used to her prescience in this respect that he offered no comment. She "kenned" his approach always, and at times when his life had been in danger—and these were not of infrequent occurrence—Mary Kerry, if sleeping, had awakened, trembling, though the scene of peril were a hundred miles away, and if awake had blanched and known a deadly sudden fear.

"Ye'll be goin' to bed?" she asked.

"For three hours, Mary. Don't fail to rouse me if I oversleep."

"Is it clear to ye yet?"

"Nearly clear. The dark thing you saw behind it all, Mary, was dope! Kazmah's is a secret drug-syndicate. They've appointed a Home Office agent, and he's working independently of us, but ..."

His teeth came together with a snap.

"Oh, Dan," said his wife, "it's a race? Drugs? A Home Office agent? Dan, they think the Force is in it?"

"They do!" rapped Kerry. "I'm for Leman Street in three hours. If there's double-dealing behind it, then the mugs are in the East End, and it's folly, not knavery, I'm looking for. It's a race, Mary, and the credit of the Service is at stake! No, my dear, I'll have a snack when I wake. You're going shopping?"

"I am, Dan. I'd ha' started, but I wanted to see ye when ye came hame. If ye've only three hours go straight up the now. I'll ha' something hot a' ready when ye waken."

Ten minutes later Kerry was in bed, his short clay pipe between his teeth, and *The Meditations of Marcus Aurelius* in his hand. Such was his customary sleeping-draught, and it had never been known to fail. Half a pipe of Irish twist and three pages of the sad imperial author invariably plunged Chief Inspector Kerry into healthy slumber.

CHAPTER XXV

NIGHT-LIFE OF SOHO

It was close upon midnight when Detective-Sergeant Coombes appeared in a certain narrow West End thoroughfare, which was lined with taxicabs and private cars. He wore a dark overcoat and a tweed cap, and although his chin was buried in the genial folds of a woollen comforter, and his cap was pulled down over his eyes, his sly smile could easily be detected even in the dim light afforded by the car lamps. He seemed to have business of a mysterious nature among the cabmen; for with each of them in turn he conducted a brief conversation, passing unobtrusively from cab to cab, and making certain entries in a notebook. Finally he disappeared. No one actually saw him go, and no one had actually seen him arrive. At one moment, however, he was there; in the next he was gone.

Five minutes later Chief Inspector Kerry entered the street. His dark overcoat and white silk muffler concealed a spruce dress suit, a fact betrayed by black, braided trousers, unusually tight-fitting, and boots which almost glittered. He carried the silver-headed malacca cane, and had retained his narrow-brimmed bowler at its customary jaunty angle.

Passing the lines of waiting vehicles, he walked into the entrance of a popular night-club which faced the narrow street. On a lounge immediately inside the doorway a heated young man was sitting fanning his dancing partner and gazing into her weakly pretty face in vacuous adoration.

Kerry paused for a moment, staring at the pair. The man returned his stare, looking him up and down in a manner meant to be contemptuous. Kerry's fierce, intolerant gaze became transferred to the face and then the figure of the woman. He tilted his hat further forward and turned aside. The woman's glance followed him, to the marked disgust of her companion.

"Oh," she whispered, "what a delightfully savage man! He looks positively uncivilized. I have no doubt he drags women about by their hair. I *do* hope he's a member!"

Mollie Gretna spoke loudly enough for Kerry to hear her, but unmoved by her admiration he stepped up to the reception office. He was in high good humor. He had spent the afternoon agreeably, interviewing certain officials charged with policing the East End of London, and had succeeded, to quote his own language, "in getting a gale up." Despite the coldness of the weather, he had left two inspectors and a speechlessly indignant superintendent bathed in perspiration.

"Are you a member, sir?" inquired the girl behind the desk.

Kerry smiled genially. A newsboy thrust open the swing-door, yelling: "Bond Street murder! A fresh development. Late speshul!"

"Oh!" cried Mollie Gretna to her companion, "get me a paper. Be quick! I am so excited!"

Kerry took up a pen, and in large bold hand-writing inscribed the following across two pages of the visitors' book:

"Chief Inspector Kerry. Criminal Investigation Department."

He laid a card on the open book, and, thrusting his cane under his arm, walked to the head of the stairs.

"Cloak-room on the right, sir," said an attendant.

Kerry paused, glancing over his shoulder and chewing audibly. Then he settled his hat more firmly upon his red head and descended the stairs. The attendant went to inspect the visitors' book, but Mollie Gretna was at the desk before him, and:

"Oh, Bill!" she cried to her annoyed cavalier, "it's Inspector Kerry— who is in charge of poor Lucy's murder! Oh, Bill! this is lovely! Something is going to happen! Do come down!"

Followed by the obedient but reluctant "Bill," Mollie ran downstairs, and almost into the arms of a tall dark girl, who, carrying a purple opera cloak, was coming up.

"You're not going yet, Dickey?" said Mollie, throwing her arm around the other's waist.

"Ssh!" whispered "Dickey." "Inspector Kerry is here! You don't want to be called as a witness at nasty inquests and things, do you?"

"Good heavens, my dear, no! But why should I be?"

"Why should any of us? But don't you see they are looking for the people who used to go to Kazmah's? It's in the paper tonight. We shall all be served with *subpoenas*. I'm off!"

Escaping from Mollie's embrace, the tall girl ran up the stairs, kissing her hand to Bill as she passed. Mollie hesitated, looking all about the crowded room for Chief Inspector Kerry. Presently she saw him, standing nearly opposite the stairway, his intolerant blue eyes turning right and left, so that the fierce glance seemed to miss nothing and no one in the room. Hands thrust in his overcoat pockets and his cane held under his arm, he inspected the place and its occupants as a very aggressive country cousin might inspect the monkey-house at the Zoo. To Mollie's intense disappointment he persistently avoided looking in her direction.

Although a popular dance was on the point of commencing, several visitors had suddenly determined to leave. Kerry pretended to be ignorant of the sensation which his appearance had created, passing slowly along the room and submitting group after group to deliberate scrutiny; but as news flies through an Eastern bazaar the name of the celebrated detective, whose association with London's latest crime was mentioned by every evening paper in the kingdom, sped now on magic wings, so that there was a muted *charivari* out of which, in every key from bass to soprano, arose ever and anon the words "Chief Inspector Kerry."

"It's perfectly ridiculous but characteristically English," drawled one young man, standing beside Mollie Gretna, "to send out a bally red-headed policeman in preposterous glad-rags to look for a clever criminal. Kerry is well known to all the crooks, and nobody could mistake him. Damn silly—damn silly!"

As "damn silly" Kerry's open scrutiny of the members and visitors must have appeared to others, but it was a deliberate policy very popular with the Chief Inspector, and termed by him "beating." Possessed of an undisguisable personality, Kerry had found a way of employing his natural physical peculiarities to his professional advantage. Where other investigators worked in the dark, secretly, Red Kerry sought the limelight—at the right time. That every hour lost in getting on the track of the mysterious Kazmah was a point gained by the equally mysterious man from Whitehall he felt assured, and although the elaborate but hidden mechanism of New Scotland Yard was at work seeking out the patrons of the Bond Street drug-shop, Kerry was indisposed to await the result.

He had been in the night club only about ten minutes, but during those ten minutes fully a dozen people had more or less hurriedly departed. Because of the arrangements already made by Sergeant

Coombes, the addresses of many of these departing visitors would be in Kerry's possession ere the night was much older. And why should they have fled, incontinent, if not for the reason that they feared to become involved in the Kazmah affair? All the cabmen had been warned, and those fugitives who had private cars would be followed.

It was a curious scene which Kerry surveyed, a scene to have interested philosopher and politician alike. For here were representatives of every stratum of society, although some of those standing for the lower strata were suitably disguised. The peerage was well represented, so was Judah; there were women entitled to wear coronets dancing with men entitled to wear the broad arrow, and men whose forefathers had signed Magna Charta dancing with chorus girls from the revues and musical comedies.

Waiting until the dance was fully in progress, Inspector Kerry walked slowly around the room in the direction of the stair. Parties seated at tables were treated each to an intolerant stare, alcoves were inspected, and more than one waiter meeting the gaze of the steely eyes, felt a prickling of conscience and recalled past peccadilloes.

Bill had claimed Mollie Gretna for the dance, but:

"No, Bill," she had replied, watching Kerry as if enthralled; "I don't want to dance. I am watching Chief Inspector Kerry."

"That's evident," complained the young man. "Perhaps you would like to spend the rest of the night in Bow Street?"

"Oh," whispered Mollie, "I should love it! I have never been arrested, but if ever I am I hope it will be by Chief Inspector Kerry. I am positive he would haul me away in handcuffs!"

When Kerry came to the foot of the stairs, Mollie quite deliberately got in his way, murmured an apology, and gave him a sidelong gaze through lowered lashes, which was more eloquent than any thesis. He smiled with fierce geniality, looked her up and down, and proceeded to mount the stairs, with never a backward glance.

His genius for criminal investigation possessed definite limitations. He could not perhaps have been expected in tactics so completely opposed to those which he had anticipated to recognize the presence of a valuable witness. Student of human nature though undoubtedly he was, he had not solved the mystery of that outstanding exception which seems to be involved in every rule.

Thus, a fellow with a low forehead and a weakly receding chin, Kerry classified as a dullard, a witling, unaware that if the brow were but low enough and the chin virtually absent altogether he might stand in the presence of a second Daniel. Physiognomy is a subtle science, and the exceptions to its rules are often of a sensational character. In the same way Kerry looked for evasion, and, where possible, flight, on the part of one possessing a guilty conscience. Mollie Gretna was a phenomenal exception to a rule otherwise sound. And even one familiar with criminal psychology might be forgiven for failing to detect guilt in a woman anxious to make the acquaintance of a prominent member of the Criminal Investigation Department.

Pausing for a moment in the entrance of the club, and chewing reflectively, Kerry swung open the door and walked out into the street. He had one more cover to "beat," and he set off briskly, plunging into the mazes of Soho crossing Wardour Street into old Compton Street, and proceeding thence in the direction of Shaftesbury Avenue. Turning to the right on entering the narrow thoroughfare for which he was bound, he stopped and whistled softly. He stood in the entrance to a court; and from further up the court came an answering whistle.

Kerry came out of the court again, and proceeded some twenty paces along the street to a restaurant. The windows showed no light, but the door remained open, and Kerry entered without hesitation, crossed a darkened room and found himself in a passage where a man was seated in a little apartment like that of a stage-door keeper. He stood up, on hearing Kerry's tread, peering out at the newcomer.

"The restaurant is closed, sir."

"Tell me a better one," rapped Kerry. "I want to go upstairs."

"Your card, sir."

Kerry revealed his teeth in a savage smile and tossed his card on to the desk before the concierge. He passed on, mounting the stairs at the end of the passage. Dimly a bell rang; and on the first landing Kerry met a heavily built foreign gentleman, who bowed.

"My dear Chief Inspector," he said gutturally, "what is this, please? I trust nothing is wrong, eh?"

"Nothing," replied Kerry. "I just want to look round."

"A few friends," explained the suave alien, rubbing his hands together and still bowing, "remain playing dominoes with me."

"Very good," rapped Kerry. "Well, if you think we have given them time to hide the 'wheel' we'll go in. Oh, don't explain. I'm not worrying about sticklebacks tonight. I'm out for salmon."

He opened a door on the left of the landing and entered a large room which offered evidence of having been hastily evacuated by a considerable company. A red and white figured cloth of a type much used in Continental cafés had been spread upon a long table, and three foreigners, two men and an elderly woman, were bending over a row of dominoes set upon one corner of the table. Apparently the men were playing and the woman was watching. But there was a dense cloud of cigar smoke in the room, and mingled with its pungency were sweeter scents. A number of empty champagne bottles stood upon a sideboard and an elegant silk theatre-bag lay on a chair.

"H'm," said Kerry, glaring fiercely from the bottles to the players, who covertly were watching him. "How you two smarts can tell a domino from a door-knocker after cracking a dozen magnums gets me guessing."

He took up the scented bag and gravely handed it to the old woman.

"You have mislaid your bag, madam," he said. "But, fortunately, I noticed it as I came in."

He turned the glance of his fierce eyes upon the man who had met him on the landing, and who had followed him into the room.

"Third floor, von Hindenburg," he rapped. "Don't argue. Lead the way."

For one dangerous moment the man's brow lowered and his heavy face grew blackly menacing. He exchanged a swift look with his friends seated at the disguised roulette table. Kerry's jaw muscles protruded enormously.

"Give me another answer like that," he said in a tone of cold ferocity, "and I'll kick you from here to Paradise."

"No offense—no offense," muttered the man, quailing before the savagery of the formidable Chief Inspector. "You come this way, please. Some ladies call upon me this evening, and I do not want to frighten them."

"No," said Kerry, "you wouldn't, naturally." He stood aside as a door at the further end of the room was opened. "After you, my friend. I said 'lead the way.'"

They mounted to the third floor of the restaurant. The room which they had just quitted was used as an auxiliary dining and supper-room before midnight, as Kerry knew. After midnight the centre table was unmasked, and from thence onward to dawn, sometimes, was surrounded by roulette players. The third floor he had never visited, but he had a shrewd idea that it was not entirely reserved for the private use of the proprietor.

A babel of voices died away as the two men walked into a room rather smaller than that below and furnished with little tables, café fashion. At one end was a grand piano and a platform before which a velvet curtain was draped. Some twenty people, men and women, were in the place, standing looking towards the entrance. Most of the men and all the women but one were in evening dress; but despite this common armor of respectability, they did not all belong to respectable society.

Two of the women Kerry recognized as bearers of titles, and one was familiar to him as a screen-beauty. The others were unclassifiable, but all were fashionably dressed with the exception of a masculine-looking lady who had apparently come straight off a golf course, and who later was proved to be a well-known advocate of woman's rights. The men all belonged to familiar types. Some of them were Jews.

Kerry, his feet widely apart and his hands thrust in his overcoat pockets, stood staring at face after face and chewing slowly. The proprietor glanced apologetically at his patrons and shrugged. Silence fell upon the company. Then:

"I am a police officer," said Kerry sharply. "You will file out past me, and I want a card from each of you. Those who have no cards will write name and address here."

He drew a long envelope and a pencil from a pocket of his dinner jacket. Laying the envelope and pencil on one of the little tables:

"Quick march!" he snapped. "You, sir!" shooting out his forefinger in the direction of a tall, fair young man, "step out!"

Glancing helplessly about him, the young man obeyed, and approaching Kerry:

"I say, officer," he whispered nervously, "can't you manage to keep my name out of it? I mean to say, my people will kick up the deuce. Anything up to a tenner...."

The whisper faded away. Kerry's expression had grown positively ferocious.

"Put your card on the table," he said tersely, "and get out while my hands stay in my pockets!"

Hurriedly the noble youth (he was the elder son of an earl) complied, and departed. Then, one by one, the rest of the company filed past the Chief Inspector. He challenged no one until a Jew smilingly laid a card on the table bearing the legend: "Mr. John Jones, Lincoln's Inn Fields."

"Hi!" rapped Kerry, grasping the man's arm. "One moment, Mr. 'Jones'! The card I want is in the other case. D'you take me for a mug? That 'Jones' trick was tried on Noah by the blue-faced baboon!"

His perception of character was wonderful. At some of the cards he did not even glance; and upon the women he wasted no time at all. He took it for granted that they would all give false names, but since each of them would be followed it did not matter. When at last the room was emptied, he turned to the scowling proprietor, and:

"That's that!" he said. "I've had no instructions about your establishment, my friend, and as I've seen nothing improper going on I'm making no charge, at the moment. I don't want to know what sort of show takes place on your platform, and I don't want to know anything about you that I don't know already. You're a Swiss subject and a dark horse."

He gathered up the cards from the table, glancing at them carelessly. He did not expect to gain much from his possession of these names and addresses. It was among the women that he counted upon finding patrons of Kazmah and Company. But as he was about to drop the cards into his overcoat pocket, one of them, which bore a written note, attracted his attention.

At this card he stared like a man amazed; his face grew more and more red, and:

"Hell!" he said—"Hell! which of 'em was it?"

The card contained the following:—

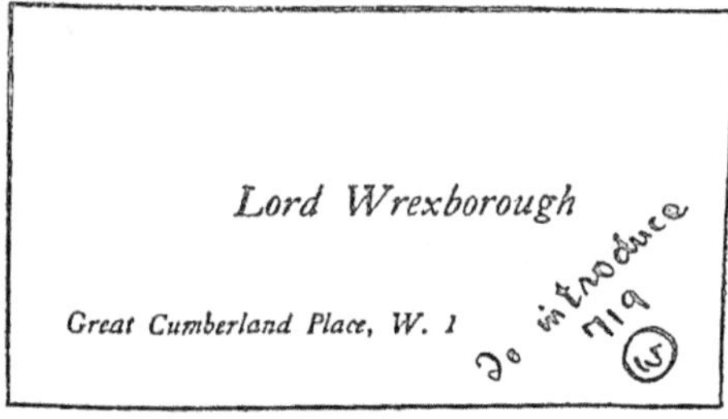

CHAPTER XXVI

THE MOODS OF MOLLIE

Early the following morning Margaret Halley called upon Mollie Gretna.

Mollie's personality did not attract Margaret. The two had nothing in common, but Margaret was well aware of the nature of the tie which had bound Rita Irvin to this empty and decadent representative of English aristocracy. Mollie Gretna was entitled to append the words "The Honorable" to her name, but not only did she refrain from doing so but she even preferred to be known as "Gretna"—the style of one of the family estates.

This pseudonym she had adopted shortly after her divorce, when she had attempted to take up a stage career. But although the experience had proved disastrous, she had retained the *nom de guerre*, and during the past four years had several times appeared at war charity garden-parties as a classical dancer—to the great delight of the guests and greater disgust of her family. Her maternal uncle, head of her house, said to be the most blasé member of the British peerage and known as "the noble tortoise," was generally considered to have pronounced the final verdict upon his golden-haired niece when he declared "she is almost amusing."

Mollie received her visitor with extravagant expressions of welcome.

"My dear Miss Halley," she cried, "how perfectly sweet of you to come to see me! of course, I can guess what you have called about. Look! I have every paper published this morning in London! Every one! Oh! poor, darling little Rita! What *can* have become of her!"

Tears glistened upon her carefully made-up lashes, and so deep did her grief seem to be that one would never have suspected that she had spent the greater part of the night playing bridge at a "mixed" club in Dover Street, and from thence had proceeded to a military "breakfast-dance."

"It is indeed a ghastly tragedy," said Margaret. "It seems incredible that she cannot be traced."

"Absolutely incredible!" declared Mollie, opening a large box of cigarettes. "Will you have one, dear?"

"No, thanks. By the way, they are not from Buenos Ayres, I suppose?"

Mollie, cigarette in hand, stared, round-eyed, and:

"Oh, my dear Miss Halley!" she cried, "what an idea! Such a funny thing to suggest."

Margaret smiled coolly.

"Poor Sir Lucien used to smoke cigarettes of that kind," she explained, "and I thought perhaps you smoked them, too."

Mollie shook her head and lighted the cigarette.

"He gave me one once, and it made me feel quite sick," she declared.

Margaret glanced at the speaker, and knew immediately that Mollie had determined to deny all knowledge of the drug coterie. Because there is no problem of psychology harder than that offered by a perverted mind, Margaret was misled in ascribing this secrecy to a desire to avoid becoming involved in a scandal. Therefore:

"Do you quite realize, Miss Gretna," she said quietly, "that every hour wasted now in tracing Rita may mean, must mean, an hour of agony for her?"

"Oh, don't! please don't!" cried Mollie, clasping her hands. "I cannot bear to think of it."

"God knows in whose hands she is. Then there is poor Mr. Irvin. He is utterly prostrated. One shudders to contemplate his torture as the hours and the days go by and no news comes of Rita."

"Oh, my dear! you are making me cry!" exclaimed Mollie. "If only I could do something to help...."

Margaret was studying her closely, and now for the first time she detected sincere emotion in Mollie's voice—and unforced tears in her eyes. Hope was reborn.

"Perhaps you can," she continued, speaking gently. "You knew all Rita's friends and all Sir Lucien's. You must have met the woman called Mrs. Sin?"

"Mrs. Sin," whispered Mollie, staring in a frightened way so that the pupils of her eyes slowly enlarged. "What about Mrs. Sin?"

"Well, you see, they seem to think that through Mrs. Sin they will be able to trace Kazmah; and wherever Kazmah is one would expect to find poor Rita."

Mollie lowered her head for a moment, then glanced quickly at the speaker, and quickly away again.

"Please let me explain just what I mean," continued Margaret. "It seems to be impossible to find anybody in London who will admit having known Mrs. Sin or Kazmah. They are all afraid of being involved in the case, of course. Now, if you can help, don't hesitate for that reason. A special commission has been appointed by Lord Wrexborough to deal with the case, and their agent is working quite independently of the police. Anything which you care to tell him will be treated as strictly confidential; but think what it may mean to Rita."

Mollie clasped her hands about her right knee and rocked to and fro in her chair.

"No one knows who Kazmah is," she said.

"But a number of people seem to know Mrs. Sin. I am sure you must have met her?"

"If I say that I know her, shall I be called as a witness?"

"Certainly not. I can assure you of that."

Mollie continued to rock to and fro.

"But if I were to tell the police I should have to go to court, I suppose?"

"I suppose so," replied Margaret. "I am afraid I am dreadfully ignorant of such matters. It might depend upon whether you spoke to a high official or to a subordinate one; an ordinary policeman for instance. But the Home Office agent has nothing whatever to do with Scotland Yard."

Mollie stood up in order to reach an ash-tray, and:

"I really don't think I have anything to say, Miss Halley," she declared. "I have certainly met Mrs. Sin, but I know nothing whatever about her, except that I believe she is a Jewess."

Margaret sighed, looking up wistfully into Mollie's face. "Are you quite sure?" she pleaded. "Oh, Miss Gretna, if you know anything—anything—don't hide it now. It may mean so much."

"Oh, I quite understand that," cried Mollie. "My heart simply aches and aches when I think of poor, sweet little Rita. But—really I don't think I can be of the least tiny bit of use."

Their glances met, and Margaret read hostility in the shallow eyes. Mollie, who had been wavering, now for some reason had become confirmed in her original determination to remain silent. Margaret stood up.

"It is no good, then," she said. "We must hope that Rita will be traced by the police. Good-bye, Miss Gretna. I am so sorry you cannot help."

"And so am I!" declared Mollie. "It is perfectly sweet of you to take such an interest, and I feel a positive *worm*. But what can I do?"

As Margaret was stepping into her little runabout car, which awaited her at the door, a theory presented itself to account for Mollie's sudden hostility. It had developed, apparently, as a result of Margaret's reference to the Home Office inquiry. Of course! Mollie would naturally be antagonistic to a commission appointed to suppress the drug traffic.

Convinced that this was the correct explanation, Margaret drove away, reflecting bitterly that she had been guilty of a strategical error which it was now too late to rectify.

In common with others, Kerry among them, who had come in contact with that perverted intelligence, she misjudged Mollie's motives. In the first place, the latter had no wish to avoid publicity, and in the second place—although she sometimes wondered vaguely what she should do when her stock of drugs became exhausted—Mollie was prompted by no particular animosity toward the Home Office inquiry. She had merely perceived a suitable opportunity to make the acquaintance of the fierce red Chief Inspector, and at the same time to secure notoriety for herself.

Ere Margaret's car had progressed a hundred yards from the door, Mollie was at the telephone.

"City 400, please," she said.

An interval elapsed, then:

"Is that the Commissioner's office, New Scotland Yard?" she asked.

A voice replied that it was.

"Could you put me through to Chief Inspector Kerry?"

"What name?" inquired the voice.

Mollie hesitated for three seconds, and then gave her family name.

"Very well, madam," said the voice respectfully. "Please hold on, and I will enquire if the Chief Inspector is here."

Mollie's heart was beating rapidly with pleasurable excitement, and she was as confused as a maiden at her first rendezvous. Then:

"Hello," said the voice.

"Yes?"

"I am sorry, madam. But Chief Inspector Kerry is off duty."

"Oh, dear!" sighed Mollie, "what a pity. Can you tell me where I could find him?"

"I am afraid not, madam. It is against the rules to give private addresses of members of any department."

"Oh, very well." She sighed again. "Thank you."

She replaced the receiver and stood biting her finger thoughtfully. She was making a mental inventory of her many admirers and wondering which of them could help her. Suddenly she came to a decision on the point. Taking up the receiver:

"Victoria 8440, please," she said.

Still biting one finger she waited, until:

"Foreign Office," announced a voice.

"Please put me through to Mr. Archie Boden-Shaw," she said.

Ere long that official's secretary was inquiring her name, and a moment later:

"Is that you, Archie?" said Mollie. "Yes! Mollie speaking. No, please listen, Archie! You can get to know everything at the Foreign Office, and I want you to find out for me the private address of Chief Inspector Kerry, who is in charge of the Bond Street murder case. Don't be silly! I've asked Scotland Yard, but they won't tell me. *You* can find out.... It doesn't matter why I want to know.... Just ring me up and tell me. I *must* know in half an hour. Yes, I shall be seeing you tonight. Good-bye...."

Less than half an hour later, the obedient Archie rang up, and Mollie, all excitement, wrote the following address in a dainty scented notebook which she carried in her handbag.

CHIEF INSPECTOR KERRY,
67 Spenser Road, Brixton.

CHAPTER XXVII

CROWN EVIDENCE

The appearance of the violet-enamelled motor brougham upholstered in cream, and driven by a chauffeur in a violet and cream livery, created some slight sensation in Spenser Road, S.E. Mollie Gretna's conspicuous car was familiar enough to residents in the West End of London, but to lower middle-class suburbia it came as something of a shock. More than one window curtain moved suspiciously, suggesting a hidden but watchful presence, when the glittering vehicle stopped before the gate of number 67; and the lady at number 68 seized an evidently rare opportunity to come out and polish her letter-box.

She was rewarded by an unobstructed view of the smartest woman in London (thus spake society paragraphers) and of the most expensive set of furs in Europe, also of a perfectly gowned slim figure. Of Mollie's disdainful face, with its slightly uptilted nose, she had no more than a glimpse.

A neat maid, evidently Scotch, admitted the dazzling visitor to number 67; and Spenser Road waited and wondered. It was something to do with the Bond Street murder! Small girls appeared from doorways suddenly opened and darted off to advise less-watchful neighbors.

Kerry, who had been at work until close upon dawn in the mysterious underworld of Soho was sleeping, but Mrs. Kerry received Mollie in a formal little drawing-room, which, unlike the cosy, homely dining-room, possessed that frigid atmosphere which belongs to uninhabited apartments. In a rather handsome cabinet were a number of trophies associated with the detective's successful cases. The cabinet itself was a present from a Regent Street firm for whom Kerry had recovered valuable property.

Mary Kerry, dressed in a plain blouse and skirt, exhibited no trace of nervousness in the presence of her aristocratic and fashionable caller. Indeed, Mollie afterwards declared that "she was quite a ladylike person. But rather tin tabernacley, my dear."

"Did ye wish to see Chief Inspector Kerry parteecularly?" asked Mary, watching her visitor with calm, observant eyes.

"Oh, most particularly!" cried Mollie, in a flutter of excitement. "Of course I don't know *what* you must think of me for calling at such a preposterous hour, but there are some things that simply can't wait."

"Aye," murmured Mrs. Kerry. "'Twill be yon Bond Street affair?"

"Oh, yes, it is, Mrs. Kerry. Doesn't the very name of Bond Street turn your blood cold? I am simply shivering with fear!"

"As the wife of a Chief Inspector I am maybe more used to tragedies than yoursel', madam. But it surely is a sair grim business. My husband is resting now. He was hard at work a' the night. Nae doubt ye'll be wishin' tee see him privately?"

"Oh, if you please. I am so sorry to disturb him. I can imagine that he must be literally exhausted after spending a whole night among dreadful people."

Mary Kerry stood up.

"If ye'll excuse me for a moment I'll awaken him," she said. "Our household is sma'."

"Oh, of course! I quite understand, Mrs. Kerry! So sorry. But so good of you."

"Might I offer ye a glass o' sherry an' a biscuit?"

"I simply couldn't *dream* of troubling you! Please don't suggest such a thing. I feel covered with guilt already. Many thanks nevertheless."

Mary Kerry withdrew, leaving Mollie alone. As soon as the door closed Mollie stood up and began to inspect the trophies in the cabinet. She was far too restless and excited to remain sitting down. She looked at the presentation clock on the mantelpiece and puzzled over the signatures engraved upon a large silver dish which commemorated the joy displayed by the Criminal Investigation Department upon the occasion of Kerry's promotion to the post of Chief Inspector.

The door opened and Kerry came in. He had arisen and completed his toilet in several seconds less than five minutes. But his spotlessly neat attire would have survived inspection by the most lynx-eyed martinet in the Brigade of Guards. As he smiled at his visitor with fierce geniality, Mollie blushed like a young girl.

Chief Inspector Kerry was a much bigger man than she had believed him to be. The impression left upon her memory by his brief appearance at the night club had been that of a small, dapper figure. Now, as he stood in the little drawing-room, she saw that he was not much if anything below the average height of Englishmen, and that he possessed wonderfully broad shoulders. In fact, Kerry was deceptive. His compact neatness and the smallness of his feet and hands, together with those swift, lithe movements which commonly belong to men of light physique, curiously combined to deceive the beholder, but masked eleven stones of bone and muscle.

"Very good of you to offer information, miss," he said. "I'm willing to admit that I can do with it."

He opened a bureau and took out a writing-block and a fountain pen.

Then he turned and stared hard at Mollie. She quickly lowered her eyes.

"Excuse me," said Kerry, "but didn't I see you somewhere last night?"

"Yes," she said. "I was sitting just inside the door at—"

"Right! I remember," interrupted Kerry. He continued to stare. "Before you say any more, miss, I have to remind you that I am a police officer, and that you may be called upon to swear to the truth of any information you may give me."

"Oh, of course! I know."

"You know? Very well, then; we can get on. Who gave you my address?"

At the question, so abruptly asked, Mollie felt herself blushing again. It was delightful to know that she could still blush. "Oh—I... that is, I asked Scotland Yard—"

She bestowed a swift, half-veiled glance at her interrogator, but he offered her no help, and:

"They wouldn't tell me," she continued. "So—I had to find out. You see, I heard you were trying to get information which I thought perhaps I could give."

"So you went to the trouble to find my private address rather than to the nearest police station," said Kerry. "Might I ask you from whom you heard that I wanted this information?"

"Well—it's in the papers, isn't it?"

"It is certainly. But it occurred to me that someone ... connected might have told you as well."

"Actually, someone did: Miss Margaret Halley."

"Good!" rapped Kerry. "Now we're coming to it. She told you to come to me?"

"Oh, no!" cried Mollie—"she didn't. She told me to tell *her* so that she could tell the Home Office."

"Eh?" said Kerry, "eh?" He bent forward, staring fiercely. "Please tell me exactly what Miss Halley wanted to know."

The intensity of his gaze Mollie found very perturbing, but:

"She wanted me to tell her where Mrs. Sin lived," she replied.

Kerry experienced a quickening of the pulse. In the failure of the C.I.D. to trace the abode of the notorious Mrs. Sin he had suspected double-dealing. He counted it unbelievable that a figure so conspicuous in certain circles could evade official quest even for forty-eight hours. K Division's explanation, too, that there were no less than eighty Chinamen resident in and about Limehouse whose names either began or ended with Sin, he looked upon as a paltry evasion. That very morning he had awakened from a species of nightmare wherein "719" had affected the arrest of Kazmah and Mrs. Sin and had rescued Mrs.

Irvin from the clutches of the former. Now—here was hope. "719" would seem to be as hopelessly in the dark as everybody else.

"You refused?" he rapped.

"Of course I did, Inspector," said Mollie, with a timid, tender glance. "I thought you were the proper person to tell."

"Then you know?" asked Kerry, unable to conceal his eagerness.

"Yes," sighed Mollie. "Unfortunately—I know. Oh Inspector, how can I explain it to you?"

"Don't trouble, miss. Just give me the address and I'll ask no questions!"

His keenness was thrilling, infectious. As a result of the night's "beating" he had a list of some twenty names whose owners might have been patrons of Kazmah and some of whom might know Mrs. Sin. But he had learned from bitter experience how difficult it was to induce such people to give useful evidence. There was practically no means of forcing them to speak if they chose, from selfish motives, to be silent. They could be forced to appear in court, but anything elicited in public was worse than useless. Furthermore, Kerry could not afford to wait. Mollie replied excitedly:

"Oh, Inspector, I know you will think me simply an appalling person when I tell you; but I have been to Mrs. Sin's house—'The House of a Hundred Raptures' she calls it—"

"Yes, yes! But—the address?"

"However can I tell you the address, Inspector? I could drive you there, but I haven't the very haziest idea of the name of the horrible street! One drives along dreadful roads where there are stalls and Jews for quite an interminable time, and then over a sort of canal, and then round to the right all among ships and horrid Chinamen. Then, there is a doorway in a little court, and Mrs. Sin's husband sits inside a smelly room with a positively ferocious raven who shrieks about legs and policemen! Oh! Can I ever forget it!"

"One moment, miss, one moment," said Kerry, keeping an iron control upon himself. "What is the name of Mrs. Sin's husband?"

"Oh, let me think! I can always remember it by recalling the croak of the raven." She raised one hand to her brow, posing reflectively, and began to murmur:

"Sin Sin Ah... Sin Sin Jar... Sin Sin—Oh! I have it! Sin Sin *Wa!*"

"Good!" rapped Kerry, and made a note on the block. "Sin Sin *Wa*, and he has a pet raven, you say, who talks?"

"Who positively talks like some horrid old woman!" cried Mollie. "He has only one eye."

"The raven?"

"The raven, yes—and also the Chinaman."

"What!"

"Oh! it's a nightmare to behold them together!" declared Mollie, clasping her hands and bending forward.

She was gaining courage, and now looked almost boldly into the fierce eyes of the Chief Inspector.

"Describe the house," he said succinctly. "Take your time and use your own words."

Thereupon Mollie launched into a description of Sin Sin Wa's opium-house. Kerry, his eyes fixed upon her face, listened silently. Then:

"These little rooms are really next door?" he asked.

"I suppose so, Inspector. We always went through the back of a cupboard!"

"Can you give me names of others who used this place?"

"Well"—Mollie hesitated—"poor Rita, of course and Sir Lucien. Then, Cyrus Kilfane used to go."

"Kilfane? The American actor?"

"Yes."

"H'm. He's back in America, Sir Lucien is dead, and Mrs. Irvin is missing. Nobody else?"

Mollie shook her head.

"Who first took you there?"

"Cyrus Kilfane."

"Not Sir Lucien?"

"Oh, no. But both of them had been before."

"What was Kazmah's connection with Mrs. Sin and her husband?"

"I have no idea, Inspector. Kazmah used to supply cocaine and veronal and trional and heroin, but those who wanted to smoke opium he sent to Mrs. Sin."

"What! he gave them her address?"

"No, no! He gave her *their* address."

"I see. She called?"

"Yes. Oh, Inspector"—Mollie bent farther forward—"I can see in your eyes that you think I am fabulously wicked! Shall I be arrested?"

Kerry coughed drily and stood up.

"Probably not, miss. But you may be required to give evidence."

"Oh, actually?" cried Mollie, also standing up and approaching nearer.

"Yes. Shall you object?"

Mollie looked into his eyes.

"Not if I can be of the slightest assistance to *you*, Inspector."

A theory to explain why this social butterfly had sought him out as a recipient of her compromising confidences presented itself to Kerry's mind. He was a modest man, having neither time nor inclination for gallantries, and this was the first occasion throughout his professional career upon which he had obtained valuable evidence on the strength of his personal attractions. He doubted the accuracy of his deduction. But, Mollie at that moment lowering her lashes and then rapidly raising them again, Kerry was compelled to accept his own astonishing theory.

"And she is the daughter of a peer!" he reflected. "No wonder it has been hard to get evidence."

He glanced rapidly in the direction of the door. There were several details which were by no means clear, but he decided to act upon the information already given and to get rid of his visitor without delay. Where some of the most dangerous criminals in Europe and America had failed, Mollie Gretna had succeeded in making Red Kerry nervous.

"I am much indebted to you, miss," he said, and opened the door.

"Oh, it has been delightful to confess to you, Inspector!" declared Mollie. "I will give you my card, and I shall expect you to come to me for any further information you may want. If I have to be brought to court, *you* will tell me, won't you?"

"Rely upon me, miss," replied Kerry shortly.

He escorted Mollie to her brougham, observed by no less than six discreetly hidden neighbors. And as the brougham was driven off she waved her hand to him! Kerry felt a hot flush spreading over his red countenance, for the veiled onlookers had not escaped his attention. As he re-entered the house:

"Yon's a bad woman," said his wife, emerging from the dining-room.

"I believe you may be right, Mary," replied Kerry confusedly.

"I kenned it when fairst I set een upon her painted face. I kenned it the now when she lookit sideways at ye. If yon's a grand lady, she's a woman o' puir repute. The Lord gi'e us grace."

CHAPTER XXVIII

THE GILDED JOSS

London was fog-bound. The threat of the past week had been no empty one. Towards the hour of each wintry sunset had come the yellow racks, hastening dusk and driving folks more speedily homeward to their firesides. The dull reports of fog-signals had become a part of the metropolitan bombilation, but hitherto the choking mist had not secured a strangle-hold.

Now, however, it had triumphed, casting its thick net over the city as if eager to stifle the pulsing life of the new Babylon. In the neighborhood of the Docks its density was extraordinary, and the purlieus of Limehouse became mere mysterious gullies of smoke impossible to navigate unless one were very familiar with their intricacies and dangers.

Chief Inspector Kerry, wearing a cardigan under his oilskins, tapped the pavement with the point of his malacca like a blind man. No glimmer of light could he perceive. He could not even see his companion.

"Hell!" he snapped irritably, as his foot touched a brick wall, "where the devil are you, constable?"

"Here beside you, sir," answered P.C. Bryce, of K Division, his guide.

"Which side?"

"Here, sir."

The constable grasped Kerry's arm.

"But we've walked slap into a damn brick wall!"

"Keep the wall on your left, sir, and it's all clear ahead."

"Clear be damned!" said Kerry. "Are we nearly there?"

"About a dozen paces and we shall see the lamp—if it's been lighted."

"And if not we shall stroll into the river, I suppose?"

"No danger of that. Even if the lamp's out, we shall strike the iron pillar."

"I don't doubt it," said Kerry grimly.

They proceeded at a slow pace. Dull reports and a vague clangor were audible. These sounds were so deadened by the clammy mist that they might have proceeded from some gnome's workshop deep in the bowels of the earth. The blows of a pile-driver at work on the Surrey shore suggested to Kerry's mind the phantom crew of Hendrick Hudson at their game of ninepins in the Katskill Mountains. Suddenly:

"Is that you, Bryce?" he asked.

"I'm here, sir," replied the voice of the constable from beside him.

"H'm, then there's someone else about." He raised his voice. "Hi, there! have you lost your way?"

Kerry stood still, listening. But no one answered to his call.

"I'll swear there was someone just behind us, Bryce!"

"There was, sir. I saw someone, too. A Chinese resident, probably. Here we are!"

A sound of banging became audible, and on advancing another two paces, Kerry found himself beside Bryce before a low closed door.

"Hello! hello!" croaked a dim voice. "Number one p'lice chop, lo! Sin Sin Wa!"

The flat note of a police whistle followed.

"Sin Sin is at home," declared Bryce. "That's the raven."

"Does he take the thing about with him, then?"

"I don't think so. But he puts it in a cupboard when he goes out, and it never talks unless it can see a light."

Bolts were unfastened and the door was opened. Out through the moving curtain of fog shone the red glow from a stove. A grotesque silhouette appeared outlined upon the dim redness.

"You wantchee me?" crooned Sin Sin Wa.

"I do!" rapped Kerry. "I've called to look for opium."

He stepped past the Chinaman into the dimly lighted room. As he did so, the cause of an apparent deformity which had characterized the outline of Sin Sin Wa became apparent. From his left shoulder the raven partly arose, moving his big wings, and:

"Smartest leg!" it shrieked in Kerry's ear and rattled imaginary castanets.

The Chief Inspector started, involuntarily.

"Damn the thing!" he muttered. "Come in, Bryce, and shut the door. What's this?"

On a tea-chest set beside the glowing stove, the little door of which was open, stood a highly polished squat wooden image, gilded and colored red and green. It was that of a leering Chinaman, possibly designed to represent Buddha, and its jade eyes seemed to blink knowingly in the dancing rays from the stove.

"Sin Sin Wa's Joss," murmured the proprietor, as Bryce closed the outer door. "Me shinee him up; makee Joss glad. Number one piecee Joss."

Kerry turned and stared into the pock-marked smiling face. Seen in that dim light it was not unlike the carved face of the image, save that the latter possessed two open eyes and the Chinaman but one. The details of the room were indiscernible, lost in yellowish shadow, but the eye of the raven and the eye of Sin Sin Wa glittered like strange jewels.

"H'm," said Kerry. "Sorry to interrupt your devotions. Light us."

"Allee velly proper," crooned Sin Sin Wa.

He took up the joss tenderly and bore it across the room. Opening a little cupboard set low down near the floor he discovered a lighted lantern. This he took out and set upon the dirty table. Then he placed the image on a shelf in the cupboard and turned smilingly to his visitors.

"Number one p'lice!" shrieked the raven.

"Here!" snapped Kerry. "Put that damn thing to bed!"

"Velly good," murmured Sin Sin Wa complacently.

He raised his hand to his shoulder and the raven stepped sedately from shoulder to wrist. Sin Sin Wa stooped.

"Come, Tling-a-Ling," he said softly. "You catchee sleepee."

The raven stepped down from his wrist and walked into the cupboard.

"So fashion, lo!" said Sin Sin Wa, closing the door.

He seated himself upon a tea-chest beside the useful cupboard, resting his hands upon his knees and smiling.

Kerry, chewing steadily, had watched the proceedings in silence, but now:

"Constable Bryce," he said crisply, "you recognize this man as Sin Sin Wa, the occupier of the house?"

"Yes, sir," replied Bryce.

He was not wholly at ease, and persistently avoided the Chinaman's oblique, beady eye.

"In the ordinary course of your duty you frequently pass along this street?"

"It's the limit of the Limehouse beat, sir. Poplar patrols on the other side."

"So that at this point, or hereabout, you would sometimes meet the constable on the next beat?"

"Well, sir," Bryce hesitated, clearing his throat, "this street isn't properly in his district."

"I didn't say it was!" snapped Kerry, glaring fiercely at the embarrassed constable. "I said you would sometimes meet him here."

"Yes, sometimes."

"Sometimes. Right. Did you ever come in here?"

The constable ventured a swift glance at the savage red face, and:

"Yes, sir, now and then," he confessed. "Just for a warm on a cold night, maybe."

"Allee velly welcome," murmured Sin Sin Wa.

Kerry never for a moment removed his fixed gaze from the face of Bryce.

"Now, my lad," he said, "I'm going to ask you another question. I'm not saying a word about the warm on a cold night. We're all human. But—did you ever see or hear or smell anything suspicious in this house?"

"Never," affirmed the constable earnestly.

"Did anything ever take place that suggested to your mind that Sin Sin Wa might be concealing something—upstairs, for instance?"

"Never a thing, sir. There's never been a complaint about him."

"Allee velly proper," crooned Sin Sin Wa.

Kerry stared intently for some moments at Bryce; then, turning suddenly to Sin Sin Wa:

"I want to see your wife," he said. "Fetch her."

Sin Sin Wa gently patted his knees.

"She velly bad woman," he declared. "She no hab topside pidgin."

"Don't talk!" shouted Kerry. "Fetch her!"

Sin Sin Wa turned his hands palms upward.

"Me no hab gotchee wifee," he murmured.

Kerry took one pace forward.

"Fetch her," he said; "or—" He drew a pair of handcuffs from the pocket of his oilskin.

"Velly bad luck," murmured Sin Sin Wa. "Catchee trouble for wifee no got."

He extended his wrists, meeting the angry glare of the Chief Inspector with a smile of resignation. Kerry bit savagely at his chewing-gum, glancing aside at Bryce.

"Did you ever see his wife?" he snapped.

"No, sir. I didn't know he had one."

"No habgotchee," murmured Sin Sin Wa, "velly bad woman."

"For the last time," said Kerry, stooping and thrusting his face forward so that his nose was only some six inches from that of Sin Sin Wa, "where's Mrs. Sin?"

"Catchee lun off," replied the Chinaman blandly. "Velly bad woman. Tlief woman. Catchee stealee alla my dollars!"

"Eh!"

Kerry stood upright, moving his shoulders and rattling the handcuffs.

"Comee here when Sin Sin Wa hab gone for catchee shavee, liftee alla my dollars, and—*pff! chee*-lo!"

He raised his hand and blew imaginary fluff into space. Kerry stared down at him with an expression in which animal ferocity and helplessness were oddly blended. Then:

"Bryce," he said, "stay here. I'm going to search the house."

"Very good, sir."

Kerry turned again to the Chinaman.

"Is there anyone upstairs?" he demanded.

"Nobody hab. Sin Sin Wa alla samee lonesome. Catchee shinum him joss."

Kerry dropped the handcuffs back into the pocket of his overall and took out an electric torch. With never another glance at Sin Sin Wa he went out into the passage and began to mount the stairs, presently finding himself in a room filled with all sorts of unsavory rubbish and containing a large cupboard. He uttered an exclamation of triumph.

Crossing the littered floor, and picking his way amid broken cane chairs, tea-chests, discarded garments and bedlaths, he threw open the cupboard door. Before him hung a row of ragged clothes and a number of bowler hats. Directing the ray of the torch upon the unsavory collection, he snatched coats and hats from the hooks upon which they depended and hurled them impatiently upon the floor.

When the cupboard was empty he stepped into it and began to bang upon the back. The savagery of his expression grew more marked than usual, and as he chewed his maxillary muscles protruded extraordinarily.

"If ever I sounded a brick wall," he muttered, "I'm doing it now."

Tap where he would—and he tapped with his knuckles and with the bone ferrule of his cane—there was nothing in the resulting sound to suggest that that part of the wall behind the cupboard was less solid than any other part.

He examined the room rapidly, then passed into another one adjoining it, which was evidently used as a bedroom. The latter faced towards the court and did not come in contact with the wall of the neighboring house. In both rooms the windows were fastened, and judging from the state of the fasteners were never opened. In that containing the cupboard outside shutters were also closed. Despite this sealing-up of the apartments, traces of fog hung in the air. Kerry descended the stairs.

Snapping off the light of his torch, he stood, feet wide apart, staring at Sin Sin Wa. The latter, smiling imperturbably, yellow hands resting upon knees, sat quite still on the tea-chest. Constable Bryce was seated on a corner of the table, looking curiously awkward in his tweed overcoat and bowler hat, which garments quite failed to disguise the policeman. He stood up as Kerry entered. Then:

"There used to be a door between this house and the next," said Kerry succinctly. "My information is exact and given by someone who has often used that door."

"Bloody liar," murmured Sin Sin Wa.

"What!" shouted Kerry. "What did you say, you yellow-faced mongrel!"

He clenched his fists and strode towards the Chinaman.

"Sarcee feller catchee pullee leg," explained the unmoved Sin Sin Wa. "Velly bad man tellee lie for makee bhoberry—getchee poor Chinaman in tlouble."

In the fog-bound silence Kerry could very distinctly be heard chewing. He turned suddenly to Bryce.

"Go back and fetch two men," he directed. "I should never find my way."

"Very good, sir."

Bryce stepped to the door, unable to hide the relief which he experienced, and opened it. The fog was so dense that it looked like a yellow curtain hung in the opening.

"Phew!" said Bryce. "I may be some little time, sir."

"Quite likely. But don't stop to pick daisies."

The constable went out, closing the door. Kerry laid his cane on the table, then stooped and tossed a cud of chewing-gum into the stove. From his waistcoat pocket he drew out a fresh piece and placed it between his teeth. Drawing a tea-chest closer to the stove, he seated himself and stared intently into the glowing heart of the fire.

Sin Sin Wa extended his arm and opened the little cupboard.

"Number one p'lice," croaked the raven drowsily.

"You catchee sleepee, Tling-a-Ling," said Sin Sin Wa.

He took out the green-eyed joss, set it tenderly upon a corner of the table, and closed the cupboard door. With a piece of chamois leather, which he sometimes dipped into a little square tin, he began to polish the hideous figure.

CHAPTER XXIX

DOUBTS AND FEARS

Monte Irvin raised his head and stared dully at Margaret Halley. It was very quiet in the library of the big old-fashioned house at Prince's Gate. A faint crackling sound which proceeded from the fire was clearly audible. Margaret's grey eyes were anxiously watching the man whose pose as he sat in the deep, saddle-back chair so curiously suggested collapse.

"Drugs," he whispered. "Drugs."

Few of his City associates would have recognized the voice; all would have been shocked to see the change which had taken place in the man.

"You really understand why I have told you, Mr. Irvin, don't you?" said Margaret almost pleadingly. "Dr. Burton thought you should not be told, but then Dr. Burton did not know you were going to ask me point blank. And *I* thought it better that you should know the truth, bad as it is, rather than—"

"Rather than suspect—worse things," whispered Irvin. "Of course, you were right, Miss Halley. I am very, very grateful to you for telling me. I realize what courage it must have called for. Believe me, I shall always remember—"

He broke off, staring across the room at his wife's portrait. Then:

"If only I had known," he added.

Irvin exhibited greater composure than Margaret had ventured to anticipate. She was confirmed in her opinion that he should be told the truth.

"I would have told you long ago," she said, "if I had thought that any good could result from my doing so. Frankly, I had hoped to cure Rita of the habit, and I believe I might have succeeded in time."

"There has been no mention of drugs in connection with the case," said Monte Irvin, speaking monotonously. "In the Press, I mean."

"Hitherto there has not," she replied. "But there is a hint of it in one of this evening's papers, and I determined to give you the exact facts so far as they are known to me before some garbled account came to your ears."

"Thank you," he said, "thank you. I had felt for a long time that I was getting out of touch with Rita, that she had other confidants. Have you any idea who they were, Miss Halley?"

He raised his eyes, looking at her pathetically. Margaret hesitated, then:

"Well," she replied, "I am afraid Nina knew."

"Her maid?"

"I think she must have known."

He sighed.

"The police have interrogated her," he said. "Probably she is being watched."

"Oh, I don't think she knows anything about the drug syndicate," declared Margaret. "She merely acted as confidential messenger. Poor Sir Lucien Pyne, I am sure, was addicted to drugs."

"Do you think"—Irvin spoke in a very low voice—"do you think he led her into the habit?"

Margaret bit her lip, staring down at the red carpet.

"I would hate to slander a man who can never defend himself," she replied finally. "But—I have sometimes thought he did."

Silence fell. Both were contemplating a theory which neither dared to express in words.

"You see," continued Margaret, "it is evident that this man Kazmah was patronized by people so highly placed that it is hopeless to look for information from them. Again, such people have influence. I don't suggest that they are using it to protect Kazmah, but I have no doubt they are doing so to protect themselves."

Monte Irvin raised his eyes to her face. A weary, sad look had come into them.

"You mean that it may be to somebody's interest to hush up the matter as much as possible?"

Margaret nodded her head.

"The prevalence of the drug habit in society—especially in London society—is a secret which has remained hidden so long from the general public," she replied, "that one cannot help looking for bribery and corruption. The stage is made the scapegoat whenever the voice of scandal breathes the word 'dope,' but we rarely hear the names of the worst offenders even whispered. I have thought for a long time that the authorities must know the names of the receivers and distributors of cocaine, veronal, opium, and the other drugs, huge quantities of which find their way regularly to the West End of London. Pharmacists sometimes experience the greatest difficulty in obtaining the drugs which they legitimately require, and the prices have increased extraordinarily. Cocaine, for instance, has gone up from five and sixpence an ounce to eighty-seven shillings, and heroin from three and sixpence to over forty shillings, while opium that was once about twenty shillings a pound is now eight times the price."

Monte Irvin listened attentively.

"In the course of my Guildhall duties," he said slowly, "I have been brought in contact frequently with police officers of all ranks. If influential people are really at work protecting these villains who deal illicitly in drugs, I don't think, and I am not prepared to believe, that they have corrupted the police."

"Neither do I believe so, Mr. Irvin!" said Margaret eagerly.

"But," Irvin pursued, exhibiting greater animation, "you inform me that a Home Office commissioner has been appointed. What does this mean, if not that Lord Wrexborough distrusts the police?"

"Well, you see, the police seemed to be unable, or unwilling, to do anything in the matter. Of course, this may have been due to the fact that the traffic was so skilfully handled that it defied their inquiries."

"Take, as an instance, Chief Inspector Kerry," continued Irvin. "He has exhibited the utmost delicacy and consideration in his dealings with me, but I'll swear that a whiter man never breathed."

"Oh, really, Mr. Irvin, I don't think for a moment that men of that class are suspected of being concerned. Indeed, I don't believe any active collusion is suspected at all."

"Lord Wrexborough thinks that Scotland Yard hasn't got an officer clever enough for the dope people?"

"Quite possibly."

"I take it that he has put up a secret service man?"

"I believe—that is, I know he has."

Monte Irvin was watching Margaret's face, and despite the dull misery which deadened his usually quick perceptions, he detected a heightened color and a faint change of expression. He did not question her further upon the point, but:

"God knows I welcome all the help that offers," he said. "Lord Wrexborough is your uncle, Miss Halley; but do you think this secret commission business quite fair to Scotland Yard?"

Margaret stared for some moments at the carpet, then raised her grey eyes and looked earnestly at the speaker. She had learned in the brief time that had elapsed since this black sorrow had come upon him to understand what it was in the character of Monte Irvin which had attracted Rita. It afforded an illustration of that obscure law governing the magnetism which subsists between diverse natures. For not all the agony of mind which he suffered could hide or mar the cleanness and honesty of purpose which were Monte Irvin's outstanding qualities.

"No," Margaret replied, "honestly, I don't. And I feel rather guilty about it, too, because I have been urging uncle to take such a step for quite a long time. You see"—she glanced at Irvin wistfully—"I am brought in contact with so many victims of the drug habit. I believe the police are hampered; and these people who deal in drugs manage in some way to evade the law. The Home Office agent will report to a committee appointed by Lord Wrexborough, and then, you see, if it is found necessary to do so, there will be special legislation."

Monte Irvin sighed wearily, and his glance strayed in the direction of the telephone on the side-table. He seemed to be constantly listening for something which he expected but dreaded to hear. Whenever the toy spaniel which lay curled up on the rug before the fire moved or looked towards the door, Irvin started and his expression changed.

"This suspense," he said jerkily, "this suspense is so hard to bear."

"Oh, Mr. Irvin, your courage is wonderful," replied Margaret earnestly. "But he"—she hastily corrected herself—"everybody is convinced that Rita is safe. Under some strange misapprehension regarding this awful tragedy she has run away into hiding. Probably she has been induced to do so by those interested in preventing her from giving evidence."

Monte Irvin's eyes lighted up strangely. "Is that the opinion of the Home Office agent?" he asked.

"Yes."

"Inspector Kerry shares it," declared Irvin. "Please God they are right."

"It is the only possible explanation," said Margaret. "Any hour now we may expect news of her."

"You don't think," pursued Monte Irvin, "that anybody—anybody—suspects Rita of being concerned in the death of Sir Lucien?"

He fixed a gaze of pathetic inquiry upon her face.

"Of course not!" she cried. "How ridiculous it would be."

"Yes," he murmured, "it would be ridiculous."

Margaret stood up.

"I am quite relieved now that I have done what I conceived to be my duty, Mr. Irvin," she said. "And, bad as the truth may be, it is better than doubt, after all. You must look after yourself, you know. When Rita comes back we shall have a big task before us to wean her from her old habits." She met his glance frankly. "But we shall succeed."

"How you cheer me," whispered Monte Irvin emotionally. "You are the truest friend that Rita ever had, Miss Halley. You will keep in touch with me, will you not?"

"Of course. Next to yourself there is no one so sincerely interested as I am. I love Rita as I should have loved a sister if I had had one. Please don't stand up. Dr. Burton has told you to avoid all exertion for a week or more, I know."

Monte Irvin grasped her outstretched hand.

"Any news which reaches me," he said, "I will communicate immediately. Thank you. In times of trouble we learn to know our real friends."

CHAPTER XXX

THE FIGHT IN THE DARK

Towards eleven o'clock at night the fog began slightly to lift. As Kerry crossed the bridge over Limehouse Canal he could vaguely discern the dirty water below, and street lamps showed dimly, surrounded each by a halo of yellow mist. Fog signals were booming on the railway, and from the great docks in the neighborhood mechanical clashings and hammerings were audible.

Turning to the right, Kerry walked on for some distance, and then suddenly stepped into the entrance to a narrow cul-de-sac and stood quite still.

A conviction had been growing upon him during the past twelve hours that someone was persistently and cleverly dogging his footsteps. He had first detected the presence of this mysterious follower outside the house of Sin Sin Wa, but the density of the fog had made it impossible for him to obtain a glimpse of the man's face. He was convinced, too, that he had been followed back to Leman Street, and from there to New Scotland Yard. Now, again he became aware of this persistent presence, and hoped at last to confront the spy.

Below footsteps, the footsteps of someone proceeding with the utmost caution, came along the pavement. Kerry stood close to the wall of the court, one hand in a pocket of his overall, waiting and chewing.

Nearer came the footsteps—and nearer. A shadowy figure appeared only a yard or so away from the watchful Chief Inspector. Thereupon he acted.

With one surprising spring he hurled himself upon the unprepared man, grasped him by his coat collar, and shone the light of an electric torch fully into his face.

"Hell!" he snapped. "The smart from Spinker's!"

The ray of the torch lighted up the mean, pinched face of Brisley, blanched now by fright, gleamed upon the sharp, hooked nose and into the cunning little brown eyes. Brisley licked his lips. In Kerry's muscular grip he bore quite a remarkable resemblance to a rat in the jaws of a terrier.

"Ho, ho!" continued the Chief Inspector, showing his teeth savagely. "So we let Scotland Yard make the pie, and then we steal all the plums, do we?"

He shook the frightened man until Brisley's broad-brimmed bowler was shaken off, revealing the receding brow and scanty neutral-colored hair.

"We let Scotland Yard work night and day, and then we present our rat-faced selves to Mr. Monte Irvin and say we have 'found the lady' do we?" Another vigorous shake followed. "We track Chief Inspectors of the Criminal Investigation Department, do we? We do, eh? We are dirty, skulking mongrels, aren't we? We require to be kicked from Limehouse to Paradise, don't we?" He suddenly released Brisley. "So we shall be!" he shouted furiously.

Hot upon the promise came the deed.

Brisley sent up a howl of pain as Kerry's right brogue came into violent contact with his person. The assault almost lifted him off his feet, and hatless as he was he set off, running as a man runs whose life depends upon his speed. The sound of his pattering footsteps was echoed from wall to wall of the cul-de-sac until finally it was swallowed up in the fog.

Kerry stood listening for some moments, then, directing a furious kick upon the bowler which lay at his feet, he snapped off the light of the torch and pursued his way. The lesser mystery was solved, but the greater was before him.

He had made a careful study of the geography of the neighborhood, and although the fog was still dense enough to be confusing, he found his way without much difficulty to the street for which he was bound. Some fifteen paces along the narrow thoroughfare he came upon someone standing by a closed door set in a high brick wall. The street contained no dwelling houses, and except for the solitary figure by the door was deserted and silent. Kerry took out his torch and shone a white ring upon the smiling countenance of Detective-Sergeant Coombes.

"If that smile gets any worse," he said irritably, "they'll have to move your ears back. Anything to report?"

"Sin Sin Wa went to bed an hour ago."

"Any visitors?"

"No."

"Has he been out?"

"No."

"Got the ladder?"

"Yes."

"All quiet in the neighborhood?"

"All quiet."

"Good."

The street in which this conversation took place was one running roughly parallel with that in which the house of Sin Sin Wa was situated. A detailed search of the Chinaman's premises had failed to bring to light any scrap of evidence to show that opium had ever been smoked there. Of the door described by Mollie Gretna, and said to communicate with the adjoining establishment, not a trace could be found. But the fact that such a door had existed did not rest solely upon Mollie's testimony. From one of the "beat-ups" interviewed that day, Kerry had succeeded in extracting confirmatory evidence.

Inquiries conducted in the neighborhood of Poplar had brought to light the fact that four of the houses in this particular street, including that occupied by Sin Sin Wa and that adjoining it, belonged to a certain Mr. Jacobs, said to reside abroad. Mr. Jacob's rents were collected by an estate agent, and sent to an address in San Francisco. For some reason not evident to this man of business, Mr. Jacobs demanded a rental for the house next to Sin Sin Wa's, which was out of all proportion to the value of the property. Hence it had remained vacant for a number of years. The windows were broken and boarded up, as was the door.

Kerry realized that the circumstance of the landlord of "The House of a Hundred Raptures" being named Jacobs, and the lessee of the Cubanis Cigarette Company's premises in old Bond Street being named

Isaacs, might be no more than a coincidence. Nevertheless it was odd. He had determined to explore the place without unduly advertising his intentions.

Two modes of entrance presented themselves. There was a trap on the roof, but in order to reach it access would have to be obtained to one of the other houses in the row, which also possessed a roof-trap; or there were four windows overlooking a little back yard, two upstairs and two down.

By means of a short ladder which Coombes had brought for the purpose Kerry climbed on to the wall and dropped into the yard.

"The jemmy!" he said softly.

Coombes, also mounting, dropped the required implement. Kerry caught it deftly, and in a very few minutes had wrenched away the rough planking nailed over one of the lower windows, without making very much noise.

"Shall I come down?" inquired Coombes in muffled tones from the top of the wall.

"No," rapped Kerry. "Hide the ladder again. If I want help I'll whistle. Catch!"

He tossed the jemmy up to Coombes, and Coombes succeeded in catching it. Then Kerry raised the glass-less sash of the window and stepped into a little room, which he surveyed by the light of his electric torch. It was filthy and littered with rubbish, but showed no sign of having been occupied for a long time. The ceiling was nearly black, and so were the walls. He went out into a narrow passage similar to that in the house of Sin Sin Wa and leading to a stair.

Walking quietly, he began to ascend. Mollie Gretna's description of the opium-house had been most detailed and lurid, and he was prepared for some extravagant scene.

He found three bare, dirty rooms, having all the windows boarded up.

"Hell!" he said succinctly.

Resting his torch upon a dust-coated ledge of the room, which presumably was situated in the front of the house, he deposited a cud of chewing-gum in the empty grate and lovingly selected a fresh piece from the packet which he always carried. Once more chewing he returned to the narrow passage, which he knew must be that in which the secret doorway had opened.

It was uncarpeted and dirty, and the walls were covered with faded filthy paper, the original color and design of which were quite lost. There was not the slightest evidence that a door had ever existed in any part of the wall. Following a detailed examination Kerry returned his magnifying glass to the washleather bag and the bag to his waistcoat pocket.

"H'm," he said, thinking aloud, "Sin Sin Wa may have only one eye, but it's a good eye."

He raised his glance to the blackened ceiling of the passage, and saw that the trap giving access to the roof was situated immediately above him. He directed the ray of the torch upon it. In the next moment he had snapped off the light and was creeping silently towards the door of the front room.

The trap had moved slightly!

Gaining the doorway, Kerry stood just inside the room and waited. He became conscious of a kind of joyous excitement, which claimed him at such moments; an eagerness and a lust of action. But he stood perfectly still, listening and waiting.

There came a faint creaking sound, and a new damp chilliness was added to the stale atmosphere of the passage. Someone had quietly raised the trap.

Cutting through the blackness like a scimitar shone a ray of light from above, widening as it descended and ending in a white patch on the floor. It was moved to and fro. Then it disappeared. Another vague creaking sound followed—that caused by a man's weight being imposed upon a wooden framework.

Finally came a thud on the bare boards of the floor.

Complete silence ensued. Kerry waited, muscles tense and brain alert. He even suspended the chewing operation. A dull, padding sound reached his ears.

From the quality of the thud which had told of the intruder's drop from the trap to the floor, Kerry had deduced that he wore rubber-soled shoes. Now, the sound which he could hear was that of the stranger's furtive footsteps. He was approaching the doorway in which Kerry was standing.

Just behind the open door Kerry waited. And unheralded by any further sound to tell of his approach, the intruder suddenly shone a ray of light right into the room. He was on the threshold; only the door concealed him from Kerry, and concealed Kerry from the new-comer.

The disc of light cast into the dirty room grew smaller. The man with the torch was entering. A hand which grasped a magazine pistol appeared beyond the edge of the door, and Kerry's period of inactivity came to an end. Leaning back he adroitly kicked the weapon from the hand of the man who held it!

There was a smothered cry of pain, and the pistol fell clattering on the floor. The light went out, too. As it vanished Kerry leapt from his hiding-place. Snapping on the light of his own pocket lamp, he ran out into the passage.

Crack! came the report of a pistol.

Kerry dropped flat on the floor. He had not counted on the intruder being armed with *two* pistols! His pocket lamp, still alight, fell beside him, and he lay in a curiously rigid attitude on his side, one knee drawn up and his arm thrown across his face.

Carefully avoiding the path of light cast by the fallen torch, the unseen stranger approached silently. Pistol in hand, he bent, nearer and nearer, striving to see the face of the prostrate man. Kerry lay deathly still. The other dropped on one knee and bent closely over him....

Swiftly as a lash Kerry's arm was whipped around the man's neck, and helpless he pitched over on to his head! Uttering a dull groan, he lay heavy and still across Kerry's body.

"Flames!" muttered the Chief Inspector, extricating himself; "I didn't mean to break his neck."

He took up the electric torch, and shone it upon the face of the man on the floor. It was a dirty, unshaven face, unevenly tanned, as though the man had worn a beard until quite recently and had come from a hot climate. He was attired in a manner which suggested that he might be a ship's fireman save that he wore canvas shoes having rubber soles.

Kerry stood watching him for some moments. Then he groped behind him with one foot until he found the pistol, the second pistol which the man had dropped as he pitched on his skull. Kerry picked it up, and resting the electric torch upon the crown of his neat bowler hat— which lay upon the floor—he stooped, pistol in hand, and searched the pockets of the prostrate man, who had begun to breathe stertorously. In the breast pocket he found a leather wallet of good quality; and at this he stared, a curious expression coming into his fierce eyes. He opened it, and found Treasury notes, some official-looking papers, and a number of cards. Upon one of these cards be directed the light, and this is what he read:

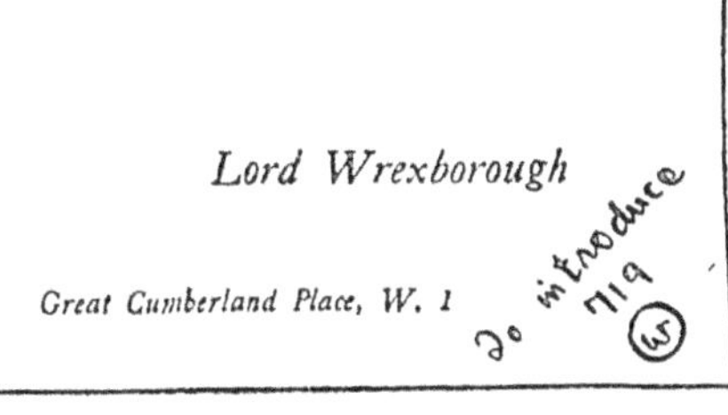

"God's truth!" gasped Kerry. "It's the man from Whitehall!"

The stertorous breathing ceased, and a very dirty hand was thrust up to him.

"I'm glad you spoke, Chief Inspector Kerry," drawled a vaguely familiar voice. "I was just about to kick you in the back of the neck!"

Kerry dropped the wallet and grasped the proffered hand. "719" stood up, smiling grimly. Footsteps were clattering on the stairs. Coombes had heard the shot.

"Sir," said Kerry, "if ever you need a testimonial to your efficiency at this game, my address is Sixty-seven Spenser Road, Brixton. We've met before."

"We have, Chief Inspector," was the reply. "We met at Kazmah's, and later at a certain gambling den in Soho."

The pseudo fireman dragged a big cigar-case from his hip-pocket.

"I'm known as Seton Pasha. Can I offer you a cheroot?"

CHAPTER XXXI

THE STORY OF 719

In a top back room of the end house in the street which also boasted the residence of Sin Sin Wa, Seton Pasha and Chief Inspector Kerry sat one on either side of a dirty deal table. Seton smoked and Kerry chewed. A smoky oil-lamp burned upon the table, and two notebooks lay beside it.

"It is certainly odd," Seton was saying, "that you failed to break my neck. But I have made it a practice since taking up my residence here to wear a cap heavily padded. I apprehend sandbags and pieces of loaded tubing."

"The tube is not made," declared Kerry, "which can do the job. You're harder to kill than a Chinese-Jew."

"Your own escape is almost equally remarkable," added Seton. "I rarely miss at such short range. But you had nearly broken my wrist with that kick."

"I'm sorry," said Kerry. "You should always bang a door wide open suddenly before you enter into a suspected room. Anybody standing behind usually stops it with his head."

"I am indebted for the hint, Chief Inspector. We all have something to learn."

"Well, sir, we've laid our cards on the table, and you'll admit we've both got a lot to learn before we see daylight. I'll be obliged if you'll put me wise to your game. I take it you began work on the very night of the murder?"

"I did. By a pure accident—the finding of an opiated cigarette in Mr. Gray's rooms—I perceived that the business which had led to my recall from the East was involved in the Bond Street mystery. Frankly, Chief Inspector, I doubted at that time if it were possible for you and me to work together. I decided to work alone. A beard which I had worn in the East, for purposes of disguise, I shaved off; and because the skin was whiter where the hair had grown than elsewhere, I found it necessary after shaving to powder my face heavily. This accounts for the description given to you of a man with a pale face. Even now the coloring is irregular, as you may notice.

"Deciding to work anonymously, I went post haste to Lord Wrexhorough and made certain arrangements whereby I became known to the responsible authorities as '719.' The explanation of these figures is a simple one. My name is Greville Seton. G is the seventh letter in the alphabet, and S the nineteenth; hence—'seven-nineteen.'

"The increase of the drug traffic and the failure of the police to cope with it had led to the institution of a Home Office inquiry, you see. It was suspected that the traffic was in the hands of Orientals, and in looking about for a confidential agent to make certain inquiries my name cropped up. I was at that time employed by the Foreign Office, but Lord Wrexborough borrowed me." Seton smiled at his own expression. "Every facility was offered to me, as you know. And that my investigations led me to the same conclusion as your own, my presence as lessee of this room, in the person of John Smiles, seaman, sufficiently demonstrates."

"H'm," said Kerry, "and I take it your investigations have also led you to the conclusion that our hands are clean?"

Seton Pasha fixed his cool regard upon the speaker.

"Personally, I never doubted this, Chief Inspector," he declared. "I believed, and I still believe, that the people who traffic in drugs are clever enough to keep in the good books of the local police. It is a case of clever camouflage, rather than corruption."

"Ah," snapped Kerry. "I was waiting to hear you mention it. So long as we know. I'm not a man that stands for being pointed at. I've got a boy at a good public school, but if ever he said he was ashamed of his father, the day he said it would be a day he'd never forget!"

Seton Pasha smiled grimly and changed the topic.

"Let us see," he said, "if we are any nearer to the heart of the mystery of Kazmah. You were at the Regent Street bank today, I understand, at which the late Sir Lucien Pyne had an account?"

"I was," replied Kerry. "Next to his theatrical enterprises his chief source of income seems to have been a certain Jose Santos Company, of Buenos Ayres. We've traced Kazmah's account, too. But no one at the bank has ever seen him. The missing Rashid always paid in. Checks were signed 'Mohammed el-Kazmah,' in which name the account had been opened. From the amount standing to his credit there it's evident that the proceeds of the dope business went elsewhere."

"Where do you think they went?" asked Seton quietly, watching Kerry.

"Well," rapped Kerry, "I think the same as you. I've got two eyes and I can see out of both of them."

"And you think?"

"I think they went to the Jose Santos Company, of Buenos Ayres!"

"Right!" cried Seton. "I feel sure of it. We may never know how it was all arranged or who was concerned, but I am convinced that Mr. Isaacs, lessee of the Cubanis Cigarette Company offices, Mr. Jacobs (my landlord!), Mohammed el-Kazmah—whoever he may be—the untraceable Mrs. Sin Sin Wa, and another, were all shareholders of the Jose Santos company."

"I'm with you. By 'another' you mean?"

"Sir Lucien! It's horrible, but I'm afraid it's true."

They became silent for a while. Kerry chewed and Seton smoked. Then:

"The significance of the fact that Sir Lucien's study window was no more than forty paces across the leads from a well-oiled window of the Cubanis Company will not have escaped you," said Seton. "I performed the journey just ahead of you, I believe. Then Sir Lucien had lived in Buenos Ayres; that was before he came into the title, and at a time, I am told, when he was not overburdened with wealth. His man, Mareno, is indisputably some kind of a South American, and he can give no satisfactory account of his movements on the night of the murder.

"That we have to deal with a powerful drug syndicate there can be no doubt. The late Sir Lucien may not have been a director, but I feel sure he was financially interested. Kazmah's was the distributing office, and the importer—"

"Was Sin Sin Wa!" cried Kerry, his eyes gleaming savagely. "He's as clever and cunning as all the rest of Chinatown put together. Somewhere not a hundred miles from this spot where we are now there's a store of stuff big enough to dope all Europe!"

"And there's something else," said Seton quietly, knocking a cone of grey ash from his cheroot on to the dirty floor. "Kazmah is hiding there in all probability, if he hasn't got clear away—and Mrs. Monte Irvin is being held a prisoner!"

"If they haven't—"

"For Irvin's sake I hope not, Chief Inspector. There are two very curious points in the case—apart from the mystery which surrounds the man Kazmah: the fact that Mareno, palpably an accomplice, stayed to face the music, and the fact that Sin Sin Wa likewise has made no effort to escape. Do you see what it means? They are covering the big man—Kazmah. Once he and Mrs. Irvin are out of the way, we can prove nothing against Mareno and Sin Sin Wa! And the most we could do for Mrs. Sin would be to convict her of selling opium."

"To do even that we should have to take a witness to court," said Kerry gloomily; "and all the satisfaction we'd get would be to see her charged ten pounds!"

Silence fell between them again. It was that kind of sympathetic silence which is only possible where harmony exists; and, indeed, of all the things strange and bizarre which characterized the inquiry, this sudden amity between Kerry and Seton Pasha was not the least remarkable. It represented the fruit of a mutual respect.

There was something about the lean, unshaven face of Seton Pasha, and something, too, in his bright grey eyes which, allowing for difference of coloring, might have reminded a close observer of Kerry's fierce countenance. The tokens of iron determination and utter indifference to danger were perceptible in both. And although Seton was dark and turning slightly grey, while Kerry was as red as a man well could be, that they possessed several common traits of character was a fact which the dissimilarity of their complexions wholly failed to conceal. But while Seton Pasha hid the grimness of his nature beneath a sort of humorous reserve, the dangerous side of Kerry was displayed in his open truculence.

Seated there in that Limehouse attic, a smoky lamp burning on the table between them, and one gripping the stump of a cheroot between his teeth, while the other chewed steadily, they presented a combination which none but a fool would have lightly challenged.

"Sin Sin Wa is cunning," said Seton suddenly. "He is a very clever man. Watch him as closely as you like, he will never lead you to the 'store.' In the character of John Smiles I had some conversation with him this morning, and I formed the same opinion as yourself. He is waiting for something; and he is certain of his ground. I have a premonition, Chief Inspector, that whoever else may fall into the net, Sin Sin Wa will slip out. We have one big chance."

"What's that?" rapped Kerry.

"The dope syndicate can only have got control of 'the traffic' in one way—by paying big prices and buying out competitors. If they cease to carry on for even a week they lose their control. The people who bring the stuff over from Japan, South America, India, Holland, and so forth will sell somewhere else if they can't sell to Kazmah and Company. Therefore we want to watch the ships from likely ports, or, better still, get among the men who do the smuggling. There must be resorts along the riverside used by people of that class. We might pick up information there."

Kerry smiled savagely.

"I've got half a dozen good men doing every dive from Wapping to Gravesend," he answered. "But if you think it worth looking into personally, say the word."

"Well, my dear sir,"—Seton Pasha tossed the end of his cheroot into the empty grate—"what else can we do?"

Kerry banged his fist on the table.

"You're right!" he snapped. "We're stuck! But anything's better than nothing. We'll start here and now; and the first joint we'll make for is Dougal's."

"Dougal's?" echoed Seton Pasha.

"That's it—Dougal's. A danger spot on the Isle of Dogs used by the lowest type of sea-faring men and not barred to Arabs, Chinks, and other gaily-colored fowl. If there's any chat going on about dope, we'll hear it in Dougal's."

Seton Pasha stood up, smiling grimly. "Dougal's it shall be," he said.

CHAPTER XXXII

ON THE ISLE OF DOGS

As the police boat left Limehouse Pier, a clammy south-easterly breeze blowing up-stream lifted the fog in clearly defined layers, an effect very singular to behold. At one moment a great arc-lamp burning above the Lavender Pond of the Surrey Commercial Dock shot out a yellowish light across the Thames. Then, as suddenly as it had come, the light vanished again as a stratum of mist floated before it.

The creaking of the oars sounded muffled and ghostly, and none of the men in the boat seemed to be inclined to converse. Heading across stream they made for the unseen promontory of the Isle of Dogs. Navigation was suspended, and they reached midstream without seeing a ship's light. Then came the damp wind again to lift the fog, and ahead of them they discerned one of the General Steam Navigation Company's boats awaiting an opportunity to make her dock at the head of Deptford Creek. The clamor of an ironworks on the Millwall shore burst loudly upon their ears, and away astern the lights of the Surrey Dock shone out once more. Hugging the bank they pursued a southerly course, and from Limehouse Reach crept down to Greenwich Reach.

Fog closed in upon them, a curtain obscuring both light and sound. When the breeze came again it had gathered force, and it drove the mist before it in wreathing banks, and brought to their ears a dull lowing and to their nostrils a farmyard odor from the cattle pens. Ghostly flames, leaping and falling, leaping and falling, showed where a gasworks lay on the Greenwich bank ahead.

Eastward swept the river now, and fresher blew the breeze. As they rounded the blunt point of the "Isle" the fog banks went swirling past them astern, and the lights on either shore showed clearly ahead. A ship's siren began to roar somewhere behind them. The steamer which they had passed was about to pursue her course.

Closer in-shore drew the boat, passing a series of wharves, and beyond these a tract of waste, desolate bank very gloomy in the half light and apparently boasting no habitation of man. The activities of the Greenwich bank seemed remote, and the desolation of the Isle of Dogs very near, touching them intimately with its peculiar gloom.

A light sprang into view some little distance inland, notable because it shone lonely in an expanse of utter blackness. Kerry broke the long silence.

"Dougal's," he said. "Put us ashore here."

The police boat was pulled in under a rickety wooden structure, beneath which the Thames water whispered eerily; and Kerry and Seton disembarked, mounting a short flight of slimy wooden steps and crossing a roughly planked place on to a shingly slope. Climbing this, they were on damp waste ground, pathless and uninviting.

"Dougal's is being watched," said Kerry. "I think I told you?"

"Yes," replied Seton. "But I have formed the opinion that the dope gang is too clever for the ordinary type of man. Sin Sin Wa is an instance of what I mean. Neither you nor I doubt that he is a receiver of drugs—perhaps *the* receiver; but where is our case? The only real link connecting him with the West-End habitué is his wife. And she has conveniently deserted him! We cannot possibly prove that she hasn't while he chooses to maintain that she has."

"H'm," grunted Kerry, abruptly changing the subject. "I hope I'm not recognized here."

"Have you visited the place before?"

"Some years ago. Unless there are any old hands on view tonight, I don't think I shall be spotted."

He wore a heavy and threadbare overcoat, which was several sizes too large for him, a muffler, and a weed cap—the outfit supplied by Seton Pasha; and he had a very vivid and unpleasant recollection of his appearance as viewed in his little pocket-mirror before leaving Seton's room. As they proceeded across the muddy wilderness towards the light which marked the site of Dougal's, they presented a picture of a sufficiently villainous pair.

The ground was irregular, and the path wound sinuously about mounds of rubbish; so that often the guiding light was lost, and they stumbled blindly among nondescript litter, which apparently represented the accumulation of centuries. But finally they turned a corner formed by a stack of rusty scrap iron, and found a long, low building before them. From a ground-floor window light streamed out upon the fragments of rubbish strewing the ground, from amid which sickly weeds uprose as if in defiance of nature's laws. Seton paused, and:

"What is Dougal's exactly?" he asked; "a public house?"

"No," rapped Kerry. "It's a coffee-shop used by the dockers. You'll see when we get inside. The place never closes so far as I know, and if we made 'em close there would be a dock strike."

He crossed and pushed open the swing door. As Seton entered at his heels, a babel of coarse voices struck upon his ears and he found himself in a superheated atmosphere suggestive of shag, stale spirits, and imperfectly washed humanity.

Dougal's proved to be a kind of hut of wood and corrugated iron, not unlike an army canteen. There were two counters, one at either end, and two large American stoves. Oil lamps hung from the beams, and the furniture was made up of trestle tables, rough wooden chairs, and empty barrels. Coarse, thick curtains covered all the windows but one. The counter further from the entrance was laden with articles of food, such as pies, tins of bully-beef, and "saveloys," while the other was devoted to liquid refreshment in the form of ginger-beer and cider (or so the casks were conspicuously labelled), tea, coffee, and cocoa.

The place was uncomfortably crowded; the patrons congregating more especially around the two stoves. There were men who looked like dock laborers, seamen, and riverside loafers; lascars, Chinese, Arabs, and dagoes; and at the "solid" counter there presided a red-armed, brawny woman, fierce of mien and ready of tongue, while a huge Irishman, possessing a broken nose and deficient teeth, ruled the "liquid" department with a rod of iron and a flow of language which shocked even Kerry. This formidable ruffian, a retired warrior of the ring, was Dougal, said to be the strongest man from Tower Hill to the River Lea.

As they entered, several of the patrons glanced at them curiously, but no one seemed to be particularly interested. Kerry wore his cap pulled well down over his fierce eyes, and had the collar of his topcoat turned up.

He looked about him, as if expecting to recognize someone; and as they made their way to Dougal's counter, a big fellow dressed in the manner of a dock laborer stepped up to the Chief Inspector and clapped him on the shoulder.

"Have one with me, Mike," he said, winking. "The coffee's good."

Kerry bent towards him swiftly, and:

"Anybody here, Jervis?" he whispered.

"George Martin is at the bar. I've had the tip that he 'traffics.' You'll remember he figured in my last report, sir."

Kerry nodded, and the trio elbowed their way to the counter. The pseudo-dock hand was a detective attached to Leman Street, and one who knew the night birds of East End London as few men outside their own circles knew them.

"Three coffees, Pat," he cried, leaning across the shoulder of a heavy, red-headed fellow who lolled against the counter. "And two lumps of sugar in each."

"To hell wid yer sugar!" roared Dougal, grasping three cups deftly in one hairy hand and filling them from a steaming urn. "There's no more sugar tonight."

"Not any *brown* sugar?" asked the customer.

"Yez can have one tayspoon of brown, and no more tonight," cried Dougal.

He stooped rapidly below the counter, then pushed the three cups of coffee towards the detective. The latter tossed a shilling down, at which Dougal glared ferociously.

"'Twas wid sugar ye said!" he roared.

A second shilling followed. Dougal swept both coins into a drawer and turned to another customer, who was also clamoring for coffee. Securing their cups with difficulty, for the red-headed man surlily refused to budge, they retired to a comparatively quiet spot, and Seton tasted the hot beverage.

"H'm," he said. "Rum! Good rum, too!"

"It's a nice position for me," snapped Kerry. "I *don't* think! I would remind you that there's a police station actually on this blessed island. If there was a dive like Dougal's anywhere West it would be raided as a matter of course. But to shut Dougal's would be to raise hell. There are two laws in England, sir; one for Piccadilly and the other for the Isle of Dogs!" He sipped his coffee with appreciation. Jervis looked about him cautiously, and:

"That's George—the red-headed hooligan against the counter," he said. "He's been liquoring up pretty freely, and I shouldn't be surprised to find that he's got a job on tonight. He has a skiff beached below here, and I think he's waiting for the tide."

"Good!" rapped Kerry. "Where can we find a boat?"

"Well," Jervis smiled. "There are several lying there if you didn't come in an R.P. boat."

"We did. But I'll dismiss it. We want a small boat."

"Very good, sir. We shall have to pinch one!"

"That doesn't matter," declared Kerry glancing at Seton with a sudden twinkle discernible in his steely eyes. "What do you say, sir?"

"I agree with you entirely," replied Seton quietly. "We must find a boat, and lie off somewhere to watch for George. He should be worth following."

"We'll be moving, then," said the Leman Street detective. "It will be high tide in an hour."

They finished their coffee as quickly as possible; the stuff was not far below boiling-point. Then Jervis returned the cups to the counter. "Good night, Pat!" he cried, and rejoined Seton and Kerry.

As they came out into the desolation of the scrap heaps, the last traces of fog had disappeared and a steady breeze came up the river, fresh and salty from the Nore. Jervis led them in a north-easterly direction, threading a way through pyramids of rubbish, until with the wind in their teeth they came out upon the river bank at a point where the shore shelved steeply downwards. A number of boats lay on the shingle.

"We're pretty well opposite Greenwich Marshes," said Jervis. "You can just see one of the big gasometers. The end boat is George's."

"Have you searched it?" rapped Kerry, placing a fresh piece of chewing-gum between his teeth.

"I have, sir. Oh, he's too wise for that!"

"I propose," said Seton briskly, "that we borrow one of the other boats and pull down stream to where that short pier juts out. We can hide behind it and watch for our man. I take it he'll be bound up-stream, and the tide will help us to follow him quietly."

"Right," said Kerry. "We'll take the small dinghy. It's big enough."

He turned to Jervis.

"Nip across to the wooden stairs," he directed, "and tell Inspector White to stand by, but to keep out of sight. If we've started before you return, go back and join him."

"Very good, sir."

Jervis turned and disappeared into the mazes of rubbish, as Seton and Kerry grasped the boat and ran it down into the rising tide. Kerry boarding, Seton thrust it out into the river and climbed in over the stern.

"Phew! The current drags like a tow-boat!" said Kerry.

They were being drawn rapidly up-stream. But as Kerry seized the oars and began to pull steadily, this progress was checked. He could make little actual headway, however.

"The tide races round this bend like fury," he said. "Bear on the oars, sir."

Seton thereupon came to Kerry's assistance, and gradually the dinghy crept upon its course, until, below the little pier, they found a sheltered spot, where it was possible to run in and lie hidden. As they won this haven:

"Quiet!" said Seton. "Don't move the oars. Look! We were only just in time!"

Immediately above them, where the boats were beached, a man was coming down the slope, carrying a hurricane lantern. As Kerry and Seton watched, the man raised the lantern and swung it to and fro.

"Watch!" whispered Seton. "He's signalling to the Greenwich bank!"

Kerry's teeth snapped savagely together, and he chewed but made no reply, until:

"There it is!" he said rapidly. "On the marshes!"

A speck of light in the darkness it showed, a distant moving lantern on the curtain of the night. Although few would have credited Kerry with the virtue, he was a man of cultured imagination, and it seemed to him, as it seemed to Seton Pasha, that the dim light symbolized the life of the missing woman, of the woman who hovered between the gay world from which tragically she had vanished and some Chinese hell upon whose brink she hovered. Neither of the watchers was thinking of the crime and the criminal, of Sir Lucien Pyne or Kazmah, but of Mrs. Monte Irvin, mysterious victim of a mysterious tragedy. "Oh, Dan! ye must find her! ye must find her! Puir weak hairt—dinna ye ken how she is suffering!" Clairvoyantly, to Kerry's ears was borne an echo of his wife's words.

"The traffic!" he whispered. "If we lose George Martin tonight we deserve to lose the case!"

"I agree, Chief Inspector," said Seton quietly.

The grating sound made by a boat thrust out from a shingle beach came to their ears above the whispering of the tide. A ghostly figure in the dim light, George Martin clambered into his craft and took to the oars.

"If he's for the Greenwich bank," said Seton grimly, "he has a stiff task."

But for the Greenwich bank the boat was headed; and pulling mightily against the current, the man struck out into mid-stream. They watched him for some time, silently, noting how he fought against the tide, sturdily heading for the point at which the signal had shown. Then:

"What do you suggest?" asked Seton. "He may follow the Surrey bank up-stream."

"I suggest," said Kerry, "that we drift. Once in Limehouse Reach we'll hear him. There are no pleasure parties punting about that stretch."

"Let us pull out, then. I propose that we wait for him at some convenient point between the West India Dock and Limehouse Basin."

"Good," rapped Kerry, thrusting the boat out into the fierce current. "You may have spent a long time in the East, sir, but you're fairly wise on the geography of the lower Thames."

Gripped in the strongly running tide they were borne smoothly up-stream, using the oars merely for the purpose of steering. The gloomy mystery of the London river claimed them and imposed silence upon them, until familiar landmarks told of the northern bend of the Thames, and the light above the Lavender Pond shone out upon the unctuously moving water.

Each pulling a scull they headed in for the left bank.

"There's a wharf ahead," said Seton, looking back over his shoulder. "If we put in beside it we can wait there unobserved."

"Good enough," said Kerry.

They bent to the oars, stealing stroke by stroke out of the grip of the tide, and presently came to a tiny pool above the wharf structure, where it was possible to lie undisturbed by the eager current.

Those limitations which are common to all humanity and that guile which is peculiar to the Chinese veiled the fact from their ken that the deserted wharf, in whose shelter they lay, was at once the roof and the gateway of Sin Sin Wa's receiving office!

As the boat drew in to the bank, a Chinese boy who was standing on the wharf retired into the shadows. From a spot visible down-stream but invisible to the men in the boat, he signalled constantly with a hurricane lantern.

Three men from New Scotland Yard were watching the house of Sin Sin Wa, and Sin Sin Wa had given no sign of animation since, some hours earlier, he had extinguished his bedroom light. Yet George, drifting noiselessly up-stream, received a signal to the effect "police" while Seton Pasha and Chief Inspector Kerry lay below the biggest dope cache in London. Seton sometimes swore under his breath. Kerry chewed incessantly. But George never came.

At that eerie hour of the night when all things living, from the lowest to the highest, nor excepting Mother Earth herself, grow chilled, when all Nature's perishable handiwork feels the touch of death—a wild, sudden cry rang out, a wailing, sorrowful cry, that seemed to come from nowhere, from everywhere, from the bank, from the stream; that rose and fell and died sobbing into the hushed whisper of the tide.

Seton's hand fastened like a vise on to Kerry's shoulder, and:

"Merciful God!" he whispered; "what was it? *Who* was it?"

"If it wasn't a spirit it was a woman," replied Kerry hoarsely; "and a woman very near to her end."

"Kerry!"—Seton Pasha had dropped all formality—"Kerry—if it calls for all the men that Scotland Yard can muster, we must search every building, down to the smallest rathole in the floor, on this bank—and do it by dawn!"

"We'll do it," rapped Kerry.

PART FOURTH

THE EYE OF SIN SIN WA

CHAPTER XXXIII

CHINESE MAGIC

Detective-Sergeant Coombes and three assistants watched the house of Sin Sin Wa, and any one of the three would have been prepared to swear "on the Book" that Sin Sin Wa was sleeping. But he who watches a Chinaman watches an illusionist. He must approach his task in the spirit of a psychical inquirer who seeks to trap a bogus medium. The great Robert Houdin, one of the master wizards of modern times, quitted Petrograd by two gates at the same hour according to credible witnesses; but his performance sinks into insignificance beside that of a Chinese predecessor who flourished under one of the Ming emperors. The palace of this potentate was approached by gates, each having twelve locks, and each being watched by twelve guards. Nevertheless a distinguished member of the wizard family not only gained access to the imperial presence but also departed again unseen by any of the guards, and leaving all the gates locked behind him! If Detective-Sergeant Coombes had known this story he might not have experienced such complete confidence.

That door of Sin Sin Wa's establishment which gave upon a little backyard was oiled both lock and hinge so that it opened noiselessly. Like a shadow, like a ghost, Sin Sin Wa crept forth, closing the door behind him. He carried a sort of canvas kit-bag, so that one observing him might have concluded that he was "moving."

Resting his bag against the end wall, he climbed up by means of holes in the neglected brickwork until he could peer over the top. A faint smell of tobacco smoke greeted him: a detective was standing in the lane below. Soundlessly, Sin Sin Wa descended again. Raising his bag he lifted it lovingly until it rested upright upon the top of the wall and against the side of the house. The night was dark and still. Only a confused beating sound on the Surrey bank rose above the murmur of sleeping London.

From the rubbish amid which he stood, Sin Sin Wa selected a piece of rusty barrel-hoop. Cautiously he mounted upon a wooden structure built against the end wall and raised himself upright, surveying the prospect. Then he hurled the fragment of iron far along the lane, so that it bounded upon a strip of corrugated roofing in a yard twice removed from his own, and fell clattering among a neighbor's rubbish.

A short exclamation came from the detective in the lane. He could be heard walking swiftly away in the direction of the disturbance. And ere he had gone six paces, Sin Sin Wa was bending like an inverted U over the wall and was lowering his precious bag to the ground. Like a cat he sprang across and dropped noiselessly beside it.

"Hello! Who's there?" cried the detective, standing by the wall of the house which Sin Sin Wa had selected as a target.

Sin Sin Wa, bag in hand, trotted, soft of foot, across the lane and into the shadow of the dock-building. By the time that the C.I.D. man had decided to climb up and investigate the mysterious noise, Sin Sin Wa was on the other side of the canal and rapping gently upon the door of Sam Tûk's hairdressing establishment.

The door was opened so quickly as to suggest that someone had been posted there for the purpose. Sin Sin Wa entered and the door was closed again.

"Light, Ah Fung," he said in Chinese. "What news?"

The boy who had admitted him took a lamp from under a sort of rough counter and turned to Sin Sin Wa.

"George came with the boat, master, but I signalled to him that the red policeman and the agent who has hired the end room were watching."

"They are gone?"

"They gather men at the head depot and are searching house from house. She who sleeps below awoke and cried out. They heard her cry."

"George waits?"

"He waits, master. He will wait long if the gain is great."

"Good."

Sin Sin Wa shuffled across to the cellar stairs, followed by Ah Fung with the lamp. He descended, and, brushing away the carefully spread coal dust, inserted the piece of bent wire into the crevice and raised the secret trap. Bearing his bag upon his shoulder he went down into the tunnel.

"Reclose the door, Ah Fung," he said softly; "and be watchful."

As the boy replaced the stone trap, Sin Sin Wa struck a match. Then, having the lighted match held in one hand and carrying the bag in the other, he crept along the low passage to the door of the cache. Dropping the smouldering match-end, he opened the door and entered that secret warehouse for which so many people were seeking.

Seated in a cane chair by the oil-stove was the shrivelled figure of Sam Tûk, his bald head lolling sideways so that his big horn-rimmed spectacles resembled a figure 8. On the counter was set a ship's lantern. As Sin Sin Wa came in Sam Tûk slowly raised his head.

No greetings were exchanged, but Sin Sin Wa untied the neck of his kit-bag and drew out a large wicker cage. Thereupon: "Hello! hello!" remarked the occupant drowsily. "Number one p'lice chop lo! Sin Sin Wa—Sin Sin...."

"Come, my Tling-a-Ling," crooned Sin Sin Wa.

He opened the front of the cage and out stepped the raven onto his wrist. Sin Sin Wa raised his arm and Tling-a-Ling settled himself contentedly upon his master's shoulder.

Placing the empty cage on the counter. Sin Sin Wa plunged his hand down into the bag and drew out the gleaming wooden joss. This he set beside the cage. With never a glance at the mummy figure of Sam Tûk, he walked around the counter, raven on shoulder, and grasping the end of the laden shelves, he pulled the last section smoothly to the left, showing that it was attached to a sliding door. The establishments of Sin Sin Wa were as full of surprises as a Sicilian trinketbox.

The double purpose of the timbering which had been added to this old storage vault was now revealed. It not only served to enlarge the store-room, but also shut off from view a second portion of the cellar, smaller than the first, and containing appointments which indicated that it was sometimes inhabited.

There was an oil-stove in the room, which, like that adjoining it, was evidently unprovided with any proper means of ventilation. A paper-shaded lamp hung from the low roof. The floor was covered with matting, and there were arm-chairs, a divan and other items of furniture, which had been removed from Mrs. Sin's sanctum in the dismantled House of a Hundred Raptures. In a recess a bed was placed, and as Sin Sin Wa came in Mrs. Sin was standing by the bed looking down at a woman who lay there.

Mrs. Sin wore her kimona of embroidered green silk and made a striking picture in that sordid setting. Her black hair she had dyed a fashionable shade of red. She glanced rapidly across her shoulder at Sin Sin Wa—a glance of contempt with which was mingled faint distrust.

"So," she said, in Chinese, "you have come at last." Sin Sin Wa smiled. "They watched the old fox," he replied. "But their eyes were as the eyes of the mole."

Still aside, contemptuously, the woman regarded him, and:

"Suppose they are keener than you think?" she said. "Are you sure you have not led them—here?"

"The snail may not pursue the hawk," murmured Sin Sin Wa; "nor the eye of the bat follow his flight."

"Smartest leg," remarked the raven.

"Yes, yes, my little friend," crooned Sin Sin Wa, "very soon now you shall see the paddy-fields of Ho-Nan and watch the great Yellow River sweeping eastward to the sea."

"Pah!" said Mrs. Sin. "Much—very much—you care about the paddy-fields of Ho-Nan, and little, oh, very little, about the dollars and the traffic! You have my papers?"

"All are complete. With those dollars for which I care not, a man might buy the world—if he had but enough of the dollars. You are well known in Poplar as 'Mrs. Jacobs,' and your identity is easily established—as 'Mrs. Jacobs.' You join the *Mahratta* at the Albert Dock. I have bought you a post as stewardess."

Mrs. Sin tossed her head. "And Juan?"

"What can they prove against your Juan if *you* are missing?"

Mrs. Sin nodded towards the bed.

With slow and shuffling steps Sin Sin Wa approached. He continued to smile, but his glittering eye held even less of mirth than usual. Tucking his hands into his sleeves, he stood and looked down—at Rita Irvin.

Her face had acquired a waxen quality, but some of her delicate coloring still lingered, lending her a ghastly and mask-like aspect. Her nostrils and lips were blanched, however, and possessed a curiously pinched appearance. It was impossible to detect the fact that she breathed, and her long lashes lay motionless upon her cheeks.

Sin Sin Wa studied her silently for some time, then:

"Yes," he murmured, "she is beautiful. But women are like adder's eggs. He is a fool who warms them in his bosom." He turned his slow regard upon Mrs. Sin. "You have stained your hair to look even as hers. It was discreet, my wife. But one is beautiful and many-shadowed like a copper vase, and the other is like a winter sunset on the poppy-fields. You remind me of the angry red policeman, and I tremble."

"Tremble as much as you like," said Mrs. Sin scornfully, "but *do* something, think; don't leave everything to me. She screamed tonight— and someone heard her. They are searching the river bank from door to door."

"Lo!" murmured Sin Sin Wa, "even this I had learned, nor failed to heed the beating of a distant drum. And why did she scream?"

"I was—keeping her asleep; and the prick of the needle woke her."

"*Tchée, tchée,*" crooned Sin Sin Wa, his voice sinking lower and lower and his eye nearly closing. "But still she lives—and is beautiful."

"Beautiful!" mocked Mrs. Sin. "A doll-woman, bloodless and nerveless!"

"So—so. Yet she, so bloodless and nerveless, unmasked the secret of Kazmah, and she, so bloodless and nerveless, struck down—"

Mrs. Sin ground her teeth together audibly.

"Yes, yes!" she said in sibilant Chinese. "She is a robber, a thief, a murderess." She bent over the unconscious woman, her jewel-laden fingers crooked and menacing. "With my bare hands I would strangle her, but—"

"There must be no marks of violence when she is found in the river. *Tchée, chée*—it is a pity."

"Number one p'lice chop, lo!" croaked the raven, following this remark with the police-whistle imitation.

Mrs. Sin turned and stared fiercely at the one-eyed bird.

"Why do you bring that evil, croaking thing here?" she demanded. "Have we not enough risks?"

Sin Sin Wa smiled patiently.

"Too many," he murmured. "For failure is nothing but the taking of seven risks when six were enough. Come—let us settle our affairs. The 'Jacobs' account is closed, but it is only a question of hours or days before the police learn that the wharf as well as the house belongs to someone of that name. We have drawn our last dollar from the traffic, my wife. Our stock we are resigned to lose. So let us settle our affairs."

"Smartest—smartest," croaked Tling-a-Ling, and rattled ghostly castanets.

CHAPTER XXXIV

ABOVE AND BELOW

"Thank the guid God I see ye alive, Dan," said Mary Kerry.

Having her husband's dressing-gown over her night attire, and her usually neat hair in great disorder, she stood just within the doorway of the little dining-room at Spenser Road, her face haggard and the fey light in her eyes. Kerry, seated in the armchair dressed as he had come in from the street, a parody of his neat self with mud on his shoes and streaks of green slime on his overall, raised his face from his hands and stared at her wearily.

"I awakened wi' a cry at some hour afore the dawn," she whispered stretching out her hands and looking like a wild-eyed prophetess of old. "My hairt beat sair fast and then grew caud. I droppit on my knees and prayed as I ha' ne'er prayed afore. Dan, Dan, I thought ye were gene from me."

"I nearly was," said Kerry, a faint spark of his old truculency lighting up the weary eyes. "The man from Whitehall only missed me by a miracle."

"'Twas the miracle o' prayer, Dan," declared his wife in a low, awe-stricken voice. "For as I prayed, a great comfort came to me an' a great peace. The second sight was wi' me, Dan, and I saw, no' yersel'—whereby I seemed to ken that ye were safe—but a puir dying soul stretched on a bed o' sorrow. At the fuit o' the bed was standing a fearsome figure o' a man—yellow and wicked, wi' his hands tuckit in his sleeves. I thought 'twas a veesion that was opening up tee me and that a' was about to be made clear, when as though a curtain had been droppit before my een, it went awe' an' I kenned it nae more; but plain—plain, I heerd the howling o' a dog."

Kerry started and clutched the arms of the chair.

"A dog!" he said. "A dog!"

"The howling o' a sma' dog," declared his wife; "and I thought 'twas a portent, an' the great fear came o'er me again. But as I prayed 'twas unfolder to me that the portent was no' for yersel' but for her—the puir weak hairt ye ha' tee save."

She ceased speaking and the strange fey light left her eyes. She dropped upon her knees beside Kerry, bending her head and throwing her arms about him. He glanced down at her tenderly and laid his hands upon her shoulders; but he was preoccupied, and the next moment, his jaws moving mechanically, he was staring straight before him.

"A dog," he muttered, "a dog!"

Mary Kerry did not move; until, a light of understanding coming into Kerry's fierce eyes, he slowly raised her and stood upright himself.

"I have it!" he said. "Mary, the case is won! Twenty men have spent the night and early morning beating the river bank so that the very rats have been driven from their holes. Twenty men have failed where a dog would have succeeded. Mary, I must be off."

"Ye're no goin' out again, Dan. Ye're weary tee death."

"I must, my dear, and it's you who send me."

"But, Dan, where are ye goin'?"

Kerry grabbed his hat and cane from the sideboard upon which they lay, and:

"I'm going for the dog!" he rapped.

Weary as he was and travel-stained, for once neglectful of that neatness upon which he prided himself, he set out, hope reborn in his heart. His assertion that the very rats had been driven from their holes was scarce an exaggeration. A search-party of twenty men, hastily mustered and conducted by Kerry and Seton Pasha, had explored every house, every shop, every wharf, and, as Kerry believed, every cellar adjoining the bank, between Limehouse Basin and the dock gates. Where access had been denied them or where no one had resided they had never hesitated to force an entrance. But no trace had they found of those whom they sought.

For the first time within Kerry's memory, or, indeed, within the memory of any member of the Criminal Investigation Department, Detective-Sergeant Coombes had ceased to smile when the appalling truth was revealed to him that Sin Sin Wa had vanished—that Sin Sin Wa had mysteriously joined that invisible company which included Kazmah, Mrs. Sin and Mrs. Monte Irvin. Not a word of reprimand did the Chief Inspector utter, but his eyes seemed to emit sparks. Hands plunged deeply in his pockets he had turned away, and not even Seton Pasha had dared to speak to him for fully five minutes.

Kerry began to regard the one-eyed Chinaman with a superstitious fear which he strove in vain to stifle. That any man could have succeeded in converting a *chandu-khân* such as that described by Mollie Gretna into a filthy deserted dwelling such as that visited by Kerry, within the space of some thirty-six hours, was well nigh incredible. But the Chief Inspector had deduced (correctly) that the exotic appointments depicted by Mollie were all of a detachable nature—merely masking the filthiness beneath; so that at the shortest notice the House of a Hundred Raptures could be dismantled. The communicating door was a larger proposition, but that it was one within the compass of Sin Sin Wa its effectual disappearance sufficiently demonstrated.

Doubtless (Kerry mused savagely) the appointments of the opium-house had been smuggled into that magically hidden cache which now concealed the conjurer Sin Sin Wa as well as the other members of the Kazmah company. How any man of flesh and blood could have escaped from a six-roomed house surrounded by detectives surpassed Kerry's powers of imagination. How any apartment large enough to contain a mouse, much less half a dozen human beings, could exist anywhere within the area covered by the search-party he failed to understand, nor was he prepared to admit it humanly possible.

Kerry chartered a taxicab by Brixton Town Hall and directed the man to drive to Prince's Gate. To the curious glances of certain of his neighbors who had never before seen the Chief Inspector otherwise than a model of cleanliness and spruceness he was indifferent. But the manner in which the taxi-driver looked him up and down penetrated through the veil of abstraction which hitherto had rendered Kerry impervious to all external impressions, and:

"Give me another look like that, my lad," he snapped furiously, "and I'll bash your head through your blasted wind-screen."

A ready retort trembled upon the cabman's tongue, but a glance into the savage blue eyes reduced him to fearful silence. Kerry entered the cab and banged the door; and the man drove off positively trembling with indignation.

Deep in reflection the Chief Inspector was driven westward through the early morning traffic. Fine rain was falling, and the streets presented that curiously drab appearance which only London streets can present in all its dreary perfection. Workers bound Cityward fought for places inside trams and buses. A hundred human comedies and tragedies were to be witnessed upon the highways; but to all of them Kerry was blind as he was deaf to the din of workaday Babylon. In spirit he was roaming the bank of old Father Thames where the river sweeps eastward below Limehouse Causeway—wonder-stricken before the magic of the one-eyed wizard who could at will efface himself as an artist rubs out a drawing, who could camouflage a drug warehouse so successfully that human skill, however closely addressed to the task, failed utterly to detect its whereabouts. Above the discord of the busy streets he heard again and again that cry in the night which had come from a hapless prisoner whom they were powerless to succor. He beat his cane upon the floor of the cab and swore savagely and loudly. The intimidated cabman, believing these demonstrations designed to urge him to a greater speed, performed feats of driving calculated to jeopardize his license. But still the savage passenger stamped and cursed, so that the cabby began to believe that a madman was seated behind him.

At the corner of Kennington Oval Kerry was effectually aroused to the realities. A little runabout car passed his cab, coming from a southerly direction. Proceeding at a rapid speed it was lost in the traffic ahead. Unconsciously Kerry had glanced at the occupants and had recognized Margaret Halley and Seton Pasha. The old spirit of rivalry between himself and the man from Whitehall leapt up hotly within Kerry's breast.

"Now where the hell has *he* been!" he muttered.

As a matter of fact, Seton Pasha, acting upon a suggestion of Margaret's had been to Brixton Prison to interview Juan Mareno who lay there under arrest. Contents bills announcing this arrest as the latest public development in the Bond Street murder case were to be seen upon every news-stand; yet the problem of that which had brought

Seton to the south of London was one with which Kerry grappled in vain. He had parted from the Home Office agent in the early hours of the morning, and their parting had been one of mutual despair which neither had sought to disguise.

It was a coincidence which a student of human nature might have regarded as significant, that whereas Kerry had taken his troubles home to his wife, Seton Pasha had sought inspiration from Margaret Halley; and whereas the guidance of Mary Kerry had led the Chief Inspector to hurry in quest of Rita Irvin's spaniel, the result of Seton's interview with Margaret had been an equally hurried journey to the big jail.

Unhappily Seton had failed to elicit the slightest information from the saturnine Mareno. Unmoved alike by promises or threats, he had coolly adhered to his original evidence.

So, while the authorities worked feverishly and all England reading of the arrest of Mareno inquired indignantly, "But who is Kazmah, and where is Mrs. Monte Irvin?" Sin Sin Wa placidly pursued his arrangements for immediate departure to the paddyfields of Ho-Nan, and sometimes in the weird crooning voice with which he addressed the raven he would sing a monotonous chant dealing with the valley of the Yellow River where the opium-poppy grows. Hidden in the cunning vault, the search had passed above him; and watchful on a quay on the Surrey shore whereto his dinghy was fastened, George Martin awaited the signal which should tell him that Kazmah and Company were ready to leave. Any time after dark he expected to see the waving lantern and to collect his last payment from the traffic.

At the very hour that Kerry was hastening to Prince's Gate, Sin Sin Wa sat before the stove in the drug cache, the green-eyed joss upon his knee. With a fragment of chamois leather he lovingly polished the leering idol, crooning softly to himself and smiling his mirthless smile. Perched upon his shoulder the raven studied this operation with apparent interest, his solitary eye glittering bead-like. Upon the opposite side of the stove sat the ancient Sam Tûk and at intervals of five minutes or more he would slowly nod his hairless head.

The sliding door which concealed the inner room was partly open, and from the opening there shone forth a dim red light, cast by the paper-shaded lamp which illuminated the place. The coarse voice of the Cuban-Jewess rose and fell in a ceaseless half-muttered soliloquy, indescribably unpleasant but to which Sin Sin Wa was evidently indifferent.

Propped up amid cushions on the divan which once had formed part of the furniture of the House of a Hundred Raptures, Mrs. Sin was smoking opium. The long bamboo pipe had fallen from her listless fingers, and her dark eyes were partly glazed. Buddha-like immobility was claiming her, but it had not yet effaced that expression of murderous malice with which the smoker contemplated the unconscious woman who lay upon the bed at the other end of the room.

As the moments passed the eyes of Mrs. Sin grew more and more glazed. Her harsh voice became softened, and presently: "Ah!" she whispered; "so you wait to smoke with me?"

Immobile she sat propped up amid the cushions, and only her full lips moved.

"Two pipes are nothing to Cy," she murmured. "He smokes five. But you are not going to smoke?"

Again she paused, then:

"Ah, my Lucy. You smoke with *me?*" she whispered coaxingly.

Chandu had opened the poppy gates. Mrs. Sin was conversing with her dead lover.

"Something has changed you," she sighed. "You are different—lately. You have lots of money now. Your investments have been good. You want to become—respectable, eh?"

Slightly—ever so slightly—the red lips curled upwards. No sound of life came from the woman lying white and still in the bed. But through the partly open door crept snatches of Sin Sin Wa's crooning melody.

"Yet once," she murmured, "yet once I seemed beautiful to you, Lucy. For La Belle Lola you forgot that English pride." She laughed softly. "You forgot Sin Sin Wa. If there had been no Lola you would never have escaped from Buenos Ayres with your life, my Lucy. You forgot that English pride, and did not ask me where I got them from—the ten thousand dollars to buy your 'honor' back."

She became silent, as if listening to the dead man's reply. Finally:

"No—I do not reproach you, my dear," she whispered. "You have paid me back a thousand fold, and Sin Sin Wa, the old fox, grows rich and fat. Today we hold the traffic in our hands, Lucy. The old fox cares only for his money. Before it is too late let us go—you and I. Do you remember Havana, and the two months of heaven we spent there? Oh, let us go back to Havana, Lucy. Kazmah has made us rich. Let Kazmah die.... You smoke with me?"

Again she became silent, then:

"Very likely," she murmured; "very likely I know why you don't smoke. You have promised your pretty little friend that you will stay awake and see that nobody tries to cut her sweet white throat."

She paused momentarily, then muttered something rapidly in Spanish, followed by a short, guttural phrase in Chinese.

"Why do you bring her to the house?" she whispered hoarsely. "And you brought her to Kazmah's. Ah! I see. Now everybody says you are changed. Yes. She is a charming friend."

The Buddha-like face became suddenly contorted, and as suddenly grew placid again.

"I know! I know!" Mrs. Sin muttered harshly. "Do you think I am blind! If she had been like any of the others, do you suppose it would have mattered to *me?* But you *respect* her—you *respect*...." Her voice died away to an almost inaudible whisper: "I don't believe you. You are telling me lies. But you have always told me lies; one more does not matter, I suppose.... How strong you are. You have hurt my wrists. You will smoke with me now?"

She ceased speaking abruptly, and abruptly resumed again:

"And I do as you wish—I do as you wish. How can I keep her from it except by making the price so high that she cannot afford to buy it? I tell you I do it. I bargain for the pink and white boy, Quentin, because I want her to be indebted to him—because I want her to be so sorry for him that she lets him take her away from *you!* Why should you *respect* her—"

Silence fell upon the drugged speaker. Sin Sin Wa could be heard crooning softly about the Yellow River and the mountain gods who sent it sweeping down through the valleys where the opium-poppy grows.

"Go, Juan," hissed Mrs. Sin. "I say—*go!*"

Her voice changed eerily to a deep, mocking bass; and Rita Irvin lying, a pallid wraith of her once lovely self, upon the untidy bed, stirred slightly—her lashes quivering. Her eyes opened and stared straightly upward at the low, dirty ceiling, horror growing in their shadowy depths.

CHAPTER XXXV

BEYOND THE VEIL

Rita Irvin's awakening was no awakening in the usually accepted sense of the word; it did not even represent a lifting of the veil which cut her off from the world, but no more than a momentary perception of the existence of such a veil and of the existence of something behind it. Upon the veil, in grey smoke, the name "Kazmah" was written in moving characters. Beyond the veil, dimly divined, was life.

As of old the victims of the Inquisition, waking or dreaming, beheld ever before them the instrument of their torture, so before this woman's racked and half-numbed mind panoramically passed, an endless pageant, the incidents of the night which had cut her off from living men and women. She tottered on the border-line which divides sanity from madness. She was learning what Sir Lucien had meant when, once, long long ago, in some remote time when she was young and happy and had belonged to a living world, he had said "a day is sure to come." It had come, that "day." It had dawned when she had torn the veil before Kazmah—and that veil had enveloped her ever since. All that had preceded the fatal act was blotted out, blurred and indistinct; all that had succeeded it lived eternally, passing, an endless pageant, before her tortured mind.

The horror of the moment when she had touched the hands of the man seated in the big ebony chair was of such kind that no subsequent terrors had supplanted it. For those long, slim hands of the color of old ivory were cold, rigid, lifeless—the hands of a corpse! Thus the pageant began, and it continued as hereafter, memory and delusion taking the stage in turn.

Complete darkness came.

Rita uttered a wild cry of horror and loathing, shrinking back from the thing which sat in the ebony chair. She felt that consciousness was slipping from her; felt herself falling, and shrieked to know herself helpless and alone with Kazmah. She groped for support, but found none; and, moaning, she sank down, and was unconscious of her fall.

A voice awakened her. Someone knelt beside her in the darkness, supporting her; someone who spoke wildly, despairingly, but with a strange, emotional reverence curbing the passion in his voice.

"Rita—my Rita! What have they done to you? Speak to me.... Oh God! Spare her to me.... Let her hate me for ever, but spare her—spare her. Rita, speak to me! I tried, heaven hear me, to save you little girl. I only want you to be happy!"

She felt herself being lifted gently, tenderly. And as though the man's passionate entreaty had called her back from the dead, she reentered into life and strove to realize what had happened.

Sir Lucien was supporting her, and she found it hard to credit the fact that it was he, the hard, nonchalant man of the world she knew, who had spoken. She clutched his arm with both hands.

"Oh, Lucy!" she whispered. "I am so frightened—and so ill."

"Thank God," he said huskily, "she is alive. Lean against me and try to stand up. We must get away from here."

Rita managed to stand upright, clinging wildly to Sir Lucien. A square, vaguely luminous opening became visible to her. Against it, silhouetted, she could discern part of the outline of Kazmah's chair. She drew back, uttering a low, sobbing cry. Sir Lucien supported her, and:

"Don't be afraid, dear," he said reassuringly. "Nothing shall hurt you."

He pushed open a door, and through it shone the same vague light which she had seen in the opening behind the chair. Sir Lucien spoke rapidly in a language which sounded like Spanish. He was answered by a perfect torrent of words in the same tongue.

Fiercely he cried something back at the hidden speaker.

A shriek of rage, of frenzy, came out of the darkness. Rita felt that consciousness was about to leave her again. She swayed forward dizzily, and a figure which seemed to belong to delirium—a lithe shadow out of which gleamed a pair of wild eyes—leapt upon her. A knife glittered....

In order to have repelled the attack, Sir Lucien would have had to release Rita, who was clinging to him, weak and terror-stricken. Instead he threw himself before her.... She saw the knife enter his shoulder....

Through absolute darkness she sank down into a land of chaotic nightmare horrors. Great bells clanged maddeningly. Impish hands plucked at her garments, dragged her hair. She was hurried this way and that, bruised, torn, and tossed helpless upon a sea of liquid brass. Through vast avenues lined with yellow, immobile Chinese faces she was borne upon a bier. Oblique eyes looked into hers. Knives which glittered greenly in the light of lamps globular and suspended in immeasurable space, were hurled at her in showers....

Sir Lucien stood before her, supporting her; and all the knives buried themselves in his body. She tried to cry out, but no sound could she utter. Darkness fell again....

A Chinaman was bending over her. His hands were tucked in his loose sleeves. He smiled, and his smile was hideous but friendly. He was strangely like Sin Sin Wa, save that he did not lack an eye.

Rita found herself lying in an untidy bed in a room laden with opium fumes and dimly lighted. On a table beside her were the remains of a meal. She strove to recall having partaken of food, but was unsuccessful....

There came a blank—then a sharp, stabbing pain in her right arm. She thought it was the knife, and shrieked wildly again and again....

Years seemingly elapsed, years of agony spent amid oblique eyes which floated in space unattached to any visible body, amid reeking fumes and sounds of ceaseless conflict. Once she heard the cry of some bird, and thought it must be the parakeet which eternally sat on a branch of a lonely palm in the heart of the Great Sahara.... Then, one night, when she lay shrinking from the plucking yellow hands which reached out of the darkness:

"Tell me your dream," boomed a deep, mocking voice; "and I will read its portent!"

She opened her eyes. She lay in the untidy bed in the room which was laden with the fumes of *chandu*. She stared upward at the low, dirty ceiling.

"Why do you come to *me* with your stories of desperation?" continued the mocking voice. "You have insisted upon seeing me. I am here."

Rita managed to move her head so that she could see more of the room.

On a divan at the other end of the place, propped up by a number of garish cushions, Rita beheld Mrs. Sin. The long bamboo pipe had fallen from her listless fingers. Her face wore an expression of mystic rapture, like that characterizing the features of some Chinese Buddhas....

In the other corner of the divan, contemplating her from under heavy brows, sat *Kazmah*....

CHAPTER XXXVI

SAM TÛK MOVES

Chinatown was being watched as Chinatown had never been watched before, even during the most stringent enforcement of the Defence of the Realm Act. K Division was on its mettle, and Scotland Yard had sent to aid Chief Inspector Kerry every man that could be spared to the task. The River Police, too, were aflame with zeal; for every officer in the service whose work lay east of London Bridge had appropriated to himself the stigma implied by the creation of Lord Wrexborough's commission.

"Corners" in foodstuffs, metals, and other indispensable commodities are appreciated by every man, because every man knows such things to exist; but a corner in drugs was something which the East End police authorities found very difficult to grasp. They could not free their minds of the traditional idea that every second Chinaman in the Causeway was a small importer. They were seeking a hundred lesser stores instead of one greater one. Not all Seton's quiet explanations nor Kerry's savage language could wean the higher local officials from their ancient beliefs. They failed to conceive the idea of a wealthy syndicate conducted by an educated Chinaman and backed, covered, and protected by a crooked gentleman and accomplished man of affairs.

Perhaps they knew and perhaps they knew not, that during the period ruled by D.O.R.A. as much as £25 was paid by habitués for one pipe of *chandu*. The power of gold is often badly estimated by an official whose horizon is marked by a pension. This is mere lack of imagination, and no more reflects discredit upon a man than lack of hair on his crown or of color in his cheeks. Nevertheless, it may prove very annoying.

Towards the close of an afternoon which symbolized the worst that London's particular climate can do in the matter of drizzling rain and gloom, Chief Inspector Kerry, carrying an irritable toy spaniel, came out of a turning which forms a V with Limehouse Canal, into a narrow street which runs parallel with the Thames. He had arrived at the conclusion that the neighborhood was sown so thickly with detectives that one could not throw a stone without hitting one. Yet Sin Sin Wa had quietly left his abode and had disappeared from official ken.

Three times within the past ten minutes the spaniel had tried to bite Kerry, nor was Kerry blind to the amusement which his burden had occasioned among the men of K Division whom he had met on his travels. Finally, as he came out into the riverside lane, the ill-tempered little animal essayed a fourth, and successful, attempt, burying his wicked white teeth in the Chief Inspector's wrist.

Kerry hooked his finger into the dog's collar, swung the yapping animal above his head, and hurled it from him into the gloom and rain mist.

"Hell take the blasted thing!" he shouted. "I'm done with it!"

He tenderly sucked his wounded wrist, and picking up his cane, which he had dropped, he looked about him and swore savagely. Of Seton Pasha he had had news several times during the day, and he was aware that the Home Office agent was not idle. But to that old rivalry which had leapt up anew when he had seen Seton near Kennington oval had succeeded a sort of despair; so that now he would have welcomed the information that Seton had triumphed where he had failed. A furious hatred of the one-eyed Chinaman around whom he was convinced the mystery centred had grown up within his mind. At that hour he would gladly have resigned his post and sacrificed his pension to know that Sin Sin Wa was under lock and key. His outlook was official, and accordingly peculiar. He regarded the murder of Sir Lucien Pyne and the flight or abduction of Mrs. Monte Irvin as mere minor incidents in a case wherein Sin Sin Wa figured as the chief culprit. Nothing had acted so powerfully to bring about this conviction in the mind of the Chief Inspector as the inexplicable disappearance of the Chinaman under circumstances which had apparently precluded such a possibility.

A whimpering cry came to Kerry's ears; and because beneath the mask of ferocity which he wore a humane man was concealed: "Flames!" he snapped; "perhaps I've broken the poor little devil's leg."

Shaking a cascade of water from the brim of his neat bowler, he set off through the murk towards the spot from whence the cries of the spaniel seemed to proceed. A few paces brought him to the door of a dirty little shop. In a window close beside it appeared the legend:

SAM TÛK,
BARBER.

The spaniel crouched by the door whining and scratching, and as Kerry came up it raised its beady black eyes to him with a look which, while it was not unfearful, held an unmistakable appeal. Kerry stood watching the dog for a moment, and as he watched he became conscious of an exhilarated pulse.

He tried the door and found it to be open. Thereupon he entered a dirty little shop, which he remembered to have searched in person in the grey dawn of the day which now was entering upon a premature dusk. The dog ran in past him, crossed the gloomy shop, and raced down into a tiny coal cellar, which likewise had been submitted during the early hours of the morning to careful scrutiny under the directions of the Chief Inspector.

A Chinese boy, who had been the only occupant of the place on that occasion and who had given his name as Ah Fung, was surprised by the sudden entrance of man and dog in the act of spreading coal dust with his fingers upon a portion of the paved floor. He came to his feet with a leap and confronted Kerry. The spaniel began to scratch feverishly upon the spot where the coal dust had been artificially spread. Kerry's eyes gleamed like steel. He shot out his hand and grasped the Chinaman by his long hair. "Open that trap," he said, "or I'll break you in half!"

Ah Fung's oblique eyes regarded him with an expression difficult to analyze, but partly it was murder. He made no attempt to obey the order. Meanwhile the dog, whining and scratching furiously, had exposed the greater part of a stone slab somewhat larger than those adjoining it, and having a large crack or fissure in one end.

"For the last time," said Kerry, drawing the man's head back so that his breath began to whistle through his nostrils, "open that trap."

As he spoke he released Ah Fung, and Ah Fung made one wild leap towards the stairs. Kerry's fist caught him behind the ear as he sprang, and he went down like a dead man upon a small heap of coal which filled the angle of the cellar.

Breathing rapidly and having his teeth so tightly clenched that his maxillary muscles protruded lumpishly, Kerry stood looking at the fallen man. But Ah Fung did not move. The dog had ceased to scratch, and now stood uttering short staccato barks and looking up at the Chief Inspector. Otherwise there was no sound in the house, above or below.

Kerry stooped, and with his handkerchief scrupulously dusted the stone slab. The spaniel, resentment forgotten, danced excitedly beside him and barked continuously.

"There's some sort of hook to fit in that crack," muttered Kerry.

He began to hunt about among the debris which littered one end of the cellar, testing fragment after fragment, but failing to find any piece of scrap to suit his purpose. By sheer perseverance rather than by any process of reasoning, he finally hit upon the piece of bent wire which was the key to this door of Sin Sin Wa's drug warehouse.

One short exclamation of triumph he muttered at the moment that his glance rested upon it, and five seconds later he had the trapdoor open and was peering down into the narrow pit in which wooden steps rested. The spaniel began to bark wildly, whereupon Kerry grasped him, tucked him under his arm, and ran up to the room above, where he deposited the furiously wriggling animal. He stepped quickly back again and closed the upper door. By this act he plunged the cellar into complete darkness, and accordingly he took out from the pocket of his rain-drenched overall the electric torch which he always carried. Directing its ray downwards into the cellar, he perceived Ah Fung move and toss his hand above his head. He also detected a faint rattling sound.

"Ah!" said Kerry.

He descended, and stooping over the unconscious man extracted from the pocket of his baggy blue trousers four keys upon a ring. At these Kerry stared eagerly. Two of them belonged to yale locks; the third was a simple English barrel-key, which probably fitted a padlock; but the fourth was large and complicated.

"Looks like the key of a jail," he said aloud.

He spoke with unconscious prescience. This was the key of the door of the vault. Removing his overall, Kerry laid it with his cane upon the scrap-heap, then he climbed down the ladder and found himself in the mouth of that low timbered tunnel, like a trenchwork, which owed its existence to the cunning craftsmanship of Sin Sin Wa. Stooping uncomfortably, he made his way along the passage until the massive door confronted him. He was in no doubt as to which key to employ; his mental condition was such that he was indifferent to the dangers which probably lay before him.

The well-oiled lock operated smoothly. Kerry pushed the door open and stepped briskly into the vault.

His movements, from the moment that he had opened the trap, had been swift and as nearly noiseless as the difficulties of the task had permitted. Nevertheless, they had not been so silent as to escape the attention of the preternaturally acute Sin Sin Wa. Kerry found the place occupied only by the aged Sam Tûk. A bright fire burned in the stove, and a ship's lantern stood upon the counter. Dense chemical fumes rendered the air difficult to breathe; but the shelves, once laden with the largest illicit collection of drugs in London, were bare.

Kerry's fierce eyes moved right and left; his jaws worked automatically. Sam Tûk sat motionless, his hands concealed in his sleeves, bending decrepitly forward in his chair. Then:

"Hi! Guy Fawkes!" rapped Kerry, striding forward. "Who's been letting off fire-works?"

Sam Tûk nodded senilely, but spoke not a word.

Kerry stooped and stared into the heart of the fire. A dense coat of white ash lay upon the embers. He grasped the shoulder of the aged Chinaman, and pushed him back so that he could look into the bleared eyes behind the owlish spectacles.

"Been cleaning up the 'evidence,' eh?" he shouted. "This joint stinks of opium and a score of other dopes. Where are the gang?" He shook the yielding, ancient frame. "Where's the smart with one eye?"

But Sam Tûk merely nodded, and as Kerry released his hold sank forward again, nodding incessantly.

"H'm, you're a hard case," said the Chief Inspector. "A couple of witnesses like you and the jury would retire to Bedlam!"

He stood glaring fiercely at the limp frame of the old Chinaman, and as he glared his expression changed. Lying on the dirty floor not a yard from Sam Tûk's feet was a ball of leaf opium!

"Ha!" exclaimed Kerry, and he stooped to pick it up.

As he did so, with a lightning movement of which the most astute observer could never have supposed him capable, Sam Tûk whipped a loaded rubber tube from his sleeve and struck Kerry a shrewd blow across the back of the skull.

The Chief Inspector, without word or cry, collapsed upon his knees, and then fell gently forward—forward—and toppled face downwards before his assailant. His bowler fell off and rolled across the dirty floor.

Sam Tûk sank deeply into his chair, and his toothless jaws worked convulsively. The skinny hand which clutched the piece of tubing twitched and shook, so that the primitive deadly weapon fell from its wielder's grasp.

Silently, that set of empty shelves nearest to the inner wall of the vault slid open, and Sin Sin Wa came out. He, too, carried his hands tucked in his sleeves, and his yellow, pock-marked face wore its eternal smile.

"Well done," he crooned softly in Chinese. "Well done, bald father of wisdom. The dogs draw near, but the old fox sleeps not."

CHAPTER XXXVII

SETON PASHA REPORTS

At about the time that the fearless Chief Inspector was entering the establishment of Sam Tûk Seton Pasha was reporting to Lord Wrexborough in Whitehall. His nautical disguise had served its purpose, and he had now finally abandoned it, recognizing that he had to deal with a criminal of genius to whom disguise merely afforded matter for amusement.

In his proper person, as Greville Seton, he afforded a marked contrast to that John Smiles, seaman, who had sat in a top room in Limehouse with Chief Inspector Kerry. And although he had to report failure, the grim, bronzed face and bright grey eyes must have inspired in the heart of any thoughtful observer confidence in ultimate success. Lord Wrexborough, silver-haired, florid and dignified, sat before a vast table laden with neatly arranged dispatch-boxes, books, documents tied with red tape, and the other impressive impedimenta which characterize the table of a Secretary of State. Quentin Gray, unable to conceal his condition of nervous excitement, stared from a window down into Whitehall.

"I take it, then, Seton," Lord Wrexborough was saying, "that in your opinion—although perhaps it is somewhat hastily formed—there is and has been no connivance between officials and receivers of drugs?"

"That is my opinion, sir. The traffic has gradually and ingeniously been 'ringed' by a wealthy group. Smaller dealers have been bought out or driven out, and today I believe it would be difficult, if not impossible, to obtain opium, cocaine, or veronal illicitly anywhere in London. Kazmah and Company had the available stock cornered. Of course, now that they are out of business, no doubt others will step in.

It is a trade that can never be suppressed under existing laws."

"I see, I see," muttered Lord Wrexborough, adjusting his pince-nez. "You also believe that Kazmah and Company are in hiding within what you term"—he consulted a written page—"the 'Causeway area'? And you believe that the man called Sin Sin Wa is the head of the organization?"

"I believe the late Sir Lucien Pyne was the actual head of the group," said Seton bluntly. "But Sin Sin Wa is the acting head. In view of his physical peculiarities, I don't quite see how he's going to escape us, either, sir. His wife has a fighting chance, and as for Mohammed el-Kazmah, he might sail for anywhere tomorrow, and we should never know. You see, we have no description of the man."

"His passports?" murmured Lord Wrexborough.

Seton Pasha smiled grimly.

"Not an insurmountable difficulty, sir," he replied, "but Sin Sin Wa is a marked man. He has the longest and thickest pigtail which I ever saw on a human scalp. I take it he is a Southerner of the old school; therefore, he won't cut it off. He has also only one eye, and while there are many one-eyed Chinamen, there are few one-eyed Chinamen who possess pigtails like a battleship's hawser. Furthermore, he travels with a talking raven, and I'll swear he won't leave it behind. On the other hand, he is endowed with an amount of craft which comes very near to genius."

"And—Mrs. Monte Irvin?"

Quentin Gray turned suddenly, and his boyish face was very pale.

"Seton, Seton!" he said. "For God's sake tell me the truth! Do you think—"

He stopped, choking emotionally. Seton Pasha watched him with that cool, confident stare which could either soothe or irritate; and:

"She was alive this morning, Gray," he replied quietly, "we heard her. You may take it from me that they will offer her no violence. I shall say no more."

Lord Wrexborough cleared his throat and took up a document from the table.

"Your remark raises another point, Quentin," he said sternly, "which has to be settled today. Your appointment to Cairo was confirmed this morning. You sail on Tuesday."

Quentin Gray turned again abruptly and stared out of the window.

"You're practically kicking me out, sir," he said. "I don't know what I've done."

"You have done nothing," replied Lord Wrexborough "which an honorable man may not do. But in common with many others similarly circumstanced, you seem inclined, now that your military duties are at an end, to regard life as a sort of perpetual 'leave.' I speak frankly before Seton because I know that he agrees with me. My friend the Foreign Secretary has generously offered you an appointment which opens up a career that should not—I repeat, that should not prove less successful than his own."

Gray turned, and his face had flushed deeply.

"I know that Margaret has been scaring you about Rita Irvin," he said, "but on my word, sir, there was no need to do it."

He met Seton Pasha's cool regard, and:

"Margaret's one of the best," he added. "I know you agree with me?"

A faint suggestion of added color came into Seton's tanned cheeks.

"I do, Gray," he answered quietly. "I believe you are good enough to look upon me as a real friend; therefore allow me to add my advice, for what it is worth, to that of Lord Wrexborough and your cousin: take the Egyptian appointment. I know where it will lead. You can do no good by remaining in London; and when we find Mrs. Irvin your presence would be an embarrassment to the unhappy man who waits for news at Prince's Gate. I am frank, but it's my way."

He held out his hand, smiling. Quentin Gray's mercurial complexion was changing again, but:

"Good old Seton!" he said, rather huskily, and gripped the outstretched hand. "For Irvin's sake, save her!"

He turned to his father.

"Thank you, sir," he added, "you are always right. I shall be ready on Tuesday. I suppose you are off again, Seton?"

"I am," was the reply. "Chief Inspector Kerry is moving heaven and earth to find the Kazmah establishment, and I don't want to come in a poor second."

Lord Wrexborough cleared his throat and turned in the padded revolving chair.

"Honestly, Seton," he said, "what do you think of your chance of success?"

Seton Pasha smiled grimly.

"Many ascribe success to wit," he replied, "and failure to bad luck; but the Arab says 'Kismet.'"

CHAPTER XXXVIII

THE SONG OF SIN SIN WA

Mrs. Sin, aroused by her husband from the deep opium sleep, came out into the fume-laden vault. Her dyed hair was disarranged, and her dark eyes stared glassily before her; but even in this half-drugged state she bore herself with the lithe carriage of a dancer, swinging her hips lazily and pointing the toes of her high-heeled slippers.

"Awake, my wife," crooned Sin Sin Wa. "Only a fool seeks the black smoke when the jackals sit in a ring."

Mrs. Sin gave him a glance of smiling contempt—a glance which, passing him, rested finally upon the prone body of Chief Inspector Kerry lying stretched upon the floor before the stove. Her pupils contracted to mere pin-points and then dilated blackly. She recoiled a step, fighting with the stupor which her ill-timed indulgence had left behind.

At this moment Kerry groaned loudly, tossed his arm out with a convulsive movement, and rolled over on to his side, drawing up his knees.

The eye of Sin Sin Wa gleamed strangely, but he did not move, and Sam Tûk who sat huddled in his chair where his feet almost touched the fallen man, stirred never a muscle. But Mrs. Sin, who still moved in a semi-phantasmagoric world, swiftly raised the hem of her kimona, affording a glimpse of a shapely silk-clad limb. From a sheath attached to her garter she drew a thin stilletto. Curiously feline, she crouched, as if about to spring.

Sin Sin Wa extended his hand, grasping his wife's wrist.

"No, woman of indifferent intelligence," he said in his queer sibilant language, "since when has murder gone unpunished in these British dominions?"

Mrs. Sin snatched her wrist from his grasp, falling back wild-eyed.

"Yellow ape! yellow ape!" she said hoarsely. "One more does not matter—now."

"One more?" crooned Sin Sin Wa, glancing curiously at Kerry.

"They are here! We are trapped!"

"No, no," said Sin Sin Wa. "He is a brave man; he comes alone."

He paused, and then suddenly resumed in pidgin English:

"You likee killa him, eh?"

Perhaps unconscious that she did so, Mrs. Sin replied also in English:

"No, I am mad. Let me think, old fool!"

She dropped the stiletto and raised her hand dazedly to her brow.

"You gotchee tired of knifee chop, eh?" murmured Sin Sin Wa.

Mrs. Sin clenched her hands, holding them rigidly against her hips; and, nostrils dilated, she stared at the smiling Chinaman.

"What do you mean?" she demanded.

Sin Sin Wa performed his curious oriental shrug.

"You putta topside pidgin on Sir Lucy alla lightee," he murmured. "Givee him hell alla velly proper."

The pupils of the woman's eyes contracted again, and remained so. She laughed hoarsely and tossed her head.

"Who told you that?" she asked contemptuously. "It was the doll-woman who killed him—I have said so."

"*You* tella me so—*hoi, hoi!* But old Sin Sin Wa catchee wonder. Lo!"— he extended a yellow forefinger, pointing at his wife—"Mrs. Sin make him catchee die! No bhobbery, no palaber. Sin Sin Wa gotchee you sized up allee timee."

Mrs. Sin snapped her fingers under his nose then stooped, picked up the stiletto, and swiftly restored it to its sheath. Her hands resting upon her hips, she came forward, until her dark evil face almost touched the yellow, smiling face of Sin Sin Wa.

"Listen, old fool," she said in a low, husky voice; "I have done with you, ape-man, for good! Yes! I killed Lucy, *I* killed him! He belonged to *me*—until that pink and white thing took him away. I am glad I killed him. If I cannot have him neither can she. But I was mad all the same."

She glanced down at Kerry, and:

"Tie him up," she directed, "and send him to sleep. And understand, Sin, we've shared out for the last time—You go your way and I go mine. No stinking Yellow River for me. New York is good enough until it's safe to go to Buenos Ayres."

"Smartest leg in Buenos Ayres," croaked the raven from his wicker cage, which was set upon the counter.

Sin Sin Wa regarded him smilingly.

"Yes, yes, my little friend," he crooned in Chinese, while Tling-a-Ling rattled ghostly castanets. "In Ho-Nan they will say that you are a devil and I am a wizard. That which is unknown is always thought to be magical, my Tling-a-Ling."

Mrs. Sin, who was rapidly throwing off the effects of opium and recovering her normal self-confident personality, glanced at her husband scornfully.

"Tell me," she said, "what has happened? How did he come here?"

"Blinga filly doggy," murmured Sin Sin Wa. "Knockee Ah Fung on him head and comee down here, lo. Ah Fung allee lightee now—topside. Chasee filly doggy. Allee velly proper. No bhobbery."

"Talk less and act more," said Mrs. Sin. "Tie him up, and if you *must* talk, talk Chinese. Tie him up."

She pointed to Kerry. Sin Sin Wa tucked his hands into his sleeves and shuffled towards the masked door communicating with the inner room.

"Only by intelligent speech are we distinguished from the other animals," he murmured in Chinese.

Entering the inner room, he began to extricate a long piece of thin rope from amid a tangle of other materials with which it was complicated. Mrs. Sin stood looking down at the fallen man. Neither Kerry nor Sam Tûk gave the slightest evidence of life. And as Sin Sin Wa disentangled yard upon yard of rope from the bundle on the floor by the bed where Rita Irvin lay in her long troubled sleep, he crooned a queer song. It was in the Ho-Nan dialect and intelligible to himself alone.

"Shöa, the evil woman (he chanted), the woman of many strange loves....
Shöa, the ghoul....
Lo, the Yellow River leaps forth from the nostrils of the mountain god....
Shöa, the betrayer of men....
Blood is on her brow.
Lo, the betrayer is betrayed. Death sits at her elbow.
See, the Yellow River bears a corpse upon its tide...
Dead men hear her secret.
Shöa, the ghoul....
Shöa, the evil woman. Death sits at her elbow.
Black, the vultures flock about her....
Lo, the Yellow River leaps forth from the nostrils of the mountain god."

Meanwhile Kerry, lying motionless at the feet of Sam Tûk was doing some hard and rapid thinking. He had recovered consciousness a few moments before Mrs. Sin had come into the vault from the inner room. There were those, Seton Pasha among them, who would have regarded the groan and the convulsive movements of Kerry's body with keen suspicion. And because the Chief Inspector suffered from no illusions respecting the genius of Sin Sin Wa, the apparent failure of the one-eyed Chinaman to recognize these preparations for attack nonplussed the Chief Inspector. His outstanding vice as an investigator was the directness of his own methods and of his mental outlook, so that he frequently experienced great difficulty in penetrating to the motives of a tortuous brain such as that of Sin Sin Wa.

That Sin Sin Wa thought him to be still unconscious he did not believe. He was confident that his tactics had deceived the Jewess, but he entertained an almost superstitious respect for the cleverness of the Chinaman. The trick with the ball of leaf opium was painfully fresh in his memory.

Kerry, in common with many members of the Criminal Investigation Department, rarely carried firearms. He was a man with a profound belief in his bare hands—aided when necessary by his agile feet. At the moment that Sin Sin Wa had checked the woman's murderous and half insane outburst Kerry had been contemplating attack. The sudden change of language on the part of the Chinaman had arrested him in the act; and, realizing that he was listening to a confession which placed the hangman's rope about the neck of Mrs. Sin, he lay still and wondered.

Why had Sin Sin Wa forced his wife to betray herself? To clear Mareno? To clear Mrs. Irvin—or to save his own skin?

It was a frightful puzzle for Kerry. Then—where was Kazmah? That Mrs. Irvin, probably in a drugged condition, lay somewhere in that mysterious inner room Kerry felt fairly sure. His maltreated skull was humming like a bee-hive and aching intensely, but the man was tough as men are made, and he could not only think clearly, but was capable of swift and dangerous action.

He believed that he could tackle the Chinaman with fair prospects of success; and women, however murderous, he habitually disregarded as adversaries. But the mummy-like, deceptive Sam Tûk was not negligible, and Kazmah remained an unknown quantity.

From under that protective arm, cast across his face, Kerry's fierce eyes peered out across the dirty floor. Then quickly he shut his eyes again.

Sin Sin Wa, crooning his strange song, came in carrying a coil of rope—and a Mauser pistol!

"P'licemanee gotchee catchee sleepee," he murmured, "or maybe he catchee die!"

He tossed the rope to his wife, who stood silent tapping the floor with one slim restless foot.

"Number one top-side tie up," he crooned. "Sin Sin Wa watchee withum gun!"

Kerry lay like a dead man; for in the Chinaman's voice were menace and warning.

CHAPTER XXXIX

THE EMPTY WHARF

The suspected area of Limehouse was closely invested as any fortress of old when Seton Pasha once more found himself approaching that painfully familiar neighborhood. He had spoken to several pickets, and had gathered no news of interest, except that none of them had seen Chief Inspector Kerry since some time shortly before dusk. Seton, newly from more genial climes, shivered as he contemplated the misty, rain-swept streets, deserted and but dimly lighted by an occasional lamp. The hooting of a steam siren on the river seemed to be in harmony with the prevailing gloom, and the most confirmed optimist must have suffered depression amid those surroundings.

He had no definite plan of action. Every line of inquiry hitherto followed had led to nothing but disappointment. With most of the details concerning the elaborate organization of the Kazmah group either gathered or in sight, the whereabouts of the surviving members remained a profound mystery. From the Chinese no information could be obtained. Distrust of the police resides deep within the Chinese heart; for the Chinaman, and not unjustly, regards the police as ever ready to accuse him and ever unwilling to defend him; knows himself for a pariah capable of the worst crimes, and who may therefore be robbed, beaten and even murdered by his white neighbors with impunity. But when the police seek information from Chinatown, Chinatown takes its revenge—and is silent.

Out on the river, above and below Limehouse, patrols watched for signals from the Asiatic quarter, and from a carefully selected spot on the Surrey side George Martin watched also. Not even the lure of a neighboring tavern could draw him from his post. Hour after hour he waited patiently—for Sin Sin Wa paid fair prices, and tonight he bought neither opium nor cocaine, but liberty.

Seton Pasha, passing from point to point, and nowhere receiving news of Kerry, began to experience a certain anxiety respecting the safety of the intrepid Chief Inspector. His mind filled with troubled conjectures, he passed the house formerly occupied by the one-eyed Chinaman—where he found Detective-Sergeant Coombes on duty and very much on the alert—and followed the bank of the Thames in the direction of Limehouse Basin. The narrow, ill-lighted street was quite deserted. Bad weather and the presence of many police had driven the

Asiatic inhabitants indoors. But from the river and the docks arose the incessant din of industry. Whistles shrieked and machinery clanked, and sometimes remotely came the sound of human voices.

Musing upon the sordid mystery which seems to underlie the whole of this dingy quarter, Seton pursued his way, crossing inlets and circling around basins dimly divined, turning to the right into a lane flanked by high eyeless walls, and again to the left, finally to emerge nearly opposite a dilapidated gateway giving access to a small wharf.

All unconsciously, he was traversing the same route as that recently pursued by the fugitive Sin Sin Wa; but now he paused, staring at the empty wharf. The annexed building, a mere shell, had not escaped examination by the search party, and it was with no very definite purpose in view that Seton pushed open the rickety gate. Doubtless Kismet, of which the Arabs speak, dictated that he should do so.

The tide was high, and the water whispered ghostly under the pile-supported structure. Seton experienced a new sense of chill which did not seem to be entirely physical as he stared out at the gloomy river prospect and listened to the uncanny whisperings of the tide. He was about to turn back when another sound attracted his attention. A dog was whimpering somewhere near him.

At first he was disposed to believe that the sound was due to some other cause, for the deserted wharf was not a likely spot in which to find a dog, but when to the faint whimpering there was added a scratching sound, Seton's last doubts vanished.

"It's a dog," he said, "a small dog."

Like Kerry, he always carried an electric pocket-lamp, and now he directed its rays into the interior of the building.

A tiny spaniel, whining excitedly, was engaged in scratching with its paws upon the dirty floor as though determined to dig its way through. As the light shone upon it the dog crouched affrightedly, and, glancing in Seton's direction, revealed its teeth. He saw that it was covered with mud from head to tail, presenting a most woe-begone appearance, and the mystery of its presence there came home to him forcibly.

It was a toy spaniel of a breed very popular among ladies of fashion, and to its collar was still attached a tattered and muddy fragment of ribbon.

The little animal crouched in a manner which unmistakably pointed to the fact that it apprehended ill-treatment, but these personal fears had only a secondary place in its mind, and with one eye on the intruder it continued to scratch madly at the floor.

Seton acted promptly. He snapped off the light, and, replacing the lamp in his pocket, stepped into the building and dropped down upon his knees beside the dog. He next lay prone, and having rapidly cleared a space with his sleeve of some of the dirt which coated it, he applied his ear to the floor.

In spite of that iron control which habitually he imposed upon himself, he became aware of the fact that his heart was beating rapidly. He had learned at Leman Street that Kerry had brought Mrs. Irvin's dog from Prince's Gate to aid in the search for the missing woman. He did not doubt that this was the dog which snarled and scratched excitedly beside him. Dimly he divined something of the truth. Kerry had fallen into the hands of the gang, but the dog, evidently not without difficulty, had escaped. What lay below the wharf?

Holding his breath, he crouched, listening; but not a sound could he detect.

"There's nothing here, old chap," he said to the dog.

Responsive to the friendly tone, the little animal began barking loudly with high staccato notes, which must have been audible on the Surrey shore.

Seton was profoundly mystified by the animal's behavior. He had personally searched every foot of this particular building, and was confident that it afforded no hiding-place. The behavior of the dog, however, was susceptible of only one explanation; and Seton recognizing that the clue to the mystery lay somewhere within this ramshackle building, became seized with a conviction that he was being watched.

Standing upright, he paused for a moment, irresolute, thinking that he had detected a muffled shriek. But the riverside noises were misleading and his imagination was on fire.

That almost superstitious respect for the powers of Sin Sin Wa, which had led Chief Inspector Kerry to look upon the Chinaman as a being more than humanly endowed, began to take possession of Seton Pasha. He regretted having entered the place so overtly, he regretted having shown a light. Keen eyes, vigilant, regarded him. It was perhaps a delusion, bred of the mournful night sounds, the gloom, and the uncanny resourcefulness, already proven, of the Kazmah group. But it operated powerfully.

Theories, wild, improbable, flocked to his mind. The great dope cache lay beneath his feet—and there must be some hidden entrance to it which had escaped the attention of the search-party. This in itself was not improbable, since they had devoted no more time to this building than to any other in the vicinity. That wild cry in the night which had struck so mournful a chill to the hearts of the watchers on the river had seemed to come out of the void of the blackness, had given but slight clue to the location of the place of captivity. Indeed, they could only surmise that it had been uttered by the missing woman. Yet in their hearts neither had doubted it.

He determined to cause the place to be searched again, as secretly as possible; he determined to set so close a guard over it and over its approaches that none could enter or leave unobserved.

Yet Kismet, in whose omnipotence he more than half believed, had ordained otherwise; for man is merely an instrument in the hand of Fate.

CHAPTER XL

COIL OF THE PIGTAIL

The inner room was in darkness and the fume-laden air almost unbreathable. A dull and regular moaning sound proceeded from the corner where the bed was situated, but of the contents of the place and of its other occupant or occupants Kerry had no more than a hazy idea. His imagination supplied those details which he had failed to observe. Mrs. Monte Irvin, in a dying condition, lay upon the bed, and someone or some *thing* crouched on the divan behind Kerry as he lay stretched upon the matting-covered floor. His wrists, tied behind him, gave him great pain; and since his ankles were also fastened and the end of the rope drawn taut and attached to that binding his wrists, he was rendered absolutely helpless. For one of his fiery temperament this physical impotence was maddening, and because his own handkerchief had been tied tightly around his head so as to secure between his teeth a wooden stopper of considerable size which possessed an unpleasant chemical taste and smell, even speech was denied him.

How long he had lain thus he had no means of judging accurately; but hours—long, maddening hours—seemed to have passed since, with the muzzle of Sin Sin Wa's Mauser pressed coldly to his ear, he had submitted willy-nilly to the adroit manipulations of Mrs. Sin. At first he had believed, in his confirmed masculine vanity, that it would be a simple matter to extricate himself from the fastenings made by a woman; but when, rolling him sideways, she had drawn back his heels and run the loose end of the line through the loop formed by the lashing of his wrists behind him, he had recognized a Chinese training, and had resigned himself to the inevitable. The wooden gag was a sore trial, and if it had not broken his spirit it had nearly caused him to break an artery in his impotent fury.

Into the darkened inner chamber Sin Sin Wa had dragged him, and there Kerry had lain ever since, listening to the various sounds of the place, to the coarse voice, often raised in anger, of the Cuban-Jewess, to the crooning tones of the imperturbable Chinaman. The incessant moaning of the woman on the bed sometimes became mingled with another sound more remote, which Kerry for long failed to identify; but ultimately he concluded it to be occasioned by the tide flowing under the wharf. The raven was silent, because, imprisoned in his wicker cage, he had been placed in some dark spot below the counter. Very dimly from time to time a steam siren might be heard upon the river, and once the thudding of a screw-propeller told of the passage of a large vessel along Limehouse Reach.

In the eyes of Mrs. Sin Kerry had read menace, and for all their dark beauty they had reminded him of the eyes of a cornered rat. Beneath the contemptuous nonchalance which she flaunted he read terror and remorse, and a foreboding of doom—panic ill repressed, which made her dangerous as any beast at bay. The attitude of the Chinaman was more puzzling. He seemed to bear the Chief Inspector no personal animosity, and indeed, in his glittering eye, Kerry had detected a sort of mysterious light of understanding which was almost mirthful, but which bore no relation to Sin Sin Wa's perpetual smile. Kerry's respect for the one-eyed Chinaman had increased rather than diminished upon closer acquaintance. Underlying his urbanity he failed to trace any symptom of apprehension. This Sin Sin Wa, accomplice of a murderess self-confessed, evident head of a drug syndicate which had led to the establishment of a Home Office inquiry—this badly "wanted" man, whose last hiding-place, whose keep, was closely invested by the agents of the law, was the same Sin Sin Wa who had smilingly extended his wrists, inviting the manacles, when Kerry had first made his acquaintance under circumstances legally very different.

Sometimes Kerry could hear him singing his weird crooning song, and twice Mrs. Sin had shrieked blasphemous execrations at him because of it. But why should Sin Sin Wa sing? What hope had he of escape? In the case of any other criminal Kerry would have answered "None," but the ease with which this one-eyed singing Chinaman had departed from his abode under the very noses of four detectives had shaken the Chief Inspector's confidence in the efficiency of ordinary police methods where this Chinese conjurer was concerned. A man who could convert an elaborate opium house into a dirty ruin in so short a time, too, was capable of other miraculous feats, and it would not have surprised Kerry to learn that Sin Sin Wa, at a moment's notice, could disguise himself as a chest of tea, or pass invisible through solid walls.

For evidence that Seton Pasha or any of the men from Scotland Yard had penetrated to the secret of Sam Tûk's cellar Kerry listened in vain. What was about to happen he could not imagine, nor if his life was to be spared. In the confession so curiously extorted from Mrs. Sin by her husband he perceived a clue to this and other mysteries, but strove in vain to disentangle it from the many maddening complexities of the case.

So he mused, wearily, listening to the moaning of his fellow captive, and wondering, since no sign of life came thence, why he imagined another presence in the stuffy room or the presence of someone or of some *thing* on the divan behind him. And in upon these dreary musings broke an altercation between Mrs. Sin and her husband.

"Keep the blasted thing covered up!" she cried hoarsely.

"Tling-a-Ling wantchee catchee bleathee sometime," crooned Sin Sin Wa.

"Hello, hello!" croaked the raven drowsily. "Smartest—smartest—smartest leg."

"You catchee sleepee, Tling-a-Ling," murmured the Chinaman. "Mrs. Sin no likee you palaber, lo!"

"Burn it!" cried the woman, "burn the one-eyed horror!"

But when, carrying a lighted lantern, Sin Sin Wa presently came into the inner room, he smiled as imperturbably as ever, and was unmoved so far as external evidence showed.

Sin Sin Wa set the lantern upon a Moorish coffee-table which once had stood beside the divan in Mrs. Sin's sanctum at the House of a Hundred Raptures. A significant glance—its significance an acute puzzle to the recipient—he cast upon Chief Inspector Kerry. His hands tucked in the loose sleeves of his blouse, he stood looking down at the woman who lay moaning on the bed; and:

"Tchée, tchée," he crooned softly, "you hab no catchee die, my beautiful. You sniffee plenty too muchee 'white snow,' *hoi, hoi!* Velly bad woman tly makee you catchee die, but Sin Sin Wa no hab got for killee chop. Topside pidgin no good enough, lo!"

His thick, extraordinary long pigtail hanging down his back and gleaming in the rays of the lantern, he stood, head bowed, watching Rita Irvin. Because of his position on the floor, Mrs. Irvin was invisible from Kerry's point of view, but she continued to moan incessantly, and he knew that she must be unconscious of the Chinaman's scrutiny.

"Hurry, old fool!" came Mrs. Sin's harsh voice from the outer room. "In ten minutes Ah Fung will give the signal. Is she dead yet—the doll-woman?"

"She hab no catchee die," murmured Sin Sin Wa, "She still vella beautiful—*tchée!*"

It was at the moment that he spoke these words that Seton Pasha entered the empty building above and found the spaniel scratching at the paved floor. So that, as Sin Sin Wa stood looking down at the wan face of the unfortunate woman who refused to die, the dog above, excited by Seton's presence, ceased to whine and scratch and began to bark.

Faintly to the vault the sound of the high-pitched barking penetrated.

Kerry tensed his muscles and groaned impotently feeling his heart beating like a hammer in his breast. Complete silence reigned in the outer room. Sin Sin Wa never stirred. Again the dog barked, then:

"Hello, hello!" shrieked the raven shrilly. "Number one p'lice chop, lo! Sin Sin Wa! Sin Sin Wa!"

There came a fierce exclamation, the sound of something being hastily overturned, of a scuffle, and:

"Sin—Sin—Wa!" croaked the raven feebly.

The words ended in a screeching cry, which was followed by a sound of wildly beating wings. Sin Sin Wa, hands tucked in sleeves, turned and walked from the inner room, closing the sliding door behind him with a movement of his shoulder.

Resting against the empty shelves, he stood and surveyed the scene in the vault.

Mrs. Sin, who had been kneeling beside the wicker cage, which was upset, was in the act of standing upright. At her feet, and not far from the motionless form of old Sam Tûk who sat like a dummy figure in his chair before the stove, lay a palpitating mass of black feathers. Other detached feathers were sprinkled about the floor. Feebly the raven's wings beat the ground once, twice—and were still.

Sin Sin Wa uttered one sibilant word, withdrew his hands from his sleeves, and, stepping around the end of the counter, dropped upon his knees beside the raven. He touched it with long yellow fingers, then raised it and stared into the solitary eye, now glazed and sightless as its fellow. The smile had gone from the face of Sin Sin Wa.

"My Tling-a-Ling!" he moaned in his native mandarin tongue. "Speak to me, my little black friend!"

A bead of blood, like a ruby, dropped from the raven's beak. Sin Sin Wa bowed his head and knelt awhile in silence; then, standing up, he reverently laid the poor bedraggled body upon a chest. He turned and looked at his wife.

Hands on hips, she confronted him, breathing rapidly, and her glance of contempt swept him up and down.

"I've often threatened to do it," she said in English. "Now I've done it.

They're on the wharf. We're trapped—thanks to that black, squalling horror!"

"*Tchée, tchée!*" hissed Sin Sin Wa.

His gleaming eye fixed upon the woman unblinkingly, he began very deliberately to roll up his loose sleeves. She watched him, contempt in her glance, but her expression changed subtly, and her dark eyes grew narrowed. She looked rapidly towards Sam Tûk but Sam Tûk never stirred.

"Old fool!" she cried at Sin Sin Wa. "What are you doing?"

But Sin Sin Wa, his sleeves rolled up above his yellow, sinewy forearms, now tossed his pigtail, serpentine, across his shoulder and touched it with his fingers, an odd, caressing movement.

"Ho!" laughed Mrs. Sin in her deep scoffing fashion, "it is for *me* you make all this bhobbery, eh? It is *me* you are going to chastise, my dear?"

She flung back her head, snapping her fingers before the silent Chinaman. He watched her, and slowly—slowly—he began to crouch, lower and lower, but always that unblinking regard remained fixed upon the face of Mrs. Sin.

The woman laughed again, more loudly. Bending her lithe body forward in mocking mimicry, she snapped her fingers, once—again—and again under Sin Sin Wa's nose. Then:

"Do you think, you blasted yellow ape, that you can frighten *me?*" she screamed, a swift flame of wrath lighting up her dark face.

In a flash she had raised the kimona and had the stiletto in her hand. But, even swifter than she, Sin Sin Wa sprang ...

Once, twice she struck at him, and blood streamed from his left shoulder. But the pigtail, like an executioner's rope, was about the woman's throat. She uttered one smothered shriek, dropping the knife, and then was silent ...

Her dyed hair escaped from its fastenings and descended, a ruddy torrent, about her as she writhed, silent, horrible, in the death-coil of the pigtail.

Rigidly, at arms-length, he held her, moment after moment, immovable, implacable; and when he read death in her empurpled face, a miraculous thing happened.

The "blind" eye of Sin Sin Wa opened!

A husky rattle told of the end, and he dropped the woman's body from his steely grip, disengaging the pigtail with a swift movement of his head. Opening and closing his yellow fingers to restore circulation, he stood looking down at her. He spat upon the floor at her feet.

Then, turning, he held out his arms and confronted Sam Tûk.

"Was it well done, bald father of wisdom?" he demanded hoarsely.

But old Sam Tûk seated lumpish in his chair like some grotesque idol before whom a human sacrifice has been offered up, stirred not. The length of loaded tubing with which he had struck Kerry lay beside him where it had fallen from his nerveless hand. And the two oblique, beady eyes of Sin Sin Wa, watching, grew dim. Step by step he approached the old Chinaman, stooped, touched him, then knelt and laid his head upon the thin knees.

"Old father," he murmured, "Old bald father who knew so much. Tonight you know all."

For Sam Tûk was no more. At what moment he had died, whether in the excitement of striking Kerry or later, no man could have presumed to say, since, save by an occasional nod of his head, he had often simulated death in life—he who was so old that he was known as "The Father of Chinatown."

Standing upright, Sin Sin Wa looked from the dead man to the dead raven. Then, tenderly raising poor Tling-a-Ling, he laid the great dishevelled bird—a weird offering—upon the knees of Sam Tûk.

"Take him with you where you travel tonight, my father," he said. "He, too, was faithful."

A cheap German clock commenced a muted clangor, for the little hammer was muffled.

Sin Sin Wa walked slowly across to the counter. Taking up the gleaming joss, he unscrewed its pedestal. Then, returning to the spot where Mrs. Sin lay, he coolly detached a leather wallet which she wore beneath her dress fastened to a girdle. Next he removed her rings, her bangles and other ornaments. He secreted all in the interior of the joss—his treasure-chest. He raised his hands and began to unplait his long pigtail, which, like his "blind" eye, was camouflage—a false queue attached to his own hair, which he wore but slightly longer than some Europeans and many Americans. With a small pair of scissors he clipped off his long, snake-like moustaches....

CHAPTER XLI

THE FINDING OF KAZMAH

At a point just above the sweep of Limehouse Reach a watchful river police patrol observed a moving speck of light on the right bank of the Thames. As if in answer to the signal there came a few moments later a second moving speck at a point not far above the district once notorious in its possession of Ratcliff Highway. A third light answered from the Surrey bank, and a fourth shone out yet higher up and on the opposite side of the Thames.

The tide had just turned. As Chief Inspector Kerry had once observed, "there are no pleasure parties punting about that stretch," and, consequently, when George Martin tumbled into his skiff on the Surrey shore and began lustily to pull up stream, he was observed almost immediately by the River Police.

Pulling hard against the stream, it took him a long time to reach his destination—stone stairs near the point from which the second light had been shown. Rain had ceased and the mist had cleared shortly after dusk, as often happens at this time of year, and because the night was comparatively clear the pursuing boats had to be handled with care.

George did not disembark at the stone steps, but after waiting there for some time he began to drop down on the tide, keeping close inshore.

"He knows we've spotted him," said Sergeant Coombes, who was in one of the River Police boats. "It was at the stairs that he had to pick up his man."

Certainly, the tactics of George suggested that he had recognized surveillance, and, his purpose abandoned, now sought to efface himself without delay. Taking advantage of every shadow, he resigned his boat to the gentle current. He had actually come to the entrance of Greenwich Reach when a dock light, shining out across the river, outlined the boat yellowly.

"He's got a passenger!" said Coombes amazedly.

Inspector White, who was in charge of the cutter, rested his arm on Coombes' shoulder and stared across the moving tide.

"I can see no one," he replied. "You're over anxious, Detective-Sergeant—and I can understand it!"

Coombes smiled heroically.

"I may be over anxious, Inspector," he replied, "but if *I* lost Sin Sin

Wa, the River Police had never even *heard* of him till the C.I.D. put 'em wise."

"H'm!" muttered the Inspector. "D'you suggest we board him?"

"No," said Coombes, "let him land, but don't trouble to hide any more. Show him we're in pursuit."

No longer drifting with the outgoing tide, George Martin had now boldly taken to the oars. The River Police boat close in his wake, he headed for the blunt promontory of the Isle of Dogs. The grim pursuit went on until:

"I bet I know where he's for," said Coombes.

"So do I," declared Inspector White; "Dougal's!"

Their anticipations were realized. To the wooden stairs which served as a water-gate for the establishment on the Isle of Dogs, George Martin ran in openly; the police boat followed, and:

"You were right!" cried the Inspector, "he has somebody with him!"

A furtive figure, bearing a burden upon its shoulder, moved up the slope and disappeared. A moment later the police were leaping ashore. George deserted his boat and went running heavily after his passenger.

"After them!" cried Coombes. "That's *Sin Sin Wa!*"

Around the mazey, rubbish-strewn paths the pursuit went hotly. In sight of Dougal's Coombes saw the swing door open and a silhouette— that of a man who carried a bag on his shoulder—pass in. George Martin followed, but the Scotland Yard man had his hand upon his shoulder.

"Police!" he said sharply. "Who's your friend?"

George turned, red and truculent, with clenched fists.

"Mind your own bloody business!" he roared.

"Mind yours, my lad!" retorted Coombes warningly. "You're no Thames waterman. Who's your friend?"

"Wotcher mean?" shouted George. "You're up the pole or canned you are!"

"Grab him!" said Coombes, and he kicked open the door and entered the saloon, followed by Inspector White and the boat's crew.

As they appeared, the Inspector conspicuous in his uniform, backed by the group of River Police, one of whom grasped George Martin by his coat collar:

"*Splits!*" bellowed Dougal in a voice like a fog-horn.

Twenty cups of tea, coffee and cocoa, too hot for speedy assimilation, were spilled upon the floor.

The place as usual was crowded, more particularly in the neighborhood of the two stoves. Here were dock laborers, seamen and riverside loafers, lascars, Chinese, Arabs, negroes and dagoes. Mrs.

Dougal, defiant and red, brawny arms folded and her pose as that of one contemplating a physical contest, glared from behind the "solid" counter. Dougal rested his hairy hands upon the "wet" counter and revealed his defective teeth in a vicious snarl. Many of the patrons carried light baggage, since a P and O boat, an oriental, and the *S. S. Mahratta*, were sailing that night or in the early morning, and Dougal's was the favorite house of call for a *doch-an-dorrich* for sailormen, particularly for sailormen of color.

Upon the police group became focussed the glances of light eyes and dark eyes, round eyes, almond-shaped eyes, and oblique eyes. Silence fell.

"We are police officers," called Coombes formally. "All papers, please."

Thereupon, without disturbance, the inspection began, and among the papers scrutinized were those of one, Chung Chow, an able-bodied Chinese seaman. But since his papers were in order, and since he possessed two eyes and wore no pigtail, he excited no more interest in the mind of Detective-Sergeant Coombes than did any one of the other Chinamen in the place.

A careful search of the premises led to no better result, and George Martin accounted for his possession of a considerable sum of money found upon him by explaining that he had recently been paid off after a long voyage and had been lucky at cards.

The result of the night's traffic, then, spelled failure for British justice, the *S.S. Mahratta* sailed one stewardess short of her complement; but among the Chinese crew of another steamer Eastward bound was one, Chung Chow, formerly known as Sin Sin Wa. And sometimes in the night watches there arose before him the picture of a black bird resting upon the knees of an aged Chinaman. Beyond these figures dimly he perceived the paddy-fields of Ho-Nan and the sweeping valley of the Yellow River, where the opium poppy grows.

It was about an hour before the sailing of the ship which numbered Chung Chow among the yellow members of its crew that Seton Pasha returned once more to the deserted wharf whereon he had found Mrs. Monte Irvin's spaniel. Afterwards, in the light of ascertained facts, he condemned himself for a stupidity passing the ordinary. For while he had conducted a careful search of the wharf and adjoining premises, convinced that there was a cellar of some kind below, he had omitted to look for a water-gate to this hypothetical cache.

Perhaps his self-condemnation was deserved, but in justice to the agent selected by Lord Wrexborough, it should be added that Chief Inspector Kerry had no more idea of the existence of such an entrance, and exit, than had Seton Pasha.

Leaving the dog at Leman Street then, and learning that there was no news of the missing Chief Inspector, Seton had set out once more. He had been informed of the mysterious signals flashed from side to side of the Lower Pool, and was hourly expecting a report to the effect that Sin Sin Wa had been apprehended in the act of escaping. That Sin Sin Wa had dropped into the turgid tide from his underground hiding-place, and pushing his property—which was floatable—before him, encased in a waterproof bag, had swum out and clung to the stern of George Martin's boat as it passed close to the empty wharf, neither Seton Pasha nor any other man knew—except George Martin and Sin Sin Wa.

At a suitably dark spot the Chinaman had boarded the little craft, not without difficulty, for his wounded shoulder pained him, and had changed his sodden attire for a dry outfit which awaited him in the locker at the stern of the skiff. The cunning of the Chinese has the simplicity of true genius.

Not two paces had Seton taken on to the mystifying wharf when:

"Sam Tûk barber! Entrance in cellar!" rapped a ghostly, muffled voice from beneath his feet. "Sam Tûk barber! Entrance in cellar!"

Seton Pasha stood still, temporarily bereft of speech. Then, *"Kerry!"* he cried. "Kerry! Where are you?"

But apparently his voice failed to reach the invisible speaker, for:

"Sam Tûk barber! Entrance in cellar!" repeated the voice.

Seton Pasha wasted no more time. He ran out into the narrow street. A man was on duty there.

"Call assistance!" ordered Seton briskly, "Send four men to join me at the barber's shop called Sam Tûk's! You know it?"

"Yes, sir; I searched it with Chief Inspector Kerry."

The note of a police whistle followed.

Ten minutes later the secret of Sam Tûk's cellar was unmasked. The place was empty, and the subterranean door locked; but it succumbed to the persistent attacks of axe and crowbar, and Seton Pasha was the first of the party to enter the vault. It was laden with chemical fumes....

He found there an aged Chinaman, dead, seated by a stove in which the fire had burned very low. Sprawling across the old man's knees was the body of a raven. Lying at his feet was a woman, lithe, contorted, the face half hidden in masses of bright red hair.

"End case near the door!" rapped the voice of Kerry. "Slides to the left!"

Seton Pasha vaulted over the counter, drew the shelves aside, and entered the inner room.

By the dim light of a lantern burning upon a moorish coffee-table he discerned an untidy bed, upon which a second woman lay, pallid.

"God!" he muttered; "this place is a morgue!"

"It certainly isn't healthy!" said an irritable voice from the floor. "But I think I might survive it if you could spare a second to untie me."

Kerry's extensive practice in chewing and the enormous development of his maxillary muscles had stood him in good stead. His keen, strong teeth had bitten through the extemporized gag, and as a result the tension of the handkerchief which had held it in place had become relaxed, enabling him to rid himself of it and to spit out the fragments of filthy-tasting wood which the biting operation had left in his mouth.

Seton turned, stooped on one knee to release the captive ... and found himself looking into the face of someone who sat crouched upon the divan behind the Chief Inspector. The figure was that of an oriental, richly robed. Long, slim, ivory hands rested upon his knees, and on the first finger of the right hand gleamed a big talismanic ring. But the face, surmounted by a white turban, was wonderful, arresting in its immobile intellectual beauty; and from under the heavy brows a pair of abnormally large eyes looked out hypnotically.

"My God!" whispered Seton, then:

"If you've finished your short prayer," rapped Kerry, "set about *my* little job."

"But, Kerry—Kerry, behind you!"

"I haven't any eyes in my back hair!"

Mechanically, half fearfully, Seton touched the hands of the crouching oriental. A low moan came from the woman in the bed, and:

"It's *Kazmah!*" gasped Seton. "Kerry ... Kazmah is—a *wax figure!*"

"Hell!" said Chief Inspector Kerry.

CHAPTER XLII

A YEAR LATER

Beneath an awning spread above the balcony of one of those modern elegant flats, which today characterize Heliopolis, the City of the Sun, site of perhaps the most ancient seat of learning in the known world, a party of four was gathered, awaiting the unique spectacle which is afforded when the sun's dying rays fade from the Libyan sands and the violet wonder of the afterglow conjures up old magical Egypt from the ashes of the desert.

"Yes," Monte Irvin was saying, "only a year ago; but, thank God, it seems more like ten! Merciful time effaces sadness but spares joy."

He turned to his wife, whose flower-like face peeped out from a nest of white fur. Covertly he squeezed her hand, and was rewarded with a swift, half coquettish glance, in which he read trust and contentment. The dreadful ordeal through which she had passed had accomplished that which no physician in Europe could have hoped for, since no physician would have dared to adopt such drastic measures. Actuated by deliberate cruelty, and with the design of bringing about her death from apparently natural causes, the Kazmah group had deprived her of cocaine for so long a period that sanity, life itself, had barely survived; but for so long a period that, surviving, she had outlived the drug craving. Kazmah had cured her!

Monte Irvin turned to the tall fair girl who sat upon the arm of a cane rest-chair beside Rita.

"But nothing can ever efface the memory of all you have done for Rita, and for me," he said, "nothing, Mrs. Seton."

"Oh," said Margaret, "my mind was away back, and that sounded—so odd."

Seton Pasha, who occupied the lounge-chair upon the broad arm of which his wife was seated, looked up, smiling into the suddenly flushed face. They were but newly returned from their honeymoon, and had just taken possession of their home, for Seton was now stationed in Cairo. He flicked a cone of ash from his cheroot.

"It seems to me that we are all more or less indebted to one another," he declared. "For instance, I might never have met you, Margaret, if I had not run into your cousin that eventful night at Princes; and Gray would not have been gazing abstractedly out of the doorway if Mrs. Irvin had joined him for dinner as arranged. One can trace almost every episode in life right back, and ultimately come—"

"To Kismet!" cried his wife, laughing merrily. "So before we begin dinner tonight—which is a night of reunion—I am going to propose a toast to Kismet!"

"Good!" said Seton, "we shall all drink it gladly. Eh, Irvin?"

"Gladly, indeed," agreed Monte Irvin. "You know, Seton," he continued, "we have been wandering, Rita and I; and ever since your wife handed her patient over to me as cured we have covered some territory. I don't know if you or Chief Inspector Kerry has been responsible, but the press accounts of the Kazmah affair have been scanty to baldness. One stray bit of news reached us—in Colorado, I think."

"What was that, Mr. Irvin?" asked Margaret, leaning towards the speaker.

"It was about Mollie Gretna. Someone wrote and told me that she had eloped with a billiard marker—a married man with five children!"

Seton laughed heartily, and so did Margaret and Rita.

"Right!" cried Seton. "She did. When last heard of she was acting as barmaid in a Portsmouth tavern!"

But Monte Irvin did not laugh.

"Poor, foolish girl!" he said gravely. "Her life might have been so different—so useful and happy."

"I agree," replied Seton, "if she had had a husband like Kerry."

"Oh, please don't!" said Margaret. "I almost fell in love with Chief Inspector Kerry myself."

"A grand fellow!" declared her husband warmly. "The Kazmah inquiry was the triumph of his career."

Monte Irvin turned to him.

"*You* did your bit, Seton," he said quietly. "The last words Inspector Kerry spoke to me before I left England were in the nature of a splendid tribute to yourself, but I will spare your blushes."

"Kerry is as white as they're made," replied Seton, "but we should never have known for certain who killed Sir Lucien if he had not risked his life in that filthy cellar as he did."

Rita Irvin shuddered slightly and drew her furs more closely about her shoulders.

"Shall we change the conversation, dear?" whispered Margaret.

"No, please," said Rita. "You cannot imagine how curious I am to learn the true details—for, as Monte says, we have been out of touch with things, and although we were so intimately concerned, neither of us really knows the inner history of the affair to this day. Of course, we know that Kazmah was a dummy figure, posed in the big ebony chair. He never moved, except to raise his hand, and this was done by someone seated in the inner room behind the figure. But who was seated there?"

Seton glanced inquiringly at his wife, and she nodded, smiling.

"Right-o!" he said. "If you will excuse me for a moment I will get my notes. Hello, here's Gray!"

A little two-seater came bowling along the road from Cairo, and drew up beneath the balcony. It was the car which had belonged to Margaret when in practice in Dover Street. Quentin Gray jumped out, waving his hand cheerily to the quartette above, and went in at the doorway. Seton walked through the flat and admitted him.

"Sorry I'm late!" cried Gray, impetuous and boyish as ever, although he looked older and had grown very bronzed. "The chief detained me."

"Go through to them," said Seton informally. "I'm getting my notes; we're going to read the thrilling story of the Kazmah mystery before dinner."

"Good enough!" cried Gray. "I'm in the dark on many points."

He had outlived his youthful infatuation, although it was probable enough that had Rita been free he would have presented himself as a suitor without delay. But the old relationship he had no desire to renew. A generous self-effacing regard had supplanted the madness of his earlier passion. Rita had changed too; she had learned to know herself and to know her husband.

So that when Seton Pasha presently rejoined his guests, he found the most complete harmony to prevail among them. He carried a bulky notebook, and, tapping his teeth with his monocle:

"Ladies and gentlemen," he began whimsically, "I will bore you with a brief account of the extraordinary facts concerning the Kazmah case."

Margaret was seated in the rest-chair which her husband had vacated, and Seton took up a position upon the ledge formed by one of the wide arms. Everyone prepared to listen, with interest undisguised.

"There were three outstanding personalities dominating what we may term the Kazmah group," continued Seton. "In order of importance they were: Sin Sin Wa, Sir Lucien Pyne and Mrs. Sin."

Rita Irvin inhaled deeply, but did not interrupt the speaker.

"I shall begin with Sir Lucien," Seton went on. "For some years before his father's death he seems to have lived a very shady life in many parts of the world. He was a confirmed gambler, and was also somewhat unduly fond of the ladies' society. In Buenos Ayres—the exact date does not matter—he made the acquaintance of a variety artiste known as La Belle Lola, a Cuban-Jewess, good-looking and unscrupulous. I cannot say if Sir Lucien was aware from the outset of his affair with La Belle that she was a married woman. But it is certain that her husband, Sin Sin Wa, very early learned of the intrigue, and condoned it.

"How Sir Lucien came to get into the clutches of the pair I do not know. But that he did so we have ascertained beyond doubt. I think, personally, that his third vice—opium—was probably responsible. For Sin Sin Wa appears throughout in the character of a drug dealer.

"These three people really become interesting from the time that La Belle Lola quitted the stage and joined her husband in the conducting of a concern in Buenos Ayres, which was the parent, if I may use the term, of the Kazmah business later established in Bond Street. From a music-hall illusionist, who came to grief during a South American tour, they acquired the oriental waxwork figure which subsequently mystified so many thousands of dupes. It was the work of a famous French artist in wax, and had originally been made to represent the Pharaoh, Rameses II., for a Paris exhibition. Attired in Eastern robes, and worked by a simple device which raised and lowered the right hand, it was used, firstly, in a stage performance, and secondly, in the character of 'Kazmah the Dream-reader.'

"Even at this time Sir Lucien had access to good society, or to the best society which Buenos Ayres could offer, and he was the source of the surprising revelations made to patrons by the 'dream-reader.' At first, apparently, the drug business was conducted independently of the Kazmah concern, but the facilities offered by the latter for masking the former soon became apparent to the wily Sin Sin Wa. Thereupon the affair was reorganized on the lines later adopted in Bond Street. Kazmah's became a secret dope-shop, and annexed to it was an elaborate *chandu-khân*, conducted by the Chinaman. Mrs. Sin was the go-between.

"You are all waiting to hear—or, to be exact, two are waiting to hear, Gray and Margaret already know—who spoke as Kazmah through the little window behind the chair. The deep-voiced speaker was Juan Mareno, Mrs. Sin's brother! Mrs. Sin's maiden name was Lola Mareno.

"Many of these details were provided by Mareno, who, after the death of his sister, to whom he was deeply attached, volunteered to give crown evidence. Most of them we have confirmed from other sources.

"Behold 'Kazmah the dream-reader,' then, established in Buenos Ayres. The partners in the enterprise speedily acquired considerable wealth. Sir Lucien—at this time plain Mr. Pyne—several times came home and lived in London and elsewhere like a millionaire. There is no doubt, I think, that he was seeking a suitable opportunity to establish a London branch of the business."

"My God!" said Monte Irvin. "How horrible it seems!"

"Horrible, indeed!" agreed Seton. "But there are two features of the case which, in justice to Sir Lucien, we should not overlook. He, who had been a poor man, had become a wealthy one and had tasted the sweets of wealth; also he was now hopelessly in the toils of the woman Lola.

"With the ingenious financial details of the concern, which were conducted in the style of the 'Jose Santos Company,' I need not trouble you now. We come to the second period, when the flat in Albemarle Street and the two offices in old Bond Street became vacant and were promptly leased by Mareno, acting on Sir Lucien's behalf, and calling himself sometimes Mr. Isaacs, sometimes Mr. Jacobs, and at other times merely posing as a representative of the Jose Santos Company in some other name.

"All went well. The concern had ample capital, and was organized by clever people. Sin Sin Wa took up new quarters in Limehouse; they had actually bought half the houses in one entire street as well as a wharf! And Sin Sin Wa brought with him the good-will of an illicit drug business which already had almost assumed the dimensions of a control.

"Sir Lucien's household was a mere bluff. He rarely entertained at home, and lived himself entirely at restaurants and clubs. The private entrance to the Kazmah house of business was the back window of the Cubanis Cigarette Company's office. From thence down the back stair to Kazmah's door it was a simple matter for Mareno to pass unobserved. Sir Lucien resumed his role of private inquiry agent, and Mareno recited the 'revelations' from notes supplied to him.

"But the 'dream reading' part of the business was merely carried on to mask the really profitable side of the concern. We have recently learned that drugs were distributed from that one office alone to the amount of thirty thousand pounds' worth annually! This is excluding the profits of the House of a Hundred Raptures and of the private *chandu* orgies organized by Mrs. Sin.

"The Kazmah group gradually acquired control of the entire market, and we know for a fact that at one period during the war they were actually supplying smuggled cocaine, indirectly, to no fewer than twelve R.A.M.C. hospitals! The complete ramifications of the system we shall never know.

"I come, now, to the tragedy, or series of tragedies, which brought about the collapse of the most ingenious criminal organization which has ever flourished, probably, in any community. I will dare to be frank. Sir Lucien was the victim of a woman's jealousy. Am I to proceed?"

Seton paused, glancing at his audience; and:

"If you please," whispered Rita. "Monte knows and I know—why— she killed him. But we don't know—"

"The nasty details," said Quentin Gray. "Carry on, Seton. Are you agreeable, Irvin?"

"I am anxious to know," replied Irvin, "for I believe Sir Lucien deserved well of me, bad as he was."

Seton clapped his hands, and an Egyptian servant appeared, silently and mysteriously as is the way of his class.

"Cocktails, Mahmoud!"

The Egyptian disappeared.

"There's just time," declared Margaret, gazing out across the prospect, "before sunset."

CHAPTER XLIII

THE STORY OF THE CRIME

"You are all aware," Seton continued, "that Sir Lucien Pyne was an admirer of Mrs. Irvin. God knows, I hold no brief for the man, but this love of his was the one redeeming feature of a bad life. How and when it began I don't profess to know, but it became the only pure thing which he possessed. That he was instrumental in introducing you, Mrs. Irvin, to the unfortunately prevalent drug habit, you will not deny; but that he afterwards tried sincerely to redeem you from it I can positively affirm. In seeking your redemption he found his own, for I know that he was engaged at the time of his death in extricating himself from the group. You may say that he had made a fortune, and was satisfied; that is *your* view, Gray. I prefer to think that he was anxious to begin a new life and to make himself more worthy of the respect of those he loved.

"There was one obstacle which proved too great for him—Mrs. Sin. Although Juan Mareno was the spokesman of the group, Lola Mareno was the prompter. All Sir Lucien's plans for weaning Mrs. Irvin from the habits which she had acquired were deliberately and malignantly foiled by this woman. She endeavored to inveigle Mrs. Irvin into indebtedness to you, Gray, as you know now. Failing in this, she endeavored to kill her by depriving her of that which had at the time become practically indispensable. A venomous jealousy led her to almost suicidal measures. She risked exposure and ruin in her endeavors to dispose of one whom she looked upon as a rival.

"During Sir Lucien's several absences from London she was particularly active, and this brings me to the closing scene of the drama. On the night that you determined, in desperation, Mrs. Irvin, to see Kazmah personally, you will recall that Sir Lucien went out to telephone to him?"

Rita nodded but did not speak.

"Actually," Seton explained, "he instructed Mareno to go across the leads to Kazmah's directly you had left the flat, and to give you a certain message as 'Kazmah.' He also instructed Mareno to telephone certain orders to Rashid, the Egyptian attendant. In spite of the unforeseen meeting with Gray, all would have gone well, no doubt, if Mrs. Sin had not chanced to be on the Kazmah premises at the time that the message was received!

"I need not say that Mrs. Sin was a remarkable woman, possessing many accomplishments, among them that of mimicry. She had often amused herself by taking Mareno's place at the table behind Kazmah, and, speaking in her brother's oracular voice, had delivered the 'revelations.' Mareno was like wax in his sister's hands, and on this fateful night, when he arrived at the place—which he did a few minutes before Mrs. Irvin, Gray and Sir Lucien—Mrs. Sin peremptorily ordered him to wait upstairs in the Cubanis office, and *she* took her seat in the room from which the Kazmah illusions were controlled.

"So carefully arranged was every detail of the business that Rashid, the Egyptian, was ignorant of Sir Lucien's official connection with the Kazmah concern. He had been ordered—by Mareno speaking from Sir Lucien's flat—to admit Mrs. Irvin to the room of séance and then to go home. He obeyed and departed, leaving Sir Lucien in the waiting-room.

"Driven to desperation by 'Kazmah's' taunting words, we know that Mrs. Irvin penetrated to the inner room. I must slur over the details of the scene which ensued. Hearing her cry out, Sir Lucien ran to her assistance. Mrs. Sin, enraged by his manner, lost all control of her insane passion. She attempted Mrs. Irvin's life with a stiletto which habitually she carried—and Sir Lucien died like a gentleman who had lived like a blackguard. He shielded her—"

Seton paused. Margaret was biting her lip hard, and Rita was looking down so that her face could not be seen.

"The shock consequent upon the deed sobered the half crazy woman," continued the speaker. "Her usual resourcefulness returned to her. Self-preservation had to be considered before remorse. Mrs. Irvin had swooned, and"—he hesitated—"Mrs. Sin saw to it that she did not revive prematurely. Mareno was summoned from the room above. The outer door was locked.

"It affords evidence of this woman's callous coolness that she removed from the Kazmah premises, and—probably assisted by her brother, although he denies it—from the person and garments of the dead man, every scrap of evidence. They had not by any means finished the task when *you* knocked at the door, Gray. But they completed it, faultlessly, after you had gone.

"Their unconscious victim, and the figure of Kazmah, as well as every paper or other possible clue, they carried up to the Cubanis office, and from thence across the roof to Sir Lucien's study. Next, while Mareno went for the car, Mrs. Sin rifled the safe, bureaus and desks in Sir Lucien's flat, so that we had the devil's own work, as you know, to find out even the more simple facts of his everyday life.

"Not a soul ever came forward who noticed the big car being driven into Albemarle Street or who observed it outside the flat. The chances run by the pair in conveying their several strange burdens from the top floor, down the stairs and out into the street were extraordinary. Yet they succeeded unobserved. Of course, the street was imperfectly lighted, and is but little frequented after dusk.

"The journey to Limehouse was performed without discovery—aided, no doubt, by the mistiness of the night; and Mareno, returning to the West End, ingeniously inquired for Sir Lucien at his club. Learning, although he knew it already, that Sir Lucien had not been to the club that night, he returned the car to the garage and calmly went back to the flat.

"His reason for taking this dangerous step is by no means clear. According to his own account, he did it to gain time for the fugitive Mrs. Sin. You see, there was really only one witness of the crime (Mrs. Irvin) and she could not have sworn to the identity of the assassin. Rashid was warned and presumably supplied with sufficient funds to enable him to leave the country.

"Well, the woman met her deserts, no doubt at the hands of Sin Sin Wa. Kerry is sure of this. And Sin Sin Wa escaped, taking with him an enormous sum of ready money. He was the true genius of the enterprise. No one, his wife and Mareno excepted—we know of no other—suspected that the real Sin Sin Wa was clean-shaven, possessed two eyes, and no pigtail! A wonderfully clever man!"

The native servant appeared to announce that dinner was served; African dusk drew its swift curtain over the desert, and a gun spoke sharply from the Citadel. In silence the party watched the deepening velvet of the sky, witnessing the birth of a million stars, and in silence they entered the gaily lighted dining-room.

Seton Pasha moved one of the lights so as to illuminate a small oil painting which hung above the sideboard. It represented the head and shoulders of a savage-looking red man, his hair close-cropped like that of a pugilist, and his moustache trimmed in such a fashion that a row of large, fierce teeth were revealed in an expression which might have been meant for a smile. A pair of intolerant steel-blue eyes looked squarely out at the spectator.

"What a time I had," said Seton, "to get him to sit for that! But I managed to secure his wife's support, and the trick was done. You are down to toast Kismet, Margaret, but I am going to propose the health, long life and prosperity of Chief Inspector Kerry, of the Criminal Investigation Department."

THE END

YELLOW SHADOWS

— — —

SAX ROHMER

FOREWORD

Some objection may be legitimately raised to my choice of a title for this story. I want to confess and to make clear that "Yellow Shadows" from the time of its conception underwent considerable changes before reaching actual parturition. Those dead yellow faces in which only the slit-like eyes live, those elusive figures which merge with the mists of Limehouse, have often seemed to me to be kin of the shadows; to be indeed those shadows—yellow shadows. And if, in this story, I set out to paint a Whistler Nocturne, and because of a changing purpose or because my characters ran away with me, I have rather accomplished no more than a sketch in charcoal and ochre, I feel that this apology is called for.

Sax Rohmer.
Funchal, Madeira.

CHAPTER I

SLANTING EYES

The 8:5 from Blackwall was more than an hour late.

Since the chilly coming of dusk, London had battled with her pet demon, King Fog. Slowly but surely he was conquering. Intervals of comparative visibility were growing more rare; the enemy was establishing a stranglehold.

Even under ideal conditions, this service—one of the oldest in England—does not cater for *voyageurs de luxe.* But the frequent and jerky stoppages of the last train from Blackwall ("Fast to Fenchurch Street") on this occasion had irritated the sole occupant of a certain first-class compartment to an extraordinary degree. Indeed, the irregular movements of the train were not without actual danger to him. For he was engaged in shaving!

It was not a corridor compartment which he occupied, and toilet facilities were accordingly limited. A shaving glass, safety razor, and water from a thermos flask enabled him, however, to achieve his object; and when, amid a dismal rattling of brakes, the 8:5 settled down as if abandoned to despair, he arose and surveyed himself in the fog-fouled mirror above the seat, sponged his upper lip, which alone had engaged his attention, with a moistened handkerchief, and smiled at his reflection joyously.

A grip lay open upon the seat, and into this he put the thermos flask, shaving mirror, and other accessories, and reclosed the case. Finally, he opened a window, with the result that the compartment became laden with yellow vapour, and threw something out, quickly shutting the window again. Fog signals were booming eerily as he sank into a corner seat and lighted a cigarette.

The now clean-shaven traveller abandoned himself to pleasant speculations which a close observer would have said related to the future. Nor were these dissociated from his light baggage, reposing upon the rack in front of him. For some time he stared almost tenderly at an attaché case which, with a topcoat and the grip, constituted his visible possessions.

In spirit he was far from present surroundings, yet these were not without interest of a kind; for this last and most formidable bank of fog had delayed the train on the very borders of Chinatown. Lost in roseate dreams, he sat within a stone's throw of Little Asia. Only the fog banks obscured from his view streets which after dark were honoured by double patrols.

A muffled signal boomed somewhere ahead. The 8:5 came to life again. But not before the man in the corner had been recalled from his waking dreams by what sounded like a police whistle blown at no great distance from the line.

He sat up alertly, peering into the yellow void, then he glanced at his wrist watch and uttered an impatient exclamation. The train, however, was moving slowly onward. Dimly he became aware of shouts out there in the fog. He could not be sure from which side they came, nor sure indeed that he was not deceiving himself. Nevertheless, an impulse prompted him to cross and open the window.

Immediately, he regretted the action. Evil-smelling mist swept in at him menacingly. The train was gaining speed, and, now, he could detect no sound above the rattle which it made. Upon a powerful current of air, vapour, visible like smoke, swept into the compartment. Hastily he reclosed the window. A door banged behind him—and he turned in a flash.

"Good God!"

His hand went to his right jacket pocket, his glance momentarily was directed to the attaché case upon the rack. Then, dumb with astonishment, he stood there staring. The train now was proceeding at something like twenty miles an hour—but he was no longer alone.

A woman had entered the compartment, and she stood by the opposite window confronting him!

"Please!" she said, "please!" and stretched out her hands in a gesture of appeal. "Don't be angry with me. I will explain."

The expression in her long, narrow, dark eyes was not entirely in accordance with the music of her voice, and so for a moment the man did not relax his tense attitude. Each studied the other.

The woman saw a man of medium height and slight build, wearing a well-cut double-breasted blue serge suit, which, nevertheless, was not new. It was still fashionable, however, and had obviously been made by a tailor in the Mayfair district. Its wearer appeared to be about thirty-five, and although the rest of his face was slightly sunburned, his upper lip was not. He was handsome in an intellectual fashion, having the high brow of imagination, and dark hair receding at the temples.

His observant gaze showed him a woman who wore a dark, fur-trimmed coat fitting closely to her slim figure, and a small, modish hat which, like a pierrot's cap, entirely concealed her hair. Even in the imperfect light he saw that her fawn stockings and dainty, high-heeled shoes were mud stained; indeed, one of her stockings was torn. But her face particularly engaged his attention.

She was pale with a pallor resembling ivory, and her long, almond-shaped eyes possessed a marked peculiarity: they slanted in a manner rarely met with in the Western races. Her lips were full and very red, or by artifice were rendered so. She wore no gloves, and because, as if in agitation, she constantly moved her hands, he noted that they were long and slender and of the same ivory pallor as her face and neck.

Chelsea would have acclaimed her a beauty; but her good looks were of a type too unusual to appeal to every man. Her fellow traveller laughed shortly.

"I shall be glad to hear your explanation," he said.

His change of tone seemed to reassure her, and:

"You will find it very hard to believe," she replied; "yet you must, you must believe me! So much depends upon it."

Her voice, like her nationality, puzzled him. It possessed an unfamiliar music, and he knew that this woman, who like a phantom had appeared out of the fog, in despite of her perfect English, had first seen the light far from the misty shores of Britain.

"Please sit down," he said. "I don't know that you really owe me any explanation. But"—he laughed again whimsically—"I had not anticipated the pleasure of meeting you."

The woman seated herself, but did not respond to his mood. Her long, dark eyes remained sombre and watchful.

"Thank you," she responded, as her fellow traveller sank into a seat and faced her. "There were several people in the compartments to right and left of this one, and so I decided to throw myself on your mercy." She bent forward, watching him intently. "I have escaped from the gravest peril in which a woman can be—a peril into which my own folly led me. If my husband even suspected—" She made a gesture with her eloquent white hands: "I dare not think of it."

"But, madam—pardon my curiosity—what prompted you to attempt so dangerous a thing as to climb up on to a railway track and mount a moving train?"

The long, slanting eyes continued to regard him fixedly, and:

"Fear!" the woman replied.

But she spoke the word in such a way that something of its quality was conveyed eerily to the listener.

"A good fortune which I do not deserve brought this train to a standstill at that point. They were behind me—not ten yards behind me."

The man's astonishment was growing by leaps and bounds.

"They?" he echoed, "who were *they?*"

She bent farther forward, until her pale, beautiful face was very near to his own. Then:

"The Chinese!" she whispered. "I cannot, I dare not, tell you more. But I had ventured into a place"—she moved her hand vaguely—"down there. O God!" She shuddered and covered her face in sudden, violent agitation.

"If he knew—if he suspected! I am not safe yet, I am not safe yet!"

She looked up again, and resting one of those long, slender hands upon her companion's knee:

"You are a gentleman," she said. "You could not torture a woman. I have been tortured enough already. Help me, now. I will be grateful to you all my life."

The man was moved indefinably. He could not marshal his own emotions. It was an appeal to his chivalry, but it was not his chivalry which it had awakened. The watching dark eyes, the touch of the sensitive fingers, the whole aura of the woman, reacted upon him in a manner which he found his brain in too great a turmoil to examine. Ostensibly she addressed herself to the good that was in him; but it was some deep, buried evil, hitherto only dimly suspected by himself, which responded.

"Help me," she whispered. "You shall not regret having helped me."

He shook himself free—the effort was a conscious one—from the peculiar spell of her personality. He forced a smile to his lips.

"Madam," he said, "it is to the railway company you must justify yourself, not to me."

She shrank back, inhaling sibilantly, but:

"Please don't be offended," he added hastily. "Rest assured that I will do anything in my power to help you. Believe me"—he spoke earnestly—"I only strove to reassure you. In anything I can do, command me."

He aimed to put his companion at her ease but was not at ease himself. His first idea, which had manifested itself in that rapid glance at the attaché case, he had not yet wholly dismissed. But if this woman with the bell-like voice and the unforgettable slender hands should prove to be a criminal, then he thought he would never trust experience or instinct again. She was silent for a while, but finally:

"Where does this train go to?" she asked.

"To Fenchurch Street. It is not supposed to stop between West India Docks and the terminus."

"How can I ask you?" she went on, her voice lowered almost to a whisper. "I am ashamed, I am ashamed."

She looked up at him suddenly.

"Don't you understand? I have no ticket—and I am penniless."

He met her glance. His first fears, he determined, had been childish, groundless. This was an ingenious variation of the confidence trick!

In order to confirm his suspicions:

"I quite understand," he returned gravely, and was taking out his pocket case, when came the pleading voice:

"You surely don't want to humiliate me?"

He paused in astonishment.

"I don't understand."

"Yet I ask so little of you," she said. "Consider." She glanced down at her muddy shoes. "Consider the attention I should attract at Fenchurch Street—the interview with the officials—the particulars as to where I lost my ticket—in short, the undesirable publicity. I beg of you, sir, to give up your ticket to me. If you will also give me your card I will see that the amount of the fare reaches you by first post in the morning."

Subtly, she had secured an advantage. Perhaps it was merely strategy on her part, but she had destroyed the premises upon which his second theory rested, and he found himself thrown back again upon vague speculation. Whatever the truth of the matter, he reflected, the price of a first-class ticket from West India Docks to Fenchurch Street was a small one to pay for so singular an experience; the exact amount being fourpence!

"I shall be delighted to do as you suggest," he replied, "and if it would be a convenience to you, I propose that you share my taxi to your destination."

The dark eyes rested upon him, momentarily, with a new expression in their depths.

"It is very good of you," said his strange companion; "but as, thanks to your kindness, you will have to delay to buy a ticket, it would be very unwise for me to wait."

"By which," he retorted, "I understand that you do not desire me to know your name. Is not that a little unkind?"

She was watching him intently again; and:

"I should not like you to think so," she replied, "but if you will promise never to breathe a word to any one of our meeting and to make no endeavour to trace me, I will give you an opportunity, if you care to avail yourself, of meeting me again."

Entering into the spirit of this fantastic adventure:

"I promise," he said simply, handing her his railway ticket and visiting card. "I think we are just running into Fenchurch Street."

Their glances met for a few moments, and:

"Thank you," came the musical voice.

Delicate ivory hands gripped his shoulders, and just as the first of the station lights burst dully through the fog, he found languorous, heavy-lidded eyes close to him and red lips pressed to his own in a lingering kiss, the memory of which was to haunt him through many long days to come.

CHAPTER II

THE MAN WITH NO TICKET

She disappeared almost as mysteriously as she had appeared. At one moment she was with him; in the next he was alone. He wondered— and was unsatisfied. Her indiscretion—"If my husband even suspected"—what could it have been? And why was she penniless?

"Ah, well," he muttered.

He had resumed his topcoat, and, carrying the attaché case and grip, he proceeded slowly along the platform.

Few first-class passengers had been on the train, and no porter presented himself. The greater number of the travellers by the belated 8:5 were dock officials and members of the railway staff. It was a bedraggled and dejected company. By a small stack of luggage conveniently near to the barrier, the man with no ticket set down his grip, which was uncomfortably heavy.

The fact had suddenly been borne home to him that something unusual was taking place at the station, or was expected to take place.

Yellow, choking vapour draping the ugly building enhanced this peculiar atmosphere of mystery, so that an indefinable foreboding clutched at his heart. Through the windows of the train which he had just quitted he could see the platform on the other side.

It was deserted, except for two constables; and vaguely he wondered what they could be doing there. Then, as he moved nearer to the exit, he saw the guard of the train in conversation with the station master; and standing immediately behind the collector, closely examining the faces of outgoing passengers, was a thick-set, florid man buttoned up in a fawn-coloured raincoat and wearing a bowler hat—almost certainly a detective.

A frightful suspicion entered his mind. They were looking for his late companion!

Perhaps he had been travelling in the company of a notorious international criminal—some agent of the Terrorists! But, if this were so, why had they allowed her to pass? For certainly she had been among the first to leave the platform, since she was nowhere in sight. There were less than a dozen people ahead of him, now, and as if in further contradiction of his latest theory, he noticed that the man behind the barrier was scrutinizing the faces of the male passengers but paying little attention to the few women.

He gripped his case nervously and felt his heart beginning to beat with unusual rapidity. He had attached little importance to his "loss" of a four-penny ticket, but now, at the prompting of a nameless fear which beset him, he determined to search for it in that half-absent and half-apprehensive manner which characterizes the average traveller on such occasions.

Therefore, by the gateway and in view of the officials, he plunged his hand into pocket after pocket, whilst a file of fellow passengers passed out unchallenged and he found himself a focus of interest for the watchful group; in fact, as he abandoned the spurious search, he surprised an exchange of significant glances between the stationmaster and the detective.

The constables who had been on the farther platform were now searching the train, compartment by compartment. He stepped up to the stationmaster, whose gaze was fixed upon him in open hostility, in time to detect the whispered words of one of the four men at the barrier:

"We've got him!"

A sort of anger which he thought must resemble that of a cornered rat restored his courage, and:

"I fear I have lost my ticket," he said. His tone was just a shade too casual—"As I am to blame, it will save time if I pay the fare from Blackwall."

He placed the attaché case on the platform beside him and thrust his hand into his pocket.

"I forget the exact amount," he added. "I actually joined the train at West India Docks."

It was not the stationmaster but the man in the raincoat who answered.

"Kindly step this way," he remarked, but:

"Stationmaster!" said the passenger sharply, "I addressed you. Will you be good enough to answer? My time is of some value."

"I have asked you kindly to step this way, sir," the previous speaker interrupted patiently. He had good-humoured blue eyes and a conciliatory manner which was disarming. "I regret the inconvenience, but no doubt the matter can be settled in a few minutes."

"It can surely be settled at once if I give you sixpence or whatever the fare is?"

"That might suit *you!*" said the guard, chuckling excitedly.

Whereupon the other lost his temper.

"What the devil do you mean!" he cried. "I am not accustomed to rudeness from railway employees!"

The man flushed, looking at him darkly, and would have retorted, but:

"Hold your tongue, my lad!" said the wearer of the raincoat, an unsuspected note of authority coming into his voice. He turned to the angry passenger. "I must request you to answer a few questions. I am a police officer."

Observing that a considerable group of people had collected beyond the barrier, principally composed of fellow passengers who had sensed the fact that something unusual was afoot, the angry traveller determined that this was neither the time nor place for a further display of spleen, and, once more grasping his precious case, he proceeded in silence to the stationmaster's office. There, resting his elbow upon the desk, he faced the stationmaster and the detective; and:

"Perhaps," he requested, "in common justice you will be good enough to explain the position. Why am I detained in this way? Since when has it been a crime to lose one's railway ticket?"

For a moment neither man answered him. The stationmaster stood just inside the door, looking peculiarly ill at ease, and the detective, having removed his bowler, leaned against the mantelpiece. He possessed a head of very bristly upstanding black hair which was seen to advantage against a coloured background afforded by a map of the London, Tilbury & Southend Railway Company's routes. Nature had palpably designed him for a humorist, and he now approached his delicate official task with a distaste which he was unable wholly to conceal.

"No one has accused you of committing a crime," he said. "May I ask your name?"

"My name can have nothing whatever to do with the fact that I have lost my ticket. By what right do you ask?"

"I have told you by what right."

"The mere fact that you are attached to the police force does not entitle you to detain me without reason. My time is of value. You ask me for my name. I ask you for yours. I also ask of what I am accused."

"So far," the other replied patiently, "you are accused of nothing. My name is Sowerby—Detective Inspector Sowerby of the Criminal Investigation Department. I have official reasons for wishing to know yours."

"Very well, Inspector," the passenger replied slowly; "I suppose you are within your rights. I will give you my card."

He took out his case, paused, and immediately realized that he had committed a blunder. He had given the last card in the case to his mysterious travelling companion!

"I am sorry," he said, returning the wallet to his pocket. "My name is Bernard Hope."

The stationmaster coughed drily, and Inspector Sowerby gazed down speculatively at the floor as though inspiration might lurk in the nearly defaced pattern of the linoleum. When he looked up again, the effect was as though a comedian had looked through a mask of tragedy. In other words, the Inspector's face had assumed the prescribed official expression, but his eyes smiled.

"Very well, Mr. Hope," he said. "It's a funny world. Do you live in London?"

"Yes."

"What is your business at the docks?"

"I have none, ordinarily. To-night I had gone to see a friend."

"At the West India Docks?"

"Yes—on the *Port Royal,* lying there."

"And when did you leave your friend, Mr. Hope?"

"I didn't see him. He had come up to London."

"He wasn't expecting you, then?"

"No. He did not even know that I was in England."

"How did you find out he was not on board?"

"From his steward."

The Inspector paused for a moment; then:

"As this is a very serious matter," he said, "perhaps you would like to make quite sure that the ticket is really lost."

"I *am* quite sure," Hope declared wearily, "but, nevertheless, I will look again."

Accordingly he turned out all his pockets, and then, shrugging his shoulders:

"You see," he said, "it is gone."

"Was it a return-half?"

"No. It was a single ticket—from the Docks station."

"You were travelling first class?"

"Yes."

"Were you alone in the compartment?"

Almost imperceptibly Hope hesitated before replying:

"No. There was one other passenger, a lady."

"Known to you?"

"Unknown to me."

Inspector Sowerby turned to the stationmaster.

"Have all the first-class coaches searched," he directed, "for a ticket issued at West India Docks."

The stationmaster nodded and went out; and, as the door closed:

"Now, Mr. Hope," said the Inspector, moving restlessly from foot to foot, "before you answer any more questions, you are entitled to know why I have detained you. A man was robbed and murdered down in the Chinatown district to-night, and someone was seen climbing up the railway embankment while the 8:5 was held up there by fog. Now, from the time the train moved on, it didn't stop again until it reached Fenchurch Street. All the exits have been watched—and you are the only passenger without a ticket!"

"Good heavens!" Hope exclaimed; and he experienced the curious sensation of feeling himself turn pale. "But—but this is preposterous! I have never been in Chinatown in my life!"

"That, I am afraid," the Inspector returned, "I shall have to ask you to prove. However, I have warned you. You will probably find it quite easy to substantiate the statements you have made. What is the name of your friend on the *Port Royal?*"

"Captain Markham."

"The commander?"

"Yes."

"Did you go down by train?"

"No," Hope replied slowly, "I came by road from Dover."

"From Dover!"

Detective Inspector Sowerby's expressive features registered acute astonishment.

"Yes. I have been abroad. I left Paris at noon, and some people whose acquaintance I made on the boat offered to drive me up. They had arranged for a car to meet them at Dover."

"I see," Sowerby murmured; but his expression indicated that such was not the case. "I should like to point out that the Dover Road does not run through Limehouse."

"I agree, Inspector. We reached the Docks by way of Blackwall Tunnel. These people were going to join a liner for the East."

"Coming from Paris? Why not join it at Marseilles?"

"The very point I raised when I heard of their plans. But I learned that the lady—they were a Mr. and Mrs. Eldred of New York—disliked Continental railway travelling. I accepted their offer, as I thought it would just enable me to catch Markham before he sailed."

"I see," Sowerby murmured again. "So they dropped you at the West India Docks and went on down to the Royal Albert? This all seems fairly reasonable. It's a pity you have no card, but there are many people in London who can identify you?"

"Certainly."

"Have you such a thing as an hotel bill?" Sowerby suggested helpfully.

"I am afraid I always destroy them."

"H'm! Anything else? A theatre ticket, for instance?"

"No. By some fatality I seem to have scrapped everything that could have assisted me now."

Inspector Sowerby turned his speculative gaze upon the floor once more. The door opened and the stationmaster entered, shaking his head.

"Nothing," he reported.

There was a moment of silence, and then, in a strained voice:

"I can only assure you," said Hope, "that I know nothing whatever about this matter. Good heavens, Inspector! As you say that the murderer was seen escaping, surely you have some description of his appearance?"

"I have," the Inspector replied sorrowfully. "A slight, dark man, very active, and wearing a blue suit."

"Good heavens!" said Hope again. "But, Inspector, if you believe me to be the man who boarded the train in the fog, how do you account for my having baggage with me?"

Inspector Sowerby glanced down at the attaché case upon the floor beside the speaker.

"That is easily handled," he replied; "in fact, the wanted man was actually carrying something— which might have been a small bag and an overcoat."

"But my suitcase!" Hope cried triumphantly— "what of my heavy suitcase?"

"Eh!" the Inspector exclaimed, looking blankly at the stationmaster, "Have *you* seen any suitcase?"

The other shook his head.

"Where did you leave this suitcase?" Sowerby inquired.

"I put it down on the platform near some other luggage. It was too heavy to carry far, and I intended to go back for it when I had paid for my ticket."

"Surely you didn't know you had lost your ticket at that time?" the stationmaster broke in. "I saw you looking for it just by the barrier. You had no suitcase with you then."

"But," Hope exclaimed confusedly, "this can all be settled by sending out for my grip! I can enumerate the whole of its contents."

The Inspector turned to the stationmaster.

"Will you make sure?" he said.

"Certainly," was the reply.

The other went out. As the door closed upon his exit:

"You know, Mr. Hope," Inspector Sowerby continued, his hands clasped behind him and his eyes now fixed upon the suspect, "your story is beginning to wear a little bit thin. You have not yet produced one shred of evidence to show that you have been in Paris, nor one shred of evidence to show that you were on the train when it left West India Docks. There was a time when I thought I had made a mistake, but I am beginning to change my mind. If this suitcase is not forthcoming, I warn you that things will have taken on a very serious aspect."

"My suitcase is there. I put it down on the platform myself."

"Very well; we shall see. But in the meantime, there is one small point, Mr. Hope, which should help us to settle the question once and for all about your being in Paris. Where's your passport?"

Bernard Hope's expression changed. Perhaps, in crises of our lives, we become clairvoyant; perhaps a shadowy foreknowledge of what was to be came to him. Certainly, he paused for several seconds, watching Sowerby, who had put his last question almost pathetically. Then:

"It is in my suitcase," he replied.

And even as he spoke the words the door opened again, and the stationmaster entered.

"Not a scrap of baggage on the platform," he announced. "Everything cleared away."

At that, Bernard Hope lost control of himself.

"My God!" he cried, "this is like some dreadful nightmare! It must have been stolen! I am not blaming you, Inspector, but your suspicions are absurd. I know nothing—*nothing* whatever—about this matter!"

His mind was in a turmoil. What possible connection could exist between the murderer and the woman who had climbed into the train, he could not imagine. He remained sane enough to realize that the fatality which seemed to be dogging his footsteps had nullified the value of every statement he had made. To admit now that he had not told the whole truth, and to offer as his explanation a promise to a strange woman, could in no way improve his case. Indeed, he realized that the fantastic story would certainly not be credited. He determined to seek expert advice.

"I fully realize my position," he said, forcing himself to speak calmly, "and so, before I answer any more questions, I should like to communicate with a friend who is a counsel of long experience in such matters."

"You may communicate with any one you wish in a moment," the Inspector replied, "but as a very large sum of ready money is believed to have been stolen from the murdered man, I must first ask you" — pointing to the attaché case—"to open that."

As Sowerby spoke it was possible, even in the badly lighted office, to detect the fact that Bernard Hope had grown pale. The stationmaster, catching the Inspector's glance, nodded grimly.

"Unlock it, please," the Inspector repeated sorrowfully.

A figure of detected guilt, moving like an automaton, Bernard Hope took out a key ring, selected a key, and opened the attaché case. A voice, he could not have said whose voice it was, exclaimed:

"That settles it."

The case was packed with English banknotes and Treasury notes, neatly tied together in little bundles!

CHAPTER III

YVETTE GOES EAST

Some two hours prior to these dramatic happenings at Fenchurch Street, Yvette Chalmers sat before the mirror in her dressing room at the Riviera Theatre crushing a fashionably small hat down on her short, closely waving hair, which gleamed with mahogany tints in the lamplight. She was otherwise dressed ready to go out. For, as she was wont to explain to her friends who expressed surprise at meeting her during the evening, she had the misfortune to be murdered in the first act.

She wore a dark, fur-trimmed coat, which fitted her slim figure perfectly, and as she sat there arranging her hair beneath the inadequate brim of her hat, she must have afforded a very charming study for an artist not obsessed by the modern cult of ugliness.

Yvette had gray-blue eyes whose habitual expression was one of quizzical self-dissatisfaction, and a freshness of colouring which was the despair of her professional sisters. To-night, one would have said that she was preoccupied. Indeed, when presently the door opened and the dresser entered, her sudden start and the way in which she glanced over her shoulder might almost have been termed apprehensive.

"Good heavens! You quite startled me. My mind was miles and miles away. What have you got there?"

Mrs. Walters laid a card upon the table; and:

"The gentleman asked me to remind you that he was leaving England to-night," she said.

Yvette glanced at the card, and a little frown of perplexity appeared between her level brows. Methodically she tore the card into fragments and dropped the fragments upon the floor. Then, looking up at the woman:

"How frightfully awkward," she murmured. "I don't quite know what to do."

"Shall I ask him to come up?"

"Oh! no, no!" Yvette cried urgently. "Wait—I must think. Did you say I was still here?"

"Yes, miss. I didn't know you wouldn't want to see him. You have always seen him before."

"I know I have. But to-night, you see— Well"—she laughed in an embarrassed fashion—"it's very difficult. I have to go somewhere else."

"Then why not tell him so?"

"Well, he might want to come with me."

"Oh!" said the dresser; "yes. That's reasonable."

"At the same time, I don't want to offend him. I had quite forgotten it was his last night in town, or I wouldn't have made the arrangement."

Mrs. Walters, a kindly looking woman of vast experience, thought that she understood, and:

"Suppose I say you must have gone out through the front?" she suggested. "He won't know any different."

"He would be sure to ask the commissionaire," Yvette declared; "he is very persevering."

"That's all right," said the other reassuringly. "It's getting foggy. You might easily have slipped out unnoticed."

"Foggy?" cried Yvette with concern. "Oh, dear! I'm sorry to hear that. Does it look like being a really thick one?"

"It might be," said Mrs. Walters guardedly.

"Rapkin tells me if the wind shifts to the northeast, we shall be in for a regular choker."

Rapkin, the stage doorkeeper, was the theatre oracle, and Yvette received this pronouncement with suitable respect.

"I hope the wind stays in the west," she commented, "or wherever it may be at the moment, if that is the case."

She glanced again into the mirror and stood up.

"I'm awfully afraid you will have to do as you suggest," she said. "I hate doing it, but I must. Yes, tell him I have gone out through the front."

Mrs. Walters smiled knowingly and retired, whilst Yvette, making certain that her purse, powder puff, and other necessities were in her bag, prepared to depart as soon as the signal "all clear" should be received.

The second act of the play had just commenced, and the rooms to right and left of her were deserted, so that she stood quite alone in the corridor until Mrs. Walters's leisurely steps sounded upon the stone stairs and Mrs. Walters reappeared.

"He didn't believe me," that lady reported, "but he's gone."

"You are quite sure?"

Yvette looked at her eagerly.

"Well, he went out."

"Do you know if Rapkin got me my cab?"

"Yes."

"The usual one?"

"Yes, miss," said the dresser, staring curiously. "I heard his voice out there as the door opened."

Yvette began to descend, and:

"I wish you would go out and ask him to come inside the stage door for a moment," she said. "You might make sure, too, that no one is waiting."

Mrs. Walters nodded comprehendingly, and, descending ahead of Yvette Chalmers, passed the doorkeeper's stronghold, pushed the swing door, and went out into the street.

There had been a belated postal delivery whilst the first act was in progress, but as the girl paused and looked into Rapkin's little room:

"No, miss," he said, and gloomily shook his head.

Indeed, Rapkin was habitually gloomy, a dark man wearing his jet-black moustache in the manner of a Viking; an odd figure in a clean-shaven age, and an incurable Romantic. He had learned to anticipate Yvette's perpetual inquiry, and, having watched her examining her letters, by a process of elimination he had learned that it was for a once familiar handwriting that she looked in vain.

She smiled at him cheerfully, hiding her disappointment.

"When Miss Chalmers looks in at my window," Rapkin had informed Mrs. Walters, "she makes the sun shine in the middle of the night."

Then, as Yvette turned aside to greet the taxi man who had entered, Rapkin shook his head sadly, replaced his spectacles which he had temporarily removed, and returned to "East Lynne," which he was reading with deep and sympathetic understanding.

"Good evening, miss," said the taxi man heartily.

He was a florid and jovial figure, and in common with most people who came in contact with Yvette Chalmers was happier in serving her than in serving, almost any one else.

As Mrs. Walters paused, significantly shaking her head:

"Thanks so much," said the girl; "you need not wait any longer." She turned again to the man, and, lowering her voice, "Is it too foggy for you to drive me to Limehouse?" she inquired.

His brown eyes opened widely in astonishment, and:

"*Limehouse,* miss?" he whispered beerily.

"Yes. Is it too foggy?"

"Well, miss"—he continued to stare, almost reproachfully—"it's coming up a bit thick, but I'll chance it, if that's where you want to go. What part of Limehouse?"

Yvette glanced about her almost furtively, and, opening her bag, took out a slip of paper upon which an address was written in pencil. She held it up.

"Do you know it?" she asked.

The cabman held the slip of paper more closely to the light, screwing up his eyes to read it; then:

"I know," he said—"off West India Dock Road. Is that right?"

"I don't know," Yvette declared. "I'm afraid you will have to find it for me."

"Right ho! Shall you be there long?"

"No, not more than half an hour or so."

"Well, cut it short," said the man, crossing and holding open the door for her. "If we got caught down there by the fog, I don't know what time we should get back."

Indeed, as she came out of the stage door, Yvette was rather alarmed at the density of the mist; so much so that before entering the cab, she hesitated. Peering along in the direction of the main road, the lighted traffic of which was already half veiled by fog, she pictured in her mind the gloomy East End thoroughfares along which the route lay.

"I think it's lifting a bit," the cabman declared optimistically. "If it's too thick when we get past Aldgate we shall have to turn back, that's all."

"Very well," said Yvette bravely, and got in.

The man, who had been waiting some time, stopped to crank his engine, and, as he did so, from a shadowy doorway a little farther up the narrow street in which the stage entrance was located, a muffled figure came out, passed the cab, which was still stationary, and disappeared in the direction of the main thoroughfare. It was that of a man buttoned up in a thick, dark overcoat, the collar raised so as to hide his features, and the brim of his soft hat pulled down. So that even one who had known him well must have failed to recognize him. The corner gained, he began keenly to scrutinize the passing traffic, and presently, discerning a disengaged taxicab:

"Hi!" he called. "Taxi!"

The man pulled up.

"I want to go to the West India Docks," said the one who had hailed him. "Is it too far for you, or too foggy?"

"Are you coming back, sir?"

"No. I shall be staying."

"It's a bit off the map," the man growled.

"I agree. But it is urgent. I'll give you double fare and five shillings over."

"If the fog thickens, I may get hung up there all night."

"If that is the case, I'll double the tip."

A moment's hesitation, then:

"Jump in. I'll risk it."

"That's not all," the fare continued. "See that cab, just coming out of the turning, yonder, from the stage door of the Riviera Theatre?"

"Eh?" the man muttered, straining his eyes to peer through the mist. "Yes, I see."

"Well, it is going the same way and I don't want you to lose sight of it."

"You mean you want me to follow that cab?"

"Exactly! Can you do it?"

"I'll try. I've got a better engine than his. But if it gets any more soupy—the answer is 'No.'"

"Do your best. Quick! They've turned the corner."

"Very good, sir. Jump in."

And so, through the growing darkness, two cabs headed for Limehouse.

CHAPTER IV

COSMO POTTER, K. C.

An awkward silence had fallen upon the bleak lofty room in New Scotland Yard. Detective Inspector Sowerby sat behind a table officially furnished with a telephone, an ink pot, a pen, and a virgin blotting pad, tapping with the pen upon the pad. Bernard Hope sat in a chair by the tall, uncurtained window, staring vaguely at his attaché case which stood upon a corner of the big table.

Inspector Sowerby was a badly puzzled man. Reason strongly indicated that the wanted party was here; instinct scoffed at reason. The discovery of several thousands of pounds of ready money in Bernard Hope's possession seemed extraordinarily like conclusive evidence, and Hope's refusal to submit to further examination without advice proved that he, too, recognized the gravity of his position.

The character of this advice had done more to convince Sowerby that he tottered on the brink of a bad blunder than anything which the suspected man hitherto had said or done. For Hope had asked for and obtained permission to endeavour to communicate with none other than Cosmo Potter, one of the most successful criminal counsels at the Bar, and, moreover, a nephew of the Assistant Commissioner, who was Sowerby's immediate chief. The facilities enjoyed by Mr. Potter in the preparation of his criminal cases were notorious throughout the Department and in some quarters were resented. That the formidable and influential counsel was a friend of Hope's added an element of complexity which Sowerby found very baffling.

By great and welcome good luck Bernard Hope had found his man; and now, to break a silence which was growing embarrassing, there sounded a rap upon the door.

"Come in," said the Inspector.

The door opened and a constable came in.

"Mr. Cosmo Potter," he announced.

Inspector Sowerby nodded.

A moment later Mr. Cosmo Potter entered. He was in full evening dress, as his white bow indicated, and wore an overcoat flawless in every line, together with an extraordinarily glossy silk hat. One hand was whitely gloved and held a malacca cane; with the other he removed the glossy hat. He looked about him inquiringly.

Mr. Cosmo Potter was above medium height— perhaps half an inch taller than Bernard Hope. But because of his stocky build he was sometimes described as a short man whilst Hope was usually regarded as being tall. His face was composed on Cubist principles, being entirely made up of angles, and as he elected to wear his hair clipped close to his skull, he was frequently mistaken for a Prussian. His light blue eyes, although large and very widely opened, had a dreamy expression only one degree removed from vacancy; and no man had ever seen his right eye naked, since this eye and a small rimless monocle were seemingly inseparable. There was some authority for the rumour that he wore his monocle in bed.

"My dear Hope," he said, "whatever is the meaning of this distressing scene?"

He glanced across at the Inspector.

"Good-evening, Sowerby. Are *you* responsible? I was dancing with a really charming woman at the Embassy when I was rudely interrupted."

"Thank God we found you, Potter!" Bernard Hope exclaimed. "I am in a most dreadful mess!"

Cosmo Potter removed his topcoat and draped it with great care across the back of a chair. Upon a ledge he placed his gleaming hat, and turned again, revealing himself in an evening suit calculated to have defied criticism from the editor of the *Tailor and Cutter*. He was miraculously well groomed, seeming to have stepped fresh out of his bath into garments newly delivered from the makers. Now, he extracted a huge case and proffered cigarettes of the size of cigars. They were declined, however, whereupon, fixing one in an amber holder, he lighted up, tossed the match into the hearth, and sighed deeply.

"This all seems so unnecessary, Sowerby," he said.

"It does, sir," the Inspector agreed. "It's a funny world, but"—glancing uneasily at his watch—"there is a lot to be done and it's getting late. Now, Mr. Hope, I have warned you of the danger of your position, and, quite properly, you asked me to delay further questions until Mr. Potter could attend. We have been fortunate enough to get him along, so now, perhaps, we can go ahead."

"Am I to understand," Potter inquired, "that you have *detained* Hope for some reason?"

"Oh! it's preposterous!" Bernard Hope groaned. "Let me try to explain."

"One moment!" Potter raised the long cigarette like a conductor raising his baton. "Inspector Sowerby"—he turned to the latter—"will you please state your case against Mr. Hope? Hope, be silent!"

He had dropped the blasé manner. Although his expression remained abstracted and dreamy, his voice was that of one keenly alert.

"I want you to understand, sir," said the Inspector, "that I have made no charge. I am merely anxious to give Mr. Hope an opportunity to establish an alibi."

"An alibi!" said Potter frigidly. "What is the crime? Please enlighten me."

"Murder and suspected robbery," was the reply. "At about half-past nine to-night, a man known as Burma Chang was killed at his house in the Chinatown area."

"Burma Chang!" Hope murmured dazedly, and again: "Burma Chang!"

An unmistakable expression of horror began to steal over his face, and Sowerby, hearing the words and noting the look, asked sharply:

"You know him?"

Hope raised his hand to his brow, when:

"Hope! For the last time!" Potter said peremptorily, "be silent. Your turn will come in a moment. Be good enough to proceed, Inspector. By what means was this man's death brought about?"

Detective Inspector Sowerby, who, for all his good-humoured manner, was not a man to be browbeaten, flushed to a shade of red deeper than normal.

Almost, it was spoken—some sharp retort which trembled on his lips; but because his cardinal virtue was patience he suppressed it, coughed, and:

"On that point, sir," he answered quietly, "I am waiting for further information. The only facts which I have, so far, were communicated over the telephone from Limehouse. I was put in charge and I proceeded straight to Fenchurch Street."

"Why?" Potter inquired.

"Because a plain clothes officer on duty outside Burma Chang's house saw a man climb over the wall and run off in the fog. This man carried some kind of bundle, and he was described as being of slight build, dark, and wearing a blue suit."

"Quite," said Potter; "but why did you proceed to Fenchurch Street? Enlighten me."

"Because the officer gave chase, lost his man between the house and the railway, then heard a police whistle, joined up with a constable whose name I forget at the moment, and found that he, the constable, had just seen someone scale the fence and scramble up the railway embankment on to the line. At this time the 8:5 from Blackwall— already over an hour late—was detained there by fog, but had proceeded when Simmons, the plain clothes man, reached the spot."

"I see," Potter murmured. "They 'phoned to the terminus and the railway people applied to you?"

"That's it."

"But one moment," Potter interrupted; "a point occurs to me. Why was the plain clothes man outside the house of this Burma Chang? By accident?"

"Oh! no," Sowerby answered, "Chang had applied for protection and K Division were watching his house."

"Why did he apply for protection?"

"According to his own account," was the reply, "because he possessed valuables and had reason to believe that an attempt was to be made to rob him."

"He was a rich man, then?"

The Inspector nodded.

"Supposed to be the richest man in Chinatown."

Cosmo Potter dropped cigarette ash into the hearth; and:

"What was the source of this wealth of his?" he inquired. "Of course, you know?"

"There you have me, sir. I don't know."

"Really," Potter murmured; "and I thought there were some good men in K Division."

"So there are," the Inspector returned warmly, his colour rising again; "but they are only human, after all, and when the whole Chinese community act together in covering up a certain thing, it's not an easy job to find that thing out."

Cosmo Potter bowed.

"I accept the rebuke, Sowerby," he said; "no doubt I deserved it. Burma Chang was a man of mystery. But am I to understand that this officer—Simmons, I think you said his name was—seeing someone escaping over the wall of Chang's house, ran off into the fog without troubling to inquire what had happened *inside* the house?"

"Not at all. He left that part of the inquiry to the constable on point duty at the corner."

"There were two men watching the house, then?"

"Not exactly. The constable had been detailed for that duty, and Simmons, amongst other jobs, was keeping an eye upon the place as well."

"I quite understand. Please go on."

"When Simmons got back to the house of Chang, he discovered that murder had been done. I have no details, but this much I learned before leaving the Yard, as I had half an hour to spare before the train was due at Fenchurch Street. I arranged to have it watched from the time it slowed into the station, and no one left it except by the usual platform."

"You are sure of this?"

"Perfectly certain. There was only one person on the train who had no ticket, and that person was Mr. Hope. Mr. Hope carried no baggage."

"I did!" Hope cried angrily.

"One moment, Hope, if you please." Potter raised his cigarette. "I am acting for you now; leave this to me. Had no baggage, you say, Sowerby?"

"Exactly," the Inspector went on. "His explanation on this point, as well as regarding the loss of his ticket, was most unsatisfactory, or seemed so to me. I might not have gone so far as to detain him if it had not been"—pointing to the attaché case—"for that. On top of all the other suspicious circumstances, when I found what Mr. Hope was so carefully guarding in his bag, there was really no other course open to me."

"What he was guarding in his bag, Sowerby? What *was* he guarding in his bag? Enlighten me."

"Six thousand pounds in notes!"

"I have already told you," Hope burst in excitedly, but:

"One moment, if you please, one moment!" Potter interrupted sharply. "You have definite evidence, Sowerby, of a theft of money from the house of this man Chang?"

"Not definite evidence, but enough to make it pretty clear that a theft took place. In the room where his body was found, I understand, a safe had been opened, and it contained a large amount of ready money."

"What leads you to suppose that a thief, especially one so desperate as to commit murder, would leave any ready money behind?"

"Well," the Inspector hesitated, "he might have had no means of carrying any more."

Potter smoked his enormous cigarette in silence for a while, and then:

"In short, I gather," he said, "that you have no evidence of a theft at all?"

"Well, in one sense you are right," the Inspector admitted grudgingly; "although robbery was most likely the motive. In fact, it would be a waste of time to look for any other in the circumstances. You must remember that Chang had applied for protection because he was afraid of robbery."

"Or so he said," Potter murmured. "Humanity is so disappointing,

Sowerby. You are certain that there was ready money in the safe?"

"Yes. Simmons said so distinctly."

"The logical deduction to my mind, therefore, would be, not that a theft had been committed, but that a theft had *not* been committed. However, as neither of us is in possession of all the facts, how hopeless to attempt to arrive at any sane conclusion. Briefly, I take it that this is the outline of your case against Mr. Bernard Hope?"

"It is, sir. And when you hear his explanations of all these things which look so black against him, I think you will agree that I acted quite rightly in asking him to prove his story."

CHAPTER V

BERNARD HOPE EXPLAINS

"And now, Hope," said Potter, "with Inspector Sowerby's permission, I propose to cross-examine you, in order to establish the fact, of which I, personally, have no doubt, that you know nothing whatever about this crime."

The telephone bell rang, and:

"Just a moment, sir," said Sowerby, taking up the instrument. "Hello! Yes! Speaking. Is that you, Peel?"

He listened awhile, nodding, his expression one of humorous perplexity; and with a pencil which he drew from his waistcoat he made notes upon a writing block. Presently:

"Don't tell me any more, now," he said; "I want to form my own impressions. Be careful that nothing is moved. Is the fog very thick down that way?"

As he listened to the reply, he nodded constantly, serio-comic concern written upon his florid face; and at last:

"It may take me a long while to get down," he declared, "but I shall be there as soon as possible. Good-bye." He hung up the receiver. "Divisional Inspector Peel, speaking from Burma Chang's house," he explained. "There are certain developments in that quarter, and the sooner I can start out the better." Once more he consulted his watch. "Now, sir, I am at your service."

"Very good." Potter flicked more cigarette ash into the hearth, and:

"Now, Hope," he went on, as the latter, who had begun to look very haggard, watched him almost distractedly, "before we begin, is there anything which in your very natural excitement and alarm, finding yourself suspected of such a crime as this, you omitted from your earlier statement?”

For one long dramatic moment Hope hesitated and then:

“Yes, there is!” he confessed.

“Oh! *Is* there!” Sowerby muttered, frowningly.

“Wait!” Potter held up his diminishing cigarette. “Did you omit this information intentionally?”

“At the time, no,” Hope replied. “I thought it had no bearing upon the matter. Later I hesitated to mention it because, firstly, I did not think I should be believed, and secondly, to be quite honest, because I was in a funk. Everything I had said had been turned against me and that was why I determined to wait for you.”

He would have gone on, but Potter checked him again.

“Very well,” he said, coolly, “let us have this additional information when we come to it. But to begin at the end”—he pointed to the attaché case—“where did you obtain this large sum of ready money?”

“At Monte Carlo,” came the reply, promptly.

“You won it?”

“I won it, yes.”

“At the Casino?”

“Yes.”

“At roulette?”

“Yes.”

“And why did you change your winnings into notes?”

Hope laughed unmirthfully.

“The reason was so fantastic that I know it will sound like another misstatement,” he said, “but it was this: I wanted to surprise”—he hesitated—“someone who has inspired and helped me and who deserves to share in my good fortune. To-night I had intended to pour out my winnings before her. It was there I was going, when—”

“H’m,” Potter murmured, staring vacantly at the speaker. “Your craving after dramatic situations, Hope, has led you into a pretty mess. Did you realize the risk which you were incurring—in view of the very peculiar circumstances—by travelling from Monte Carlo to London with six thousand pounds in a handbag?”

“Yes, I was a fool. But I’ve always been a fool in money matters.”

“Where did you obtain the English notes?”

“At Cook’s in Monte Carlo.”

“Did you win it all at one sitting?”

“No, at several.”

“Did you change the entire amount at the same time?”

“Yes. At one point my winnings were rather more, but on the last occasion that I went to the Casino, I lost. I was playing on a system, but at this final session I came to the conclusion that extraordinary good luck and not the system had made me win. Accordingly, I changed the remainder of my money—about six thousand pounds—at Cook's on the following morning and left for Paris in the afternoon."

"Therefore, Cook's Monte Carlo Office would probably remember the transaction as a somewhat unusual one, I should presume?"

"They would probably remember it, yes."

"And could identify you?"

Bernard Hope raised his hand to his head wearily.

"I fear they would not be able to identify me," he replied.

Potter turned to him sharply.

"Why not? Enlighten me."

"I was wearing a moustache at that time and tortoise-shell rimmed glasses."

Inspector Sowerby's expression was so eloquent that:

"Damn it! On my word of honour, I am speaking the truth!" Hope cried desperately. "It's true, every word of it! I know how improbable it must sound, but it's true!"

"All right, Hope," said Potter. "I cannot recall having contradicted you. Please don't get excited. It won't help anybody. You were, in short, disguised. For what reason?"

Hope made an effort to control himself, and then:

"I must go back a little way to make you understand," he said slowly. "I have a play which several managements had offered to produce, but I had declined their offers, although I was at the end of my resources."

"Why?"

"Because I had determined that a certain lady, whom I hope to marry one day, should play the leading part. Indeed, it was written for her. But since she has her reputation to make, none of the managements would consent to cast her for lead. As, otherwise, she has nothing whatever to do with this horrible affair, I hope you will allow me to withhold her name—at least for the present.

"Rather more than two months ago, when I was all but despairing, I turned my attention to a system upon which, in a desultory fashion, I had been working for some time. Perhaps desperation spurred me, but in a few hours I had completed it."

"You refer to a roulette system?" Potter interjected.

"Yes. I had just the minimum amount to spare which I required to give it a trial. I am not a gambler by instinct—as the result shows; but I believed that I had found a way of beating the bank. Therefore, I borrowed a sum, sufficient to cover my expenses, knowing that, if the worst came, I could repay it in two months' time, when certain royalties fall due to me."

"One moment," Sowerby interrupted. "You say you borrowed your expenses, Mr. Hope—"

Cosmo Potter raised his cigarette, and:

"I object!" he said sharply. "Hope, does this loan in any way concern the matter in hand?"

"Well," Hope replied wearily, "in a way, it does."

"Very good. I withdraw my objection. What do you want to know, Sowerby?"

"The name of the person Mr. Hope borrowed from."

"You have heard of him already, Inspector," Hope said; "I borrowed from a very old friend. Captain Markham. You know him, Potter?"

The latter nodded.

"Go on," he directed.

"Very well. I went to Markham, who, unlike myself, is a born gambler, only on the understanding that he was backing me to win. In other words, I made an effort to-night to catch him before he sailed because one thousand of the six in that bag belongs to him under the terms of the loan."

"Good!" Potter snapped. "Important, most important."

"As I have already told Inspector Sowerby, Markham came up to town to-night and was presumably detained by fog—"

"Stop, stop!" The dwindling cigarette was uplifted urgently. "Please continue your statement from the point where, having decided to test this system, you set out for Monte Carlo."

"All right, Potter. Let me think." Hope raised his hand again to his brow. "Oh, yes—my object, then, was to raise sufficient capital to produce my own play. Now, there are quite a number of people to whom I am known. They are aware, most of them, that I cannot afford a Riviera holiday. I did not want to be called upon to explain what I was doing in Monte Carlo. Therefore, I went down to a little bungalow at Shoreham, which belongs to my sister, and let my moustache grow! Having told the lady in whose interests I was really behaving in this mad way a story to account for my absence, I proceeded to Monte Carlo, where I booked under another name."

"What name?" Inspector Sowerby interrupted.

"Arthur Morton," Hope replied. "My full names being Bernard Arthur Morton Hope."

"Go on," said the Inspector, whose expression of bewilderment was becoming extravagant.

"My moustache went unchallenged by the passport people, and while actually in Monaco I wore spectacles, as I have said already. I left

Monte Carlo on Wednesday afternoon, and finding no opportunity of shaving off my moustache without attracting attention on the journey, I determined to travel from Dover by a slow train, find a carriage to myself, and perform the metamorphosis on the way. With this object in view, I provided myself with hot water on the boat, filling my thermos flask. However, my plans were altered as a result of a chance acquaintance.

"I was naturally most anxious that Markham should share my good fortune, and I had studied the movements of his ship, the *Port Royal,* of the Port Line, as closely as possible. I realized that he would be sailing on the very night of my return. I had intended to leave my suitcase in the cloakroom at Victoria and to 'phone from there for a good car to get me down to the Docks.

"As I have explained to Inspector Sowerby, I met some people who were coming by road from Dover to join a liner for the East. They offered me a lift, as a result of my mentioning these plans to catch Markham. But, being deposited with my two bags at West India Docks, my real troubles began. In the first place, from the time that we approached the river, the fog had grown steadily worse. We were fully an hour late. Then, having found a dock official to mind my suitcase, I made my way on board the *Port Royal*—only to learn that Markham had gone up to town and was not back.

"I might have waited—I wish to Heaven I had— but Markham's steward asked me how I proposed to get home. Frankly, I had not thought of this, and I was very anxious to pay another visit.

"'If you take my advice,' said the steward, 'you'll run for the 8:5. It's the last train up—and it's been held for over an hour by some fog trouble farther along the line. It's standing in the Dock Station now, but may leave at any minute. There are no cabs—so make up your mind.'

"I took his advice. To leave a thousand pounds in cash in Markham's cabin was more than I cared to risk. Therefore, I scribbled a note and bolted along to the platform. I got my other bag from the man who was minding it, bought a ticket, and some five minutes later, the train started. I was given to understand that it would run through, direct, to Fenchurch Street; so, being anxious to appear in town clean shaven, as soon as we started I got out nail scissors, shaving kit, and the thermos flask "

"You shaved off your moustache in the train?" said Potter.

"I did, and threw the fragments of the operation out on to the line."

"Ah!" Potter murmured, withdrawing from the case another of his gigantic cigarettes, "we come now to what took place at Fenchurch

Street."

"No, not yet," Hope said nervously. "We come first to an incident so extraordinary that I am quite prepared to be disbelieved."

Thereupon, speaking rapidly, as if he feared interruption, Hope related his adventure with the mysterious woman who had entered the train out of the fog. He omitted the episode of the kiss, and, in conclusion:

"Since it is now fairly obvious," he said, "that this woman must have been concerned in some way with the crime, I count myself justified in breaking the promise which I made."

A moment of complete silence followed. Cosmo Potter turned to Inspector Sowerby, whose ruddy face expressed blank incredulity, and:

"You were at the gate of the platform," he snapped. "You saw this woman?"

"Well!"—Sowerby hesitated—"there were only three women on the train, and one was certainly young and well dressed. But—"

"All I want to know!" said Potter. "Go on, Hope."

"When I reached the station," Hope resumed wearily, "I put down my suitcase and walked in the direction of the exit with the idea of paying my fare. It dawned upon me that the passengers were being watched. Inspector Sowerby I recognized for a police officer at once, and it occurred to me that they must be looking for my mysterious acquaintance. Foolishly—I admit I rather lost my head—I pretended to hunt for my ticket. That is all. Palpably my suitcase was stolen during the time that I was in the stationmaster's office."

Silence fell again—a silence which seemed to be rendered even more oppressive by the deadening effect of the fog, which had invested the building and traces of which were to be seen in the room. At last:

"What do you mean," Sowerby inquired, "when you say that you found no opportunity of shaving off your moustache until you reached England? You could surely have done it in a hotel somewhere."

"What!" cried Potter, staring across at the speaker. "Enter a foreign hotel wearing a moustache and come out clean shaven? My dear Sowerby, you know better than that. Humanity is so distrustful."

Inspector Sowerby drew out a handkerchief and blew his nose loudly.

"A point occurs to me," Potter resumed, turning to Hope; "the bungalow at Shoreham belonging to your sister. Enlighten me. Your sister can testify to the fact that you grew a moustache during your stay there?"

"My sister is in Switzerland," Hope replied in a dreary voice. "She left the keys with me before she went."

"Hard luck!" said Potter. "It reduces us to Markham, who knew you were going; to your boat acquaintances and a steward on the *Port Royal* (who knew you came back); and to the dark lady of the 8.5."

"I have put it all in hand," Sowerby declared, staring oddly at Hope. "A man has been sent to try to get aboard the *Port Royal* before she sails. The fog should make it easy. I have also taken up the matter of Mr. and Mrs. Eldred and the car from Dover. Monte Carlo will soon know what's required; so that by midday to-morrow we should have tested Mr. Hope's story in every link."

"In the meantime," said Potter, "I should be glad if you would allow me to use the telephone. I want to make things as smooth as possible for you, Hope, and I propose to ask the Assistant Commissioner if I can give you a lift as far as Limehouse, Inspector."

"Very good, sir," Sowerby replied resignedly.

"But!" cried Hope, "does all this mean—"

"It means," Sowerby took him up sharply, "that Mr. Potter has forgotten one small point."

Cosmo Potter, his hand on the telephone, paused, staring vacantly at the speaker, who had risen and now confronted him.

"Really?" he murmured. "Enlighten me."

"That's easily done, sir." Sowerby turned to Hope. "You haven't told us—and Mr. Potter has forgotten to remind you—what you know about Burma Chang."

There was a note of challenge in Sowerby's voice, and:

"Hope!" Potter snapped, "you need not do so at this stage."

"I should prefer it," Hope replied, speaking in a tired, toneless way. "I never met Burma Chang. But in some way he had made the acquaintance of—the lady to whom I have already referred."

"Eh!" murmured Potter, and then, aside, "O Lord!"

"Did you object?" Sowerby persisted.

"I objected, yes."

"Recently?"

"Yes."

A moment of silence, then:

"As I am afraid we may require her as a witness, then," Sowerby resumed, "I must ask you for this lady's name."

"Miss Yvette Chalmers," Hope answered dully, "at present playing at the Riviera Theatre."

CHAPTER VI

BEHIND THE CURTAIN

In and adjoining that district of London which is sometimes called Chinatown survive some few examples of country mansions, undevoured by the greedy maw of commercialism; for, once, where dockland stretches its grimy fingers over the river bank and disturbs with its ceaseless clangour the sleepy quiet of old Thames, were broad meadows and prosperous farmsteads. At least one great monastery thrived here, too, amid a rustic peace first broken by the rapacity of the eighth Henry.

Such a survival was the house of Burma Chang, a house now closely invested by the Asiatic settlement, its very existence unsuspected by the casual visitor, and its entrance a door in a long blank wall. Promising nothing, this wall concealed a fine old manor which had known much tumult and many changes, none stranger than that which had come to it with the invasion of yellow settlers from China.

As Cosmo Potter's car proceeded farther East, the density of the fog grew greater, and in creating a mutual sympathy this yellow investment had the effect of bringing the two travellers more closely together.

The genial Sowerby would have been less or more than human if he had been capable of welcoming the interference of Cosmo Potter in a case already bristling with difficulties. Potter's kinship with the Assistant Commissioner and the frank advantage which he took of it had shadowed the path of Detective Inspector Sowerby prior to the present occasion, and whilst he knew his hands to be tied, he was none the less resentful. He deplored the irregularity of the whole thing. Yet because the Detective Inspector was very much a human being, he found it difficult to maintain an attitude of resentment where Potter was concerned; and marooned with his elegant companion in a yellow sea of fog, he had early proclaimed an armistice.

"God knows if we'll ever get there!" he said, when, at some point in Whitechapel, the fog presented a seemingly impassable barrier, and the chauffeur opened the door to consult with his employer. "Unless the wind veers round, Mr. Potter, I can see us spending the night in the High Street, here."

"It looks like that to me," the chauffeur agreed, shivering.

But because it was written so, at that very moment a cool breeze blew in at the door, and, magically, a squalid vista opened up.

"Look! It has lifted, Burton, already," cried Cosmo Potter. "Go ahead. We shall do it all right."

And so that strange journey was resumed, the suspect's accuser and his advocate being borne eastward to the scene of the crime which had brought them together.

Sowerby expanded more and more.

"I have never been in Burma Chang's house," he said, "but it has been described to me by the Superintendent and others; and although accounts vary, there is no doubt that it contains valuable stuff."

He warmed to his topic.

"There is more money in that little section of London than most people suspect," he went on. "When I say that Burma Chang was the wealthiest man in the district, I am saying something."

"It is incredible to me," Cosmo Potter declared, "that the life of a man like that could remain a mystery to the police. You must have had suspicions, at least. Was he a dope dealer?"

"No," Sowerby replied emphatically; "of that I am certain. It wasn't dope."

"A fence?" Potter suggested. "Overseas stuff, maybe?"

"Well"—the detective stroked his upstanding hair, apparently in a hopeless attempt to make it lie down—"there are possibilities in that idea, I admit, sir. Yet, from all I have heard, I don't think it covers the ground. He was some kind of big among the Chinese. There is always one sure indication to a thing of that sort—their silence. And where Burma Chang was concerned, it seemed impossible to get a word out of any Chink in the neighbourhood."

Cosmo Potter contemplated the smouldering end of a huge cigarette for some moments, then:

"What aged man was this Burma Chang?" he asked; "and was he pure Chinese?"

"He was a Chinaman," Sowerby replied, "with a streak of something else in his make-up, which may or may not have been Burmese. I should put his age at forty-five to fifty."

"I take it, then," said Potter, "the man was fairly well known to the C. I. D.?"

Sowerby nodded.

"In a general way, yes," he admitted. "He was recognized to be a central figure in the Chinese quarter without ever having come upon the books. Do you see what I mean, sir? It's a funny world. He might have been with us or against us—we never knew which. But his name was always cropping up."

He glanced out of the window.

"Thank goodness!" he said, "for a time, at least, it's comparatively clear."

Such was indeed the case, and Burton, the chauffeur, taking advantage of this, they went bowling along Commercial Road East at racing speed—a fairly safe proceeding, since the lateness of the hour and the fog had emptied those dreary streets of pedestrians and vehicular traffic alike.

Inspector Sowerby's words regarding Burma Chang recurred, oddly, to Potter, as presently they swung to the right, riverward, plunging into the purlieus of Chinatown proper and meeting again threatening banks of vapour which seemed to sweep up from the Thames. For now the solitude became broken by isolated figures—shadows thrown exaggeratedly against that yellow curtain by the chance rays of some street lamp, or the headlights of the car. Single figures—pairs—and, presently, groups; some motionless, some moving—and those that were moving all moved in the same direction—mysteriously, like ghosts. A turn to the left, a northern incline, a sense of space both right and left—some main artery of dockland smudged out by the fog—and the ghostly shadows grew in number.

Once more the way became impassable, and Burton stopped. Now, all about the car, where silence had been, were murmurous voices and sibilant whispers and movements as of many observers.

"What the devil is this?" Cosmo Potter murmured.

"It's the Chinese," Sowerby replied, uneasily. "Peel told me. All Chinatown is out to-night."

And now the strangeness of this hidden vigilance took a powerful hold upon Potter's imagination. He opened a door.

"What are they all waiting for?" he said; "and why are they so furtive? If the murdered man was a leader among them, they should welcome us—yet I have a distinct impression, Sowerby, that our presence is resented. Where are we?"

"I'm not sure," the Inspector muttered.

He got out. Burton was standing at the step.

"Where are we?" the Inspector asked. "You said you knew this district."

"I know it fairly well," the chauffeur replied. "We're somewhere near the top end of Ropemakers' Fields."

Detective Inspector Sowerby whistled softly, peering into the mist where lurking shadows lived.

"That's funny," he said; "I don't understand it at all. We are nearly there, and Simmons should be here to meet us."

Cosmo Potter stepped down out of the car.

"Hi!" he shouted, "can any of you direct us to the house of Burma

Chang?"

There was no reply. The moving shadows in the mist, the murmurs, the whispers, seemed to fade away. Then the Inspector tried, and:

"Simmons!" he cried. "Sergeant Simmons!"

No one answered. A breeze from the river banked up yellow mist around them.

"Impossible to go on, sir," came Burton's voice.

As he ceased speaking, the three stood there listening. There was no sound. Even the ceaseless activities of dockland were muted by the fog: they might have been in the heart of a desert.

"What the devil do we do now?" Cosmo Potter inquired.

"Sound the horn," said Burton. "They may hear it."

The speaker acting upon this suggestion, the note of the horn seemed to be buffeted back upon them, mournfully, forbiddingly, by the walls of fog.

"Stop now, and listen!" cried Sowerby.

Silence came—a heavy, unbroken silence.

"Try again."

The signal was repeated; and presently—very faintly—from far, far away it seemed—a cry was heard.

"What is it?" Potter demanded.

"I think it's Simmons calling my name," Inspector Sowerby replied, and, using his cupped hands as a megaphone, he shouted:

"Sergeant Simmons!"

As if in answer came the cry again, as faintly as before.

"Try the horn once more."

This was done, and presently the answering cry grew clearer and resolved itself into the shouted words, "Inspector Sowerby!"

"It *is* Simmons," said the latter—then: "Hullo! What's that!"

"It's another car!" Burton replied, "there goes the horn again!"

"Which way is it coming?" Potter asked, helplessly. "It seems to be all around."

"Yes"—Burton was the speaker—"I think it's at the end of a narrow alley which makes an echo. But, listen, Simmons is coming nearer."

This was the case, but so deceptive was the fog that when, following a cry which might have come from a hundred yards away, a thick-set, light-coated figure appeared in the beam of the headlight, it was hard to believe that this was the one who had shouted.

"At last!" said Sowerby, and went forward to meet him.

A short colloquy took place between them, during which regular muffled notes sounded from the unseen car out in the mist. Cosmo Potter moved forward.

"He was at Leman Street," he heard the newcomer say. "He's only just arrived."

"In form?"—from Sowerby.

"Mustard!" was the reply, as Potter came up.

"Is there any hope of driving on?" he asked.

Sowerby turned to him, and:

"Yes," he answered. "That horn is intended to guide us. We haven't far to go."

His expression was compounded of expectancy and semi-tragic consternation, as might be read by the light of the car lamps; therefore:

"Is there some new development?" Potter asked.

Sowerby nodded, looking at the speaker almost pathetically.

"Sure," he said. "The Superintendent is here!"

CHAPTER VII

SUPERINTENDENT KERRY

An impression of hidden vigilance was strong upon every member of the party. The fog had assumed the properties of a moving yellow curtain behind which, shadowly, some hidden intelligence studied their every movement. So that, when at last they came to the door set in the high wall which promised so little but concealed so much, the interior revealed when the door was opened, despite its strangeness, offered harbourage from the whispering evil of the fog.

This was a spacious lobby, lofty, and crossed by an oaken gallery at the farther end, the gallery being approached by twin staircases, also of polished oak, the whole carried out in the manner of Grinling Gibbons. Perforated brass lamps suspended from the ceiling afforded the only light, and, except for a few rugs and one or two characteristically Oriental ornaments, the hall remained substantially as it had been when broad meadows surrounded the house and Chinatown was not.

Before a fine open fireplace in which, incongruously, an American stove burned, a police inspector stood talking to another man; and, as the door was opened by a constable and the new arrivals entered, this other man turned and stared at them.

He was little above medium height; he could perhaps have given half an inch to Cosmo Potter; but by reason of a lightness of poise and a sort of spruce slimness, he seemed much the taller man. He wore his hair cropped nearly as close to his skull as did that distinguished counsel, and this hair was brilliantly, uncompromisingly red, as was his short, wiry moustache. He was nearly as ruddy-of complexion as Sowerby, and he surveyed the newcomers with a pair of unblinking, steel-blue eyes.

His athletic figure was muffled in a big double-breasted, woolly overcoat. A neat bowler hat and a silver-mounted malacca cane lay upon the little table beside him. He appeared to be chewing, and the act of mastication revealed a perfect set of large and very white teeth.

"Now for it!" Sowerby muttered.

The words, and the manner in which they were spoken, constituted a complete criticism of the methods which had enabled a self-educated Irishman from the boglands of Munster to raise himself out of the ranks to the coveted post which he now held.

In short, there was one crime—slackness—for which no conceivable excuse existed in the eyes of the celebrated Superintendent Kerry.

"Good-evening, Superintendent," said Sowerby.

"Good-evening," Kerry rapped, continuing to chew.

"I had not anticipated seeing you here, Superintendent," Cosmo Potter declared.

"Really?" said Kerry. "Then we are both surprised! Sowerby," he went on, fixing his fierce gaze upon the Inspector, "how does it happen that a case which was handed over to Scotland Yard at 9:30 remains unattended to at a quarter of an hour after midnight?"

But this was more than the Yorkshireman could stomach. His colour perceptibly deepened, his black hair seemed to stand up more straightly, and:

"Eh!" he exclaimed indignantly—"unattended to? Well—ask Mr. Potter if it's been unattended to!"

"Mr. Potter has nothing whatever to do with the matter. No doubt he will presently explain why he is here. My question was put to *you*. I happened to have business at Leman Street, and hearing that a highly important case was being neglected, I came along immediately."

"*Neglected!*" Sowerby's indignation was affecting his voice. "You don't seem to realize, Superintendent, that a suspect has been detained."

"Release him!" said Kerry savagely. "You've got the wrong man! It was your plain duty, Sowerby, to leave all that railway station routine to a subordinate officer and to proceed to the scene of the crime—"

"He could have done no more than has been done," the uniformed inspector interpolated.

"I disagree with you," Kerry snapped. "Detective Inspector Sowerby, when his brains are not stupefied by fog, is a competent officer. A man climbed out of a window of this house to-night—a man we want to know—and you have allowed half K Division to fox-trot all over his footprints!"

He turned aside, disgustedly.

"I have been here less than five minutes," he declared, "and I have heard of four blunders." He faced Cosmo Potter. "You are acting for the detained man, sir?"

"Yes," Potter replied, meeting the fierce stare with his own dreamy regard.

"So," said Kerry, turning to Sowerby, "you have charged this Mr. Bernard Hope?"

"No. I have not charged him."

"Then why is he represented?"

"For this reason, Superintendent," Potter replied quietly: "That he is unjustly suspected, and there is a certain amount of circumstantial evidence against him. He is a very old friend of mine, and I have arranged with the Assistant Commissioner—"

"Quite!" Kerry interrupted irritably. "Please say no more, Mr. Potter."

"The evidence," Sowerby began—but:

"I don't want to hear it," Kerry snapped. "I like to see, with my own eyes, that a murder has been committed, before I start to hang anybody. But I want a few facts. Sergeant Simmons!"

Sergeant Simmons came forward. He was a sallow-complexioned man invested with a permanent air of gloom.

"Give me," Kerry directed, "a brief account of what took place to-night."

Simmons nodded, took out his notebook, cleared his throat, and:

"You know, sir," he said, "that the dead man, Burma Chang, had applied for police protection. There has been a constable on night duty outside the house for more than a week past. I have been keeping an eye on the place as well. To-night, just as the fog began to thicken"—he was referring, now, to his notes, and his voice took on that sing-song intonation often heard in a police court when a constable is giving evidence—"P. C. Smith—"

"Don't say P. C. Smith!" Kerry interrupted. "You are not before a magistrate, and to me P. C. means nothing. Call him Smith."

"Very good, Superintendent."

Simmons returned gloomily to his notes, and resumed:

"Smith was on duty in front of the house, and as I happened to walk round at the back, I noticed a light in the window of a room which I knew to be used as an office by Burma Chang. I watched this window for some time—because it was open at the bottom—just trying to find out who was in the room. It seemed funny for a window to be open, as the fog was coming up pretty badly. I thought I could see shadows on the wall, as though several people were moving up there. Then, presently, I saw a figure cross right over to the window—"

"What figure?" came crisply from Cosmo Potter.

Superintendent Kerry glared at the speaker, opened his mouth, hesitated, and then, depositing a wad of chewing-gum in the hearth, unbuttoned his topcoat and took out a packet containing fresh wafers of the fragrant mint.

"Impossible to say, sir," Simmons replied. "The light was behind him, and it was more than half dark outside."

"Him? It was a man?"

"Oh, yes, it was a man, for, as I watched, he climbed over the ledge and disappeared."

"How do you mean he disappeared?" Kerry demanded, pausing in the act of unwrapping a piece of gum.

"I mean he dropped out of sight. The high wall prevented me seeing any more."

"Right. Go on."

"I started for the back door—by which I expected to see him come out. At the same time I blew my whistle to attract the attention of P. C.—of Smith—on point at the front of the house."

"That was damn silly," said Kerry uncompromisingly.

"Perhaps it was, Superintendent," Simmons replied gloomily; "but one man can't surround a big house. Anyway, as soon as he arrived— he came running—I gave him his instructions and got back to the corner just as the man dropped from the top of the wall and ran off. He was swallowed up at once by the fog, but for a time I could hear his footsteps ahead of me. Once, by a street lamp, I almost overtook him. But he doubled on me down a court, and just dimly I heard his footsteps going off again in the direction of the railway. I had almost given it up when I heard a whistle. Thinking that a constable had made a capture, I ran along and found one of our men named Adams standing beside the line. He reported that just as a train was held up by signals at that point, a figure ran across the street only a few yards in front of him, climbed the fence and disappeared up the embankment.

"At the same moment the train began to move again, and hearing my shouts—I was yelling 'Stop him!' in the hope that someone might round up the man I was after—the constable blew his whistle. I concluded that our man had boarded the train, and hurrying back here as fast as the fog would allow, I got through to the station and they got through to Fenchurch Street."

"Right," snapped Kerry. "Now tell me what you found when you came back here."

"I found that Smith had entered the premises and had already telephoned to Limehouse."

"Where is Smith?"

"He's off duty."

"He should not be off duty!" Kerry shouted.

"One moment," said Inspector Peel, "one moment. I was here myself in seven or eight minutes, and I can give you all the particulars."

"I don't want particulars. I want to see the man who first entered the house! Go on, Simmons."

"I found," Simmons continued, "Smith standing here in the hall with four native servants."

"What sort of native servants?"

"They are all locked up in their quarters," said Peel; "you can see them for yourself."

"Where are their quarters?"

"In the basement."

"Go on, Simmons."

"He explained," the latter continued, "that Burma Chang was lying dead upstairs in his room. I should mention that this was the room in which I had seen the light, and from which I had seen the man climb out. I went up there and found it to be as he described. I found—"

"Stop!" Kerry raised his hand. "There was no one there but the dead man?"

"No one."

"Simmons and Smith were just coming down," Inspector Peel interrupted, "when I arrived."

Voices sounded from above, and two figures appeared upon the balcony.

Kerry turned his fierce eyes upward. Then, directing his glance upon Peel:

"Who in hell are these two smarts?" he demanded. "Are you charging twopence to see the peep show?"

"The divisional surgeon, and another medical man from the Asiatic Hospital," Peel replied angrily.

"You authorized this?"

"I did."

"Why?"

"Because Doctor Anderton was puzzled. He said the case was unusual and that there was a chance of a special opinion by one of the biggest authorities on this sort of thing—Doctor Van Stüy. Doctor Van Stüy is at present working at the Asiatic Hospital and has had many years' experience in the Dutch East Indies."

Kerry's fierce eyes remained fixed upon the speaker, then:

"There is some doubt about the cause of death?" he asked.

"Doubt!" said Peel, and laughed. "Go and see for yourself!"

The two medical men were about to descend, but:

"Gentlemen!" cried Kerry. They paused. "Be good enough to wait a moment. I will join you."

CHAPTER VIII

THE SIGHING DEATH

Doctor Anderton, the divisional surgeon, a large-boned, untidy Scot, whose misanthropic outlook made him even more gloomy than Simmons, greeted the Superintendent, with whom he was acquainted.

"Good-evening," said he. "A very strange, suspicious case. You should know my friend, Doctor Van Stüy."

He indicated his companion, a spare little man having very yellow, wrinkled skin, a high, bald head fringed with curly white hair, and extraordinarily intelligent eyes magnified by the powerful, black-rimmed glasses which he wore.

The Superintendent and the Dutch doctor bowed.

"You will be wanting to view the corpse?" Doctor Anderton continued.

"Just one moment!" Kerry snapped grimly.

He turned. Cosmo Potter and Inspector Sowerby were mounting the stair.

"Mr. Potter," he said, "it is not my place to dispute your privileges, but be good enough to remain in the lobby until I have made my first examination."

Cosmo Potter's angular face flushed, and the paradoxical blue eyes, which habitually seemed so vacant, were vacant no longer. It was Greek meeting Greek, for in character these two had at least one common trait: colossal self-assurance. Contact with polite society had taught Potter to conceal his aggressiveness beneath a cloak of indifference; Kerry had never found it necessary to stoop to such compromises. His untrammelled savagery gave him an undoubted advantage at times, and Cosmo Potter recognized that this was one of them.

"Thank you, Superintendent," he murmured, turning. "You might possibly have mentioned your wishes less publicly." He glanced at Sowerby. "Humanity is so crude at times."

But, ignoring his words:

"Sowerby," Kerry rapped, "you are in charge, below. No one is to leave that lobby and no one to come in until I return."

Sowerby nodded.

"Very good," he muttered. "It's a funny world."

Kerry rejoined the two doctors.

"I should be glad if you gentlemen would come with me," he said.

And so presently the three stood in a long, low room which combined certain features that were voluptuously Oriental with others that were purely commercial.

Thus, it was lighted by two silk-shaded lanterns of typically Chinese pattern, but a heavy safe of American manufacture, open, stood beside a roll-top desk which, with its orderly appointments, might have belonged to a stockbroker or a solicitor. The floor was richly covered, having the warm silence of opulent rugs. And there were some few choice pieces of porcelain in the shadows which emphasized the predominant Eastern note of the apartment. Through a widely opened window, fog penetrated damply.

Something in the attitude of the medical men had prepared Kerry for a scene unusually horrible, but in this strangely still room, faintly perfumed in a way that was reminiscent of sandalwood, but not entirely innocent of opium, were few evidences of violence.

He had looked for blood and confusion. He found tranquillity; but was conscious of a curious watchfulness from the doctors who accompanied him.

As became immediately evident, the safe had been hurriedly ransacked and several drawers of the writing desk were open. A finely carved chair which had stood before this desk was overturned, and near to it, stretched upon the carpet, and wearing a plain blue robe and red Arab slippers, lay Burma Chang, as if asleep. His straight black hair swept undisturbed back from his yellow forehead, his slanting eyes were closed. One arm lay relaxed beside him, the hand resting palm upward and the fingers half curled, as if in a final gesture. His left hand was raised to his throat. His face was in shadow.

So he lay, this mystery man of Chinatown, and Kerry, pausing within some six feet of him, turned startled eyes upon Doctor Anderton.

"Doctor," he whispered—"listen!"

Doctor Anderton nodded.

"I know," he replied. "Van Stüy will explain."

The man upon the floor was breathing softly and regularly!

"He's not dead!" cried Kerry angrily. "What the devil's the meaning of it!"

He looked swiftly from face to face.

"Ah!" Doctor Van Stüy raised his hand protestingly. "I know. Even my friend Doctor Anderton is puzzled—"

"Puzzled!" Kerry snapped in a manner little short of ferocious. "Are you both mad? That man's *doped,* he's not dead!"

The others exchanged glances, and Kerry, for all his intrepidity, became aware that, insidiously, an unfamiliar chill of horror seemed to be creeping through his veins, freezing his blood. He stood upon the threshold of unknown things, and the recognition awed him. He thought of the attitude of the Divisional Inspector and of his vague answers to certain questions. What did it all mean? Stricken silent, he looked down at Burma Chang and listened to that regular, ghastly breathing....

"His heart had ceased beating when I arrived." Anderton's voice seemed to come from a distance. "The automatic breathing puzzled me, although I've met with something of the sort before. But there were other symptoms—"

His voice seemed to die away. Vaguely, Kerry heard the words, "Artificial respiration ... heart massage ..." and then to his ears nothing came but the sighing—sighing—sighing—of Burma Chang.

Doctor Van Stüy was speaking now.

"I joined my friend Doctor Anderton very gladly. These cases are so rare. Indeed, I do never meet another in England. In Batavia I know two—in Sumatra, one. He has been dead, this man, for quite two hours, and breathes, although he is dead. In the Dutch East Indies they call it the 'Sighing Death.'"

And now Superintendent Kerry recovered something of his normal efficiency.

"What is it?" he demanded, looking down at the dead man who seemed to live. "Is it a disease?"

Doctor Van Stüy shrugged his shoulders.

"In my opinion," he replied, "it is a parasite."

"A parasite?"

"Yes. In this I disagree with all my colleagues who study the subject. All but one. But I believe it to be due to the bite of a minute insect."

Kerry chewed vigorously. As all who had worked with him knew, this indicated irritability.

"But you say you have met with it in the East?" he exclaimed. "Therefore, if your theory is right, Doctor, your insect would be a tropical insect. I mean, you would not expect to meet him in Limehouse Causeway."

Again Van Stüy gave his eloquent shrug.

"There are many objects"—he indicated the dimly lighted room—"from the East here. Some may have recently come. Who can say? And in one of them, this parasite—for we do not know his host, what he lives upon—this perhaps microscopic creature may lie dormant."

"In that event," snapped Kerry, "death would be accidental?"

"But quite."

"I am certain," Doctor Anderton declared gloomily, "that death was not accidental. The like of Burma Chang is born to be murdered."

Kerry looked down at the breathing figure, and:

"I take it he lies as he was found?" he inquired.

"I believe so," Anderton answered. "He lies much as I found him when I arrived. I've told you what I did, and mentioned the absence of any reaction. I presently recognized the nature of the symptoms because of my acquaintance with Doctor Van Stüy. For the same reason I obtained his opinion."

Kerry stared about, not without a certain apprehension; and:

"If your theory is correct, Doctor Van Stüy," he said, "I am completely at sea. There may have been a struggle—we have an overturned chair—and robbery I think we may presume to have taken place, But if it is a case of murder, how was the murder committed? According to your account, it practically amounts to a fatal disease. Well, a man can't direct that. It rests with Providence."

"Possibly," the Dutchman replied. "But about it is one curious fact, although, perhaps—who can say?—peculiar in my own small experience."

"What is that?" Kerry asked curiously, and the divisional surgeon's interest was palpably intense.

"It is," Van Stüy replied, "that all the victims of this Sighing Death are *Chinamen.*"

He peered oddly from the face of the detective to that of his colleague, as if intending to emphasize some covert meaning in his words.

"But"—following a short silence—"this doesn't particularly enlighten me," Kerry confessed. "I suppose there are other diseases peculiar to the Chinese?"

Doctor Van Stüy shrugged his shoulders and turned to depart.

"Not that I do know of," he replied. "Anything that can kill a Chinaman can also kill a Malay, a Burman, or one of some other race. Not with this. It is only Chinamen who die so."

"It may seem to be that way," Doctor Anderton interrupted argumentatively; "but if death is due to a minute organism, as you seem to think, it is a physiological impossibility that it should only attack members of a particular race. What's more, the like of Burma Chang are not pure Chinese. One of your two theories is wrong, Doctor. Either your theory of the organism or your theory of the immunity of everybody but the Chinese."

Doctor Van Stüy paused in the doorway, and, turning, extended his hand with an odd gesture.

"If my first theory is right," he said, "perhaps as a result of inquiries in this room, someone else, who is not Chinese, may die of the Sighing Death, so proving my second theory to be wrong."

He smiled at his own gruesome joke, bowed, and went out; whereupon:

"Hell!" said Superintendent Kerry.

He stared across at the open window.

"There's one witness," he declared, "who, if he didn't do this job himself, knows who did. The man who went out of that window could tell us all we want to know."

CHAPTER IX

YVETTE GOES EAST (CONTINUED)

Since even Superintendent Kerry was not infallible, his assertion that the man who escaped from the window "could tell us all we want to know" was not entirely accurate. The matters which had led up to this episode—the episode which first had drawn the attention of Detective Sergeant Simmons to something unusual going forward in the house of Burma Chang—had, nevertheless, been of a character to interest the investigators, could they have been placed in possession of them.

On this eventful night, two cabs had set out from the neighbourhood of the Riviera Theatre bound for Limehouse. In the first of these was Yvette Chalmers, and in the second that man of mystery destined to set a seemingly unanswerable problem to the officers of the Criminal Investigation Department.

Despite the taxi man's optimism, as the eastward journey proceeded the fog grew steadily worse. Yvette, looking out at the sordid, yellow-draped streets, thought regretfully of her own cosy flat. Twice she all but succumbed to the temptation to tell the man to turn back and to abandon the expedition, but twice conquered and allowed the journey to proceed.

As is the way of these London visitations, at one point the choking mist would be almost impenetrable, but, a little farther on, would have so far dispersed as to encourage the unwary traveller to proceed. It had not yet, however, definitely laid a stranglehold upon the metropolis, as occurred later during the night, and there was a fair amount of traffic in the eastern thoroughfares.

Yvette's second faintness of heart came in the neighbourhood of Whitechapel, where cloud banks settled so densely about the cab that the man was compelled to pull up, near to the dimly seen light of a standard lamp. He descended and opened the door.

"I think this has about done it, miss!" he said—"except that a bit of a breeze has sprung up in the northeast."

"In the northeast!" Yvette exclaimed. "But I heard that if the wind went into the northeast, the fog would grow worse."

"For a time, miss, it would, in the West End," the man replied, "where we've come from; but it would clear it ahead, and we could get on."

"But however should we get back?"

"Ah!" He made a facetious grimace. "Now you're asking something! But here it is—look! Like I said!"

And indeed, almost magically, the dreary curtain became raised and the delayed traffic was released again.

"I'm getting really alarmed," Yvette declared. "I don't know whether to go on or not."

"I should chance it now, miss," said the taxi driver; "we are more than halfway there."

And so, since Fate would have it thus, the journey was resumed. And the following cab, which was less than twenty yards behind, but which had been detained by those same dense banks in Whitechapel High Street, now took up the chase again.

On they went, these puppets in a mysterious drama, each piece upon the board boasting individuality, but each moved by Fate, that grim humorist who plays chess with human destinies.

Both cabs were within the Limehouse area when that impenetrable darkness came which, yellowly, held up the train from Blackwall and thereby allowed gruesome drama to intrude upon Bernard Hope's life.

Here, the driver of the following cab completely lost sight of the quarry. He pulled up sharply, since to have proceeded would have been suicidal. Not a light was to be seen. Only by bending forward could the man in the cab distinguish the lamp beside the taximeter. He opened the door and stepped down into the road, groping for the footpath, which, however, he failed to find for some time.

Dim noises were about him, sounds of grating mechanism, cries of warning.

"That's done it, sir!" said the taxi man. "It's what I expected."

"What I expected, too," his fare muttered grimly. "We are about a hundred yards northwest of Limehouse Causeway. Am I right?"

"About right, sir."

"I think I can find my way. You have got six shillings on your clock. We'll call it fifteen by the time you get back to civilization."

Unbuttoning his overcoat, he plunged his hand into his pocket, counted out some money by the light of the headlamp, and:

"Here are twenty-five shillings," he said. "You can get back now. Are you satisfied?"

"Very good, sir," the man replied. "That will see me right."

He took the money, and a moment later his mysterious fare had disappeared, swallowed up by the fog. The man convinced himself that he held a pound note and two half-crowns, then, transferring these to a capacious pocket, he philosophically lighted a cigarette and lay back in his seat, reconciled to fate and the elements.

His strange passenger, who was evidently well acquainted with the neighbourhood, in the meantime had found the sidewalk and was following it confidently and in the manner of one who has a definite objective in view. He had perhaps anticipated that the darkness would grow greater the nearer he approached to the Thames, but such is the waywardness of fog that it actually lifted, or became slightly less dense for a few moments, and long enough to give him a sight of a narrow turning for which he was bound.

He stood still for a while, listening, but could detect no sound of any vehicle in the immediate neighbourhood. Muted river noises there were, and faint suggestions of other pedestrians near and remote. But he pressed on, rapidly making in the direction of a high and dilapidated brick wall which skirted the grounds of an enclosed house. The house was Burma Chang's.

A comparative clarity still prevailed at the time when he came abreast of that door in the wall at which, later in the night, a man was posted. He stepped back across the lane in order to obtain a better view of a certain lighted window. And, as he did so, the figure of a woman showed in the room to which the lighted window belonged—of a woman who wore a small, tightly fitting hat, and whose silhouette suggested just such a modish coat as that in which Yvette had left the theatre!

He saw her throw up her arms, as if retreating from a threatened attack. Uttering a stifled exclamation, he crossed again to the door in the wall, threw his weight against it, but found it to be stoutly secured.

This was a sort of courtway in which he stood, and, presumably with the purpose of preventing vehicular traffic, it had three short iron posts or pillars at either end, survivals of earlier times.

In a moment he had divested himself of his heavy overcoat. Having it thrown across his shoulder, he mounted upon one of these pillars nearest to the wall of the house, with a surprising agility, suggestive of an acrobat or a sailor. The top of the wall was studded with broken glass, and over this he threw the coat as a protection. Then, reaching upward with muscular hands, he sprang, nearly fell back, but recovered himself and finally got astride of the wall.

One glance he cast up at the lighted window, which moving banks of vapour were already beginning to obscure. The woman's figure was visible no longer, but he could see her restless shadow, and it spurred him to further action. He twisted around, tearing his hands and his garments upon the jagged glass. Careless of this, he lowered himself and dropped on the soft soil beneath, dragging his coat down with him.

He took it up and ran across a small, neglected garden, or such he judged it to be, until he came to the wall of the house. A rainwater pipe with a convenient elbow afforded a grand staircase for a man of his agility.

Discarding his overcoat, he swarmed up this like a monkey. Just as he grasped the ledge the sound of a stifled shriek reached his ears. Then, pulling himself up, he looked into the room. A catlike contortion, and he was kneeling on the ledge. He thrust his elbow through a glass pane, unfastened the catch, raised the sash, and swung over into a dimly lighted apartment, fog sweeping in behind him.

CHAPTER X

THE HOUSE OF BURMA CHANG

It was Superintendent Kerry's custom to endeavour, upon the scene of a crime, to reconstruct the events which had led up to it. But in view of the nature of the medical evidence, and of the whole circumstances of this mysterious tragedy, any man must have experienced qualms in undertaking an examination of that dimly lighted and strangely furnished room.

Kerry, having requested Doctor Anderton to step downstairs for a few minutes, closed the door, removed his overcoat, and, amid a fog-muffled silence disturbed only by the sound of that ghostly breathing, proceeded to carry out his inquiry.

For a long time he stood looking down at the blue-robed figure and striving to accustom his mind to the fact that he was dead—Burma Chang was dead. Near to where he lay, and left of the writing desk, there was a narrow door. Chewing reflectively, Kerry stepped across and turned the handle; but the door was locked. He stood with his back to it looking about the room again.

Amid the more businesslike appointments of the desk a large Chinese bowl stood, incongruous, and reaching out, Kerry was about to take it up, when he recalled the words of the Dutch specialist: "There are many objects from the East here.... In one of them this ... creature may lie dormant."

He thought of a snake—some kind of small but very venomous serpent. He pictured it coiled in that very jar which he was about to touch.

"Flames!" he muttered, and drew his hand back.

A faint rustling sound from the dark interior of the safe brought him sharply about. The idea of a hidden reptile was becoming an obsession. In common with many Irishmen, Kerry feared and detested snakes. He recognized that he must do battle with this weakness in the interests of his duty. He watched intently, but could detect no movement, and as the sound was not repeated, he concluded it to have been caused by the dropping of a sheet of paper which had been disturbed when the safe was ransacked.

Stepping resolutely up to the desk, he grasped the Chinese bowl and removed the lid. It contained a very fine quality of snuff.

He turned his attention to a little porcelain dish containing yellow cigarette stumps. At these fragments he sniffed suspiciously. Replacing the tray, he dropped upon one knee, and, conquering a great revulsion, peered closely into the face of Burma Chang. Detecting the glitter of a thin gold chain about the dead man's throat, Kerry drew out from beneath the blue robe a kind of small, flat box, or reliquary, made of faded stamped leather.

Suddenly, he stood upright, facing in the direction of the open window. He had become acutely conscious, without any physical evidence, of the fact that he was being watched!

Taking an electric torch from his overcoat pocket, he crossed and examined the window.

The glass was broken; fragments lay on the floor; and faint marks were perceptible upon the dirt of the ledge outside. He could see his own moving shadow on the fog as if cast upon a yellow curtain. He hesitated, looking about him; and then, very carefully and slowly, he closed the window. Crossing the room he thrust the torch back into his topcoat where it lay on a divan, and came out upon the oaken balcony, looking into the upturned faces of the group in the lobby below.

His foot was set upon the stair—when every light in the place went out!

A moment of consternation, then:

"Hi!" cried a voice, that of Inspector Peel, "what the devil's the meaning of this?"

Kerry plunged to his pocket, only to remember that in coming out he had replaced his torch in his overcoat. He had no matches.

There came a sound of hurried footsteps.

"Sowerby!" Kerry shouted, "show a light there!"

"It's in my overall!" the reply came. "I'm trying to find it!"

"Constable! Stand by the door! Who the hell is that sand-dancing?"

"I'm trying to find my torch," came Sowerby's voice again.

"Stand still!" cried Kerry viciously. "I want to listen."

The movements ceased and not a sound could be heard in that strange house. Kerry stood clutching the rail and listening intently. Then came a crackling sound, and Cosmo Potter appeared in the darkness below, holding a lighted match.

"Go ahead, Sowerby!" Kerry cried. "Get the torch and join me here."

A moment later a white beam cut through the darkness, and Inspector Sowerby ran across the lobby and up the stairs.

"Give me the torch," snapped Kerry.

He turned, and directing the light ahead of him, rushed back to the room where Burma Chang lay. He threw the door open and leapt in, Sowerby close at his heels.

"Don't touch anything, Sowerby!" he said over his shoulder—"this place isn't healthy."

He stood looking down at the dead man. He did not appear to have been moved; nothing in the room seemed to have been touched—until:

"Hell!" Kerry cried, stooped, then came to his feet again with a bound.

He turned to his assistant, his fierce eyes lighted up by excitement. He leapt to the door beside the desk—but it was still locked. He stared across at the window—it remained closed. Then:

"There's a switch just beside you, Superintendent," said Sowerby. "Suppose you try it."

Savagely, Kerry moved the little brass knob—and the two lamps became lighted!

"Well!" Sowerby gasped—"of all the—"

"Double switches!" rapped Kerry. "But there's more behind these conjuring tricks. Stay here. Don't move."

He ran from the room, shining the light of the torch down into the lobby.

"Where are the servants?" he demanded rapidly.

Inspector Peel stared up at him. A lighted lantern stood upon a little table.

"In their own quarters, below!" he replied.

His expression was one of frank alarm.

"What do you make of this trick with the light?" he asked.

"I don't know," said Kerry shortly, "yet. Get the switch and you'll find you can turn it on again. Who is with the servants?"

"Constable Atkins."

"Good. I thought they might be alone. Sergeant Simmons, lead the way. I want to see them at once."

Simmons nodded, came forward, and led the way by a door under the gallery, descended a dark staircase, and Kerry found himself in a maze of underground passages.

"Atkins!" cried Simmons, "where the deuce are you?"

"This way!" came a voice, "this way, Sergeant!"

A door was opened, light shone out into the stone-paved passage, and Kerry entered a big kitchen, to find a group of four natives facing him and a constable standing by the door.

"Who are these people?" he inquired brusquely.

He turned to Simmons.

"I can't quite get their names," the latter replied. "Not one of them has any English, but the Inspector knows a bit of their lingo and he can tell you more about them. The big Chinaman is a cook, I believe, and the others are domestic servants of some kind."

Kerry stood chewing viciously, his fierce eyes fixed upon the group. They suffered his regard with native indifference. Two were evidently Chinese and seemed to constitute the kitchen staff. The others, who wore some kind of dark uniform, were dusky men of a lowering type, powerfully built, and having their heads swathed in blue turbans.

"What are these two beauties?" he demanded.

"Dyaks, sir," the constable replied. "I heard the Inspector say so."

"Dyaks? What is a Dyak?"

"I can't tell you, Superintendent," Simmons confessed.

"Ah!" Kerry turned again to the constable. "What happened down here when the lights went out?"

"What's that, sir?" the other asked blankly; "the lights haven't been out."

"What?"

"The lights haven't been out down here, sir."

"Then which of these four smarts did you allow out of the room?"

"No one has been out of the room."

Kerry turned angrily to the immobile group of servants. Then:

"Simmons," he said, "is Inspector Peel satisfied that this is the entire domestic staff?"

"Yes, I believe so, Superintendent."

"You have searched the premises, of course?"

"Yes."

"It's a big house. Have you been in every room?"

"Yes, every room. And there are some funny ones, too."

"No one else on the premises?"

"Not a soul."

"Men on duty at back and front?"

"Yes."

Superintendent Kerry turned and walked out of the kitchen, followed by Simmons. Arriving in the lobby, where the lights had now been turned up, he paused in front of Cosmo Potter, and:

"Mr. Potter," he said abruptly, "you have lived in the East."

"For several years."

"Do you speak Chinese?"

"A little," Potter replied. "I fear it is rather rusty."

"Nevertheless, it may prove useful," Kerry returned. "Inspector Peel, you have interrogated the servants?"

"I spoke to the Chinaman," was the reply. "I know just a few words of his lingo. But there are a couple of fellows down there who I believe are Dyaks —or so Que Foo tells me. That is the cook," he added, "and they can't or won't understand anything."

"What is a Dyak?" Kerry demanded.

"Roughly speaking," Potter replied, "a native of Borneo."

"And the other man?" Kerry continued.

"He is some kind of half-caste," was the reply.

"Where does *he* hail from?"

"Cochin-China, I believe."

"A pretty bunch of smarts! Do you trust their evidence, or what you have been able to gather?"

"No," the Inspector confessed, "I don't. Simmons has notes of it all. But, on the other hand, of one thing I am quite certain."

"What's that?"

"They are four of the most badly frightened men in Limehouse."

"Why? Because of the death of Burma Chang?"

"I suppose so. They were absolutely in a panic when I arrived. They have got some name for whatever has happened to Chang. I can't catch it, but it sounds like *'Foo-soo-chee.'*"

He looked inquiringly at Cosmo Potter, but the latter shook his head blankly.

"It means nothing to me," he murmured. "Humanity is so polyglot."

Kerry paused, chewing awhile, then:

"Inspector Peel," he said abruptly, "have you unlocked the door between the table and the safe upstairs?"

"No," was the reply; "we can't find a key to it."

"What is the room on the other side?"

"There is no room so far as I am aware."

"No room!" Kerry stared. "Then where in hell does it go to?"

"I believe to a short staircase leading into the garden. There is another locked door down there, for which no key can be found, either. There seemed to be no object in forcing the doors."

"Didn't there!" Kerry rapped savagely. "Sergeant Simmons! Take a constable round the house and force this door of which Inspector Peel speaks. See if it opens on a stair leading to the room up above. Post a man there. Report to me."

He turned to Cosmo Potter.

"Perhaps you would like to come up," he said; and crossing the lobby he mounted the stair. Over his shoulder:

"I should be obliged," he added, "if you would leave all that cigarette downstairs. Smells sometimes afford clues."

Inspector Sowerby was standing by the door, staring across in the direction of the dead man as the Superintendent entered, followed by Potter.

"Anything to report?" Kerry rapped.

"Nothing," Sowerby replied. "Except—well, it's a funny world—I feel all the time in this room as if someone was watching me!"

"Indeed?" said Kerry. "So do I!" He turned to Cosmo Potter. "Now, sir," he went on, "here's the centre of the trouble. There lies Burma Chang, the murdered man. The body has never been alone since the crime was discovered—except for less than a minute while I stood on the stair, and the lights were out."

"Most amazing," Potter murmured, looking about him with a sort of awe, "how those lights were turned out."

"*Most* amazing!" Kerry agreed, "considering that no one either entered or left the premises, and everybody is accounted for. Yet, in that time, sir, someone entered this room!"

"What!" cried Sowerby.

"Burma Chang wore a kind of amulet hung around his neck on a thin gold chain. It's gone!"

"Good God, Superintendent!" Potter whispered.

"Do you mean—"

"I mean," cried Kerry savagely, "that there's someone in this house I particularly want to meet—and I'll meet him if I have to pull the blasted place down, brick by brick!"

CHAPTER XI

A DOOR IS OPENED—AND SHUT

With an electric torch, Kerry closely examined the ledge of the room in which the dead man lay. He had again opened the window for this purpose, and turning to Sowerby who stood behind him:

"There are no fresh marks," he declared. "It was through that door he came," pointing to the door beside the safe.

He ceased speaking, and all three listened for a while to a sound of confused voices in the garden, below. The hideous breathing had subsided now and the room was uncannily still. Cosmo Potter drew a fine silk handkerchief from his pocket and raised it to his forehead.

"Whew!" he said, "this thing is a nightmare. Are you going to force the door?"

"Wait!" Kerry raised his hand. He leaned from the window, carefully avoiding effacing the marks. "Simmons!" he called, "Sergeant Simmons!"

"Hullo!" came a ghostly voice out of the fog.

"I don't want the footprints of all K Division around that door," Kerry continued violently, "and I don't want more than a hundred men on the stair—if it opens on the stair."

"There will be no footprints, Simmons's voice came back; "there's a paved path leading to it."

"Right!" cried the Superintendent. "Get on with it."

Arose a sudden noise of loud crashing. Kerry turned to his assistant.

"Now, Sowerby," he directed, "put your shoulder to that door yonder."

Inspector Sowerby nodded, scratched his head, and examined the lock; then:

"It opens outward," he muttered optimistically—"so I can do it."

Twice the door resisted his attacks, however, but the third time, with a sound of splintering, it burst suddenly open, almost precipitating Sowerby into the darkness beyond.

"Go slow," Kerry warned. "Wait for the light. What's there?"

"A sort of little lobby," the Inspector reported, peering in and ruefully rubbing his shoulder. "There's another stairway leading down, you see."

A tremendous crash sounded from the depths below, and:

"That's the outside door," Kerry muttered. "Simmons is in."

Shining the light of his torch ahead of him, Sowerby had already begun to -descend. And, over his shoulder:

"A bend just ahead," he reported; at which moment:

"Hullo, there!" came the muffled voice of Simmons.

Speaking from the bend of the stair:

"There's no one here," Sowerby declared, "only Simmons coming up."

Kerry glanced at Potter, chewing vigorously the while. At the still form on the floor he stared with grim suspicion. In despite of contrary professional opinion, a doubt was beginning to enter his mind.

"Come here, Sowerby," he cried. "I'll examine that stair, myself, in a moment."

Sowerby reentered, looking every bit as puzzled as his chief. The door remained wide open.

"Where's Simmons?" Kerry demanded.

"Just coming up."

"I suppose he left a man on duty at the bottom?"

"Yes," Sowerby replied a little absently; "I noticed the light reflected on his buttons as I shone my torch down the stair."

"Listen," the Superintendent continued in a low voice, looking down at Burma Chang, "between ourselves I don't believe this smart is dead at all! At least, I don't believe he was dead five minutes ago!"

Sowerby's surprised eyes opened more widely than ever.

"You mean you think he's been shamming? It's a funny world, but— what on earth for?"

"I don't know!" snapped Kerry savagely, "but I'm going to find out."

Sowerby dropped down suddenly upon one knee, and laid his hand upon Burma Chang's breast, exposed by the loose blue robe which he wore. He shuddered and stood up.

"That man's as dead as mutton," he declared. "He's cold."

A dull thud sounded from the stair, and:

"What the devil is Simmons about?" Kerry exclaimed irritably.

"I don't know," said Cosmo Potter.

His voice was oddly hushed. The still form on the floor possessed an uncanny fascination: he found himself constantly watching it.

"He must have discovered something," Sowerby began. "Perhaps—"

His voice died away. Slowly—as if by dint of great effort—he raised his hand, pointing.

Kerry and Potter turned together.

The door beside the safe was closed!

"Hi!" Kerry cried, "what in hell are you up to!"

He leapt to the door, hand thrust out to open it, but sharply withdrew his hand again, stifling an exclamation of pain.

"Someone's holding it!" he exclaimed.

"What!" cried Sowerby, and recovering himself, he joined in an attack upon the door.

But now it resisted their joint endeavours.

"It's bolted from the other side!" Potter cried. "Did you notice a bolt, Sowerby?"

"No, I didn't look when I broke the lock."

Kerry raced across to the window, and, craning out:

"Simmons!" he cried, "Sergeant Simmons!"

A voice answered him from somewhere below:

"Sergeant Simmons has gone round to the front to report, sir."

"Who are you?"

"Constable Smith, sir."

"Where are you?"

"I'm standing by the door."

"Have you got a light?"

"Yes, my lantern."

"Then come upstairs and unbolt the door at the top."

"Very good, sir."

In curiously tense attitudes the three men in the room waited, what time the constable's heavy footsteps might be heard upon the stair. Then, a well- oiled bolt was shot back and the door thrown open. The man stood there in the little lobby looking frankly frightened, and shining the light of his lamp all about him.

"Why did Sergeant Simmons bolt this door?" Kerry demanded.

"I don't know, sir," the constable replied.

"What did he say?"

"He said, 'Stand by, Smith. I am going round to the front to report.'"

"Those his exact words?" Kerry snapped.

"Yes, sir, as near as I remember."

Kerry's jaw muscles protruded enormously.

"Go down again," he directed, "and remain at the bottom until I send a man to relieve you."

"Very good, sir."

The constable descended, palpably very ill at ease.

"Remain here, Sowerby," Kerry continued. "I am going down into the hall to meet Simmons. This thing wants explaining."

He ran out on to the balcony. Below in the lobby, where haze floated, Doctor Anderton stood talking to Inspector Peel, who was making notes in a large notebook. A constable stood over by the door. As Kerry came out on the balcony, all eyes were turned in his direction.

"Inspector Peel," he called, "where is your sergeant?"

"You detailed him to break down the door."

"Thanks. My memory hasn't quite gone. He's done it. He came around to the front to report to you."

"Is that so?" Peel replied. "He has not arrived yet."

"He's probably stopping to pick buttercups," Kerry said savagely. "I suppose," he continued, his fierce regard fixed upon the Divisional Inspector, "you have noticed that there is a certain tendency to fog? How many men are posted around this house?"

"There are five men on duty outside. Simmons will have taken one, I expect."

"Yes," Kerry interrupted; "he's on duty at the door, now."

"Well," Peel went on. "That leaves four men who are watching the house from outside and one downstairs with the servants."

"What I mean," said Kerry, crossing to him, "is this: You are certain no one could give us the slip?"

"Absolutely certain."

"Because there is somebody in this house not yet accounted for!"

Inspector Peel stared hard.

"Are you sure of that?" he demanded.

"No," said Kerry, "I'm guessing. But I've guessed right. There is somebody in this house whose acquaintance I am particularly anxious to make."

Passing on, he opened the door, whereupon clouds of vapour swirled into the lobby. Faintly, silver buttons glittered, and:

"Who is this?" Kerry rapped.

"One of my men," Peel explained. Then, raising his voice: "Have you seen Detective Sergeant Simmons, Houghton?"

"No, sir," came a voice from the fog, "not since he went out."

On the threshold Kerry turned; and:

"Where are your other three men posted?" he demanded.

"One at the end of the lane," the Inspector replied; "one by the garden gate; one in the street outside. So that you see no one could possibly leave the house unobserved. The other, Smith, is in the garden by the door, you told me."

Kerry nodded and disappeared into the fog. First, he walked to the end of the narrow lane bordering one side of the house. A light flashed suddenly into his face.

"What do you want?" a gruff voice challenged.

"Your name," said Kerry crisply. "I'm Superintendent Kerry."

"My name is Pollock, sir."

"Good. Anything happened here?"

"Nothing, sir."

Kerry turned and retraced his footsteps. He came round the corner of the building, and proceeded along by the wall until he gained the door which gave access to the garden. There, as he groped his way, again a light shone suddenly into his face. Probably there was no member of the Metropolitan Police force to whom that face was unfamiliar, and:

"All clear here, sir," the constable reported.

"Sergeant Simmons came out this way?"

"Yes, sir—a few minutes ago."

"What did he say?"

"Just, 'Stand by.'"

"Was he in a hurry?"

"Yes."

"Wore his topcoat and hat?"

"He did."

"Which way did he go?"

"Round to the front of the house, sir."

Kerry passed on, chewing reflectively. The man on the third post had nothing to report. He had not seen Simmons. Kerry returned to the second post and entered the garden. This door had been unlocked previously, and by the aid of his torch Kerry groped his way to the point whereat Smith mounted guard. The constable challenged him at ten yards, in a voice which told of jumpy nerves; but:

"All right!" Kerry cried. "Nothing to report?"

"Nothing, sir."

"Right. I am going up."

Slowly and carefully he began to mount the mysterious stairway. As he came to the bend near the top:

"Hello there!" Sowerby challenged from the room beyond.

"All right, Sowerby. I am coming in."

He entered, to find Sowerby standing alertly watching the door, Cosmo Potter at his elbow.

"Anything happened?"

"Nothing," Sowerby replied. "Why did Simmons shoot the bolt?"

The savage expression on the Superintendent's face was momentarily disturbed, and:

"When I find Simmons, I may be able to tell you," he said.

"Eh?" Potter began; but Kerry crossed the room and came out again on to the balcony.

He looked down into the lobby. Three pairs of eyes again were turned in his direction.

"Inspector Peel," he said sharply, "has Sergeant Simmons reported?"

"No!" Peel answered in a startled voice. "Isn't he outside?"

"He is not!"

At his words, Cosmo Potter, who had followed him, advanced, and stared into the grim, red face. There was a short, dramatic silence, then:

"But you don't mean—" Potter began.

"I *do* mean!" Kerry cried savagely; "I mean that Simmons has disappeared!"

CHAPTER XII

THE MYSTERY HOUSE

"I should be obliged, Divisional Inspector," said Kerry with acid politeness, "if you would confine yourself to the facts. If I should find it necessary to put the whole of K Division in the dock, there is a barrister present and no doubt he would undertake the defence."

He turned his fierce regard upon Cosmo Potter.

This was a jaded quartette gathered in that room where the shadow of violent death lingered eerily. The body of Burma Chang had been removed, but all appointments remained untouched. The fog had lifted somewhat and dawn was not far off. Sounds of awakening riverside activity came dully to the ears of the four men gathered in this ill-omened room.

Burma Chang was dead, but London lived. The throbbing pulse of her might be heard, might be felt.

Potter smiled, and his smile seemed to light up the angular face, and went far to account for his popularity.

"After all, Superintendent," he said, "we are all very tired and consequently getting a bit jagged, I suppose. But I quite see Inspector Peel's point."

"So do I," Sowerby muttered.

Whereupon the Superintendent's fierce gaze sought him out; and:

"Did you speak?" Kerry inquired.

"I did," said Sowerby bravely. "I admit I can't see any flaw in your reasoning, but I've worked with Sergeant Simmons more than once, and to suggest that he's been 'got at' in any way—that he's in league with the people responsible for this business, I mean—well, I can't believe it."

"It is preposterous," cried Inspector Peel warmly.

Superintendent Kerry, withdrawing his gaze from Sowerby, transferred it to the face of the Divisional Inspector, who sustained it very well. Finally, he fixed it upon Cosmo Potter.

"I've listened to two opinions," he said. "What is yours?"

Potter hesitated, but finally:

"My acquaintance with Detective Sergeant Simmons," he replied, "being confined to the few words we have exchanged to-night, I am fortunately in a position to view the whole thing impartially. Your survey of the facts, Superintendent, was admirable. Whilst it would have been difficult for Sergeant Simmons to reach this room from the lobby below and to return during the time that the lights were out, it would, I confess, not have been quite impossible. In other words, neutralizing what we know of the character and record of Sergeant Simmons, it might quite conceivably have been Sergeant Simmons who entered this room and removed whatever was attached to the thin gold chain suspended about the neck of Burma Chang. This, however, is very problematical.

"Turning to your second point, Superintendent, the fact that Simmons bolted the door yonder from the outside, passed the man on duty at the bottom of the stairs, crossed the garden, and went out into the street, some three hours ago, and that he has not seen fit to report either here or at Limehouse Station since, calls for close investigation."

"A child could explain it!" cried Inspector Peel angrily. "He had picked up valuable evidence somewhere out on that stair." He pointed. "Ashe came out into the street—and we know that he went out into the street on the evidence of the constable on duty at the garden door—he was attacked; for all we know, killed and taken away. Do you realize, sir, that there's nearly a thousand pounds in ready money in that safe? There's money at the back of this job—big money. And where there's big money, people take big risks. If Simmons is alive, he is a prisoner."

There was a brief silence; then:

"It's one of the most unsatisfactory cases I have ever handled," Superintendent Kerry declared. "I've detained the four servants because I regard them as four liars. They are frightened, that is plain enough, but is their fright due to the fact that they are in the hands of the police, or due to something else?"

"In my opinion," Cosmo Potter interrupted, "due to something else."

"I am certain of it," said Inspector Peel.

Kerry looked from face to face.

"Even if I don't agree with you," he said, "I am sure of one thing. Somewhere amongst that yellow quartette there is evidence. For instance"—he turned to Cosmo Potter—"two of these men were Dyaks. Now, sir, you may know. What, exactly, is a Dyak?"

"Well," the other replied, "Dyak is a Malay, and these particular specimens are Hill Dyaks. Their dialect is quite unfamiliar to me. But considering the type of men—they are essentially a lighting stock—I confess I cannot imagine why they were included in the domestic staff of Burma Chang."

"But I am particularly remembering that their evidence," Kerry returned, "if you can call it evidence, of what happened, was obtained with Que Foo, the Chinese cook, as interpreter. Now, I ask you"—he looked around him—"what is it worth?"

"Nothing at all," said Peel. "But I might add, Superintendent, that I don't think these two Malays were in any way concerned in the death of Burma Chang. In fact, I have every reason to believe that they were most loyal to their employer."

"Oh!" Kerry snapped. "Local gossip, I suppose?"

"Local gossip, if you like, Superintendent, but local gossip in Chinatown affords valuable news."

"You know this to be true," Cosmo Potter said, pouring oil on troubled waters; "for your own experience, Superintendent, bears it out."

"It may do," Kerry replied, continuing to gaze at Inspector Peel, "but it does not satisfy me that the evidence of these Malay smarts is worth two candles in hell."

Out where the morning was breaking, craft detained by the fog began to move again; and into that strange room, the very perfume of which was redolent of China, penetrated sounds of shipping—the harsh voices of sirens—the indescribable but unforgettable turmoil of London's river, which, washing the shores of Chinatown, has known so many mysteries and borne so many secrets upon its bosom.

"As I have remarked before," said Kerry, "you allowed the most important witness to go off duty—the constable on point in front of the house. When Simmons gave him warning and then rushed off to waste his time in the fog, the man came and rang at the front door. Now, I want to refresh my memory. Who opened the door?"

"One of the Dyaks," said Peel, consulting his notebook.

"I see. And how did the officer make him understand the nature of his business, as neither of these men have any English?"

"I don't know," Peel replied shortly, "but, at any rate, he reports that the man went up to Burma Chang's room, and evidently finding the door locked and getting no reply to his knocking, came down again and summoned the other Dyak."

"And where did *he* appear from?"

"I have no information on this point."

"H'm," Kerry muttered, "a pity. What then?"

"The second Dyak carried a bunch of keys—those you have seen—

and went up and unlocked the door."

"Did the cook and the other man appear at all?"

"There is no mention of it."

"I see. And Burma Chang was already dead, or, at least, lying on the floor in the condition in which I found him on my arrival?"

"Exactly."

"Were there any sounds inside the room before the door was unlocked?"

"I don't know."

"After that, I take it, the room was never empty."

"No, not once."

Kerry moved his shoulders restlessly. For the twentieth time he peered into the open safe, turning over bundles of papers covered with Chinese writing, many of them roughly kept accounts, apparently, and inscribed with heavy, black brush strokes upon oblong strips of newspaper. But the trays of banknotes afforded the problem which defeated him. He examined several bundles. Then, over his shoulder:

"Mr. Potter," he said, "you saw the money in possession of the man detained at Scotland Yard to-night? How was it tied up?"

"It was fastened with elastic bands."

"H'm," Kerry muttered, and tossed a bundle of a hundred five-pound notes back into a tray of the safe. The bundles were uniformly tied with thin green silk. "I see no elastic here." He glanced at Sowerby. "Your first inquiry looks like a mare's nest," he commented.

"In my opinion," Cosmo Potter interrupted, "robbery was not the motive of the crime."

"Really!" said Kerry; "then what do you think was the motive? Why is this safe turned upside down as well as all the table drawers and many other receptacles in the room? What were they looking for? Pickled onions?"

"I have very little doubt," Potter replied quietly, "that they were looking for whatever was contained in the little reliquary suspended about the dead man's neck."

Superintendent Kerry chewed noisily. Then, crossing to the door beside the safe, he pushed it widely open and stared vaguely into the darkness of the landing outside.

"His applying for police protection," he said, turning to Sowerby, "would seem to indicate that Burma Chang went in fear of his life." He glanced at Peel. "Did he go about much in Limehouse?"

"Very little," was the reply, "and never at night. He was invariably accompanied by one of the Dyaks."

"Ah!" Kerry muttered, "those pretty boys were his bodyguard, then?"

"It hadn't occurred to me, but after what Mr. Potter has told us about these Hill Dyaks, I think you may be right."

"We sha'n't really get to the bottom of the business until we can find out something about Burma Chang's affairs."

"I suppose," said Cosmo Potter slowly, "he can't have been a dope dealer? That might account for the extraordinary sums of ready money in his possession."

Inspector Peel shook his head vigorously.

"No," he replied. "We know the dope merchants well enough, and I'd stake my hat Burma Chang had no sort of relations with them."

"Apart from the ready money," Potter went on musingly, "the house contains a great quantity of valuable property. He may have been a receiver of stolen goods."

"A fence?" snapped Kerry. "That explanation would hardly cover the ground, sir. The matter goes deeper. This house has always been a mystery to me."

"And to me," Inspector Peel declared. "It used to belong to a man named Zani Chada. He 'did' three years, not so long ago, but I think he's out again. Then a woman had it—a Chinese woman. In fact, it has always been in the possession of Chinese."

"Chinese property," Sowerby murmured. "I don't suppose a European could lease it."

"Ah!" Kerry turned to his subordinate. "Stay here, Sowerby," he directed. "I am going to take another look around."

He went out, Peel and Potter following, on to the balcony, and along to a door at the western end. It was a two-leaved sliding door, like many in the house, and it opened smoothly and almost noiselessly.

The room within was softly illuminated, lights being on all over the house by the Superintendent's orders.

It was sparsely furnished in the Chinese manner. In addition to that by which they had entered, there were two other doors, both of fine lacquer work. Violet and black was the scheme of decoration and the painted silken lampshades were also carried out in these colours. At one end was an ornate idol before which two huge joss sticks still smouldered. There was a sort of dais at the other end of the room with a ceremonial couch upon it, beside which stood a finely carved and inlaid table, resembling a coffee table, whereon were an ivory snuff box and a fan. There were a number of carved stools in the room the floor of which was richly and beautifully carpeted. The walls were decorated with panels in high relief, painted and gilded in the patient Chinese fashion, and the ceiling was draped with violet silk.

Beside each of the little stools was a black silk cushion, and the room possessed that curious odour resembling sandalwood which, mingling with the burning incense, spoke to their senses with the voice of the Orient.

Kerry's fierce eyes turned to right and left of him; and:

"I should say this was a sort of Board Room," he hazarded. "Meetings of some kind must have taken place here. Where do the other doors lead to?"

"One on to the stairs," Peel replied; "you have passed it from the other side, when you went up to examine the rooms above. The other into a sort of anteroom which opens on to the balcony behind us."

He crossed as he spoke, sliding the panels aside and revealing a room some fourteen feet square, furnished with chaste simplicity and having a mat-covered floor. It was lighted by a lamp of perforated brass work.

Kerry stared about him vaguely, then turned, recrossed the larger room, and went out on to the stair leading to the upper part of the house.

Once one quitted the lobby below, there was nothing European in the whole place. It was purely a Chinese house. There was a living room above, with little low tables and mats and those few simple appointments which are found in such apartments, and to right and left of it were bleak-looking native bedrooms. There was no evidence anywhere of feminine occupation.

"Have there never been any women in the house?" Kerry inquired.

"Not that I know of," said Peel. "There were none found here, at any rate."

In a long, lofty cupboard, having sliding doors, they came upon a number of magnificent robes and other articles of attire. There was also a curious library in one room which Cosmo Potter examined with interest.

It was a queer, low room, lined with shelves upon the top of which were pieces of porcelain and other oriental ornaments. Rich carpets, inlaid furniture were there, lending the place an air of exotic luxury. There was a long, narrow table, also, laden with curious objects of the East.

Kerry's teeth snapped together viciously.

"I've been in this room before," he said—"in Zani Chada's time."

He looked about him appraisingly.

"Nothing much has been altered," he mused. "Burma Chang must have taken over the whole of the furniture."

Cosmo Potter, picking up a curious little carved ivory stick, to which was attached a long green silk tassel, turned and stared hard at the

Superintendent.

"Your remark gives me an idea," he declared.

"Good!" snapped Kerry. "I can do with it."

"Has it occurred to you," Potter went on, "that this house may be a sort of official residence? A kind of No. 10 Downing Street of Chinatown?"

"Eh?" said the Superintendent. "I don't follow."

"I mean that Burma Chang might have been some kind of official, and this house, which, as you say, Inspector," turning to Peel, "has always belonged to the Chinese, may have always been occupied by such an official. For instance, you speak of Zani Chada."

"Ah!" Superintendent Kerry revealed his large teeth in a fierce smile. "I see what you are driving at. You mean that Zani Chada was this man's predecessor, and that all this wealth belongs, not to an individual, but to an organization?"

Potter shrugged his shoulders.

"Something of the kind," he said. "It's only a theory. But it seems to cover some of the facts, at any rate."

"By Jove!" said Peel, looking about him with a new interest. "Funny no man ever thought of that before. It would account, too, for the extraordinary disturbance in Chinatown to-night. Every man in the area seems to know that Burma Chang is dead. Yes, by Gad! I think you are right, sir. He was some sort of an official."

Kerry's audible chewing alone disturbed the silence for a few moments. And then:

"Official of what?" he inquired.

And, standing in that curious, low room, the three men looked at one another and wondered.

CHAPTER XIII

UNDER SURVEILLANCE

Thanks to the influence of Cosmo Potter, Bernard Hope left New Scotland Yard a free man, but, for the first time in his life, under police surveillance. This fact he could not mistake. His attaché case with its precious contents had been detained, and when Potter, entering his car with Sowerby, en route for Limehouse, had reassuringly grasped Hope by the hand, he had whispered:

"Don't forget you are followed!" Then, aloud, he had added, "Cheer up, my lad! It will all come right!"

"Thanks to you," Hope said, "I believe it will. But I shall never forgive myself for putting you to all this trouble."

"Trouble!" Potter exclaimed; "I love it! Chinatown in a fog beats the Embassy hollow!"

Through the gates of the Yard, Bernard Hope watched the car driven off. He stood alone in the misty night looking about him.

His great gamble had ended successfully. Half ashamedly he had entered upon it, concealing his identity, masking his movements even from those nearest and dearest. All this had been dictated by a fear of ridicule, by sensitiveness; but his system or his luck had stood the test, and the return he had dreamed of, the triumphant return, armed with adequate capital for the launching of his play and the establishment of Yvette Chalmers as leading woman, had been realized.

But Fate is a disastrous stage manager. He had pictured nothing like this. The great scene which his dramatic imagination had conjured up—the scene when he should appear before Yvette and pour out at her feet the fruits of his wild adventure—this could not be.

The fruits of his adventure were safely lodged within the walls of New Scotland Yard; he, himself, was a suspect; and save for the happy chance that Potter, a distinguished ornament of the Bar and relative of the Assistant Commissioner, had roomed with him in college and dugout, he might now be under lock and key in Brixton Jail!

It was an odd reflection, and not without stimulus for a man of his trade. There was a sort of perverted humour in it which appealed to him wrily. It surpassed anything he would have dared to attempt in a play, since he leaned toward realism, and even now that it had palpably come into his own life, his intellectual predilection made it difficult of acceptance.

He reviewed the situation. His sense of the dramatic prompted him to postpone his meeting with Yvette until he could triumphantly vindicate his long silence. But since she was now involved in the same unsavoury net with himself, common sense dictated that he should see her at once. He had nothing to gain by subterfuge. That he would be followed to Yvette's flat was a foregone conclusion, but that he must go there seemed to him to be equally obvious. It was his duty to tell her the facts, of which, at present, she must necessarily be ignorant. He wondered whether the cabman whom presently he chartered had been officially advised to make a note of his destination, or whether a detective in another cab would follow him. He wondered what would have happened if he had walked out into Parliament Street and mounted a bus.

At any other time than this—such is the way of life, which cruelly limits our experiences—he must have taken a delight, he told himself, in testing the methods of Scotland Yard; in learning exactly what was done in regard to a man under police surveillance.

To-night, his thirst for information about any and every phase of life had ceased to rule. He was satiated with the unfamiliar. It awakened only as he discharged the cab before Yvette's flat.

He stared hard at the man as he paid his fare, deliberately drawing him into conversation, but failing to detect anything in his manner to suggest that he had been suborned. He entered the door of the building and mounted the stairs; but from a window of the first-floor staircase he looked out. As the taxi man drove off, he descended again and peered to right and left along the street.

It was well off the main road and the hour was late. No other cab apparently had followed him, and he was reduced to one of two conjectures: either the address to which he had driven would be reported to Scotland Yard, or in some mysterious way it had been communicated to the local police, and, hidden in a dark doorway, a constable had noted his arrival. He waited there for two or three minutes and then once more mounted the stairs.

Yvette's flat was on the third floor, and before the door he paused, irresolute. Cruelly, he had been robbed of his triumph. Instead of appearing before her, joyous, with visible evidence to account for his long silence, he came as something of a fugitive, watched by the police, concerned in a case of murder, and committed to warn her that she, too, was implicated.

He looked at the familiar number upon the door, and at last, almost mechanically, pressed the bell. He knew that Yvette had no resident maid. They were both, in the real sense, Bohemians. Yet, socially, in calling upon her at this hour he was compromising her, and, acutely, because of the circumstances, this fact came home to him.

Hope was not of those who despise the Metropolitan Police Service: he had failed to detect that surveillance which he knew was being exercised, yet he did not doubt that his visit was known to the responsible authorities. He realized that the Bohemian is poorly represented upon an average jury; he realized that every step which he took now might presently be subjected to the scrutiny of a court sitting in judgment on no less a crime than murder; so that when the door was opened and Yvette stood before him, he was not entirely master of himself or his expression.

She was fully dressed as though she had but just come in, and:

"Bernard!" she exclaimed.

There was welcome in her voice and he thrilled to it, but there was something like fear in it, too.

"You did not expect me?" he said, noting her curiously rigid attitude.

"How could I?" she replied, beginning to relax. "Bernard! You have almost frightened me."

She stood aside so that he might enter.

The fog had all but disappeared. Traces of it had been visible at the outset of his journey, but, as he vaguely remembered, the way had grown clearer as they had proceeded. Yet, its legacy was here upon the staircase, damply assailing the nostrils; a lingering smell like the memory of a pestilence. Swiftly it awoke a train of reflection.

He entered the lobby, and:

"Surely, you have only just come in?" he said.

"Only a few minutes ago," Yvette replied. "Oh! Bernard! Where have you been? Why have you not written to me?"

He laughed in a short, embarrassed way, whilst Yvette closed the door and stood with her back to it, watching him.

It was so different, this meeting, from all he had pictured. In Yvette's manner he seemed to detect something furtive: mingled with that pleasure which he had recognized was some mysterious alarm.

That night Burma Chang had been murdered—and she had known Burma Chang. It ran through his mind in a sort of refrain—she had known Burma Chang. The familiar little lobby took on an unfamiliar aspect. Yvette was a stranger, and he, Bernard Hope, an intruder.

"What is the matter?" she said sharply. "Why don't you speak to me? Where have you been? Why have you not written?"

She was watching him eagerly, hopefully, doubtingly; whilst the words went drumming through his brain, to a sort of tom-tom beat—she had known Burma Chang.

"My dear," he said, "so many strange things have happened, and I have so much to tell you. May I come in awhile and talk, or are you very tired?"

His manner was stranger than he recognized.

"Please come in," Yvette replied, biting her lip in sudden agitation; "I want to know. Of course I want to know."

CHAPTER XIV

YVETTE'S VISITOR

Inspector Sowerby arrived at Yvette's flat about eleven o'clock on the following morning. Yvette, newly from her bath, and a charming figure in her negligee, stared at the card when Molly, the daily girl who constituted the sole staff of her tiny flat, brought it in to her. She was just finishing her breakfast. A morning paper lay open upon the table before her, and a number of others were strewn upon the carpet.

The Press, that singular product of civilization which never sleeps, had already secured particulars of the Limehouse murder, and one enterprising journal published a half-column article on the "Mystery Man of Chinatown." Its appearance at this time was a coincidence, fortunate for the journal in question, since it was the work of an outside contributor. Because, although no names were mentioned, it had struck the literary editor as being libellous, if (a) such a Chinese millionaire as the one described actually existed, and calculated to provoke ridicule if (b) fictitious—which he strongly suspected—it had been marked for rejection, and would have been posted back to its writer on the following day, if news of the murder of Burma Chang had not arrived to confirm its authenticity and to enhance its value.

In spite of this dreadful shadow which had come Yvette was happy, as the least observant must have noticed. Her beauty was touched with a new radiance. Bernard Hope was the big thing in her life, bigger than her work and her ambition, and his singular disappearance and long silence had raised a dreadful doubt in her mind. For she had never believed the explanation which had preceded it, and, womanlike, had leapt to the inevitable but wrong conclusion. Now, he was back again, and, better still, no longer penniless.

Because she knew him innocent, that he could possibly suffer for this ghastly crime in Chinatown was an idea which simply never entered her mind. It was annoying, of course, for him to be suspected, but ridiculous. The vital thing was that his disappearance had not been connected with another woman, but that his wild adventure at Monte Carlo had been purely prompted by his love for, and interest in, herself—after which, nothing mattered.

She frowned in her own fascinating way, looking up at Molly. Bernard had prepared her for a visit from the police, but she had not expected it to take place quite so early; for, to Yvette, eleven was quite early.

"Do I look all right, Molly?" she asked. "Dare I see him like this?"

"You look beautiful, mum," said Molly sincerely. "And he's awful nice; he's Yorkshire."

"In that event," said Yvette, drawing her wrap more closely about her, and glancing down to see that her ankles were properly covered, "perhaps you had better show him in."

A moment afterward, Sowerby came in, quite unable to conceal the embarrassment which his modest nature experienced in such circumstances.

He had never before seen at close quarters a lady dressed quite as Yvette was dressed. He thought she was very beautiful, and to beauty Detective Inspector Sowerby accorded a respect bordering upon Veneration. With his surprised red face and upstanding hair, he scarcely offered a picture of a cavalier, yet he was a very chivalrous little gentleman, and his present task, which he had set himself, was entirely opposed to his instincts.

"Good morning, miss," he said. "Perhaps you would like me to call back in half an hour?"

"Oh, not at all," Yvette declared; "please sit down, Inspector. May I give you a cup of tea?"

Sowerby sat down obediently.

"Thank you," he said, "if it is not troubling you, I should like a cup of tea."

"Molly," Yvette called, while Sowerby watched her fascinatedly, "bring another cup in for Inspector Sowerby."

Then, addressing the latter:

"You really do not mind if I finish my breakfast while you talk to me, do you?" she asked.

"Not at all, miss," he answered. "I am sorry to have interrupted you. But I don't think I need detain you very long."

"Please don't talk about *detaining* me!" said Yvette, with mock alarm. "Isn't that what you say when you lock people up?"

"Well, yes, it is," Sowerby admitted, "but I didn't mean it in that way."

Molly having brought another cup and saucer, he stared as at a novel operation, whilst Yvette poured him out a cup of tea, eliciting his wishes respecting milk and sugar.

"I don't know any time in the day," he declared, "that I don't like a cup of tea."

"You can smoke if you want to," said Yvette, "I don't mind at all."

"Thank you," Sowerby replied, "but I would rather not."

Yvette returned to her toast and marmalade while he sipped his tea appreciatively. Then, placing the cup down:

"It's a little difficult to begin, miss," he said, "but," nodding in the direction of the open newspaper, "you know that a man called Burma Chang was murdered last night?"

"I knew it before," she returned composedly. "Mr. Hope came straight from Scotland Yard and told me."

"Ah!" said Sowerby. "Yes, I know he did. Well, now, we want to find out all we can about the— about this Burma Chang, and I understand that you knew him?"

"There must be many people in London who knew him better than I did. I only met him twice."

"Only twice!" Sowerby exclaimed. "Oh! is that so? Well, he seems a funny man for a lady in your position to know. May I ask where you met him?"

"Yes," Yvette replied musingly. "It's odd, of course. I met him at a house in Wade Street."

"Wade Street," Sowerby muttered. "Where is Wade Street?"

"Limehouse, I believe," Yvette replied.

"But, might I ask, miss, what you were doing in Limehouse?"

Yvette laughed.

"It sounds very mysterious," she confessed, "but really, it's perfectly simple. During the first two years I lived in London I had a maid— Annie Prescott, her name was. She was a wonderful servant and I became very much attached to her. She had relatives living in Shadwell, or Wapping, or some of those dreadful districts down by the docks, and finally, to my astonishment and horror, she married a Chinaman."

"Oh, Lord!" Sowerby muttered; "it's a funny world."

"A very funny world, Inspector. At first, I was disgusted—I confess it—in fact, I tried to make her change her mind when I first heard of her intention, but it was no good. She married this man—his name is Ah Wong. Well, contrary to all my expectations, she was very happy. The marriage took place nearly a year ago and she wrote to me quite regularly. Then "—Yvette hesitated, glancing swiftly at Sowerby—"she told me that a little Ah Wong was anticipated, and asked me, as she had asked me many times before, to go down and see her.

"I relented and went. I met her Chinese husband; and although, of course, no ordinary woman could think of him in such a relationship, I must admit that he was quite wonderful to her. They had a dear little home, too, spotlessly clean, and in their modest way they seemed to want for nothing. He is the manager, I believe, of some kind of Chinese store. He speaks quite fair English, and Annie had learned to talk Chinese, which to me does not sound like a language at all.

"Well, in this way, Inspector, I got in touch with her again, and sometimes I used to take her down little things which I thought might be useful, and sometimes send them. Then, one day when I was there, 'Charlie'—she calls her husband 'Charlie'— went to open the door and returned very excited—that is, as excited as a Chinaman can be. He had been honoured by a visit, I understood, from one of the great men of Chinatown, and he was torn between his preposterous respect for me and his veneration of this awful being who had called. His English nearly deserted him, but Annie explained that he wanted to know if I would consent to meet the great man. Of course, I consented—and Mr. Burma Chang came in."

She paused, looking across at Sowerby.

"That was how I met him," she added simply.

"I see, miss. Well, please go on. You say you met him a second time?"

"Yes," Yvette resumed. "He paid me the honour of being very attentive. Annie, who saw him through her husband's eyes, of course, informed me by letter that after my departure he had made many inquiries and had since become a regular visitor to the house in Wade Street. She thought, poor girl, that I should be flattered, of course. But after meeting him there a second time, his attentions became so marked that, well"— she laughed in sudden embarrassment—"to tell you the truth, I was rather frightened.

"I knew, you see, that he was very wealthy, and had some kind of power amongst the Chinese, and I spoke to Mr. Hope about it. As a result, he asked me to discontinue my visits. He made some inquiries, I believe, which led him to the conclusion that Burma Chang was a dangerous man."

Following a short silence:

"And so you never saw him again?" said Sowerby.

"No, never again."

"Excuse me asking you, miss, but I've got my job to do: Did you ever see Annie again?"

"No, I have not seen her since then."

"She never came to see you?"

"She has been to see me on two or three occasions, but not since the time I have spoken about."

"Not since your second meeting with Burma Chang?"

"No. Would you like another cup of tea, Inspector?"

"No, thank you, miss," said Sowerby, a little ruefully.

He had become quite cheerful on learning the innocuous character of Yvette's association with Chinatown. But, now, something seemed to be weighing upon his mind; and:

"Is that all you have to tell me, miss?" he asked, almost pathetically.

"All I can think of," Yvette replied, looking at him in a suddenly startled way.

"Ah!" muttered Sowerby.

He stared down reflectively at the carpet. Detecting there a nervous movement of Yvette's little feet, he became suddenly self-conscious and transferred his gaze to the ceiling. Considering its whiteness studiously:

"I thought, perhaps," he went on, "that you might have taken it into your head to go down there, to see this maid of yours—last night."

He continued to regard the ceiling, thereby deliberately failing to observe how Yvette started at the words.

"But, Inspector," she said in a low voice, "really, even if I had thought of such a thing, what bearing could it have upon the matter? I mean, I have told you all I know about Burma Chang, and I have told you that I have not been to the house in Wade Street since my second meeting with him."

"I know you have, miss," Sowerby admitted. "But although you may not have been there again, I thought as there is such a lot of doubt about various people who seem to be connected with this matter, that you might have liked to mention where you went last night."

"Where I went last night?" Yvette echoed in a whisper.

The ever chivalrous Sowerby kept his gaze religiously averted.

"You see, miss," he said, "we have sources of information at the Yard. We have to have," he added apologetically; "and I sent an inquiry round the principal taxicab garages early this morning, and as a result—"

"Oh!" Yvette cried sharply, "you don't mean to tell me that my taxi man has been giving information about me ? Why, he was here at half-past eight this morning, just after Molly arrived, to ask if I was all right, because, he said, he was so alarmed about me. I can't believe he could be so mean!"

"Ah!" Sowerby murmured, now at last transferring his gaze to Yvette's flushed face. "It's a funny world." His expression was reproachful. "You might as well have been frank with me, really. It seems to me, miss, that you are talking about the man who drove you down. The man I mean is the one who drove you back."

"Oh! that one!" Yvette exclaimed.

"Yes," Sowerby went on. "There isn't much taxi traffic between Limehouse and this part of London at night—particularly a foggy night— and it was my idea to do the cab depots."

"Really," said Yvette, wide-eyed, "it was a very clever idea. I suppose you think, now, Inspector, that I have been telling you lies! But I have told you the absolute truth. Fortunately, I can prove it."

"Excuse me," said Sowerby eagerly, "I have not suggested, I wouldn't suggest, anything to the contrary!"

"Oh, dear!" Yvette sighed plaintively, "our little sins do seem to find us out, don't they? I suppose I must make a full confession. You see, Inspector, I did not want Mr. Hope to know what had happened last night! Not that there was any harm in it, but what I did was contrary to his wishes. I was rather angry with him, as a matter of fact. He had been away and had not written to me for a long time. I know the reason now, silly fellow, but I didn't know it then. And so," she paused, "I broke my promise.

"Annie sent a message to the theatre to tell me that the little Ah Wong had arrived and that she, herself, was dangerously ill. She begged me to go down and see her." She paused, watching Sowerby.

"Perhaps you won't understand an appeal like that, Inspector. But I wanted to go very badly. Bernard—Mr. Hope—seemed at that time to have forgotten my existence, and so I arranged with the taxi man who usually calls for me at the theatre to go down to Wade Street last night. Mr. Hope doesn't know this—I have not told him."

"I quite understand, miss," said Sowerby sympathetically. "Unless it passes out of my hands—you understand what I mean—this is strictly between ourselves."

"Thank you, Inspector," said Yvette, with a little emotional laugh. "Well, we started. I hadn't realized how bad the fog was. But at last, after a dreadful journey, we got to the corner of Wade Street, or what the taxi man believed to be the corner of Wade Street. I thought I recognized the houses, and, foolishly, I got out of the cab and walked in what I thought was the direction of Ah Wong's house. I had not gone ten yards before I realized that I was in a perfectly unfamiliar street!

"At once I turned to go back. Of course, I couldn't see the cab—I couldn't see a yard in front of me. And just as I did so, I heard footsteps, like those of someone who had been following! The footsteps ceased as I turned, then came slowly on. Well, of course"—she laughed nervously— "I simply got in a panic. I walked quickly across to the other side of the street, and stood quite still, listening.

"I heard the footsteps pass slowly on. When at last they died away again, I tried to find my taxi. But that one change of direction, when I crossed the street, had upset everything. I was hopelessly lost!

"Never in my life have I been so frightened! I had not been in Limehouse at night before, and I seemed to wander through an endless maze of unlighted streets. Sometimes I heard, or felt, people near me, but I always avoided them. Then, to crown my misfortunes, there suddenly came the sound of a police whistle!

"Where everything had been muffled and secretive, all about me, a tremendous uproar arose! I heard men running and shouting. One man seemed to be coming in my direction. He cried out—and in my nervous, excited frame of mind, I thought he was crying out to *me!* I heard another whistle. After which, honestly, I don't know quite what happened or what I did. In fact, I really can't imagine what would have become of me, if I had not providentially blundered upon a stranded taxicab!

"At first, when I found it, I thought it was mine, the one in which I had come. But it was another one altogether. The driver was sitting inside, smoking his pipe, prepared, so he told me, to spend the night there if the fog did not lift.

"He had driven someone down to the docks and lost his way on the return journey. He allowed me to sit in the cab for which I was really very grateful, and some little time later a man came along who succeeded in guiding us to a main thoroughfare, which the driver seemed to recognize. Of course, I had abandoned all idea of finding Annie's house. And in this way, ultimately, I got home. I had a telegram sent to her early this morning, though, and I am glad to say that she has passed the crisis and is doing well."

"Ah!" said Sowerby. "And about how long, should you think, miss, you were walking about before you found this second cab?"

"Really," Yvette declared, "it seemed an age to me! I suppose it can't have been really more than about ten minutes."

"Ah," Sowerby repeated; "that seems quite reasonable. I don't know, miss, that I need trouble you any further, beyond asking for one or two addresses."

CHAPTER XV

AT THE GATE LODGE

Bernard Hope's residence was one which a more commercial-minded playwright—and every playwright of to-day should be commercial-minded—would have turned to excellent publicity use.

It was a tiny two-roomed cottage in a southeastern suburb, invisible except for its gray slated roof and chimneys, because of the overgrown shrubbery which separated it from the roadway. It was shadowed by a perfect coppice of elms, which, choking a semi-circular piece of ground bounded on one side by the road and on the other by the sweep of the carriage drive, almost succeeded in hiding Elm House from the curious gaze of the passer-by.

Elm House was unoccupied; "To Be Let or Sold," as weather-stained boards along the road frontage announced. Behind the rambling building were neglected lawns and extensive gardens. During the lifetime of its last occupier—an eccentric aunt of Bernard's—and in the days before motor busses had rendered the district untenable for folks of spacious habits, Elm House, indeed, had been, as the Estate Agent's boards declared, a "desirable residence."

It was desirable no longer, since workmen's tenements and jerry-built houses now hemmed it in. Yet at the time that it came to him he had accepted the legacy with gratitude, but, having no use for a big house, had tried to let or sell it, but had failed dismally.

He had come to recognize it as something of a white elephant, until, his fortunes being at low ebb, he had recognized the fact that the little lodge, to which he had caused a bathroom to be added, was a cosy enough residence in which he might live rent-free. Latterly, he had received several offers for the land, one of which, failing the kindly advice of Cosmo Potter, he must have accepted.

Fortunately, Potter stepped in, and Hope learned that there was a development scheme entailing the cutting of a new road, which would emerge into the highway upon the very site of Elm House.

"Sit tight," had been Potter's advice; and he was literally following it.

He was within easy distance of the centre of things. Save for the passing of many motor busses, some ten paces from bis window—and to this he had become used—the place suited him for work. He had had a telephone installed, and the decorations of the tiny cottage having been supervised by Yvette, his miniature home was not unattractive.

Here, then, he was awakened, on the morning following his unpleasant adventures at Fenchurch Street, by the ringing of his telephone bell.

On opening his eyes, for the moment he was nonplussed. Then he realized that he must have been dreaming of his experiences of the previous night. The tiny, dimly lighted room had seemed like a cell, and he had known all the tremors of an imprisoned man. He heaved a great sigh of relief. It was not so bad as that—yet.

This was a gray, cheerless morning, threatening rain. Since he had advised no one of his return, he did not anticipate that Mrs. Upton, who normally attended daily, would be appearing, although the cleanliness of the place proved that it had not been neglected during his absence, he having left a key in her possession.

He glanced at his watch on the table beside him, and found that it was nearly nine o'clock. This dispelled his first idea, that Yvette was the caller. She rarely telephoned before eleven. He got out of bed, pulling on his dressing gown. It was probably someone from Scotland Yard, and he hoped for good news, which would enable him to reclaim his precious attaché case. Taking up the receiver:

"Hello!" he said.

He learned that his surmise had been inaccurate. The call came from his club, and the speaker apologized for troubling him, but explained that someone who had no other address had telephoned urgently requesting to be put in touch with him, and as the matter seemed to be important, they had thought it better to ring him up.

"Very extraordinary," said Hope. "Is it a man or a woman?"

"A woman."

"Did she give her name?"

"No. But she said that you would know her, and that she had something very urgent to communicate."

Bernard Hope's brain worked rapidly. An image of the woman in the train arose before him. He saw the slanting eyes near to his own, he felt again the imprint of the red lips. And he realized that a possible link with the truth was here.

She wished to speak to him. Since the papers would be full of the murder in Chinatown, this spoke eloquently for her innocence and her anxiety to assist justice, whilst not unnaturally remaining, if possible, outside the case. Therefore:

"Very well," he replied, "give her my number."

He hung up the receiver and stood looking about the little room, which was his drawing room, his dining room, and his study.

Every available inch of space was utilized. It had surprised him to find how considerable a portion of his library could be housed in this tiny apartment. Books lined two of the walls, and even a few pictures were displayed. He had had a gas fire installed, and this he proceeded to light, for the morning air was damp and chilly.

He remembered clearly, now, that the card which he had given to the mysterious woman in the train had borne no other address than that of his club.

It was She, beyond doubt.

He stood up again, looking about him, and wondering whether to light the geyser in the bathroom, or to await the call which he was expecting. He determined to wait; and, returning to his bedroom, he took a cigarette from a box which lay upon a little table beside the bed, and lighted it.

There would be no newspapers delivered this morning. Economically, he had cancelled his order with the local newsagent on the day before his departure. It was annoying, because he had learned at Scotland Yard, on the night before, that enterprising members of the Press already were upon the scene of the crime. However, he must be patient.

His tiny kitchen, which was really an enlarged cupboard, opened off this room, its presence hidden by a graceful curtain. He entered and set a kettle to boil upon the gas stove. He then explored the pantry, discovering there bread, butter, and eggs, also several rashers of bacon. There was plenty of tea and coffee, but he would be reduced to tinned milk, which he detested.

The telephone bell rang, and, setting down a tin which he was exploring in quest of sugar, he went out and took up the instrument. Once more:

"Hello!" he said.

"Is that Mr. Bernard Hope?" a voice inquired.

It was vaguely familiar, although something of its bell-like quality was lost by transmission.

"Yes," he replied, "speaking."

"You will not know my name," the voice went on, "but I will tell you. I am Suzee Che Lo. I met you last night in a train. Do you remember?"

"I remember!" said Hope.

"Something has happened, since, which makes it important for me to see you—something I must tell you—which you ought to know— which you must know."

Her curious method of speech, of construction—a unique kind of intensity which, if he had been called upon to express in words, he would have defined as passive vehemence—all were unmistakable. It was his mysterious acquaintance! He thought rapidly, and:

"It is good of you to take the trouble," he replied; but:

"You must not say that," she interrupted. "You saved me last night from something you do not know about. I want to tell you because it is right that you should be told. It is impossible on the telephone. I must see you. The papers this morning say something which makes it necessary that I should see you."

"You realize that you may become involved?" said Hope.

He heard her laugh.

"That is so silly!" she said. "But of course, you don't realize how silly it is. Believe me, I am involved already. I cannot stay here much longer. Please tell me where I can see you."

Hope hesitated, seeking to visualize the situation.

He had good reason to know that he was being watched. Probably the cottage was being watched even at this very hour. On the other hand, he could not be sure that the woman so strangely named had any direct association with the crime in Chinatown. That she had information, possibly valuable information, bearing upon it, seemed very likely. It was a delicate situation, and he wondered how Cosmo Potter would have acted.

"Please answer me," the voice pleaded.

Thereupon Hope made his mind up.

"Listen," he said, "very attentively. It will be impossible for me to see you until nightfall because —well—because the police are watching me. Do you understand?"

"I understand," she answered softly.

"Also, we must not be seen together. So when you come, be sure that you are not followed."

He then gave her careful instructions which would enable her to find a narrow lane running behind the gardens of a row of small villas, and communicating with a back entrance to the grounds of Elm House.

"At nine o'clock," he concluded. "Be very careful. I shall be at the gate to meet you."

"I shall be there," she assured him.

As he hung up the receiver, Hope smiled grimly. Perhaps he was playing with fire, yet he had acted for the best.

He remembered, ruefully, Yvette's reception of that part of his story touching the encounter in the train. He reflected that if the Black Gods should enable her to witness the meeting which he had just arranged, she would inevitably misconstrue the meaning of the tryst. But, in his present state of knowledge, certainly he must not expose Suzee Che Lo to detection by the watching officials of Scotland Yard.

"Damn!" he said aloud, "what an infernal tangle—and not of my own making."

The morning was very gloomy. He was about to turn on the light, when he hesitated, his hand touching the switch. Crossing to the little window, he peered out.

A red motor bus was passing slowly, for Elm House stood almost at the crest of a steep hill. Through the dense bushes, their leaves dripping with moisture, he saw lighted windows in the houses on the opposite side of the street. Along the pavement by the cottage a man was slowly passing: he could see his bowler hat over the top of the fence. He wondered!

Of the methods of Scotland Yard he knew little. Would surveillance be continuous? He was prepared to believe it possible, and preferred to do so until he should have consulted Cosmo Potter, from whom he expected to hear at almost any moment, now.

As a matter of fact, he had not long finished his bath and was only just beginning to prepare breakfast, when the bell rang. Looking out of the window, he saw Potter's car drawn up beyond the bushes.

He went out into the tiny hallway and opened the door, and there, in the low porch, was his friend, muffled in a fur-lined overcoat and wearing a soft hat with the brim pulled down. He had a bundle of newspapers under his arm, and a cigar holder containing a gigantic cigarette protruded from the left corner of his mouth. At Bernard Hope, still wearing his dressing gown, he gazed amusedly; and:

"Our friend Sowerby is very thorough," he murmured, entering. "I recognized one of his watchdogs on the hill as we came up."

"Good!" said Hope grimly. "Thank God, he's wasting his time. I was expecting you, Potter. But it is tremendously decent of you to come, all the same."

"Not at all," declared the other, as Hope closed the door. "Humanity is so infernally dull, Hope; these unforeseen outbreaks make life worth living. I am due in chambers in forty minutes, but I have time to give you all the important information."

"Carry on," said Hope. "I left two rashers of bacon in the pan. Go on talking whilst I attend to them."

"I suspected it," Potter murmured. "Very appetizing smell."

"Will you join me?" cried Hope.

"Well," said Potter, removing hat and coat, "1 am no breakfast man as a rule, but this rusticity seems to have aroused a latent appetite. Suppose I make some toast while you grapple with the bacon?"

As a result, the distinguished K. C. and the yet unrecognized dramatist, one in correct morning dress and the other in pajamas and loose gown, presently faced one another across a dish of bacon and eggs, prepared with their own hands in the gate lodge of what had once been a country house but was now a deserted building in a decaying suburb.

The humour of it struck them simultaneously. They both burst into hearty laughter. Cosmo Potter, his mouth full of hot bacon, murmured:

"Humanity is so improbable, Hope."

The meal dispatched, Potter fitted a cigarette into his holder, whilst Bernard Hope loaded a briar pipe; and:

"The position to date," said Potter, "is this. There is no mention of you in the Press, except for the vague statement that a man was detained by the police last night. That man, of course, is yourself. Markham has confirmed your story, corroborated by the steward whom you saw. The fog served us in this case, as also in the case of your American acquaintances. The Japanese boat was held up at Albert Dock, in fact, may not have sailed yet. So that the evidence from Monte Carlo becomes almost unnecessary.

"You are fairly entitled to the six thousand pounds, Hope, and I advise you to go up to Scotland Yard and claim it at once. I have 'phoned my uncle, and I don't think any difficulty will be raised."

"By Gad!" said Hope, "this is a tremendous relief. My thinking of you last night was a stroke of genius. But I don't understand one thing."

"What is that?"

Cosmo Potter stared at him oddly.

"Very simple," Hope continued. "Since I am no longer suspected, why am I still watched?"

"Ah!"

Potter contemplated the end of his cigarette.

"The trouble is that in certain quarters you *are* still suspected."

"What!"

"Oh, *I* know it's silly, my dear fellow, and *you* know it. To give the man his due, I think Kerry knows it, too. But Sowerby is Yorkshire. A decent fellow enough, but a one-idea man. You see, Hope," he tapped his finger upon the table, "it seems like hair-splitting, but there's a gap in your story!"

"Where?" Hope demanded incredulously.

"Between the time that you left the ship, or rather left the docks—the watchman who had charge of your bag has so far failed to materialize, I gather—and the time of your arrival at Fenchurch Street. In other words, owing to the unfortunate occurrence which you know of, there is absolutely no evidence, even now, that you were ever on the train, prior to its stoppage at the point where a constable saw someone mount the embankment.

"The theory that you robbed the safe is no longer tenable. But the possibility remains—not in my mind, but in others—that you may have been distracted from your original purpose, if you ever held such a purpose, and may have gone to Burma Chang's house. Unfortunately, there would just have been time for you to have done so, and for you to have been the man who was seen climbing out of the window. I know it's damn silly, so don't bother to tell me so. But, speaking legally, there is, even now, no real evidence that you are *not* that man. You see my point, Hope?"

"I see it with unpleasant clearness," Hope replied.

"West India Dock Station being practically deserted when you joined the train," Potter went on, "to look for any witness there is rather hopeless. I suppose, with the exception of the man from whom you bought your ticket, you encountered no other official whatever?"

"Not a soul," Hope replied. "Surely *he* would remember me?"

"He has to be found," Potter murmured. "He may remember you, of course. On the other hand, he may not. I have sent an advertisement to several newspapers, which I fear you will have to pay for, offering a reward of £20 and no questions asked, for the return of your suitcase."

"The whole contents were worth more like five!" Hope declared.

"Very likely," said Potter drily. "But a man carrying a heavy suitcase cannot scale walls; nor was the fugitive seen scrambling up the railway embankment described as carrying any baggage. The recovery of that suitcase, my dear fellow, would clear you definitely. Do you see my point?"

Hope nodded slowly.

Depression threatened him again. He perceived that the cloud was not yet lifted.

"Yes, you are right, Potter," he replied. "But isn't it rather hopeless?"

"In a way it is," the other admitted; "but whatever crook stole your case, he would never find so fine a market as that offered by us. And now, I must be off. But first, as to your own movements. What did you do when I left you last night? Tell me briefly, so that I may know how to deal with any points that may arise before we meet again."

Hope complied, outlining his movements from the time that he left New Scotland Yard up to the moment of his return to the cottage. Finally, as Potter struggled again into his fur-lined coat, he told him of the telephone message received that morning.

Potter, half in his coat and half out of it, stopped dead, and stared as one amazed.

"Great Smoke!" he said. "Hope, your luck is fabulous!"

"One moment," said Hope, "I have an inkling of what you mean, but since she has volunteered to come—"

"My dear fellow!"—Potter completely enveloped himself in the coat and raised his hand—"I am not an official of Scotland Yard. You may trust to my discretion. If I should be unable to see you again to-day, observe every possible precaution."

"You don't think I acted unwisely in agreeing to the meeting?"

"Unwisely!" Potter exclaimed. "I could not have done better myself!"

He put his hat on, and:

"You will probably hear from Yvette later," he said. "I shall be greatly surprised if Sowerby has not interviewed her this morning."

Hope nodded gloomily.

"I should like to kick myself for dragging her into this thing," he replied; "but what the devil could I do?"

"Nothing but what you did do."

Potter stepped to the door.

"Potter," said Hope, "I have been turning over in my mind your account of what took place last night at Burma Chang's house. Have you formed any sort of opinion, yourself, as to who murdered this man?"

"As to who murdered him—no," Potter replied, "but as to where the murderer *is,* yes!"

"Where he is!" Hope exclaimed. "What do you mean?"

"I mean," said Potter, opening the door and going out, "that I think I know where the murderer is to be looked for. And I think Superintendent Kerry knows, too."

CHAPTER XVI

RED KERRY AT WORK

Yvette 'phoned Hope just before noon, and in confirmation of Potter's surmise, informed him that Inspector Sowerby had been to question her. Hope arranged to meet Yvette for lunch, and then, following his friend's advice, he set out for New Scotland Yard.

Not being familiar as Potter with the officials of that institution, he suspected every second man he met upon the hill of being a detective; but when presently he entered a taxi and proceeded townward, his observations through the window in the rear availed him nothing. He could detect no sign of pursuit.

It was not entirely without trepidation that he entered the headquarters of the Metropolitan Police. Absurd though it might be, he could not disguise from himself the fact that he was a man suspected of a ghastly crime. Perhaps the very police officer to whom he gave his card on entering was already familiar with his name. Imagination suggested that such was the case.

He invested the building with the attributes of the Bastille and, doing so, marvelled at his own courage in entering it. He was presently invited to step into a lift, and, this lift stopping at the third floor, he was shown to a bleak-looking room and requested to wait.

The room, although identical in almost every particular, was, nevertheless, not that in which on the previous night he had nervously awaited the arrival of Cosmo Potter. It was rather larger, although the window commanded the same prospect. It was slightly more homely. A woolly overcoat was thrown over the back of a chair, and a neat bowler hat balanced upon it.

Against the coat rested a silver-mounted malacca cane, which automatically suggested a sergeant-major. There were a great number of papers upon the table, and a framed photograph which Hope studied with interest. It was that of a severely handsome woman, attired with strict simplicity, her hand resting upon the shoulder of a boy wearing college colours, and notable for a really remarkable pugnacity of expression.

Hope wondered why he had been shown into this room. Evidently he was not to be interviewed this morning by Sowerby; possibly, he was in Chinatown. He rather suspected that this was the apartment of a superior official. Then, suddenly, upon a smaller table in a corner, he saw his attaché case.

It was a heartening sight. Evidently Scotland Yard was prepared to return his property, and this he accounted a favourable indication. Perhaps other evidence had come to light since Potter had been in touch with them.

So he stood, staring at his case, when the door opened and a man entered.

He wore an excellently cut double-breasted blue suit, square-pointed collar, and a neat bow. His glistening shoes betrayed no evidence that they had ever known dust or mud. At the flaming redness of his close-cropped hair and moustache Hope stared in amazement with which a faint sense of familiarity began to mingle.

The newcomer smiled with a sort of savage geniality; and:

"Good-morning, Mr. Hope," he said briefly.

As he crossed and seated himself behind the big table with its neat piles of documents, Bernard Hope, from a description which had been given to him by Cosmo Potter, recognized that he stood in the presence of the celebrated Superintendent Kerry.

"Please sit down, Mr. Hope," the latter continued, running a swift glance over a typewritten paper which lay upon his blotting pad. "I take it you have come to claim your case?"

"Yes," Hope replied. "I am naturally anxious to lodge the money at my bank."

"Well, there's no objection to that," said Kerry, looking up. "I have a report here from Cook's, giving the numbers of the bank notes issued at Monte Carlo. You may regard that unpleasantness as concluded, Mr. Hope. I regret that official routine made it necessary."

Hope smiled ruefully.

"Official routine spoiled a big situation for me, Superintendent," he said. "I believe I am speaking to Superintendent Kerry?"

Kerry nodded, gratified by the recognition.

"You see," Hope went on, "I had taken a big chance. I am not a gambler by instinct, but I happened to meet the only woman I had ever wanted to marry at a time when I had scarcely a penny in the world."

Kerry rested his elbow on the table and his truculent chin in his palm, nodding sympathetically.

"I did a thing which all the world would have said was foolish—I tried to make money at roulette; not haphazard, but by means of a system which I thought I had discovered. Apparently my system was a good one; but I was so ashamed of what looked like folly, in a man as hard up as myself, that I adopted every measure I could think of to conceal my whereabouts, with the result that this thing happened to me. I did not write to a soul, not even to the lady I have mentioned. And last night, I had planned to put everything right by emptying all that money upon the table in front of her. Perhaps you will think I am mad, Superintendent—"

"No, I don't," said Kerry. "You are engaged to marry this lady, sir?"

"I am."

"I don't think you are mad at all," Kerry declared. "When a man feels that way, it's the real thing, and I know from the way you say it that it's the real thing with you, sir. I understand that the lady is an actress, and perhaps because the actresses who have come my way have not been all they might have been, I don't look on that profession quite fairly. But I quite understand."

His eyes strayed to the photograph upon the table.

"It seems like madness, Mr. Hope, but it's the best thing that can happen to a man. It only comes once, and when it comes we ought to grasp it with both hands."

Bernard Hope recognized that he was staring at the speaker almost rudely. Thereupon he smiled; and because his smile was so full of human understanding, it established an immediate link between these two so widely different personalities. Either Cosmo Potter's powers of observation were at fault for once, or this was a Superintendent Kerry whom he had never had the privilege of meeting.

The physical characteristics were as described, together with that unvarnished truthfulness of sentiment, for which Hope had been prepared. But this instant understanding of his romance had astounded the man who had looked for official stodginess mixed with ferocity.

"I am glad to hear you say so, Superintendent," he declared; "only a happily married man could speak in that way."

"You are right, Mr. Hope," snapped Kerry with a sudden energy almost startling. He turned the photograph in his visitor's direction. "My wife and son," he announced proudly. "Mrs. Kerry is Scotch and Free Church, but none the worse for that, though I say it. My boy is captain of the school, and one day he will sit in Parliament, or my name is not Daniel Kerry."

"I congratulate you, Superintendent," said Hope. "Your wife is very charming, and your son, if I may say so, looks more likely to grasp a field marshal's baton than the portfolio of a Minister."

"No, sir!" Kerry replaced the photograph. "No soldiering for my boy. In the first place, I couldn't afford it, and, in the second place, peace-time soldiering is demoralizing. No, where we want the fighters to-day, sir, is not in the army but in the House of Commons!"

He stood up, crossed the room, took up the attaché case and handed it to Hope.

"I should be glad if you would just check the contents," he said, "and sign this form."

Hope did so, and he having certified the contents to be correct:

"Now," said Kerry, "there is one point, Mr. Hope, over which, I think, you can assist me very materially. I should like to have a description from you"—he glanced at some papers upon his table—"of this foreign woman who got into the train and to whom you gave your ticket."

Bernard Hope suppressed a guilty start; but:

"Certainly, Superintendent," he replied. "What do you wish to know?"

"Well, what aged woman would she be?"

"It is rather difficult to say," Hope answered. "I think she was half an Eastern, and they mature so early. She looked about twenty-five or twenty-six."

"Tall?"

"Yes," said Hope, "she was tall; that is to say, above medium height, and slender. She had what I should describe as a fashionable figure."

"She was very dark?" Kerry went on, consulting his notes.

"Yes, quite Oriental colouring, with an ivory skin. Her eyes slanted slightly."

"You mean like a Chinese?"

"Yes," Hope replied, feeling frightfully guilty. "I think she's probably some kind of Eurasian."

"Did she speak with any accent?"

"It was very slight. She was obviously a well-educated woman."

Superintendent Kerry extracted a wafer of chewing gum from his waistcoat pocket, unwrapping it, and placed it between his large white teeth; then:

"Was her dress torn or disordered in any way?" he asked.

"No," Hope returned, "but her shoes were muddy and so were her stockings."

"Muddy?" Kerry snapped. "What sort of shoes was she wearing?

High-heeled shoes?"

"Yes."

"Ah!" Kerry made a note. "If only I had arrived an hour earlier. To what class should you say this woman belonged?"

"To what class?" Hope echoed.

"Exactly. Allowing for her colour, should you say she was a lady?"

"Well"—Hope hesitated—"I am not familiar with people of her nationality, Superintendent, so that I can hardly say."

"Was she one of the night-club sort?"

"I should hardly say so."

Kerry consulted what appeared to be a list of names. And, finally:

"Do you think she might have been a performer?" he said; "a dancer, for instance?"

"Well," Hope admitted, "that's possible."

"Were there any distinguishing marks you noticed? Any peculiar jewellery that she wore?"

"No," Hope replied. "Except her Oriental appearance, of which I have spoken, there was nothing distinctive that I remember."

He longed for escape. It appeared to him, now, that in the very moment of freedom, with the gates open before him, he was voluntarily committing himself afresh. Evidently enough, Superintendent Kerry had determined to track down this invaluable witness; and, guiltily conscious of his own appointment with her for that very evening, Bernard Hope experienced for the second time in his career a fear akin to that which, he supposed, must haunt the criminal.

If, as Kerry clearly suspected, Suzee Che Lo—he could never forget that extraordinary name—had possession of valuable information respecting the crime, was he not becoming—indeed already become— an accessory?

How, in the event of subsequent exposure, should he explain his present silence?

His position was dreadfully difficult, and rendered the more so by a very real esteem which he had formed for the formidable Superintendent, whose work was amongst sordid things, but in whom the poetry of life still flourished.

When at last he left New Scotland Yard and set out for his bank, he was conscious of a certain self-contempt. How otherwise he could have acted was not apparent, but apart from the obvious danger of such a proceeding, his double dealing in regard to this mysterious woman, who might after all be a member of a dangerous gang of criminals, was wholly contrary to his principles.

He determined that to-night he would warn her of the true state of affairs, request her to place any information she might have in the hands of the police, and, in the event of her refusing to do so, reveal the fact of the interview, first to Scotland Yard, and, second, to Yvette.

His motives were good and plain enough, but he could clearly see danger ahead in any conspiracy of silence between himself and Suzee Che Lo.

As he proceeded to the bank, he wondered if he might construe the Superintendent's attitude as meaning that the watchdogs had been called off. In view of his appointment that evening, it would have been a relief to know this to be the case. But here he entered a province of surmise. In one respect, at least, he had saved himself from the worst suspicion: he had informed Cosmo Potter.

CHAPTER XVII

SUZEE CHE LO

Bernard Hope could not understand the silence of Cosmo Potter. After seeing Yvette to the theatre, where there was a matinee that afternoon, he had gone to his club and had remained there for an hour or so.

He was still uncertain respecting the reality of his freedom, and on his return to the cottage he made a determined attempt to learn if Scotland Yard's watch upon his movements continued. In this he was successful. His new capital, so strangely acquired, had opened up possibilities hitherto closed to him; and from his return until dusk he sat at his typewriter busily engaged with correspondence. Quite a formidable bunch of letters had accumulated during his absence, and he dealt with some of these.

With Potter he could not get in touch, although he telephoned three times. Going out to post his letters, he looked carefully about him, up and down the hill, but could detect no sign of a watcher. He returned in the early dusk, bearing copies of all the evening papers, and, lighting the lamp on the table in his tiny room, he closely studied the reports of the Chinatown murder.

In one of them he found a paragraph—which reassured him somewhat—to the effect that "the man detained last night" had been released. But in the many lurid accounts which he read he could perceive nothing of an alarming nature. The Press unanimously had decided to feature the case: so much was evident. No reference to Cosmo Potter appeared anywhere, but the fact was heavily emphasized that Superintendent Kerry, one of the "Four Aces" of Scotland Yard, had charge of the case.

On the whole, it was obvious that the Press had received but scanty official information. The bulk of the space was taken up with elaborate rehashes of the article on "The Mystery Man of Chinatown" which had appeared in a morning paper.

Ordinarily, he should have dined at his club or at a restaurant, but fearful of being late for his strange appointment, he determined to content himself with a snack and to join Yvette for supper, later.

About a quarter to nine, having closely drawn the window curtains so as to make it impossible for any one to peer into the room from outside, he left his table lamp alight and slipped quietly out by the back door of the cottage, which opened on to a narrow path, roughly tiled, and communicating in one direction with a tiny paved yard, and in the other with the drive leading up to the house.

It was possible, however, to reach the back of Elm House without coming out upon the carriage sweep. There was a sort of path close under the fence bordering the property and behind dense banks of shrubbery and weed-grown flower beds, which had probably at some time been used by gardeners. This was the path which Bernard Hope intended to use.

The door by which he had come out was secured only by a bolt on the inside; therefore, he must leave it merely fastened by the latch, for to have come out by the front door would have been to invite the curiosity of any watcher who might still be on duty.

He drew the door to softly and set out without delay. Ten paces brought him to the shrubbery where he felt himself safe from observation. The clay soil underneath was very wet, but it made his going almost silent, and, skirting one wing of the deserted house, he came out on the edge of the gardens.

It was a cloudy night with a fitful moon, but dimly to the right he could see a row of French windows opening on the terrace, a line of iron scrollwork pillars and the flat front of the house rising above, the whole suggestive, in some way, of Victorian tea parties, gentlemen with Dundreary whiskers, and much-beflounced ladies. Ahead, the ground sloped down to where twinkling lights marked the back windows of houses in an avenue which ran parallel with the hill. He must bear to the left, passing through the abandoned kitchen garden, and as nearly as possible follow the boundary wall to his destination.

Exercising great caution he proceeded. On the other side of this wall were little gardens belonging to houses on the hill. But, presently, just past what once had been a chicken run and near the end of the grounds in this direction, he took a sloping path to the right, in which at intervals steps had been cut. Here had been a flower garden, and beneath the skeleton of a pergola he paused, looking back and up toward the house.

He started, uttering a stifled exclamation. Either his imagination was playing him tricks, or a figure was moving stealthily along the terrace past the French windows!

His first thought was of the door which he had been forced to leave open. This was some prowler, who, seeing him leave the cottage, was watching until he should be a safe distance off, before seeking to enter. He watched intently, but the figure, if it had ever been there, had now disappeared.

A second and even more disturbing theory supplanted the first: Any petty burglar with designs upon his few goods would almost certainly have operated during his absence, when the place was unoccupied for days and nights together. He was still being shadowed. It was a detective. Common sense told him, however, that since there was little moon, he could not very well have been seen at any point during his journey. At the outset, he might possibly have been heard.

He hurried on, and presently came to that door in the wall which opened on a narrow lane. It ran behind a row of small houses, each possessing a miniature garden. He unlocked the door and looked out cautiously.

The lane was empty. He paused, looking along in the direction of the avenue. Clocks near and remote were chiming the hour of nine. In view of what he had recently seen, he was debating upon the best course to adopt, when, like a phantom, Suzee Che Lo appeared beside him!

He started wildly. Where she could have been hiding he was unable to imagine. He almost doubted the evidence of his senses. Remembering the circumstances of their first meeting, his imagination cloaked her with witchcraft. Seemingly, she could appear and disappear at will. Then, even as he wondered, her slender, nervous hands rested upon his shoulders, the long, slanting eyes, visible in the dusk, as though they possessed chatoyant qualities, were close to his own.

And once again he thrilled strangely to a kiss, passionless, yet lingering. Then:

"Quick!" she whispered—"we must hide! Someone is following me."

His own fears temporarily forgotten, Hope held open the door and allowed her to enter. Entering behind her, he closed and rebolted it.

As if the proximity of this mysterious woman endowed him with clairvoyant powers, he seemed to see her before him in the darkness, although they both stood in black shadow. And in some way he detected the fact that she was listening intently.

"I think the police are covering my movements," he said in a low voice. "I have been watched since last night."

But, as if ignoring his words:

"Someone is following me," she repeated. "He is near us now!"

He realized that his nerves were badly jangled. To commonplace alarm, quite normal in the circumstances, a vague and indefinite kind of fear succeeded. He had read the article on Burma Chang in a morning paper; he had heard from Potter how all Chinatown had been abroad, as though, Eastern fashion, news of the man's death had passed magically from house to house. Who or what could he have been, this mysterious figure who mysteriously had met his end last night?

Here beside him in the darkness was a link with these nameless Oriental horrors which, unbidden, had intruded upon his own life.

"Someone is following me!" The words echoed through his brain. "He is near us now!"

He exercised a great effort and escaped from an uncanny atmosphere which seemed to be closing in upon him.

"There is a little shed just to the left of the door," he said, continuing to speak in a very low voice; "let me guide you. We can talk there. I am afraid to go back to the cottage. I am certain it is watched."

She made no reply, and presently they groped their way into a little hut, one side of which opened on to the garden. He was familiar with the way, or to have found it in the darkness must have been impossible.

"I dare not strike a match," he said, "or I would endeavour to find you a seat."

"Don't trouble," she replied; "it is impossible for me to stay more than a few minutes. But there is something I must tell you, and something I must ask of you."

She grasped his arm, drawing nearer.

"Perhaps after to-night," she went on, "we may not meet again—I cannot say. You have saved me from more horrible things than I can ever tell you, and in doing so, have got into trouble yourself. I have heard, and I know. There may be worse to come than you suspect, but I, too, am still in danger. If you will do something else for me you will be aiding your English justice. Will you do it?"

"Tell me what you want me to do, and if it is possible, I will do it. But first assure me on one point. Last night I doubted you—when I learned that murder had been committed."

As he spoke, her fingers tightened upon his arm.

"I broke my word," he went on grimly; "I told the police of our meeting in the train. I had no alternative. Perhaps I was wrong. If you are in no way connected with the crime committed in Chinatown last night, then certainly I was wrong."

"I am not ignorant of it," she whispered.

"What!" Hope exclaimed. "Then I was right!"

"Yes, you were right, and I forgive you."

"But, listen," he continued excitedly, "it is your plain duty to yourself and to others to tell all you know."

He reached out in the darkness and grasped her shoulder, urgently; but:

"You think so?" she replied. "It is because you do not know. Perhaps I could tell them what they seem so anxious to learn, but in the first place I don't want to, and in the second place, I dare not."

"Dare not? What do you mean?"

"Just that—I dare not."

"Do you know who killed Burma Chang?"

"I know. Yes!"

"Good God! This is awful!" Hope exclaimed. "If you are not prepared to speak, why do you tell me this? Why do you put such a responsibility upon me?"

She was silent for a moment; then:

"Where is the responsibility?" she asked. "The laws of China are not the laws of England. Perhaps"—her tone was very sad—"Burma Chang did not respect those laws. Why should the English police try to avenge him? If they knew, they might not wish to do so."

"But," Hope said desperately, raising his voice in his excitement, "I am suspected of being concerned in the matter, and I know nothing whatever about it. For my sake, at least, will you not tell what you know? Except that you entered the train last night whilst it was detained in the fog, and that I gave you my ticket, I know nothing whatever about this thing. Yet, at the present moment, to the best of my knowledge, I am being dogged by a detective from Scotland Yard!"

He drew her nearer in his anxiety and, following a few moments' silence during which that uncomfortable clairvoyant sense leaped into life again, he divined that she was listening for some sound outside the hut.

"If danger comes to you," she answered softly, "I shall speak; if it does not, I shall remain silent."

"Then why are you here?" he demanded almost harshly. "What is it that you have to say to me?"

She leaned against him in the darkness, resting her hand upon his breast caressingly.

"You are English and can never understand," she said. "Perhaps I, who am not English, do not quite understand either, but your greatest danger is not from the police—neither is mine. I am going to ask you to take charge of something for me. If I want it, I will send for it. If I do not send for it it will be because—" She paused.

"Yes?" Hope prompted.

"Because I have gone away," she said, dropping her voice again to a whisper. "It is for my protection that I ask you to take it. Lock it up somewhere; do not tell *me* where it will be—do not tell any one. Then you will be safe. So shall I."

"But I don't understand," Hope declared. "At the present moment I have nothing to reproach myself with. If I agree to what you ask, I shall blindly become an accessory to a crime in which I had no part. I don't even know who you are or in what way you are connected with this affair."

"Don't ask!" she whispered, her lips very near his own. "I tried to prevent it—that is all my connection with it. Believe me! You *must* believe me! I am suffering now for what I risked. Please believe me and let me go! I am frightened, because I am sure that someone is listening to us!"

"What!" Hope exclaimed sibilantly.

"Yes, speak softly! I must go. Tell me you will do what I ask, and let me go."

"But at least let me know where I can communicate with you."

"It is impossible," she whispered. "I must go. Walk with me to the end of the lane," she went on, "but no farther. I have a cab waiting quite near. Please don't hesitate—only do what I ask."

Hope struggled in the throes of indecision.

"You don't seem to understand," he said, "that if I am questioned again I shall be compelled to divulge the facts of this interview."

"You may do so," she replied calmly; "but if you value your life, lodge the little box in some safe place known to no one but yourself."

"But I have not agreed to take charge of this little box!"

Suddenly she clutched him tightly.

"Don't torture me!" she whispered. "I shall go mad if you try to detain me any longer! I have promised that you shall come to no danger because of me. You are exposing me to things of which you cannot even dream if you refuse to do as I ask. Please walk with me to the end of the lane. But don't come out into the road, in case you are seen."

She ceased speaking suddenly, and he divined that she was listening again. He listened also, intently, but could detect no sound other than the distant roar of London encircling them and the noise of a passing motor bus upon the hill. He believed he was committing himself to a new folly, but:

"Very well," he said. "Hold my arm. I will guide you."

A few minutes later they came out into the narrow lane, Suzee Che Lo clinging to him tightly, almost excitedly. They walked in the direction of the corner. Voices were audible, for there were several pedestrians in the avenue; a commercial lorry drove past; and in this commonplace suburban atmosphere, the murder of Burma Chang suddenly assumed in Hope's mind a fabulous quality.

It was all unreal, and this strange, slender woman, almost invisible beside him, no more than a figment of an uneasy dream. Then, abruptly, she stopped, checking him.

As her slender hands tightened upon his shoulders he knew what to expect. Even if he had been disposed to resist, resistance must have come too late. She crushed her lips against his own, for a long, thrilling moment. Then, withdrawing:

"In the breast pocket of your coat!" she whispered, turned, and ran swiftly away.

Dazed, bewildered, Bernard Hope looked in the direction of the end of the narrow lane. Following for a few paces, he stared to right and left along the avenue.

But of the waiting cab of which she had spoken, or of Suzee Che Lo, he could see no sign! Almost automatically he raised his hand to his breast pocket.

"Good heavens!" he whispered, "what is it?"

He could detect there the outline of what felt like a small box!

CHAPTER XVIII

THE GOLDEN LOTUS

Returning, Hope bolted the door. As he did so, a sound brought him sharply about.

"Who's there?" he cried.

Unmistakable footfalls were audible from the direction of the little hut! He regretted, now, that he had come unarmed, and again:

"Who's there?" he cried.

"Don't get excited, Hope," a voice replied. "I shall be with you in a moment."

"Potter!" Hope exclaimed. "Where, in Heaven's name, are you?"

"I am tangled up with some very prickly bushes!" was the reply. "But—ah!"—there came a sound of tearing—"now I shall be with you in a moment!"

Out from the shadows emerged a figure which Hope would never have recognized for Cosmo Potter. It was that of a man dressed in a rough tweed suit, a muffler and a cap. No monocle was in evidence.

"Potter!" Hope repeated. "What the devil is the meaning of this?"

"A little detective work," replied the amazing Potter. "Recognizing your romantically absurd scruples, Hope, I knew that it would be useless to suggest to you that an acceptable alibi within the meaning of the law, which hitherto you have not had, could be obtained to-night. As you have placed your defence in my hands, I acted as I thought fit in your interests. In other words, Hope, I witnessed your interview with Suzee Che Lo, and what I have heard proves that you were in the train last night when she entered it."

Hope remaining silent:

"Don't get a wrong angle on my behaviour," Potter resumed. "You are looking at the thing from the woman's point of view, which I am not altogether disregarding, either. She has not bound you to secrecy respecting this interview, remember, but all the same, if I had not witnessed it, its legal value would have been nil."

"You are right, Potter," Hope admitted. "You adopted the only possible course in the circumstances. Let us get back. There are many things calling for explanation."

"Quite!" said Potter; "I agree with you entirely. Just a moment."

From some interior pocket of his unfashionable suit he produced his monocle and set it in its usual place. Next, the cigarette case appeared, and, presently, the two resumed their way, smoking cigarettes as large as cigars.

"She is very clever," Potter went an. "She knew that I was following her. She came in a taxicab of which I have the number, but I don't suppose for a moment that the point at which she hired it is anywhere near her present place of residence. She is dangerously attractive, Hope. I would give much to know her real identity."

"She calls herself Suzee Che Lo," said Hope.

"Yes," Potter murmured, "but she is not pure Chinese, all the same. Much of your conversation was inaudible to me. I was lying along the top of the wall, above the hut. Do you mind giving me the details as well as you remember them?"

"Not at all," said Hope, "but first I want to ask you a question. Am I still under the police surveillance?"

"No," was the reply, promptly. "Kerry has made his mind up since your interview this morning, and the watchdogs are called off."

"You are certain of this?"

"Absolutely certain."

"Then how do you account for the fact that I saw someone sneaking about on the veranda of the house up yonder as I came down here to-night?"

"As you came down to meet Suzee?"

"Yes. It wasn't you by any chance?"

"I!" Potter exclaimed. "My dear fellow! I was haunting the avenue waiting for the arrival of the lady. No. This is interesting. I can assure you quite definitely, Hope, that no one from Scotland Yard is on duty here to-night."

"More extraordinary than ever," murmured Hope. "Who the devil can it have been?"

"Let us hope you haven't been burgled!" said Potter. "Although why a burglar should wait for your return from abroad to do his dirty work is not particularly clear. It might have been a tramp, of course—quite a stranger to the neighbourhood. But I am all curiosity, Hope, to learn the details of your recent conversation. I gather that something was exchanged. Now, this is very important. Have you got it?"

"Yes, in my breast pocket."

"What is it?"

"It feels like a small cardboard box."

"Good. Now for the conversation. Tell me exactly what took place. The important thing I overheard. Other things—possibly quite as important in their way—I was unable to hear."

Bernard Hope complied, recalling the conversation without much effort since it had been of so strange a character. And, all the while, the two mounted the slope, skirted the high wall, and, since concealment was no longer necessary, passed behind the bushes and came out upon the drive, returning to the lodge by way of the front door, which Hope opened with his key.

"Let us make sure that nothing has been disturbed," Potter murmured.

He was a strange figure, his rough cap pulled down over his angular face, in the right eye of which, grotesquely, the small monocle glittered.

They made a rapid survey of the premises, a simple enough matter, but everything seemed to be in order and there was no evidence that any intruder had been there. Going through and bolting the back door by which he had originally gone out, Hope returned, and from a cupboard produced whisky and syphon.

"It was awfully good of you, Potter," he declared, "to interest yourself to this extent. My absurd affairs are completely disorganizing your arrangements."

"Disorganizing!" Potter exclaimed. "My dear fellow, I love every moment of it!"

Hope poured out drinks, and:

"I must 'phone Yvette," he said; "it will be impossible for me to join her for supper to-night."

"Not at all," Potter returned. "My car is waiting not two hundred yards away. We have several things to discuss, but they need not occupy us all night. If I am not intruding, I should love you both to have supper with me at some suitably Bohemian resort, such as the Ham Bone Club, so that my absence of a collar will not provoke comment."

"I agree," said Hope, handing a glass to the speaker. "Yvette will be delighted. She is dying to discuss this business with you."

"Right!" cried Potter. "Now, first and foremost: what is this mysterious box that you have in your breast pocket?"

"Gad!" Hope exclaimed, "I had almost forgotten it."

He plunged his hand in immediately, and drew out a small, oval cardboard box bearing a gaily coloured device upon the lid, and the name of a famous firm of French perfumers. It had contained rouge or some other kind of toilet preparation.

At this both men stared in blank amazement. Hope, removing the lid, the object in the box was revealed; and at this he gazed blankly, placing the box upon the table immediately under the lighted lamp.

"What is it?" he asked. "Have you any idea, Potter?"

Cosmo Potter bent over the curious exhibit, moving the box so that the rays of the lamp shone upon it from various angles. At last:

"It is a Chinese lotus," he declared.'

"A lotus!" Hope exclaimed.

"Yes, its shape may be unfamiliar to you, but it is a Chinese artist's conception of a lotus, nevertheless."

"But the substance! I have never seen anything like it."

Potter tilted the box, and the curiously carved object which it contained fell out into the palm of his hand. He stared at it curiously.

"Quite frankly, neither have I," he confessed. "It must be some kind of precious stone."

"I don't think so," said Hope. "It is unlike any precious stone known to me. It changes colour in an extraordinary fashion."

And indeed, this was the case. In certain lights, it appeared of a dull golden colour; then, a slight movement resulted in a magical change, and it assumed a delicate blue shade, like the blue of a tropical sky, shifting and moving, until finally the blue disappeared altogether.

"Why should she have taken so much trouble to place *this* in your hands!" Potter mused aloud. "We have to suppose that she was afraid to retain it herself for some reason. But, if she is to be believed, its possession is her safeguard—provided, however, that you lodge it in a safe place, known only to yourself. This suggests several possibilities."

"Really!" Hope exclaimed. "To me, it suggests nothing. It sounds like a fairy tale."

Cosmo Potter was staring at the lotus, turning it over and over in his hand, so as to display its strange properties.

"Do your 'phoning, Hope," he said; "I want to think. There is a clue dancing like a will-o'-the wisp before my mind's eye, but I cannot focus it."

Hope nodded comprehendingly, and, taking up the telephone, asked for Yvette's number.

A few moments later he had arranged to call for her, with Potter, and, replacing the receiver, he turned to the latter, who once again was scrutinizing the singular object left with Hope by Suzee Che Lo.

The expression on the angular face was one of intense effort.

"Somewhere, somewhere," Potter murmured, "I have come across this substance before—not shaped in this way. But it is associated in my mind with—well—it sounds absurd—with something else that I cannot identify."

"It looks as though it might be valuable," said Hope; "it might almost be cut out of a phenomenal opal."

"Only a fool would destroy an opal of such size," Potter replied. "An opal big enough for the purpose would have been worth an Emperor's ransom, I should think."

He continued to turn it over and over in his palm, touching it gingerly.

"It's a beautiful thing," he muttered. "And I should think very fragile."

He replaced it in its strange receptacle.

Hope began to fill his pipe, and:

"One thing is puzzling me badly," he declared: "the identity of the individual whom I saw slinking about up here as I left."

"Yes," Potter agreed, looking around him, "in the circumstances, it is most puzzling and disturbing. Unless Sowerby is doggedly following his original idea I can assure you that the prowler had nothing to do with the police."

"Which," said Hope, striking a match, "curiously enough, I do not find reassuring. Now that my delicate interview with Suzee Che Lo has been successfully accomplished, I should enjoy a certain sense of security if I knew a police officer to be watching the cottage."

"Yes," Potter glanced at him sharply. "I quite follow what you mean.

Hang it all, man, if you *will* play the cavalier to mysterious ladies of unknown nationality, you must expect to pay the price. Frankly," he pointed at the little box, "I don't like this thing."

"Neither do I!" said Hope, in hearty endorsement.

"I have a notion," Potter went on, "that you'll know no peace whilst it's in your possession."

"She rather implied that," the other responded gloomily. "It was forced upon me—Heaven knows why; and what on earth I am to do with it to-night defeats my imagination."

He paused, suddenly struck by Potter's curiously rigid attitude. The latter, who stood upon the farther side of the room, had an unobstructed view of the window. In opening the cupboard, Hope recognized that he had disarranged the curtains, which he had carefully drawn before going out. It was upon these curtains that Potter's gaze seemed to be fixed.

"What's the matter?" he began.

But he had scarcely spoken the words when Potter put his glass down, and, springing forward, wrenched the curtains apart, revealing the small- paned window.

"Good God!" cried Hope, and sprang to his feet so suddenly as to upset the little table.

The decanter, syphon, and glasses went crashing to the floor.

A hideous Chinese face, pock-marked, mask-like, was pressed to the glass! A moment it was visible in the lamplight—a moment later it had gone!

Hope leapt over the table and started for the door, but Potter grasped his arm.

"Wait!" he said peremptorily. "I think I know what he came for."

He stooped and picked up the little powder box.

"My dear fellow," he went on, his wonted calm quite recovered. "A nebulous theory begins to present itself, and if this theory is correct—"

"Yes?" said Hope impatiently.

"And if this theory is correct," Potter repeated, "not only you, but I as well, stand in a peculiarly unenviable position."

CHAPTER XIX

SERGEANT SIMMONS REAPPEARS

Roughly, at the same time that this singular visitant looked in upon Hope and Potter in the former's cottage, Superintendent Kerry, Inspector Peel, Anderton, and a constable were standing in a bleak, lofty room in the East End.

"Just what I expected," said Peel sadly. "I hinted as much, Superintendent."

"You did," snapped Kerry.

He turned to the divisional surgeon.

"Drowning?" he inquired.

"No, no." Doctor Anderton shook his head. "The like of poor Simmons was not a man to drown. It was the blow on the back of his skull that finished him. There is no fracture. It was a sandbag, I fancy, from the bruises. But he died of the thundering concussion. He was dead before he reached the water."

"Ah!"

Kerry turned and stared again at the ghastly exhibit upon the slab.

"You said the top end of Limehouse Reach?"

He turned his fierce regard upon Inspector Peel.

"Yes."

The latter nodded.

"They brought him straight into the stair, and, of course, I got through to you at once."

Kerry's jaws worked automatically, although he was not actually chewing.

"They were returning?" he went on in his rapid fashion.

"Yes. They were due back at ten—when the next boat starts."

"I know when the next boat starts," said Kerry, savagely.

As a matter of fact, this new development had appalled him, and his irritability as a consequence was more marked than usual.

"On matters of routine I can get information direct from the River Branch, Inspector. I said the boat was returning. We may therefore assume that they overlooked the body on their way down, or that it was not then in the river."

"The tide," began Inspector Peel, but:

"Thames Conservancy keeps a record of tides!" Kerry shouted fiercely.

Peel flushed and turned aside. "How long should you say, Doctor"—

Kerry turned to the surgeon—"he had been in the water?"

"Well," the other replied slowly, contemplating the dead man with a critical eye. "It's a little difficult in the circumstances. But—" he paused, closing his eyes as if making some mysterious calculations—"I am very much inclined to think it's going on for twenty-four hours."

"What!" Kerry snapped; "I was talking to him at midnight last night!"

"I said," the Scotsman repeated slowly, "going on for twenty-four hours. And I beg leave, Superintendent, to repeat my statement: Going on for twenty-four hours."

"Thank you, Doctor," said Kerry; "I heard you the first time. The post-mortem, I suppose, will give us the facts rather more accurately?"

"Suppose no such thing," replied Doctor Anderton dourly. "A pathologist is a scientist, but not a wizard. My theory that the man died from a blow upon the skull will be proven or disproven. But the number of hours that he was in the water must remain speculative. You don't happen to carry snuff?"

"No," said Kerry. "I don't."

"I'm sorry," the doctor returned; "I left my box at home."

Kerry nodded.

"Cover him up," he said; then, turning, he walked out of the mortuary.

He seemed to have forgotten his companions. Outside on the pavement he paused for a moment; an alert, arresting figure, the collar of his woolly overcoat turned up, his bowler worn at a rakish angle, and his malacca cane tucked military fashion under his arm. A car was waiting, that in which he had come, and the chauffeur, as he appeared, sprang down and opened the door; but Kerry, who apparently had not noticed his presence, turned on his heel and walked away.

As he disappeared around the corner, the man watching him in stupefaction, Doctor Anderton and Inspector Peel came out.

Doctor Anderton, looking after the retreating figure, clicked his tongue disapprovingly, nodding his big, untidy head as he did so.

"A very rude man, that," he said, "but able. I'll not deny his ability, Inspector."

"I am afraid," returned the other sharply, "that promotion has given him a swelled head."

"I don't agree with you," said Anderton, who, indeed, never agreed with anybody. "The like of Daniel Kerry is born with a swollen head. Nothing can increase it."

But Kerry, seemingly lost in a brown study, pursued his way through the dingy streets of Chinatown until he came to that high wall guarding the mysterious premises where Burma Chang had met his end. Before the door a constable was on duty, and at sight of the spruce figure, familiar to every member of the force, he drew rigidly upright, and:

"Good-evening, sir," he said.

"Good-evening, Constable. Anything to report?"

"Nothing, sir."

Kerry rang the bell, and another constable opened the door, admitting him to the dimly lighted lobby. For a few moments he stood there, looking about him from right to left, up and down; then, removing his topcoat, he folded it neatly and laid it on a settee, placing his bowler and his cane on the top of it.

He walked upstairs and along the corridor in the direction of the room where Burma Chang had been found. The door was half open; the room was lighted; and within, seated at the desk, was Sowerby, deep in a mass of documents which he was examining.

He had heard Kerry's arrival, and glanced over his shoulder as the Superintendent entered.

"Well?" said Kerry.

"Nothing," Sowerby reported shortly. "A Chinese interpreter was here until after nine o'clock, and all this mass of accounts"—he pointed to what looked like newspapers tied together with green silk—"might relate to anything."

Kerry glanced abstractedly at one of the bundles. It consisted of twenty or thirty strips neatly cut from various newspapers. Each strip bore a column of Chinese characters written with a brush in India ink. He tossed it down again impatiently.

Sowerby, with a weary sigh, stood up.

"I've seen the Chinese Consul," he reported. "The money has been sealed up and everything is in order. There's his note." He indicated an envelope.

"Good," rapped Kerry. "What did he say about the heirs, successors, or assigns of the dead man? Anything? I mean, what becomes of this property? Who does it belong to? What becomes of all the money in the safe?"

"As far as I can make out," Sowerby answered patiently, "Burma Chang was merely an agent for some firm in China. It was not his own money; it belonged to his firm."

"Really!" said Kerry, smiling savagely. "What firm?"

"I don't know what firm. He said something about a Tong. That's a sort of secret society, isn't it?"

"It is," Kerry replied.

Automatically, he extracted from his waistcoat pocket a wafer of chewing gum and proceeded to chew. His preoccupation was evident, and, with a certain hesitancy, Sowerby intruded upon it.

"Finding poor Sergeant Simmons knocked me sideways," he remarked.

Kerry turned his fierce regard upon the speaker; then:

"I haven't got over it yet," he admitted; "but there's one thing about it that's going to help us."

"What is that?"

"Listen!" Kerry shot out a pointing finger. "You were in this room with me when Simmons went out of that door—the last time we saw him alive. Very well. How was he dressed?"

"He was wearing a light rainproof—in fact, it was nearly white—with the collar turned up, and a bowler hat."

"Right!" rapped Kerry. "When he was pulled out of the river he had *no* hat and *no* raincoat!"

He stared fixedly at Sowerby, the latter blankly returning his gaze.

"Say something," Kerry directed; "I am waiting for an intelligent remark."

"Well"—Sowerby raised his hand to his upstanding hair, inspired by that eternal optimism which led him to hope to make it lie down—"he'd evidently taken his coat off for some reason."

"I see," said Kerry, with repressed savagery. "I guessed the reason at once. He was going for a swim. He probably took his hat off because he saw a lady passing at the time."

He turned around, walking the length of the room; then:

"Sowerby," he said, once more facing the latter, "you are tired, and you're entitled to be tired; you've worked hard. But whenever you feel your brain going numb, hold up a white flag and I won't shoot."

"My brain isn't numb," Sowerby declared indignantly; "I've been dealing with another side of the case, and you've sprung this on me. You've had time to think about it. I have not."

"You are right," said Kerry; "I have been thinking about it for the last half hour. This is, let me see, Thursday night. Next Thursday morning I shall hope to have your views on the point."

But Sowerby, beneath that good-humoured exterior, possessed a dogged pugnacity of his own; and:

"Go easy, Superintendent," he said warmly; "there's nothing gained by ragging a man. I don't know that you have ever had to complain of my work. This job has got on your nerves, and it's got on mine, too. Working alone in this room to-night, I assure you, I had the jumps. To concentrate on what I had to do was hard. I'm as keen on my work as you are, Superintendent."

And now, any of those who had suffered the hazing for which Red Kerry was notorious, would have been surprised to see the genial smile which overspread his red countenance as the Yorkshireman stolidly stood up to him. As he ceased speaking:

"Good for you!" said Kerry. "I know it, and you know I know it. So that's that."

Sowerby's habitual good humour immediately reasserted itself, and he smiled apologetically.

"The truth of the matter is, Superintendent," he said, "that both of us are strung up, and it's not to be wondered at."

"It's not," Kerry snapped, his glance roving all around the room. "This is a funny house, and some funny smarts have lived in it. To-night, when I saw that poor devil on the slab—he leaves a widow and two kiddies—I got fighting mad, and noting that he had been found without hat and overcoat, I got an idea, too. I want you to help me, Sowerby. Reconstruct just what happened when Sergeant Simmons went out of this room. My recollections may not be quite accurate. I had no reason to pay particular attention to the matter at the moment. It was a big moment, and we didn't know it. Just cast your mind back, Sowerby, to the time when we forced that door."

"Right," said Sowerby; "I remember perfectly."

"You remember that it opened with a crash and that you nearly fell through?"

"Yes, I remember."

"Then," Kerry continued, "we heard the crash of the outside door."

"Yes," said Sowerby, "I went down, shining the torch ahead of me. I saw Simmons coming up."

"We both came back to this room," Kerry went on. "And you'll remember that I got the idea that Burma Chang wasn't really dead."

"Yes," Sowerby replied, speaking in a very hushed voice and looking at the spot on the carpet where Burma Chang had lain. "I remember quite well. While you were examining him we heard a thud on the stairs."

"Ah!" cried Kerry, "and then that door was closed without a sound! It wasn't opened until Constable Smith came up and unbolted it from the other side. He reported that Sergeant Simmons had gone out. Later, the man on the garden door reported to the same effect."

"Now!" Kerry's eyes were bright with excitement as he turned them in Sowerby's direction. "If Simmons *did* go out, wearing his bowler hat and his white raincoat—why, if he was afterward thrown into the river, should these have been removed?"

Sowerby, frowning heavily in a valiant effort of concentration, shook his head.

"He might have picked up some important clue upon the stair," he said hesitatingly; "and out there in the fog he might have been sandbagged. You mustn't forget, Superintendent, that this neighbour-hood was thick with Chinese last night—a point that I have not been able to explain."

"Neither have I," said Kerry, "but your conversation with the Chinese Consul has given you a point or two. Going on from your idea that he was sandbagged in the street, he would next have had to be smuggled past one of the two constables on duty outside the house, before he could be got to the river."

"Therefore," Sowerby interrupted eagerly, "they would have removed his conspicuous white coat."

"Good!" Kerry rapped. "You are waking up. That's true."

He chewed vigorously for some moments in silence.

"The fog was so thick," Sowerby went on, enlarging upon his theory, "that it would have been possible, if there were two men on the job, to carry him along on the other side of the street without attracting the attention of the constable on duty outside this house. Then—"

"Wait a minute!" Kerry rapped. "Coming around to the front of the house, he would have been within hail all the way. This attack would have had to take place out of sight and out of earshot of the man on duty at the garden door, and yet far enough from the front door to have been unheard by the constable on duty there. Think. Think hard. Do you consider that possible?"

Sowerby's mental exertions might be traced by his tortured expressions, and, finally:

"I'm not at all certain that it is," he confessed. "But aren't you rather assuming, Superintendent, that Simmons was coming round to the front of the house? He might have been going in the opposite direction—right away down the lane. How do we know what he had in his mind?"

"Good for you again," Kerry said. "That would be in the direction of the river, certainly. But it would do away with the necessity of removing his raincoat, wouldn't it?"

"I suppose it would."

"Apart from which," Kerry went on, "why in hell should they want to kill him? Think again. If he picked up valuable evidence upon the stair, his natural and proper course would have been to come into the room and to show it to me. We will suppose, however, that he preferred to show it to Inspector Peel, his immediate superior. Therefore, shutting the door in my face, he starts out with the idea of walking around the house to the front and reporting in the lobby. One of these two things he must have done, if he had had evidence. Am I right?"

"You are right, Superintendent," said Sowerby, a subtle change of expression showing upon his countenance.

"Therefore," Kerry went on, punctuating his words with vicious chewing, "if Simmons had been worth killing, by which I mean if Simmons had held valuable evidence, Simmons would have either come into this room or would have gone around to the front to report to Inspector Peel. If, as you suggest, he went the other way"—Kerry glared—"why should they have killed him?"

"He might have been chasing someone," said Sowerby.

"What!" Kerry's glare became positively ferocious. "Someone he had seen upon the stair? What about the man on duty at the door?"

"I mean, he might have fallen, into a trap," Sowerby pursued patiently.

Kerry's teeth snapped together viciously; then:

"Yes," he admitted, "it's possible. But none of your counter theories, Sowerby, can satisfactorily account for one thing. I held it up for you to throw at, but you've never said a word."

"What thing is that, Superintendent?"

"The bolting of the door!" Kerry rapped. "I'll never forgive myself. Damn it, man, don't you see? Even if he had decided to go back and report to Peel, there was no occasion for him to bolt that door."

Sowerby's eyes opened very widely; and:

"Yes!" he muttered, "I begin to see."

"I don't blame you for being slow," said Kerry. "It has come to me nearly twenty-four hours too late. It wasn't Simmons that bolted that door! Unless I am very much mistaken, poor Simmons was dead when that door was bolted!"

"What!" Sowerby whispered.

"Focus on the colour of his raincoat," Kerry rapped. "It was very conspicuous—unmistakable, even on a foggy night."

CHAPTER XX

SATSU KUHNA

A few minutes after midnight, and just as a big car drew smoothly away over the crest of the hill, a taxicab pulled up before the gate of Elm House and Bernard Hope got out. He looked sharply to right and left as he paid the man, but could detect nothing suspicious.

He walked up the drive to the lodge door, opened it with a key, and immediately turned up the light. Nothing appeared to have been disturbed—the place looked precisely as it had looked when he and Cosmo Potter had set out earlier in the evening. The gravelly ground immediately surrounding the cottage made it a waste of time to look for footprints. So that when, following the appearance of the hideous face at the window, they had searched the neighbourhood, the search had proved futile.

It was a disturbing memory, however, the memory of that evil pock-marked countenance.

Hope, having satisfied himself that no one lurked on the premises, hastily closed the front door again. He helped himself to a drink and lit his pipe. His next proceeding was to close the curtains before each of the windows, pinning them together when necessary in order that no glimpse of the interior could be obtained from outside. This accomplished, he extinguished the light in his sitting room and went into his little bedroom, frequently permitting his shadow to fall upon the drawn curtains of the window. He proceeded to undress, to the extent of removing his coat and waistcoat.

He took off his boots and put on a pair of tennis shoes, replacing the discarded garments with a jersey and Norfolk jacket, into the pocket of which he slipped an electric torch and a loaded repeater. He turned out the light as if going to bed, and then silently crept out of the room, and out by the back door on to the little paved path.

Quietly lowering the latch again, he set off without hesitation through the bushes in the darkness, in the direction of the house.

He did not pause once until he reached the slope by the gardens. There, crouching behind a bush, he looked back. But nothing stirred in the neighbourhood of the lodge.

Motor busses on this route had ceased running, and there was no sound of traffic audible upon the hill. He pressed on, bending low so as to avail himself of the concealment afforded by the undergrowth. Abreast of the wing of Elm House, which jutted out there, he pulled up again.

The night was very cloudy, but dimly he could see along the deserted veranda. One more glance back he took in the direction of the roadway, and then, dropping upon all fours, he crawled through the thick weeds of what had once been flower beds, to where a short stone stair, wet and moss grown, led down to the underground offices of the house.

He descended, came to a door at the bottom which yielded to his touch, and entered, noiselessly closing the door behind him.

Now, from his Norfolk pocket he took the electric torch, and flashed the light about an old-fashioned, stone-paved kitchen in which he stood. One glance he took to get his direction, and then, releasing the button of the torch, crossed the place in darkness to the foot of an ascending stair. He went up slowly, feeling his way.

Presently, passing a bend, he found himself in the ghostly entrance hall, eerily lighted by windows right and left of the door. Only because his eyes were now used to the darkness could he discern anything. It was possible for him to see the great staircase leading to the upper rooms and the two pillars which supported the balcony above.

In the gloom, the place seemed abnormally lofty and uncannily still. Even the slight sound made by his rubber shoes was echoed and reechoed, so that it must have reached the innermost recesses of the house.

Turning, he began to mount the stair; and, coming to the first floor, he opened a door at the end of the balcony, staring into a long, lofty room with four windows overlooking the drive.

Sharply silhouetted against one of these windows was a crouching figure!

"Hope," came a voice, "stay where you are for a moment."

It was Cosmo Potter!

"Did you see me coming?" Hope asked.

"Yes," was the reply, "but I knew where to look for you. You will notice that more light comes through those left-hand windows than through either of the others. It puzzled me at first when I got here, but I have decided that that lamp out on the hill is the cause of it. The rays reach those windows dimly, but not these. Any one appearing at those windows might be visible from outside, so I thought I had better warn you. They afford a finer view of the lodge, I admit, but failing them this is the best place, and I think if you will stand behind me it will be all right."

"Good," said Hope softly. "You have seen nothing else, Potter?"

"Nothing. It's going to be a devilish cold job."

"It is," Hope agreed, "but I don't mind, if we catch our man."

"I am very doubtful," Potter declared. "I have been here for more than half an hour, and although I'd swear no one could possibly have seen my arrival—I came through the back way as arranged—there hasn't been a sound or a movement that could not be accounted for. If there's any one hiding in the grounds, he's an expert at the job. Just consider, Hope. Humanity is so disappointing. We might have to repeat this thing for weeks before anything happens."

"As I remember pointing out," Hope added; "but the idea was your own."

"And I am perfectly prepared to stick to it," said Potter. "My reasoning may be wrong, but the notion of leaving Burton on duty with the car at the gate, until the actual moment of your return, will have held up any attempt during our absence. You saw him drive off? I am certain that the anxiety of these people—whoever they are—to recover the powder box—or whatever it is—will drive them to any extremity. I think it's a matter that can't wait."

"It would not be so bad," said Hope, "if we could smoke."

However, since this was palpably impossible, they settled down to their strange vigil.

In such circumstances, the least observant man begins to notice trifles and to magnify their importance in the scheme of things. A pedestrian plodding up the hill was watched with intense suspicion by two pairs of eyes hidden back there behind the elm trees. The sound of his footsteps seemed to die away rather abruptly, and the two men stared at one another, until the muffled bang of a distant door gave the explanation.

From the interior of the rambling old house, above and below, came, ever and anon, inexplicable noises. Once Potter clutched Hope's arm, and:

"Listen!" he whispered. "There's someone coming upstairs!"

Both listened intently, almost holding their breath. The sound continued—as of a stealthy, scuffling approach. Automatically Hope associated it in his imagination with a stooping Chinese figure.

"Move away from the window," he warned, "into the shadow."

They did so, as noiselessly as possible, and waited, watching the dimly visible door, a blacker patch in the darkness. And, as they watched, from low down on the ground a pair of brilliant green eyes looked in. Hope stifled an exclamation, but:

"Oh! murder, it's a stray cat!" burst from Cosmo Potter.

At the words, the animal turned and went racing down the stairway again for bare life.

"Whew!" said Potter, returning to his place at the window, "this midnight watching gets on one's nerves."

A car came roaring up the hill, and:

"Back from the window!" Potter said urgently. "A light may pick us out through the trees."

He ducked below the shallow ledge and Hope stepped aside, as the car swept by, beyond, and roared on to its unknown destination. A church clock chimed the hour of one.

"I had scarcely expected anything before one," Cosmo Potter murmured.

The dreary vigil proceeded. Light after light had become extinguished in the neighbouring houses which were visible; in all that respectable district it would seem that only these two remained wakeful.

A constable trudged slowly by. Potter had opened two of the windows, so that sounds from outside were clearly audible. They had not detected the footsteps until the constable was quite close. Then, by the open gateway at the right-hand horn of the drive, he paused, a ray from his lantern cutting through the darkness in the direction of the lodge porch. He moved on, but, a moment later, a gleam of light showed through the bushes. He was examining the front window.

"Do you think," said Hope in a low voice, "he has instructions to keep an eye on the place?"

"Possibly," Potter returned; "but, on the other hand, as you have been away so long, it may have become part of the routine of the men on this beat."

He ceased speaking, as if listening for some new sound which had attracted his attention; but nothing broke the silence for a long time. Then, dimly, from a long way off, came the sound of a car approaching.

They could hear it beginning to mount the slope, running slowly and with a suggestion of effort. At a point so near the gates that a ray of the headlights showed through the bushes, the car stopped.

"That's odd," Hope muttered. "Why should any one pull up at a blank wall?"

"I don't know," Potter returned. "But the explanation is probably simple enough. We are beginning to attach an exaggerated importance to trivial things. Hello! What's this?"

He drew back sharply.

"Keep out of sight!" he added.

A man had come in at the gateway—a man who wore a heavy, fur-collared overcoat and a soft hat, the brim pulled down over his eyes.

Coming to the porch of the lodge he paused, peering at the door, and then along the avenue in the direction of the house.

"Who the devil is it?" Potter murmured—"and what does he want?"

"It looks extraordinarily as though he wants *me!*" Hope replied.

This certainly appeared to be the case, for the stranger now entered the little porch and rang the bell. So complete was the silence that both men could quite easily hear it ring inside the cottage.

"This may have no connection whatever with the affair which has brought us here," said Hope. "I think I had better go and see who it is."

"Wait a moment," Potter replied, a note of excitement in his voice; "this ringing may be a ruse."

"You mean, he is trying to find out if there is any one in the place?"

"Exactly. There goes the bell again."

As he spoke, the distant purring note became audible, and this time the ringing was continued for several seconds. It had hardly ceased, however, when the visitor reappeared upon the drive. Raising his head, he seemed to stare directly up at the window behind which the two were concealed. Then, slowly, he advanced nearer.

"Without a doubt," Potter whispered, "there's some funny business here."

Certainly the man's behaviour seemed strange. Nearer and nearer he came, until he was standing immediately below them, turning his head slowly from side to side and seeming to examine the whole of the front of the building.

Then he disappeared—and they heard his footsteps as he entered the doorway below.

Echoing and reechoing drearily through the deserted building, came the clangour of an ancient bell in the hallway!

"What the devil does he want?" said Hope amazedly. "Did you see his face?"

"Yes," Potter replied. "Of course, it may be merely a trick of imagination, but to me he looked extraordinarily like a Chinaman!"

"You are right!" Hope returned grimly; "I was thinking the same thing, myself. What's the next move?"

"This," said Potter, still keeping his voice carefully lowered: "Downstairs as fast as we can go without making a noise, out through the door by which we came in, and along behind the bushes to the cottage. Then, you leave me to make my own move, and you nip over the wall, and out on to the hill. You have been for a midnight walk; you follow me?"

The clanging of the bell downstairs was repeated.

"Quite!" said Hope; "but hurry up; he may not ring again."

"Get him into the cottage," the low voice proceeded, "open the window—that is very important—and do your best to find out what he has *really* come about."

"Good," Hope muttered.

"A moment later they were both silently descending the staircase, for both wore rubber-soled shoes. Stealthily they crossed the shadowy hallway, Hope, who was familiar with the way, leading, and Potter resting one hand upon his shoulder. Down to the basement they went, and here Hope risked a brief inspection by torchlight, for there were many obstacles between them and the door. They crossed in safety, however, and mounted the wet stone steps. At the top, both paused, listening.

Faint footsteps sounded upon the drive.

"He's walking back," Potter muttered. "Quick! we must run for it now!"

Bending low, they raced across the intervening space and came upon the path behind the bushes.

"Give me a leg up," said Hope recklessly, "this is the best place to get across the wall."

Potter complied, and in a moment Hope was astride the top. Turning, he dropped into the narrow lane which divided the grounds of Elm House from the adjoining property.

It was very muddy, and he stumbled and nearly fell, but recovered himself and walked rapidly along to the roadway. He was somewhat breathless, but he succeeded in lighting a cigarette from a packet which he had in his pocket, and, this accomplished, assuming an air of nonchalance, he strolled past a smart Citroen which was drawn up by the pavement and reached the gates of the house just as the stranger came out.

A street lamp shining down upon the man's face, Hope's earlier conjecture was confirmed.

The visitor's eyes slanted unmistakably, although, in a way, he was a handsome man. His jet-black hair grew very low upon the cheekbones. In his fur-collared overcoat—beneath which it might be seen that he wore evening dress—and soft-brimmed black hat, he possessed a sort of languid distinction, a fact which did not escape the observation of the playwright.

Hope paused, simulating surprise; and:

"Good-evening," he said. "Can I do anything for you?"

The handsome, immobile face displayed no expression whatever; but:

"Perhaps," the man replied, speaking without any trace of accent. "I observed"—he turned slowly, raising one white-gloved hand—"a telephone wire connected with the lodge, here, and I had hoped to arouse someone. My car"—the languid hand now indicated the Citroen—"has betrayed me."

He smiled, and his smile possessed a sort of sinister charm.

"My own folly," he added—"no petrol. I hoped to telephone to some garage for assistance."

"I see," Hope replied, wondering if this story, which sounded plausible enough, covered some other motive. "I am sorry I was out."

"You were out?" said the other, with mild surprise. "Do you, then, reside—?"

And now the white-gloved hand indicated the lodge.

"I do," Hope answered, "odd though it may seem. And I have been for a midnight ramble. Please come in. There is a garage not three hundred yards from here, if we can get them to answer the 'phone."

"Oh, but I am very sorry," the stranger protested; "if I had known this ..."

"Please don't apologize," Hope interrupted. "The place is shut up, but it is just possible they might answer the 'phone. Failing them, there is someone at the bottom of the hill, I think, if I can succeed in remembering the name."

The stranger inclined his head gracefully.

"Thank you," he acknowledged, following Hope into the porch.

Hope entered, lighting up; and, remembering Potter's instructions:

"Smells rather stuffy," he commented—and threw open the window. "Now"—he turned—"there is the telephone, sir. I can give you the number of the neighbouring garage."

He did so. But all attempts to get through to the establishment proved futile. Thereupon the other number was tried, this time with success; and it was arranged for a man to be despatched upon a motor-cycle with the necessary fuel. This matter settled:

"Won't you sit down?" said Hope. "My name is Bernard Hope. I am not a lodge porter"—smiling quizzically—"as you may have supposed. I am a playwright."

"Really?" said the other with unemotional politeness.

He inclined his head, his smooth black hair gleaming like ebony.

"My name is Satsu Kuhna. I am from Oshima, in the Lu Chu Islands."

"The Lu Chu Islands," Hope repeated.

The name seemed in some way familiar. Indeed, he was certain he had recently heard it, but could not remember when.

"Forgive my ignorance, but I fear I have never heard of the Lu Chu Islands."

"Is that so?" Satsu Kuhna smiled his smile of sinister charm. "It is not surprising. My birthplace is rarely visited by those of the outer world, nor do I often meet compatriots during my travels."

He was looking about him with polite interest.

"Your abode, though small, is delightful, Mr. Hope. Do you live here alone?"

"Quite alone."

"Your servants, then, sleep elsewhere?"

"Yes," Hope replied, these questions confirming his worst suspicions.

Satsu Kuhna seemed to be listening intently; and although, of course, he might merely have been endeavouring to detect the approach of the man from the garage, for some reason Hope did not believe this to be the case.

"Have you far to go?" he asked.

"Only as far as the Savoy, where I am staying," was the reply.

The speaker suddenly fixed his eyes upon Hope; and the latter realized that they possessed a peculiar property. The pupil was indistinguishable from the iris. They resembled the eyes of some wild animal—although he found himself unable more closely to identify the impression.

And now, in this mental haziness, and beneath the scrutiny of those remarkable eyes, he began to find matter for alarm. A sensation unlike any he had known was stealing over him. Sharply, he withdrew his gaze, as the sound of an approaching motorcycle proclaimed the arrival of the petrol.

"Here is your man," he said—and was aware that he spoke strangely.

"I think it is so," replied Satsu Kuhna, rising. "I will go to meet him. I thank you for your hospitality. Good-night, Mr. Hope."

He bowed in his coldly formal way, and turning, walked out of the cottage.

The farewell was almost in the nature of a dismissal; and Hope, standing in the porch and looking after him, wondered what business could have brought Satsu Kuhna to that out-of-the-way place. Oddly, however, a sense of triumphant relief was uppermost in his mind.

The man on the motorcycle had stopped hard by, and presently he heard his voice. Then, a slight movement behind him made him start wildly.

Cosmo Potter crept into the porch!

"Humanity is so adaptive!" he murmured. "A little more of this sort of thing and I should grow to resemble a Red Indian!"

"Good heavens! You quite startled me. Potter, I don't trust that man! I think our suspicions were well founded."

"From what I heard of his conversation," Potter replied, "I am inclined to agree with you. My attention was distracted during the latter part, however."

"In what way?" asked Hope, curiously, as together they reentered the cottage.

"Well," Potter replied, reaching for the whisky decanter, "a horrible-looking Chinaman was hovering round the place during the whole time that your man was inside! What would have happened if they had found you alone, I tremble to imagine!"

"Good God!"

"On sighting me," Potter went on, "he disappeared like a phantom. But unless I am greatly mistaken, he is now hiding in the car. My theory was right, Hope. They came for the Lotus—and they are in a desperate hurry to recover it!"

He finished his whisky at a draught and made for the door.

"Where the devil are you going?" Hope demanded. Potter paused, his hand upon the doorknob, and turned.

"It is some years since I rode a motorcycle," he said, "but I am going to ride one to-night!"

CHAPTER XXI

THE SILVER CLOAK

Suzee Che Lo came out of the small but fashionable night club and stood glancing along the narrow street lined with waiting cars.

She was wrapped in a cloak of dark brown fur, but where light from the doorway fell upon it, it took on the sheen of silver. An inexperienced observer might have mistaken it for mink, whereas it was actually silver sea otter—a once popular hobby with Russian millionaires.

"Your car, madam?" the attendant inquired.

But Suzee Che Lo shook her dark head, so that her long jade earrings glistened curiously. She turned and walked slowly along the street.

She had deliberately given the slip to her escort, who had begun to bore her, and now, as the night was comparatively fine, she walked on through nearly deserted streets, attractive yet repellent in her dark beauty, and a figure curiously out of place in the lamplight of midnight London.

That night she had accepted an invitation with the idea of seeking forgetfulness, but the company and the surroundings had failed to produce the desired effect. She had concluded that she preferred solitude and reflection. She was in danger and she wished to arrange her plans. Afraid she was not, for fear was foreign to her nature, but artificial gaiety was not for her to-night.

Indifferent to the curiosity of the few pedestrians she met upon her way, Suzee walked on in an apparently aimless manner, avoiding main thoroughfares, however, with an instinct which betokened familiarity with this part of London.

Crossing over to the west side of Bond Street, she pursued her leisurely way as far as Bruton Street, thence coming to Berkeley Square and turning south. Crossing Berkeley Street, she went down the steps into Curzon Street.

A few moments before she reached the steps, a car which had come from Dover Street down Hay Hill crossed behind her, and the man who drove it slowed down for a moment, peering eagerly after the retreating figure. A lamp over the head of the steps painted silver highlights upon the cloak. Then, at an accelerated speed, the watcher swung round into Charles Street, and the purr of his engine died away.

Curzon Street showed deserted from end to end. The doors of the hotels were closed, and not even a policeman was in sight. Sometimes it was not so; but apparently no one in the neighbourhood was entertaining to-night.

As she passed the bottom of Queen Street, a car came out, driven slowly, and crept up level with her. She paid little attention to it, assuming that it was bound for some of the mews. Then, suddenly, steely arms were about her, a silk scarf was slipped over her head, and she was lifted lightly into the car!

Through the silk, nervous fingers caressed her throat in a manner which she knew. Therefore, she did not scream—did not struggle—but resigned herself to captivity. And, as the car moved on again, stoically she wondered whether this could be the end or merely one other adventure in her strange and disorderly life.

She was held firmly by one of her captors, but not in such a manner as to inconvenience her breathing. No words were spoken—the journey was a silent one. But when at last it was ended, she was lifted again— someone had opened a door with a key, and she was carried up a flight of stairs, and then gently laid down upon a cushioned divan.

The scarf was removed from about her head, and she looked up, with a composure which in a Western woman must have seemed miraculous, into the smiling face of the man who bent over her.

"Satsu!" she said—"I thought it was you."

She raised one slender hand, rearranging her slightly disordered hair, but otherwise did not change her position. The slanting eyes moved swiftly to right and left. She was in a small room furnished in semi-Oriental fashion, but lacking the true simplicity of the East.

Satsu Kuhna watched her, his expression unreadable.

"My gods above yours," he said, "to-night, at least. It was only a few hours ago that I learned you had taken your old flat. I was on my way to pay my respects when I recognized your cloak."

"How fortunate," she murmured, and sat upright upon the couch. "And what do you expect to gain by bringing me here?"

Satsu Kuhna, removing his heavy coat, stood before her, slim and shapely, smiling his charming, sinister smile.

"You are here," he said. "I have nothing more to gain. Let me take your cloak."

Her long ivory hands pressing the cushions, she watched him—her face an insoluble enigma. Then, shrugging her shoulders, she drew the cloak more closely about her.

"I prefer not to," she said softly; "I don't wish to remain."

She glanced again about the room, particularly at the more discordant appointments; and:

"You have strange quarters," she continued. "I had always thought you a man of taste."

Watching her, he continued to smile. He moved his hand in a languid gesture.

"What does it matter?" he replied. "I shall not be here for long. And the poor fellow to whom it belongs considers it charming."

"Yes," she murmured, "is that so? I am afraid, Satsu, we no longer interest each other very much. We are not in China now, you know. And what you have done to-night is absurd. I have many friends in London."

She stood up.

"If there is something important you have to say to me, please call to-morrow. I refuse to stay here."

Satsu Kuhna ceased to smile; but he did not move.

"I have something to say to you," he replied, his languid voice suddenly betraying a repressed energy, "and it is here that you must listen to me. We may be in England, but we are not *of* England. It is useless for you to adopt that tone. There is no one else in this building but ourselves, except that my indispensable servant Wu Fang—you remember Wu Fang?—is waiting upon the stairs below."

"Stand aside," she said. "I refuse to talk to you."

Satsu Kuhna seized her arms and thrust her forcibly back upon the divan.

She sat there looking up at him, her slanting eyes a shade narrower.

No expression seemed to rest upon his handsome Asiatic face, yet, in some way, it had grown very evil.

"I know why you are here in England!" he went on, "and perhaps you know why I am here."

Stooping swiftly to a little table beside him, he took up a copy of the *Daily Telegraph*. A paragraph was marked with blue pencil, and he held it under the woman's eyes.

"Perhaps you know more of this matter?" he suggested softly.

The paragraph was as follows:

CIVIL WAR IN CHINATOWN
Peace Treaty Signed

New York, Thursday.—In the presence of the Chinese Consul a treaty of peace finally terminating hostilities was signed to-day between two rival Chinese secret societies, which for months past have been engaged in bitter tribal warfare, causing a number of mysterious deaths and open murders of Chinese in various parts of the country. Twenty policemen supervised the proceedings in the conference room, while another hundred outside patrolled the dingy streets of New York's Chinatown to guard against possible disorders.—*Reuter.*

She glanced at the paragraph and then raised her eyes again to the man's face.

"I know," she said, "why do you show it to me?" The tone of her voice had changed suddenly. "If you will turn to another page, you will find even more interesting news from Chinatown, London!"

"Ah!"

He threw the paper upon the table again.

"You have courage, Suzee. I have always admired your courage. You know me well enough to be aware of your danger, yet you dare to taunt me. Do you think"—his delicate nostrils dilated, his face looked like that of an ancient god carven in ivory—"that these trivial matters"— his gesture indicated the newspaper upon the table—"can stand in my way? It is all so petty. But a thousand small things together make one great thing. You know for what I work, for what I strive, yet, here, alone, in my power, you taunt me. It is that in you which first made me love you."

"And it was the poetry of your mad dreams," Suzee replied, "which made me listen to you. But your dreams are not mad, my friend. They are merely bad. No great thing, like the thing of which you once told me, was ever achieved by petty intrigue. My faith in you is dead, Satsu. An emperor does not listen at keyholes."

The man's delicate features twitched convulsively, and then all at once became immobile again. But his eyes glowed as though a fire burned behind them, as he looked down at the beautiful, mocking face of the speaker.

"A tall ladder has many steps," he quoted patiently, "and some of them are not made of gold."

"I suppose I was a rung in this ladder of yours," she said softly. "Though not of gold, of course."

"Of pearl," he whispered fervently; and now the note of langour left his voice and he became the supplicant. "Suzee, without you I could never have dared so much."

"No," she answered coolly. "You have used me unmercifully, and now, even now, you cannot respect my wish to forget the past. Every confidence I ever gave you, you have violated, used as a step in this ladder of yours—a ladder, my friend, which may lead no higher than the scaffold, after all."

"Suzee!"

His burning gaze was set upon her. He took a swift step in her direction.

But Suzee Che Lo repelled him. Rising again, she walked toward the door, only to be intercepted. The smile returned to Satsu Kuhna's face;

only now it was a glittering threat. His rigid arm barred Suzee's path.

"You ask for war," he said; "it is not for me to choose. You may pretend to despise me as much as you please, but here, in this house, you must remain until ..."

"Yes?" she taunted, "until when?"

"You spoke of recent happenings in Chinatown. From Chinatown something was stolen—something I must have. I have allowed no obstacle to stand in my way hitherto. Do you understand me?"

"Even if I did," Suzee replied, "I should be unable to help you. Oh! you are wasting your anger, Satsu, and your time."

"You will tell me where it is before you leave this house."

"I don't know."

"You fool!" he grasped her roughly. "I have ways of making you speak."

The cruel grip hurt her, but she gave no sign; merely:

"Let me go," she said. "You are wasting your time and mine."

As she spoke, a sound came from the stairs as of a sudden scuffle, followed by a loud thud.

Satsu Kuhna glanced aside, but did not release his hold. There followed a moment of absolute silence, only broken by a faint silken rustling as Suzee Che Lo's cloak slipped from her bare shoulders and fell at her feet. The grip upon her arms remained viselike. But, a sinuous, gold-sheathed figure, she made no sign to tell of the pain she suffered.

A sound as of the outer door closing reached her ears. Footsteps were heard ascending.

Suzee's eyes narrowed, and her glance was upon the partly opened door of the room.

Satsu Kuhna thrust her back in the direction of the divan and stepped forward rapidly. The footsteps reached the landing, the door was thrown open—and a curious figure entered.

It was that of a stockily built man, wearing a rough tweed suit, and, in lieu of a collar, a muffler about his neck. He held a cap in his hand, and his cleanshaven, hatchet features and closely cropped hair might have created the impression that this was a professional pugilist. The misapprehension would have been corrected by the presence of a small rimless monocle in his right eye and a certain abstraction of manner not usually met with in professors of ringcraft.

Satsu Kuhna stood very still, as the newcomer bowed upon the threshold, his gaze fixed upon Suzee Che Lo.

"Madame Che Lo, I believe?" he said. "Forgive my intrusion, but allow me to introduce myself. I am called Cosmo Potter, and we have mutual friends, I know. As it is somewhat late, may I offer to escort you home?"

For the first time since she had entered that room, Suzee's full red lips parted in a smile—a smile which altered her whole expression—a smile wonderful and alluring.

"Thank you so much," she replied composedly; "it is very good of you."

Stooping, she took up her cloak unconcernedly from the floor where it lay.

"Permit me," said Cosmo Potter.

In the most natural way in the world, he placed it about her shoulders. He stood beside the open door, and inclining his head:

"If you are ready," he added.

"Thank you," Suzee returned; "I am quite ready."

She went out.

Still as a statue, Satsu Kuhna stood and watched. Only his delicate nostrils betrayed his emotion.

As Suzee Che Lo crossed the threshold, Cosmo Potter fixed his dreamy regard upon the handsome, evil face of the motionless man; and:

"Mr. Satsu Kuhna, I believe," he said. "I shall be obliged if you will attend to your servant, who is lying insensible in the passage downstairs. I much deplored the necessity, but I had to strike him with a knuckle-duster."

He turned to follow Suzee Che Lo, paused, and, once more regarding Satsu Kuhna:

"You are from the Lu Chu Islands, unless I am greatly mistaken," he remarked. "Oshima is calling—and humanity is so patriotic. If you are wise, you will answer that call, Mr. Satsu Kuhna."

He turned and followed Suzee Che Lo down the stairs.

CHAPTER XXII

SUZEE CHE LO SPEAKS

At the foot of the narrow stairs, which terminated less than six feet from the street door, a Chinaman lay apparently lifeless, his head thrown back upon the third step, so that the light shone down on a face notable and memorable for its heavy pock marks.

Suzee had paused just above him, and:

"Wait," said Potter, joining her. "Let me go first and make sure."

He passed her, and, stooping, briefly examined the insensible Wu Feng; then:

"All right," he reported, "you can come down."

Stepping daintily past the sprawling figure, Suzee Che Lo descended to the passage, and together she and Cosmo Potter went out into the narrow street.

No sound came from Satsu Kuhna, above. No one molested them. Above, through curtained windows, light shone out from the room where Satsu Kuhna still was standing.

"Carnaby Street, Soho," Potter muttered. "Did you know?"

"No," Suzee replied composedly, resting her hand upon his arm; "I was not allowed to see where they were bringing me."

"A cheap furnished flat, I should judge," Potter continued. "And now—"

He screwed his monocle more firmly into place and glanced apologetically at a very unornamental motorcycle, to which a dilapidated side-car was attached, the side-car containing an empty petrol tin.

"This is the only conveyance I have with me. We might take the Citroen"—glancing at the car drawn up on the opposite side of the street, in which Suzee Che Lo had been brought to the house—"but I am anxious, for many reasons, to avoid complications."

"I understand," she answered, continuing to hold his arm, and watching him fascinatedly.

It was a dismal thoroughfare in which they stood, ill lighted, and presenting on one side a prospect of hoardings above which scaffolding arose and from which a gantry projected over the muddy pavement, and, on the other, boarded-up shop fronts and a flat, dismal brick wall.

Only one window in the street showed any illumination—that of the room they had just left.

"I think," Potter continued, "we might leave the tin behind." He placed the petrol tin upon the pavement. "And if we can borrow a rug from their car to protect your cloak—which I strongly suspect to be worth a thousand pounds—"

"Three," Suzee corrected.

"Three thousand pounds," Potter went on, "a drive through London in a side-car will perhaps be a novelty for you."

He crossed to the Citroen, explored in the darkness, and presently returned with a rug. This he placed in the side-car, and assisted his companion to seat herself.

No sound came from the house—no shadow showed upon the curtains. The door remained open. Potter performed acrobatic feats upon the starting pedal and presently secured a noisy reaction.

"Good," he said, swinging on to the saddle.

"Market Street, off Curzon Street," said Suzee; "I will tell you where to stop."

Thereupon, a sight which provoked the curiosity of several policemen, down Beak Street they roared and out into Regent Street—a vista of brilliant lights north and south, but suggesting a city suddenly deserted in its white stillness; by Conduit Street across New Bond Street into Bruton Street and thence to Berkeley Square.

Cosmo Potter was thoroughly enjoying himself. And when, at last, pulling up, he assisted Suzee from the side-car:

"Life is not so dull, after all!" he declared.

They went up to the tiny flat which harboured this woman of mystery. It was not much larger than Hope's cottage, but the rental, no doubt, was considerably in excess of that which Hope had tried in vain to obtain for Elm House.

The invariable composure of his hostess began to amaze him. She offered no explanation. But placing him comfortably in an armchair, she set refreshment at his elbow and dropped down sphinx-like upon a low stool facing him.

Her Oriental repose, her passive acceptance of happenings calculated to reduce the average European woman to hysterics, must have put the most diffident man at his ease.

"I want to thank you," she said presently, "very sincerely. You know I am grateful, don't you?"

"Please say no more about it," Potter replied; "I welcomed the opportunity."

"How did you find me? I cannot understand what brought you to that house."

"I was following Satsu Kuhna."

"Why?" she asked.

"Because he came to see Bernard Hope and I distrusted his motive."

"He came to see Mr. Hope?" she said, her eyes narrowing slightly. "Ah! I understand."

"He was looking for the Lotus," Potter declared, watching her closely.

She gave no sign, but:

"You know about it?" she asked. "If you know where it is, please don't tell me."

"Very well," he said, "but there is so much that you could tell *me,* if you would."

"I don't know what you want to know."

He smiled, that very, very rare smile which transfigured his gaunt face.

"Hope is my friend," he explained, "and though entirely innocent, he has become involved in this unsavoury Chinatown mystery. I am making it my business to clear him."

"It is absurd," Suzee replied. "He knows nothing whatever about it.

He helped me when I was badly in need of help—that is all. He does not deserve to suffer for it."

"If you think that, why did you compromise him further by coming to see him and leaving the Lotus in his possession?"

Her reply was a strange one.

"I knew I could trust him," she said. "Such men have been rare in my life."

"Is it, then, so valuable?"

"It is irreplaceable. You see, there are only a certain number of those Lotuses, as you call them, in existence, and it is impossible to duplicate them: not because of their design, but because of the material of which they are made."

"Ah!" Potter exclaimed, "you arouse my curiosity. Might I ask what material it is?"

"I can tell you that," she replied composedly. "It is *tabashîr*."

"Tabashîr," Potter murmured; "and what is *tabashîr?*"

"I don't really know," Suzee confessed; "but this particular kind is very rare. It is something found in certain bamboos. Usually it is very brittle, I think, and the kind you have seen occurs only rarely."

"And what *are* these things?" Potter pursued; "are they amulets?"

She paused before replying; and:

"No," she said. "They are badges of office."

"Badges of office?" he echoed. "To what officials are they given?"

"To the officials of one of the Chinese Tongs. Do you know what a Tong is?"

Potter nodded.

"Yes," he replied; "I begin to understand. In fact, I have suspected this for some time. Burma Chang was an officer of this Tong?"

It was a leading question put in Cosmo Potter's most insidious manner. But Suzee Che Lo smiled her seductive smile, and:

"Yes?" she murmured. "You think so?"

"Am I right?"

"You may be. Why do you think I know?"

"I am certain of it," he said earnestly. "Won't you trust me?"

"I do trust you. I would not allow you to come here, to my home, if I did not trust you."

"Then tell me," he added, "what I want to know."

"What is it that you wish to know?" she asked slowly. "Perhaps you forget that I am Chinese. Yes, I am Chinese—I am proud to be Chinese. I am sorry that your friend who was kind to me should have suffered for it at all. But you know quite well that he is in no real danger. Not even one of your funny juries could think that he had murdered this man. And so now"—she spoke caressingly, which robbed her words of their bitterness—"you are just curious about something that does not really concern you."

"Regarding the death of Burma Chang, you may be right," he returned, his voice growing suddenly stern, "but the murder of Sergeant Simmons does not come within the prerogative of any Tong."

Suzee inhaled sibilantly; and:

"No," she whispered, "I had forgotten."

"I strongly suspect," Potter went on, "that you know the author of both these crimes. Do you realize that if I were an official of Scotland Yard and not merely a meddlesome amateur, you would probably be asked to step across to Vine Street?"

Suzee nodded. "I understand; yes," she admitted; "but why should I? I have committed no crime."

"You commit a crime by sheltering a criminal."

"I don't know who killed either of these men."

"But you know the motive!" Potter charged; "and, knowing the motive, you could probably lay your hand upon the man."

He fixed his deceptive regard upon her.

"Who is Satsu Kuhna?" he demanded abruptly.

She shrugged her shoulders. In the light from an orange-shaded lamp which hung above her the effect was as though an ivory statue had miraculously stirred, dimpled, and grown lifeless again; then:

"He is a very dangerous man," she replied simply.

"Is he a member of this Tong to which you refer?"

"No."

"What is the name of this Tong?"

"I cannot answer your question," she replied. "All I know of it I learned from my father, who is a high official. I betrayed some of their secrets once—and suffered."

"It is, then, a powerful society?"

"Very powerful."

"And wealthy?"

"The most wealthy of them all. Don't ask me any more now," she said, bending forward, a note of entreaty coming into her musical voice; "you have seen what danger there can be here in London. You will make it very hard for me, and how foolish you are to mix yourself up with what is Chinese. It will be known you have come here. You must be very, very careful when you leave."

"But you," said Potter—"you are all alone?"

She repeated the fascinating shrug and smiled that slow Eastern smile, that smile in which lay a hundred generations of woman's wisdom.

"I am safe," she replied. "To-night I was in danger, but now I am safe. You do not understand, but it is so. Talk to me of something else for a while. Please, I beg of you, no more questions. I think you have been in my country? Is it so?"

Cosmo Potter recognized defeat. To-night he could hope to learn no more. He accepted the situation gracefully, and talked of China, that childlike land which yet is so wise, so beautiful, and so cruel.

The character of Suzee Che Lo wholly enthralled him. She had the naiveté of a child allied to the cool effrontery of a hardened adventuress, and combined the passivity which belongs to the women of her race— although, as she told him, her mother had not been Chinese—with the practical worldliness of a modern American. The manner in which she touched upon these divergent notes and the skill with which sometimes she blended them into unfamiliar chords fascinated and bewildered him, accustomed though he was to unusual types.

Potter had not visited China for many years.

He wondered if Suzee Che Lo could in any way be typical of the China of to-day. Her presence in London was a mystery he was unable to solve, nor did she offer him any enlightenment. Her tacit acceptance of his friendship, although avowedly she was in possession of important information for which Scotland Yard was seeking, defeated him, for all his forensic ability.

He conjured up the grim, red face of Superintendent Kerry, and the vision was not a pleasant one. It dawned upon him that this ivory witch with the slanting eyes was weaving a spell about him. When he glanced at a little tortoise-shell clock upon the mantelpiece and realized the time that had elapsed, he stood up abruptly and determinedly.

Committed as he was to return the motorcycle to its garage, he pictured the fantastic dangers that might lie before him in his ride across deserted London.

"Wait!" said Suzee; "there is a window from which I can see right along the street."

She crossed the room and extinguished the light. Then, a mysterious, slender silhouette moved to a window, drew the curtain aside, and, bending, peered out intently.

"It is all right," she reported. "There is no one there."

The landing outside the flat was dark; but:

"I have a torch," said Potter; "I can find my way quite easily." He shone a ray of light down the stairs. "Good-night."

He turned again to Suzee.

"Promise that you will see me before you leave England."

"I think it may be necessary," she replied, "but in any event, I promise. Yes."

She rested her slender hands upon his shoulders, this woman steeped in the bloodthirsty horrors which belong to the secret societies of China, and raised her full lips, like a child asking to be kissed.

Cosmo Potter was a stoic, but when, having kissed her, he made his way down the darkened stair, his heart was beating wildly.

CHAPTER XXIII

OFFICIAL INVESTIGATIONS

Superintendent Kerry sat at his table, his fierce eyes bent upon the work before him.

He was reading through a series of documents with close attention, and, having turned over the final page, he rang a bell.

Almost immediately a constable entered.

"Inspector Sowerby," said the Superintendent briefly. The constable turned and went out.

Kerry chewed assiduously, his fierce gaze set upon the undecorated mantelpiece. Then, a knock came at the door.

"Come in," he rapped.

The door opened and Sowerby entered.

"Good-morning, Superintendent," he said, noting the fixed stare and anticipating the worst. He glanced out of the long window. "I think we are in for a fine day at last."

Kerry's gaze transferred itself to the Inspector's face.

"We need it!" he declared. "There's fungus growing on this department. It's going mouldy. Have you completed that analysis?"

"Yes," Sowerby replied, glancing down at a bundle of papers which he carried.

"Got the medical evidence?"

"In the case of Burma Chang," he answered, "but nothing has come through about Simmons."

"That doesn't matter," said Kerry. "Go ahead. There seems to be a lot of it; you had better sit down."

Sowerby sat down. And, consulting the papers:

"The examination of the body of Burma Chang," he continued, speaking in the monotonous manner of one who is putting a tax upon his memory, "shows him to have died from poison. The poison, according to medical evidence, is allied to the ptomaine tetanine, whatever that may mean, and the condition of the tongue seems to suggest that it was taken through the mouth."

"Ptomaine tetanine," said Kerry savagely, "is lockjaw. Why the devil can't these people say what they mean?"

"It's a funny world," muttered Sowerby. "In my opinion, if they said what they meant, they would say that they didn't know what killed Burma Chang, except that he was poisoned."

"Wait a minute!" Kerry banged his open palm upon the table. "That Dutch doctor said something about a parasite. Now, these people talk about the condition of the tongue. I'm just trying to put two and two together. Did you ever know a man to be bitten on the tongue by a wasp?"

"No!" Sowerby looked positively startled. "I never did."

"*I* did," Kerry replied grimly, "once. He was dead in ten minutes!"

"Burma Chang," Sowerby continued, "was president of a Tong or Society and his successor has been nominated. According to the Chinese authorities, everything is in order, but pending instructions we have refused to remove the seals."

"I want to know the name of this Tong!" said Kerry with energy. "It is useless for the Chinese authorities to infer that they can follow their usual policy of pretending to know nothing, in a case like the present. I mean to find out who killed Simmons, if I have to examine every yellow smart in London! Go ahead, Sowerby."

"Right," said the latter. "Regarding this matter of Burma Chang and the Society which he represented, I have interviewed a man called Ah Wong who lives in Wade Street, Limehouse. He was mentioned in my report, which you have, of an interview with Miss Yvette Chalmers. He married a woman who used to be her maid. I hoped to learn something in that quarter, but I drew blank. On this matter of Burma Chang, all the Chinese seem to be dumb. The domestic staff, four in number, have been set at liberty, but Inspector Peel is keeping an eye on them."

The speaker turned over a page of his manuscript, and continued:

"There is evidence to show that someone climbed up to the window of Burma Chang's room on the night of the murder, smashed the glass, and opened the window. There is no evidence to show that he actually entered the room. Fingerprints have been obtained from the pipe and the sill—they are in the hands of the fingerprint department, but have not been identified."

"Domestic staff?" Kerry rapped. "Those hangdog snarks who, I am told, are Dyaks."

" Don't correspond," Sowerby replied briefly. "They clearly belong to the man seen by Sergeant Simmons, and this is probably the man we want."

"Thank you," said Kerry; "your suggestions are invaluable."

"My interview with Ah Wong," Sowerby continued stoically, "confirmed Miss Chalmers's statements."

"Jump that," Kerry interrupted brusquely. "The mare's nest about Mr. Bernard Hope is better forgotten, I think."

"One moment, Superintendent." Sowerby's red face assumed a slightly deeper hue. "I have a note here which I should like to read to you. I know when I'm wrong, and I don't mind admitting it. Mr. Hope didn't murder Burma Chang, but I'm not sure that Mr. Hope doesn't know who did."

"What do you mean?" Kerry demanded. "Mr. Hope's story has been substantiated up to the hilt—even to the numbers of the notes. There's a gap in it, I admit. But coincidence plays a bigger part in our lives than most people are willing to admit. He's unfortunate, that's all. He knows nothing whatever about the matter."

"Perhaps you are right," Sowerby pursued doggedly, "but how do you account for this? I was thinking particularly about the woman in the train, and as I don't like to neglect any possibility, I advised P Division. Mr. Hope lives in a sort of small cottage in that district. I have here the report of a man who has been keeping an eye on the cottage, and it appears that last night a Chinaman was seen three times in the neighbourhood!"

"A Chinaman!" Kerry rapped; "what sort of Chinaman?"

"I haven't seen the constable who made the report," Sowerby replied, "and this is all the information I have. But, further, a car, some kind of French car, stood outside this cottage at about one o'clock this morning, and someone who was in it stayed for a long time with Mr. Hope. The Chinaman previously mentioned presently came out and got in the car. A man from a local garage came up the hill—the place is on top of a hill—with petrol—"

"The car had broken down, then?"

"That seems to be the idea," Sowerby agreed; "but it was presently driven off."

"Who by?"

"By someone who had been in Mr. Hope's cottage during this time."

"The Chinaman was still in the car?"

"I suppose so."

Kerry's expression was one of fierce incredulity.

"This is simply bewildering!" he declared. "I can't make head or tail of it. Have you got the number of the car?"

"Yes, the special man got it. It's a French car—I haven't traced it yet. But there's something else. As the car drove off, another man came out. He is described as roughly dressed. He made some sort of bargain with the chap who had brought the petrol on a motorcycle, and went off after the car."

"On the motorcycle?" Kerry inquired.

"Yes."

"Did the officer speak to this man who had brought the petrol?"

"He did, but could get nothing out of him, apparently."

"Flames!" said Kerry; "this doesn't fit in anywhere."

"I am glad to hear you say so, Superintendent," Sowerby admitted, "because it all means absolutely nothing to me."

He turned over another page.

"Architect's report," he went on. "Your ideas. Superintendent, about the construction of the house seem to be borne out by the report of the experts who have examined it."

"Have they found anything?"

"No, but the measurements don't tally."

"Meet me there to-night at nine o'clock," said Kerry tersely.

"Very good, Superintendent."

Awhile longer they talked, Kerry giving rapid instructions; then:

"The thing that defeats me," he declared, "is this: Why, if there is a way into that room which we haven't found yet, should the murderer have escaped by the window?"

"The marks," said Sowerby, "suggest, as you know, that he not only went out by the window, but also came in that way. He clearly broke the glass in order to open the catch."

"More bewildering than ever," Kerry cried; "because it's an established fact that someone came into that room where the dead man was lying during the time the lights were out, and removed a sort of leather amulet which Burma Chang wore upon a thin gold chain around his neck. I strongly suspect that something went from the writing table as well, but I hadn't had time to memorize all the things upon it. The point, however, is this: Why should a clever and desperate man take risks by climbing up to and down from a window when he knows of a secret way into the room? The man who did this job, Sowerby, knows that house better than we do. For instance, he knows where the control switch is, by means of which those lights were turned off—although we have not succeeded in discovering it, so far."

"No," said Sowerby reflectively. "I had to give that job up."

"Poor Simmons was positive," Kerry went on, "that it was a man who climbed down from Burma Chang's window. I think we can take it that this was the murderer."

"I don't think there is much doubt about it,"* Sowerby agreed.

"This being the murderer," Kerry resumed, speaking in his rapid, terse fashion, "what the hell has the woman got to do with it?"

"You mean the woman described by Mr. Hope?"

"Precisely. If such a woman exists, and I for one don't doubt it, it's stretching coincidence too far to suppose that she is unconnected with the crime. As nearly as I can work out, she boarded the train about five minutes after Simmons gave the alarm, having seen a man descending from the window. Now"—he fixed his fierce gaze upon Sowerby's face—"what's the connection between the man climbing from the window and the woman climbing into the train?"

Inspector Sowerby raised his hand to his head, inspired by that ceaseless optimism which one day led him to hope that his hair might be made to lie down; then:

"God knows, Superintendent," he replied, "I don't!"

"There *is* a connection," said Kerry savagely, "otherwise we should have found her by now."

"I can't quite agree with that," Sowerby ventured; "I don't mean with the facts of the matter, Superintendent, don't misunderstand me; but with your suggestion that if this woman had been innocent she would naturally have come forward as soon as reports of the case appeared in the Press. It's my experience that they very rarely come forward in such cases unless they are pushed."

Throughout this statement, Kerry's fierce regard had been set upon him; and:

"Thank you again," said the Superintendent. "Between you and Marcus Aurelius, I shall know something of human nature before I retire. You would be a good man at a party. Do you sing or recite?"

"Neither," Sowerby answered gloomily, "but I'm beginning to think that I talk too much."

"The same idea had occurred to me," said Kerry acidly; "there may be something in it."

Silence fell for a few moments, broken only by Kerry's audible chewing; then:

"Don't entirely neglect Mr. Cosmo Potter," he snapped abruptly. "That gentleman fancies himself as an amateur detective, and if he doesn't live in Baker Street it's an oversight."

"I have got a note of him."

"Good." Kerry stood up. "The other point—the man at the garage— you have also got a note of. See him yourself—make that your first job. We want a description of this untidy smart who followed the French car on a motorcycle. The movements of Mr. Bernard Hope I will inquire into personally. He isn't connected with the matter in any way whatever, but I've an idea he knows someone who is."

"Ah!" Sowerby murmured, "it's a funny world. I made the same suggestion myself a few minutes ago."

"Oh!" Kerry's challenging glance fixed itself upon him. "Is that a fact? You should take up elocution, Sowerby—you don't drive your points home."

The telephone bell rang. Kerry crossed and took up the instrument. "Yes?" he said.

He listened awhile, his expression growing even more fierce than usual; then:

"Very good, sir," he went on; "you wish me to report to you now?" He nodded. "Very good, sir," and hung up the receiver.

He placed a wad of chewing gum in a small ash tray, performing that difficult operation with the ease of long practice. From his waistcoat he took out a pink slip, unwrapped it, and placed a fresh wafer between his large and savage-looking teeth.

Throughout this operation, Inspector Sowerby stroked his hair, and stared reflectively from the window, as though the distant prospect of the Embankment fascinated him.

Kerry spoke.

"I was right!" he announced.

Sowerby turned to face the Superintendent. He could think of no comment.

"Cosmo Potter has been amusing himself again. That was the Assistant Commissioner on the 'phone. He tells me"—Kerry's expression became positively ferocious—"that he has received important information from Mr. Potter. Have you got that, Sowerby? You, actively, are in charge of this case, and the Assistant Commissioner has received important information from Mr. Potter. Wait until I come back."

He crossed the room, opened the door, went out, and slammed the door behind him.

CHAPTER XXIV

THE ONE WHO FOLLOWED

Yvette Chalmers entered the stage door of the Riviera Theatre. Rapkin, the gloomy Viking who presided there, looked up into her smiling face. He was almost as glad as the girl herself that Bernard Hope had returned to London, and his romantic soul had planned a wonderful future for the charming young actress and her lover. For of Bernard Hope Rapkin approved, and him therefore he hailed unhesitatingly as a genius whose plays should rank one day with those of Mr. George Bernard Shaw.

"One for you, miss," he said, and handed Yvette a bulky envelope.

She glanced at it with a little frown, noted the foreign postmark, and considered the large and untidy handwriting; then:

"Thank you," she said; "there seems to be a lot of it. I hope it is interesting."

She went up to her dressing room, took off her hat and coat and placed her wrist watch on the dressing table. She noted that she had ample time; therefore, sitting down, she opened her letter.

The heading gave her a clue to the writer's identity, which hitherto had puzzled her. But, as she read, her expression changed, until, presently, one watching her would have said that she had found something in the letter which positively horrified her.

Although the letter was a very long one, she read right through to the end. And then, glancing at her own reflection in the mirror in a startled way, she put the several loose pages into their right order and began to read again from the second paragraph of the first page.

I want to know what I am to do. I have not been able to get any news, so I don't know how the case stands. I have written to no one else, and I am almost afraid to trust this letter to the post. If you want me to keep quiet I will do so—if I can help in any way by saying all I know, then just pass on this letter. It was the inquiry coming through to me about the money from Monte Carlo which, together with what I had seen, told me there might be danger. I would have given anything to have been able to stop and see it through. But that, as you know, was quite impossible. Of course, you can rely upon me absolutely.

Yvette skipped several lines and then read on again:

The night I called at the theatre and you sent a message out by Mrs. Walters that you had gone, I was disappointed, of course—although I had only called to say good-bye. I just supposed you had forgotten, and should have thought no more of the matter if I had not heard a cabman standing outside the stage door mention to another man that he was waiting for you. Now, what I have to say is hard to say, because it seems a sneaking kind of thing—the kind of thing that is really quite out of my line, but it really came about accidentally, in this way:

I was moving off very slowly and wondering whether I ought to write a line and leave it for you, when I heard the cabman's voice again and walked back. You didn't see me, but I was only a few yards away when you came out, and I heard the man say, speaking of the fog: "If it's too thick when we get past Aldgate, we shall have to turn back."

Now, what I did was done from no other motive than friendship. I thought it was madness on your part to attempt that journey in such a fog, especially after what I had told you about the influence possessed by Burma Chang in that neighbourhood. I was standing in a little entry only a few yards from the stage door, and I made my mind up at once. I passed a cab—you were in it by this time—went down to the corner, and hailed another cab which was going by. I told the man that I wanted to go to West India Dock, and I had to bribe him pretty heavily to induce him to take the job on.

He tackled it at last, though. So, when you started, my cab was only a few yards behind yours. My man performed wonders, but somewhere in West India Dock Road we lost sight of you. The darkness was so dense that it was impossible to get any farther. I paid him and started off on foot.

I was really alarmed about you. The idea of a woman coming alone to that neighbourhood on such a night appalled me. I knew the street in which Ah Wong lived, and I knew a short cut to it which would take me past the back of Burma Chang's house. As you are aware, I know the district fairly well. The fog lifted a little bit as I came to the lane which runs down at the back of the house, and I saw a light in a window up above. I stepped on to the other side to get a better view—and now I come to the thing about which I have been wondering and wondering ever since: about which I want to know what I am to do.

I saw you in the room! I saw you throw up your arm and draw back from someone as though you had been attacked!

Just at this point of her re-reading, the dressing-room door opened and Mrs. Walters, the dresser, entered. Yvette started wildly, and her expression, seen in the mirror, was so strange that Mrs. Walters paused in astonishment.

"Is there anything the matter?" she asked.

"No, no!" said Yvette, forcing herself to be composed. "I was reading, and you startled me as you came in; that's all."

"So I see," said Mrs. Walters, in a non-committal tone.

She glanced at the number of dainty garments which she had laid out ready for wear, prior to Yvette's arrival. And, as the girl thrust the loose pages back into their envelope:

"You haven't too much time," she added significantly.

Yvette looked at her wrist watch on the table before her, whereupon:

"Good heavens!" she exclaimed, "I don't think I can do it!"

"Oh, yes, you can," said Mrs. Walters soothingly. "Don't get flustered. There's just time."

"I shall have to go on without any make-up," cried Yvette in dismay.

"Fortunately, it don't matter," replied the dresser composedly. "The first scene's a dark scene, and then you've got seven minutes and no change."

Nevertheless, and in spite of these soothing counsels, a stage wait was only narrowly averted; and it was a very flustered Yvette Chalmers who made her first entrance that evening. She had been on the stage only a few minutes when Bernard Hope arrived.

Hope enjoyed the freedom of the theatre, and, exchanging a cheery "Good-evening" with Rapkin, he walked upstairs to Yvette's room and sat down, having hung his hat and coat behind the door. Then, taking out a cigarette, he discovered that he had no matches, and he crossed to the dressing table to take one from a box which lay there.

He saw a bulky envelope which lay just beside the box. A loose page protruded, and, as he stooped, it was impossible to avoid reading the words written in a large untidy hand upon the top of the page. These were the words:

The sight of you in Burma Chang's house turned me cold.

He had more than once, in his writings, employed the expression, "I was literally stunned," whilst always regarding it as a somewhat exaggerated figure. Yet such, precisely, was the effect which these simple words had upon him, now. They seemed to stun him; and then, like the writer of the letter, he experienced a sensation as of a chill at his heart. His hand upon the matchbox, he stood as one petrified, looking down at those fatal words.

The writing! He knew it ... but because of a mental numbness he was quite unable to identify it. He dropped the cigarette, unlighted, upon the table and, returning to a little armchair, sat down again.

He was seated there when Yvette came running up the stairs, and his face must have been a mask of tragedy; for:

"My dear!" she cried, and stood stock still in the doorway, "whatever is the matter?"

"Nothing," he answered slowly; indeed, remembering that she had only a short wait and must presently return to the stage, he even forced a haggard smile; "nothing that cannot keep until the end of the act."

"But—" she began, staring at him helplessly.

Then, professional instinct coming uppermost as it will, she seated herself at the dressing table, and, watching Hope through the mirror:

"I was too late to make up to-night," she said, endeavouring to speak naturally, "and it is impossible to do so now, but at least I can touch myself up a bit."

Mrs. Walters came in and relieved a somewhat strained silence, greeting Hope cheerfully. Hope contrived to talk fairly naturally during the few minutes that Yvette remained in the room, but when, followed by Mrs. Walters carrying a cloak, she went out, he noticed at once that the letter had disappeared from the dressing table!

He realized that he must not see her again until she had finished. He was afraid to trust himself, afraid to ask her to explain what he had read.

Her part, though not unimportant, was confined to the first act. He determined, therefore, not to see her until the interval.

Where he went during the intervening time, he was unable subsequently to remember. He had a vague idea of walking through lighted streets and even of exchanging greetings with acquaintances. But when at last he came back to the theatre, walked upstairs, and knocked upon Yvette's door, he found that she was dressed ready to go.

She turned in her chair and stared at him.

"Yvette!" he burst out, "I won't mince words. I must come straight to the point. When I first came in"—he pointed to the dressing table— "you had left a letter lying there beside the matchbox. I went to get a match, and it was impossible to avoid reading the words on top of a page which stuck out of the envelope. I don't try to excuse myself; I simply state a fact. I read them! I read them, Yvette!"

He paused, his hands clenched, looking at her haggardly; but:

"I don't ask you to excuse yourself," she said, speaking very quietly. "What were the words you read?"

"I cannot remember them, but they stated that you had been at the house of Burma Chang."

She opened her handbag, and, taking out the letter, put it down upon the dressing table.

"Read it all," she said calmly. "Since you discuss my private affairs with other people, you might as well know the consequences."

"Discuss your affairs! What do you mean?" Hope cried hotly.

"Just what I say," Yvette returned. "This is a letter from a friend of yours who considers it his duty to follow me about."

"What do you mean?" Hope demanded again; "in what way does this explain the statement which I read?"

"It does not explain it at all," Yvette admitted. "The writer is under a misapprehension. The facts of the matter are known to the police."

"To the police!"

"That is what I said. You may or may not know—I think I told you—that Inspector Sowerby cross-examined me recently. The facts of this matter are known to him. I explained them in detail."

Hope stood looking down at her, torn between horrible doubt and his belief in this woman on whom he had placed the highest hopes in life; then:

"Yvette," he said in a changed voice, "I don't want to read one word of it. Yvette! don't be angry with me. I don't mind what you do or where you go—"

The words were defensive—and, woman-like, Yvette immediately attacked.

"You have no right to discuss me with your friends," she said indignantly.

"I don't know what you mean. With whom have I discussed you?"

"With Jack Markham! That letter is from Jack Markham."

"But I have known Jack for years—and you and he were children together! I certainly spoke to him of Burma Chang, and of the danger which you ran by visiting Chinatown since this man had become interested in you. But explain, Yvette. For God's sake explain! You told me you had seen Markham, and now, of course, I recognize his writing"—glancing at the envelope—"but what does he mean about your being at the house of Burma Chang?"

Yvette's manner had changed. She raised her hand to her face wearily.

"I don't know what he means," she said. "I got this letter to-night when I arrived at the theatre. It is the reason I was late in dressing. It simply bewildered me. You *must* read it—or I will read it to you, if you prefer that. You see, the inquiry which the police made, about your having visited the ship, evidently gave Jack the idea that you might be concerned in some way. So, poor fellow, he has written to me. He seems to be in a dreadful frame of mind."

"But what about?" Hope exclaimed helplessly. "I don't understand at all. In what way is he connected with the matter?"

"In this way," Yvette answered wearily: "He came to see me on the night"—she hesitated—"that the murder was committed in Chinatown."

"Here at the theatre?"

"Yes. Just as I was ready to go, his card was brought to me."

"That must have been about the time that I was at West India Dock," Hope muttered. "Well— what then?"

"Well," Yvette went on, "I am afraid I told him a lie. That is, Mrs. Walters told him one."

"Why?"

"Because I didn't want to see him, then. You see—" she paused again, biting her lip in embarrassment—"I want you to remember, Bernard, that you had been away for a long time and had not written to me; and so, although up to that time I had respected your wish about visiting Annie down in Limehouse, I decided that I thought more about your peace of mind than you did about mine."

"Oh! It was only natural in the circumstances."

"And so, that night I had arranged to go."

"To go down to Limehouse? At night?"

"You see, her message only reached me late in the afternoon. She sent a note to say that her baby had been born and that she was seriously ill. She begged me to go and see her. You don't seem to understand that she is very fond of me—that it meant a lot to her. I sent a telegram to say I would come down as soon as I could leave the theatre. Then, just as I was getting ready to go, Jack's card came up.

"Poor old Jack! He is always such a dear. He is a great pal to you, Bernard, because he is always such a good pal to me, and I felt the meanest thing on earth. But knowing that he shared your views on the dangers of Chinatown and at least suspecting that he knew I had promised you not to go, I put him off and went."

"Alone?"

"Yes, of course, I went alone."

"But there was a dense fog that night!"

"It was not so dense when I started," Yvette replied, "and the taxi man was a man who has driven me many times. But it became perfectly awful when we reached Limehouse. And—perhaps you may be thinking that it was because I had deserved it—I had the most terrifying adventure there. I got lost in the fog."

"You mean the cabman lost his way?"

"No. You don't understand. Let me explain." She related her

experiences on the night of the fog, adding a little bitterly:

"All of which has been substantiated by the police, I understand; for I have heard from Annie, who is fortunately better, and they have questioned her and seen my telegram. They have also examined the cabman who drove me, as well as the one who drove me back. So that now, when you read Jack Markham's letter, you will be as puzzled, and perhaps as horrified, as I was to find that he is labouring under an impression that he saw me at a window of Burma Chang's house!

"Fortunately for myself, as I realize, I can prove that he is wrong. He, poor fellow, quite naturally is worried to death. He doesn't know what to believe or what to do. Now, please"—she took up the envelope—"read his letter, Bernard, and you will see what it *might* mean for me, if I were not in a position to prove where I went that night."

Hope, a little dazedly, smoothed out the crumpled pages and began to read Jack Markham's letter. Yvette, perhaps to hide her agitation, lighted a cigarette and sat watching the reader and swinging her foot to and fro.

He read on without comment until, turning a page, he came to the fateful lines, "When I saw you in Burma Chang's house." He inhaled sibilantly and glanced at Yvette. But she was looking down at the point of her moving shoe, in apparent abstraction. He read on:

There was a door in the wall. It was bolted; but by means of an iron pillar which stood in the court, I managed to climb to the top of the wall. It was studded with glass, but I used my coat to protect my hands and knees, and presently dropped over on the other side. I crossed to the house and swarmed up a pipe to the ledge of the window. It was a hard job, but I heard a shriek which helped me on considerably.

When I looked into the room, at first I could see no one. However, I smashed the glass, opened the catch, and, raising the sash, climbed in. The breeze was bringing more fog up and a lot of it blew in at the open window.

You had gone. I could see two doors, and I tried both, but they were both locked. None of these things mattered very much at the time, and my ideas had taken quite a fresh turn.

On the floor lay Burma Chang.

I hadn't seen him for two years, but, all the same, I recognized him. I stood there with my mind in a whirl while the fog poured in at the window, looking down at him. He was writhing, choking, and making a horrible sort of gurgling noise. As I watched, he raised one hand to his throat and dropped the other flat on the carpet. He ceased to move, but went on breathing heavily.

Then, suddenly, I noticed an open safe, the contents in disorder. I saw there were stray papers on the floor. I saw an overturned chair, and I thought I heard footsteps. My mind began to work, then, and it worked rapidly.

If you had been lured into the house, apparently you had escaped, whilst if I were to be found there, I saw in a flash what my position would be. The Chinaman looked in a pretty bad way. I strongly suspected he was dying. Then there was the open safe, and the footsteps seemed to be drawing nearer. I didn't hesitate. I went out of the window again, picking up my coat and starting across the garden.

I was making for the door which I had noticed, when the sound of a police whistle came from the lane outside—apparently just outside the door. That decided me. I realized my peril and changed my tactics. The fog was coming up again very thickly, but in one corner of the yard or garden I could see a sort of shed. I mounted it without making very much noise and looked over the wall.

As I did so, a constable ran past and presently joined someone else in the court around the corner. I jagged myself badly on the broken glass, but without delay I swarmed over and dropped in the street. I was seen, I think. Someone gave chase, but I started off into the fog and was soon swallowed up by it.

There seemed to be movements all around me, but the sound of the chase had died away, when, in the light of a lamp just ahead of me, *I saw you go by.*

It was impossible to mistake you. I could have sworn to you anywhere. You were hurrying, and looked very frightened. I called to you, but apparently you didn't hear me. So I began to follow, but lost sight of you almost immediately. I had only your footsteps to guide me, and presently I stopped and listened. As I did so, you seemed to stop as well. At any rate, that was the last I heard of you. But my mind was relieved on one point—you were safe, although wandering alone in the fog in Chinatown.

Nevertheless, I had no alternative and I should have been on board before this. And somehow, guided by my knowledge of the district, I found my way to the docks and got aboard, to learn that Bernard had been looking for me and had left a message.

We were held by the fog, of course, and some hours later the police came. Their inquiry, which related to Bernard, as I have already told you, naturally gave me a dreadful shock. I didn't know quite where I stood—where you stood—or where he stood. So I was very reticent in my replies. However, they seemed to be satisfied and went away.

From then until now, I have been able to get no more news and I don't know what to do.

Bernard Hope laid the letter down, staring across at Yvette.

"By God!" he said. "What a net! What a net I And we are all tangled up in it."

CHAPTER XXV

THE SECRET VISITOR

"Who is there?"said Yvette sharply. "Hide that letter, Bernard!"

Bernard Hope slipped the letter into his pocket, as:

"Come in!" Yvette added.

The door opened, and Rapkin in person appeared.

"A very urgent message for you, sir," he announced, and held out a card to Hope.

Hope took it from him and stared in astonishment on learning that it was Cosmo Potter's card. Upon the back was written in pencil:

> Hurry home as quickly as possible. Leave the window open
> and wait for me. C. P.

He glanced into the poetic face of the doorkeeper.

"Is Mr. Potter waiting?" he asked.

"Mr. Who, sir?" said Rapkin. "It was delivered by a chauffeur."

"Is he gone?"

"Yes, he went away at once."

"Burton, I suppose," Hope muttered, turning to Yvette. "Thank you, Rapkin."

He laid the card upon the dressing table.

"There's some sudden development," he said, as the doorkeeper retired. "Let us hope it will result in this infernal business being cleared up."

Yvette, glancing up from the card, looked in a frightened way at the speaker.

"Are you sure of the writing?" she asked.

"Yes," Hope replied, "as sure as one can be of writing in pencil. Oh! I don't doubt it's from Potter. In any event, I have nothing to lose and everything to gain."

"I should have liked to come with you," Yvette said wistfully, "but, in any case, it might have been unwise. However, as it happens, I have no alternative. Do you think you will be able to join us later?"

Hope shook his head.

"I am afraid I can't say," he replied. "God knows what this means."

"But at least you will let me know when I get home? I mean, some time?"

"Of course I will."

"I have a feeling," said Yvette, "that there is some sort of silly doubt in your mind ... about me and Burma Chang."

"My dear," Hope cried, grasping her shoulders and looking into her eyes, "how can you suggest such a thing? It's a damnably baffling business, but I quite understand that Jack Markham has made an extraordinary mistake. He may have seen you in the street...."

"He very possibly did," Yvette interrupted crossly. "At one point in my wanderings I had a distinct idea that someone was following me. You remember, I mentioned it to you."

"Yes," Hope nodded.

"But he is mistaken, of course, about the figure at the window."

"What he saw was probably a mere silhouette—and I have a shrewd suspicion—"

"Yes," said Yvette eagerly. "Do you think you know who it was?"

"I do."

"Do you mean the woman in the train?" she went on.

Hope nodded again.

"How were you dressed that night?"

"Just as I am dressed now."

"Ah!" he exclaimed, "and the woman in the train wore an almost identical coat, except that I think it was of rather darker material, and a similar hat. I begin to see daylight. You are going home to dress, of course?"

"Yes," Yvette replied.

"Then I will see you that far and keep the taxi."

So it was arranged. Once more Chinatown had reached out and interfered with the plans of Bernard Hope; for he was to have made one of the party which Yvette was on her way to join.

However, whilst these dreadful doubts remained to be cleared up, the mystery surrounding the two murders in Limehouse must have a prior claim on his attention. And, at a moment when the hilly road facing his cottage chanced to be quite deserted, he paid his cabman and stood for a while watching the taxi until it had disappeared in the distance.

Since his affairs had become mysteriously entangled with those of Suzee Che Lo, his homely surroundings had assumed a subtly changed aspect. Shadows took on mysterious shapes—the movements of a stray cat became laden with significance—casual passers-by he suspected of being disguised members of some unsavoury brotherhood.

But to-night everything seemed peaceful and still. He was by no means certain in his own mind that the message had come from Potter, in spite of his assertion to Yvette. It might or might not be in Potter's hand. However, he could conceive of nothing which any one had to gain by laying a trap for him; therefore, the obvious course was to obey the message and await the result.

He opened the door and stepped inside rather nervously, automatically turning up the light before closing the door behind him.

Everything seemed to be in order, and, removing his hat and coat, he prepared himself a drink, and, reading for the twentieth time the message upon the card, shrugged his shoulders and opened that little window through which one night a hideous, pock-marked Chinese face had looked in upon them. In the reflected light he could see the rhododendron bushes which grew close up to the side of the cottage. Nothing stirred, and sitting down where he could watch the open window, he filled and lighted his pipe, sipping his whisky-and-soda reflectively, and allowing his imagination to play with the possibilities which lay before him.

Two days had elapsed since the visit of Satsu Kuhna, but although he had received a telephone message from Cosmo Potter in which he promised exciting revelations at their next meeting, he had not seen his friend.

A slight breeze stirred the leaves outside, and the sudden rustling made him start, bringing him back from useless but disturbing reflections to the possible dangers of the moment. He stared at the dark gap made by the open window—for from where he sat, so it appeared. Nothing moved in the lamplight streaming out. A car was mounting the hill—he could hear it distinctly; but when it reached the crest, it was driven on.

He could not imagine with what object Cosmo Potter had made this singular appointment. But knowing how deeply his friend's mind had become engaged with the intricacies of the Chinatown mystery, he did not doubt that the object was a sound one.

The neighbourhood, as he had noted before, seemed curiously deserted to-night, and a sense of loneliness pervaded the cottage, so that he found himself wondering if inadvertently he had offended some mysterious, invisible Chinaman, and even at that very moment was being watched by slanting eyes out of the darkness.

Then, presently, he detected a sound which was not occasioned by the wind. Someone stealthily was creeping round from the back of the cottage to the open window!

Hope, not knowing what to expect, crossed and stood just to the right of the window, where he would be concealed from any one looking into the room. The sounds of furtive approach continued; then:

"Hope, Hope!" came a whisper, "where the devil are you?"

Hope stepped forward, staring out into the darkness, but could see no one. Yet the voice was the voice of Cosmo Potter.

"Let me in by the back door," the voice went on, "but don't make any noise in doing so."

He hurried across and opened the door opening on the little yard.

Potter, wearing a soft black hat, and having the collar of his overcoat turned up, stood on the step; beside him, a dark, slender woman wrapped in some unfamiliar kind of fur. Her pale face showed strangely in the darkness, the faint light coming from the room beyond making strange glints in the slanting eyes and painting delicate high lights upon her jade earrings.

It was Suzee Che Lo!

Noiselessly as they had come they entered, and Hope quietly rebolted the door. As they came into the little sitting room, Hope placed an armchair for Suzee. She thanked him with a smile, but offered no explanation of her presence under such extraordinary circumstances.

He thought that she was a woman who never offered explanations.

"You had better close the window now," said Potter, removing his hat and coat. "I suspect followers. Humanity is so persevering."

Hope closed the window; and, turning:

"To what am I indebted," he said, addressing Suzee Che Lo, "for this charming but unexpected visit?"

"Primarily," explained Cosmo Potter, "Madame Che Lo and I arranged to meet here in order that she might recover this"—from an inside pocket he drew out the little powder box—"which you, Hope, entrusted to me for safety."

He turned and handed it to Suzee.

She thanked him smilingly, raising the lid and peeping at the curiously carved object which lay within the box. Then, glancing up at Hope:

"You see," she said, "I am returning to China to-morrow."

CHAPTER XXVI

THE GREAT TONG

"I am indebted to you both," said Suzee Che Lo, "in more ways than you know of. If one of your own countrymen had not been killed, I should never have spoken; but he died in trying to do his duty, and so, I shall speak. For I, also, have risked a lot for a duty which I undertook, and I can sympathize with another who loses all he has to lose in such a cause. I shall try to help you, then, but some things you may want to know I shall be unable to tell you."

She moved one slender hand in an odd gesture.

"If you will just allow me to talk for a while, I will talk about the things that I think may help you, except about those which are forbidden me. This little carved lotus that you have returned to me—I will tell you about this first.

"Among the Chinese there are many secret societies." She glanced at Cosmo Potter, "You know?" she asked in her naive way.

He inclined his head gravely, being engaged in inserting one of his unusual cigarettes in the holder.

"Yes," he replied, "I know."

"Sometimes there are feuds between two such societies, or Tongs; and because, amongst my people, life is counted very cheap, sometimes there are a number of deaths. This goes on from the very bottom of the underworld right up the social scale, and although, as you know, China is very unsettled just now, there is a part of the old order still prevailing and holding together.

"There is one secret society, I cannot tell you its name, which ranks above all the others, because it has no part in any of their interests. It is very ancient and revered. Except for a comparatively small community, who have never respected this order, there is not in the world a Chinaman who would willingly offend this most ancient of all the Tongs.

"The Master of the Order is descended from Confucius, and even when the Empress was on the throne, her power was less great than his. And although there is no Empire now, yet the power of the master of this Tong remains greater than that of any other one man in China.

"To illustrate what I mean—at the most secret meeting of any other society of Chinese, at a meeting of statesmen, or a council of war, if one should arrive and present this"—she opened the little powder box, affording her listeners a glimpse of the Lotus—"he would be instantly admitted, although he might wear the rags of a beggar."

She paused, smiling up at Cosmo Potter, who was standing by the window staring hard at her.

"So you see," she said, "although we are becoming modernized, there are still mysteries in my country, of which you, in Europe, know very little. Yet I admit that we are becoming modernized; otherwise I should not be here."

She turned to Hope, upon whose lips a question palpably trembled, raising her hand.

"Please don't ask me questions," she continued. "I will think what it is possible for me to say and tell you all that I dare. You must not suppose that I belong to this society. No women belong to it. But my father"— she paused again, as if searching in her mind for suitably vague phrases—"was one of them, and by accident, as will sometimes happen, I learned some of their secrets when I was too young to understand the importance of what I had discovered.

"Someone who at that time had much power over me forced me to tell something of what I knew. I have learned since that he was an impostor. His aims, as he explained them to me, were imaginary. His real object was the same as that of a river pirate, but on a larger scale.

"I realized too late what I had done, and I feared him intensely, because of the power he had of reading my mind. I asked you to hide this"—she held up the little box—"because I was afraid he would trace me and force me to tell him what had become of it."

She smiled musingly.

"I need not have feared—he has that power no longer. But I said your European influence had reached China. That I am here in England shows that it is so. Of course, I had had a European education, but once, and not so long ago, for the sin I had committed, I should have suffered a dreadful penalty. Instead, the task was laid upon me of remedying the evil. I came to London for that purpose."

"Why to London?" asked Cosmo Potter.

Suzee Che Lo turned her mysterious eyes in his direction.

"You must not ask me questions," she said softly. "The danger was in London. The man you called Burma Chang was a member of this society. I came to London to warn him of his danger, the danger in which, against my will, I had placed him."

Cosmo Potter screwed his monocle more firmly into place and stared across at Bernard Hope. The expression upon his gaunt features indicated that he was longing to cross-examine; but:

"My task was not an easy one," Suzee went on. "I had"—she repeated the odd little gesture which accompanied any hiatus in her statements—"certain credentials. I have lived in London before, I have certain duties which bring me here sometimes, and so I took up my old quarters, off Curzon Street. The night of the great fog I set out for Limehouse—Burma Chang was expecting me. I knew the house, you see; indeed, at one time I lived there for nearly a year."

"You lived there!" Hope exclaimed in amazement—"in Limehouse?"

"Yes." She turned to him composedly. "My father for a time occupied the post that later was filled by Burma Chang. Please don't question me; I will explain as much as I can.

"I had the key, then, of the little door in the wall—you know the door I mean? There have been photographs of it in some of the newspapers. I went down an hour before the time arranged and stayed with some Chinese people whom I know there. Then I went along, unlocked the door, locking it behind me, crossed the garden, and pressed the bell which rings in the room above. Burma Chang came down and admitted me."

Both her listeners were strung up to high tension, recognizing what was coming.

"Burma Chang returned to his seat at the desk which he had left to admit me," she went on. "He smoked cigarettes which contained a lot of opium— long, yellow things; the lower half was a thin cardboard tube filled with cotton wool. One of these was smouldering in an ash tray on his desk. He took it up and went on smoking. He knew that my visit must mean that he was in very grave danger, but the Chinese, you see, do not show emotion.

"I began to tell him why I had come, and to warn him what he must fear, when suddenly he stood up, raised his hand to his throat, and his face was contorted. Then, controlling himself, he pulled out from under his robe a little leather case which he wore upon a gold chain around his neck, opened it and took out the Lotus which it contained. He beckoned to me. I could see now that he was in agony.

"'Take it,' he whispered. 'There are the keys of the door. Run for your life. It is here already—I am poisoned!'

"As he spoke, a dreadful convulsion seized him, and he fell writhing upon the floor. He uttered a shrill cry of agony and I realized that he was dying.

"I knew I was in dreadful danger from more sources than one; and so, taking the keys, I unlocked the door which led on to the stair and ran down to the bottom. Locking the lower door, I went out into the garden and relocked the door behind me. Then I went out into the lane and locked the door in the wall as well.

"The fog was growing very dense, and before I had gone ten paces I heard a police whistle close behind me, and knew that in some way the death of Burma Chang must have been discovered.

"What I did after that, you know quite well. What I should have done if I had not seen a train standing upon the line in front of me, I really do not know. I could not have found the house of my friends—indeed, I was completely lost."

She paused for a moment, and then:

"I have done what was required of me," she added, "but before I return, I wish to reward those who have helped me."

"I believe you mean what you say," Cosmo Potter said gravely; "but although you have cleared up many points, there are more which remain in darkness. You have asked me not to question you, but on the understanding that you are not compelled to answer, surely there can be no harm in my trying to learn some of the things that we want to know?"

Suzee Che Lo smiled at him; and:

"Very well," she replied.

Potter gazed at the end of his smouldering cigarette; then:

"Do you know what killed Burma Chang?" he asked.

"Yes," she replied simply. "He died of what is called *Lu-chu-see*."

"Ah!" Potter exclaimed, "that was the word which so puzzled Inspector Peel. What, may I ask, is *Lu-chu-see?*"

Suzee Che Lo performed her odd little gesture.

"It is a kind of infection," she said, "or disease, which comes out of the earth. It is named after the district where it is most common. Some of the peasants of Lu Chu die in this way, apparently because of their habit of eating a certain kind of raw potato."

"This does not account for Burma Chang dying in that way?"

"No," she shook her head. "I cannot account for it."

"I presume," Potter went on, "the extraordinary excitement in Chinatown, caused by the death of Burma Chang, was due to the fact that he was known to be a member of this society to which you have referred?"

Suzee Che Lo hesitated for a moment, watching him enigmatically. Then:

"I don't know that I should really answer that question," she said, "but you are wrong. Very few of the Chinese in London know anything of this society. He was well known for another reason. He was a member of one of the lesser or ordinary Tongs, although a very powerful one of its kind."

She hesitated as if weighing her words again. And then:

"Have you heard of *Pak-a-pu?*" she asked.

Cosmo Potter nodded.

"Yes," he replied, "it is a sort of lottery game."

"It is controlled by a Canton syndicate," Suzee went on, "more wealthy than that which runs the Casino at Monte Carlo. Burma Chang was the London agent of this syndicate. I am afraid I have already told you too much; I can tell you no more."

"But surely," Potter persevered, "you can tell me this: who is Satsu Kuhna?"

Keenly he watched Suzee Che Lo as he put the question, but no perceptible change of expression occurred in the beautiful ivory face.

"On his mother's side," she replied composedly, "he belongs to a noble Chinese family. Of his father, I know nothing."

"Do you regard him as a dangerous man?"

She smiled.

"You have seen how dangerous he can be," she replied.

"I think," said Potter, "that there is something vitally important which you may be able to tell us. You said that you lived for a year in this house in Chinatown."

"Yes," she replied, "I lived there at one time." She regarded Potter in her tranquil fashion. "What is it you want to know?"

"I was just mentally reviewing a theory covering all the facts of the case," he replied, "but based on an assumption which only you can confirm."

He began to speak as though thinking aloud.

"The investigation has been handicapped from the outset," he went on, "by a false hypothesis respecting the motive of the crime. Robbery seemed to be clearly indicated, and humanity is so predatory. But now that we know that whilst robbery was certainly the motive, but not common robbery, much that was formerly obscure becomes as clear as day.

"There was a moderate fortune in negotiable form contained in that safe. But I gather that the possession of this odd little ornament would have placed the assassin above the consideration of such purely sordid matters. He came, then, for the Lotus, and Burma Chang met his death, not because he was the president of a wealthy secret society amongst the Chinese in London, or because he was custodian of their funds, but because he chanced *also* to be a member of this older and more important association, and therefore held a token which vested its possessor with unusual powers."

"If he could have secured it, he might have done much to wreck my country," Suzee Che Lo replied simply.

"Quite so," Potter went on. "It is fairly evident that although you arrived too late to save Burma Chang, you were only too late by a few minutes. In other words, the murderer must actually have been in the house at the same time that you were there."

"Why do you think so?" she asked softly.

"Because poison had evidently been administered to Burma Chang only a few minutes before your arrival; and although, very shortly after your departure, a man climbed up to the window, a man who had seen your shadow from below and mistaken it for that of someone else, by the time he reached the window, broke it, and entered the room, the safe had been opened and ransacked, also the table drawers. In other words, someone had hastily searched the room for the Lotus. This"—he raised his finger forensically—"although both doors were locked."

"How do you know this?" asked Suzee Che Lo.

"I have it in writing in my pocket now," Hope replied quietly, "signed by the man who entered the room."

"The facts as they stand," Potter resumed, "in the light of the evidence of the various persons concerned, pointedly suggest that it was none other than yourself who ransacked the table drawers. Your possession of this amulet, which you state the dead man wore suspended by a gold chain about his neck, merely strengthens this theory."

"Ah!" Suzee Che Lo looked at him with half-closed eyes. "I might also have murdered him, you think?"

"I think nothing of the kind," Potter replied; "I am merely stating the aspect of the case up to a certain point. But, to go on. At a subsequent stage of the inquiry, on the same night, the lights were turned out all over the house at a particular moment, from some control switch which, up to the present moment, so far as my information bears me, has not been discovered. This is point one.

"During the darkness so produced, someone had entered the room where the dead man lay, and removed the gold chain with its leather case to which you refer, and the existence of which was noted by Superintendent Kerry. At this time, on the evidence of Bernard Hope here, you were certainly not in Limehouse. Therefore this is point two.

"This feat was performed, then, although Superintendent Kerry stood near one door, or a little way outside, and the other was locked. This is point three.

"Finally, a man mistaken by two constables for Sergeant Simmons left the house late on the night of the murder, certainly wearing Simmons's hat and conspicuous raincoat, and disappeared, Simmons later being recovered from the Thames. This is point four, and together with the points one, two, and three, makes up, I think, conclusive evidence to show that there is a way into that room, or to the stair leading down from it, which the police, so far, have not discovered."

Suzee Che Lo, who had continued to watch him fascinatedly, now smiled slightly; but:

"Your reasoning is excellent, Potter," said Bernard Hope. "Your idea is that the murderer in some way stunned or perhaps killed Simmons on the dark stairway, took his hat and coat, and went out, thus escaping."

"Quite so." Potter's mild eyes surveyed him surprisedly. "Any objections?"

"Yes," Hope replied slowly, whilst Suzee Che Lo now transferred her gaze to his face. "Robbery of the coat and hat suggests that it was necessary for this hypothetical hidden man to pass the constable on duty at the bottom of the stairs. In other words, that this hiding-place, which you have quite reasonably constructed in the house of Burma Chang, had an exit into the room where the dead man lay, and another exit—where?"

"Where!" Potter echoed—"almost beyond doubt, on that staircase! Hence the sudden, silent, and effective attack upon Simmons."

"So far very good," Hope admitted, "because the murderer, a few moments later, disguised as the Sergeant, went down and out into the garden, deceiving the man on duty there—as was quite possible on so foggy a night. But are you not overlooking one rather important thing?"

"What is that?" Potter demanded.

"The later discovery of Simmons's body in the Thames. How did he get there?"

Potter's angular face presented a curious study in perplexity. But before he had time to reply came the ringing of a bell and a loud and peremptory knocking at the door of the cottage.

"Hello!" said Hope, "who can this be?"

Suzee Che Lo stood up hastily, but without any trace of alarm, and Potter's gaze became fixed upon the closed door.

"Don't make any bones about it!" shouted a familiar voice. "I know who is inside, and nobody has anything to gain by hiding."

"Inspector Sowerby!" Potter murmured. "Let him in."

Hope crossed to the door, opened it, and admitted the Inspector, who looked across the little lobby into the lighted room where Suzee Che Lo and Cosmo Potter stood watching him.

"It's a funny world," he said, "and it certainly seems to me that this lady, on her own admission, knows altogether too much about this business."

Suzee looked at him scornfully.

"How do you know what I know?" she asked.

"Well," said Sowerby, "I know everything you have told these gentlemen, because, you see, while Mr. Hope was out this afternoon I called to examine the meter, and at the same time fitted a little instrument which is sometimes called a Tectaphone."

Suzee's eyes seemed to grow longer and narrower.

"So you have heard all that I have said?" Her voice was very soft.

"Every word!" Sowerby answered.

And Bernard Hope, who was watching her, saw Suzee Che Lo smile triumphantly.

CHAPTER XXVII

SUPERINTENDENT KERRY ON DUTY

Once more Cosmo Potter's car threaded the narrow and unsavoury streets of Chinatown.

Except in that main thoroughfare which is an artery of Dockland, there were few people about. The law-abiding citizens of Limehouse, dock workers and the like, are early to bed. One would have thought that Chinatown slumbered. But it was not so. The night life of Chinatown is invisible to the chance visitor.

Sowerby was mildly triumphant. Kerry's criticisms of his conduct of the case had proved hard of digestion, but the information given by Cosmo Potter to the Commissioner, relative to the desirability of interviewing Satsu Kuhna, had led nowhere, that mysterious Asiatic having disappeared like a mirage.

It was particularly grateful to Sowerby's soul that the details now in his possession had come about as a result of his dogged persistence in, as he termed it, "keeping an eye on Mr. Hope."

He reflected, as the car drew near to the house of Burma Chang, through those streets where shadows sometimes flitted, indicative of furtive life—as moving shadows on the sands tell of lizards—that Superintendent Kerry, in his place, would almost certainly have detained all three of these conspirators as "accessories after the fact."

That was Kerry's way. Sowerby did not believe in it.

And so, now, the distinguished K. C. behind him, he sat, his back to the driver, alternately studying the beautiful face of Suzee Che Lo, which he thought was like an ivory carving of some Eastern goddess, and the uneasy face of Bernard Hope who sat beside her.

There had been long intervals of silence during the drive; but now:

"I cannot understand," said Potter suddenly, "why this house has been sealed up but left comparatively unprotected. I gather from this morning's papers that there is a constable on duty somewhere, but otherwise the place is deserted. Why advertise the fact?"

"Don't ask me, sir," said Sowerby. "It's the Superintendent's idea; but, as it happens, it will save us a lot of trouble to-night. Suppose we stop the car here and walk the rest of the way? We can probably slip in unobserved. If this had been Peckham or Putney, crowds would have been round the place all day and half the night. But in Limehouse, never a soul comes near the scene of a murder. Curious, isn't it?"

"Asiatic," Potter murmured. "What is there to see? After all, the Asiatic is very logical."

"There was some sort of disturbance all through Chinatown for a time," Sowerby went on. "The death of this man Chang evidently had a disorganizing effect of some sort."

Suzee Che Lo broke her long silence.

"Yes," she said, "it has stopped them gambling for a while, and the Chinaman who cannot gamble stifles."

Inspector Sowerby stared at her curiously, and might perhaps have asked her to explain her words, but, at this moment, Cosmo Potter signalled to Burton to stop.

The car drew up at the corner of a narrow street. They walked on through the darkness, presently coming to those three iron pillars which marked the end of the lane bounding the back of the house.

"Go on in," said Sowerby. "I understand you have keys of the doors, and I will slip round to the front and see the man on duty. Leave the doors open and I will join you. Don't do anything until I come."

He retired, and Suzee Che Lo, with the key which she carried, opened the door in the wall. The three entered upon that derelict patch of ground which once had been a garden. Now they crossed to the door giving access to the stairway upon which, according to Cosmo Potter's theory, poor Simmons had met his death. It had been roughly repaired and locked, but Suzee unlocked it; and:

"You have brought your torch, Hope?" said Potter.

In reply, came a beam of white light.

The three mounted the uncarpeted stair to the door at the top and shot the bolt back. Suzee Che Lo pressed a switch immediately inside and set close beside the safe, illuminating the strange room.

"Does it matter," she said, turning to Potter, "the light?"

"I don't think so," he replied, the tone of his voice betraying the excitement which possessed him.

Bernard Hope stood staring about the queer place in bewilderment; and Potter also began to look about him; when:

"Good God!" he cried, and started back—pointing—

The safe was open, and all sorts of documents lay scattered on the floor!

No one spoke for several moments, all staring at this unforeseen spectacle. The room otherwise presented a model of neatness, everything being in place. Then, Bernard Hope, staring at an ash tray upon the writing desk, pointed, silently, indicating what lay there.

Cosmo Potter glanced down at the tray, bent lower, and stared, finally, long and hard. Then, looking up:

"A piece of chewing gum," he said. "Kerry has been here! But why?" His bewildered gaze returned again to the open safe. "Why this?"

"If the money was left under seal," Bernard Hope began in a curiously hushed voice, "a strange proceeding in the circumstances, I think—is it not possible that someone acting upon the information broadcasted this morning, and evading the one man on duty at the front of the house, gained access to this room in some way? The prize is big enough to justify big risks."

"No!" Suzee Che Lo whispered, "it is not that. At least"—her expression was enigmatical—"it is, perhaps, that, but not quite as you mean. Please, be quite still and listen."

The two men stared at her as she raised one ivory hand, enjoining them to silence.

They obeyed her, and the stillness in the closed room, where yet a faint perfume of the Orient prevailed, became complete and extraordinary. Suddenly:

"I seem to hear a sound like distant shouting!" said Hope in a hushed voice.

"It is so!" Suzee nodded. "We cannot wait for Inspector Sowerby. It may be ..."

She glanced at the open safe. Then, turning to Cosmo Potter:

"Do you carry arms?"

"Yes," said he, "I have a revolver in my pocket."

"Very well. Make sure you are ready."

Suzee crossed to the safe, manipulated the lock combination in some way, moving the heavy door slightly. Then, as she pushed, the entire safe, together with the section of wall in which it was set, swung inward, revealing a low doorway through which a light shone!

At the moment this phenomenon occurred. Inspector Sowerby might be heard mounting the stairs; and whilst the two men, transfixed with astonishment, stood one on either side of the woman, looking through the opening, Sowerby entered the room.

"Hello!" he cried, "what the devil's this?"

"Hello!" echoed a voice from within. "In at the death, Sowerby!"

Suzee Che Lo shrank back; but:

"Superintendent Kerry!" cried Potter.

Stooping, he passed through the doorway, followed by Hope, Sowerby close at the latter's heels.

A scene presented itself which none of those who saw it were ever likely to forget.

They stood in a small square room, the ceiling very high. It contained a number of curious objects, including a table upon which were stacks of *Pak-a-pu* papers. It was lighted by a hanging lamp, and another lamp was on the table. Above this table was a complicated-looking keyboard, and immediately beneath it a row of small, black, round funnels, not unlike telephone mouthpieces.

The whole place was in the utmost disorder—and in a chair facing the doorway through which they had entered sat Superintendent Kerry!

For the first time in Cosmo Potter's long experience of him, Red Kerry was unshaven, untidy, and very palpably almost exhausted. The light of his fierce eyes, however, was undimmed, and, fixing them upon Sowerby:

"If you are going to tell me that Mr. Cosmo Potter led you here," he said, some of the old snap returning to his voice, "I shall throw something, although I am nearly done."

"No, Superintendent," said Sowerby warmly; "I got the information myself."

But, even as he spoke, his glance had strayed to another corner of the room, in the direction of which Hope and Potter were both staring. Now, stooping her graceful head as she entered, Suzee Che Lo came in, and instantly, as if by instinct, her inscrutable dark eyes turned in the same direction.

One sibilant word she uttered and stood, statuesque, looking at that which lay there.

It was a man, his wrists handcuffed behind him, lying on his right side, so that his features were concealed. The slender yellow hands, however, betrayed the Asiatic, as did the glossy black hair. He was breathing regularly as if asleep.

"It's Satsu Kuhna!" said Cosmo Potter, almost in a whisper.

"It is!" rapped Kerry.

He stood up, swayed, clutched the chair, and sat down again.

"Whew!" he exclaimed, "how my head swims."

"What's the matter, Superintendent?" said Sowerby, springing forward anxiously. "You look quite pale."

"Pale!" Kerry raised a small muscular hand wearily to his head. "Do you realize that I've been playing spider in the middle of this web for just upon twenty-four hours!"

"What!" Potter cried. "By Gad, I see it all, Superintendent! I congratulate you. The paragraph in the paper was merely to bait the trap?"

"Sure." Kerry nodded wearily. "I found the way into this place yesterday evening."

And as he spoke he appeared for the first time to notice the curious glances which all were casting at the man in the corner; and:

"Don't worry," he said, with all his customary savagery; "you won't wake the baby. But I should be indebted if someone would get me a brandy-and- soda, or, failing that, a glass of water."

"I'm sorry," said Sowerby, starting for the low doorway. "I don't know about the brandy, but I noticed several bottles of whisky in a room downstairs, when I was examining the place."

"I don't doubt it," Kerry murmured, lying back and closing his eyes.

As Sowerby went out, he continued to speak:

"It's none of your business," he went on, "and I shouldn't tell you a word of this, but I owe one of you a debt of gratitude for saving my life."

"Saving your life!" Hope exclaimed. "Whatever do you mean, Superintendent?"

"I mean that for a bunch of smarts who've been doubling on me all the time," declared Kerry, his eyes flicking widely open again, "you have made some amends at the finish. Your idea of helping the Law is not *my* idea. But we'll say no more about it. I found this place yesterday evening, as I was saying. When I had given certain instructions, I came into it to examine it thoroughly. It's a sort of observation room."

He moved one hand wearily.

"You can hear what goes on all over the house. That accounts for the man who was concealed here on the night of the murder picking up so much useful information. Also, from that switchboard you can control all the lights. I don't know what the object is of this arrangement. The door behind the safe is the cleverest thing of its kind I have ever seen. When I get my strength back, I am going to shake hands with myself for finding it out. The leather thing from Burma Chang's neck was lying here on the table, with the chain, complete. I know now that it was for whatever had been inside that the murder was committed. It was not for the money in the safe, as I had thought previously.

"There's an ash tray, there, too. You can see it if you look. And I know now how Burma Chang died."

"How?" said Cosmo Potter eagerly.

And Suzee Che Lo, her gaze fixed upon Satsu Kuhna, sank down upon a small chair near the table, uttering a long sigh.

"Poison, in a cigarette," Kerry returned. "He smoked cigarettes with a cardboard end filled with cotton wool. While he was out of the room— and every movement of any one in it can be traced from here—this cotton wool was dipped into a little tube. Even the tube had been left behind by the murderer in his flight. The cotton wool was then replaced. It was enough for it to touch his tongue, it seems. Ah! thank Heaven!"

He broke off as Sowerby entered carrying a well-filled tumbler. Kerry drank eagerly but sparingly; then:

"There's another door on that side of the room," he said, "which opens on to the staircase. I don't know how to open it, but the murderer did. He opened it suddenly, as Simmons stood outside— sandbagged him— there's quite an arsenal of weapons in this place, as you can see, if you look around—and pulled him through into this room. Then wearing his hat and raincoat, he passed the man at the foot of the stairs and also the man at the garden gate."

"But," Hope began, "Simmons's body—"

Kerry stood up, and this time remained standing, although holding the back of the chair.

"Somewhere under this house," he explained, "a disused drain or sewer runs, which seems to be filled at high tide. There's a trap on the other side of the table. If you lift it you can look down a sort of deep well. I don't know where it empties, but that is the way poor Simmons went. I should be prepared to take oath a good many others have gone the same way.

"Now, I suppose you wonder what I have been doing here for twenty-four hours. Well, I'll tell you. I found my way in, and, like a fool, closed the door. I spent the next five or six hours trying to find how to open it again! I failed—nor could I open the one communicating with the stairway."

Suzee Che Lo stood up.

"It is easy," she said, and, crossing, swung the safe back into place.

"Stop her!" cried Kerry, springing forward; but:

"All right," she spoke over her shoulder. "Watch."

She moved to the keyboard and pressed three buttons, counting as she did so: "One—two—three."

Silently, the door swung open again! Then:

"Look again," she said.

She pressed two other buttons, counting: "One—two."

A door low down in the wall to the right opened, lid fashion, silently, as upon well-oiled mechanism, affording a glimpse of the staircase by which they had entered.

"I see," said Kerry, some of his habitual colour returning to his cheeks, as he regarded her appreciatively. "You would be a big asset to the Criminal Investigation Department, miss."

"This is Madame Suzee Che Lo, Superintendent," said Cosmo Potter, "and you are not far out, for she is, if I mistake not, a representative, and a very talented one, of some similar institution in China. We owe much to her."

Suzee Che Lo turned to him.

"And I owe much to you," she said gracefully.

She met the fierce gaze of Superintendent Kerry; and, slightly indicating the form of Satsu Kuhna:

"When did he come?" she asked.

"He came at about eight o'clock to-night," was the reply. "Failing the big game, whatever that was, he determined to rifle the safe, I suppose. At any rate, he came, and I was waiting for him with a sandbag, as once he waited for Simmons. I made a mistake, though. He came through the other door and closed it behind him!

"It was only a chance that he would come in here at all, but I regarded it as my last hope of escaping alive. We had something of a rough-house for five or ten minutes, but I got him quiet at last. In the struggle, you can see, we did some smashing."

He paused, finished the drink which Sowerby had brought him, and then went on:

"Very like poetic justice. His fist came down on a glass tube which lay upon that table—I have mentioned it before. It wasn't a very bad wound, but, the moment I had him secured, I learned something and knew what had happened. I won't turn him over. He's not pretty to see."

"*Lu-chu-see!*" Suzee Che Lo muttered. "*Lu-chu-see!*"

"Very likely," said Kerry, staring at her curiously. "But it's the same as that which killed Burma Chang."

He nodded in the direction of the corner. "He's been dead for two hours, I should think, but he's still breathing. It isn't pleasant," he added, "to be locked in a room which promises to be your own tomb with a dead man who breathes. I shall be glad to step outside. There are a number of formalities to be dealt with and details to be cleared up."

Dawn was not far off when Cosmo Potter returned at last to his chambers. He found a small parcel awaiting him. Opening it, he stared amazedly. It was the powder box which had contained the Lotus!

Now it contained a card and jade earring. Upon the card was written:

One day you may revisit China. You have friends there.

THE END

Sax Rohmer Bibliography
(1983-1959)

Pause! (1910) [essays, monologues & dramatic sketches, published anonymously]

Little Tich (1911) [autobiography of the Music Hall entertainer ghost-written by Ward]

The Sins of Severac Bablon (1914; stories)

The Romance of Sorcery (1914; nonfiction study of the occult)

The Exploits of Captain O'Hagan (1916; stories)

Brood of the Witch Queen (1918)

Tales of Secret Egypt (1918; stories)

The Orchard of Tears (1918)

The Quest of the Sacred Slipper (1919)

The Dream Detective (1920; Moris Klaw stories)

The Green Eyes of Bâst (1920)

The Haunting of Low Fennel (1920; stories)

Tales of Chinatown (1922; stories)

Grey Face (1924)

Moon of Madness (1927)

She Who Sleeps (1928)

The Emperor of America (1929)

Yu'an Hee See Laughs (1932)

Tales of East and West (1932; stories)

The Bat Flies Low (1935)

White Velvet (1936)

Salute to Bazarada (1939)

Egyptian Nights (1944; US Title: Bimbashi-Baruk of Egypt; stories)

Hangover House (1949)

Wulfheim (1950; originally credited to Michael Furey, later printings listed as by Sax Rohmer)

The Moon is Red (1954)

The Secret of Holm Peel and Other Strange Stories (1970)

The Green Spider and Other Forgotten Tales of Mystery & Suspense (2011)

The Leopard Couch and Other Stories of the Fantastic & Supernatural (2012)

The Complete Cases of the Crime Magnet (2012; stories)

Fu Manchu series

The Mystery of Dr. Fu-Manchu (1913; US Title: The Insidious Dr. Fu-Manchu)

The Devil Doctor (1916: US Title: The Return of Dr. Fu-Manchu)

The Si-Fan Mysteries (1917; US Title: The Hand of Fu Manchu)

The Daughter of Fu Manchu (1931)

The Mask of Fu Manchu (1932)

The Bride of Fu Manchu (1933; original US Title: Fu Manchu's Bride)

The Trail of Fu Manchu (1934)

President Fu Manchu (1936)

The Drums of Fu Manchu (1939)

The Island of Fu Manchu (1941)

The Shadow of Fu Manchu (1948)

Re-enter: Fu Manchu (1957; UK Title: Re-Enter: Dr. Fu Manchu)

Emperor Fu Manchu (1959)

The Wrath of Fu Manchu and Other Stories (UK: 1973; US: 1976; 12 stories including four previously uncollected Fu Manchu stories)

Gaston Max series

The Yellow Claw (1915)

The Golden Scorpion (1919)

The Day the World Ended (1930)

Myself and Gaston Max (a series of six BBC radio plays, 1942)

Seven Sins (1943)

"Red" Kerry series
Dope (1919)
Yellow Shadows (1925)

Paul Harley series
Bat-Wing (1921)
Fire Tongue (1921)
The Voice of Kali: The Early Paul
    Harley Mysteries (2013)

Sumuru series
The Sins of Sumuru (1950; US Title:
    Nude in Mink)
The Slaves of Sumuru (1951; US
    Title: Sumuru)
Virgin in Flames (1952; US Title:
    The Fire Goddess)
Sand and Satin (1954; US Title:
    Return of Sumuru)
Sinister Madonna (1956)

Related Works:

Bianca in Black by Elizabeth Sax
    Rohmer (1958; Rohmer's wife)
Master of Villainy: A Biography of
    Sax Rohmer by Cay Van Ash and
    Elizabeth Sax Rohmer, edited by
    Robert E. Briney (1972)
Ten Years Beyond Baker Street:
    Sherlock Holmes Matches Wits
    with the Diabolical Dr. Fu Manchu
    by Cay Van Ash (1984)
The Fires of Fu Manchu by Cay Van
    Ash (1987)
The Terror of Fu Manchu by William
    Patrick Maynard (2009)
The Destiny of Fu Manchu by
    William Patrick Maynard (2012)
The Triumph of Fu Manchu by
    William Patrick Maynard (2015;
    unpublished)

More exotic tales of mystery and suspense by

SAX ROHMER

"...thrillers, supernatural tales, borderline science fiction, occult novels, and crime stories, most of them exhibiting the same atmosphere of strangeness and menace and the same inventiveness of exotic detail that characterize the best of the Fu Manchu stories."—Robert E. Briney

Bat Wing / Fire-Tongue $15.95
"The nearest approach to the pure detective-story that Sax ever made."
—Cay Van Ash & Elizabeth Sax Rohmer, *Master of Villainy*

The Yellow Claw / The Golden Scorpion $15.95
"... sets up an intriguing mystery that titillates the reader with its strong hints of sordid drug and sex scandals among the upper class..."—William Patrick Maynard

Brood of the Witch Queen / The Quest of the Sacred Slipper $15.95
"...fast-paced, clever, ingeniously contrived and thoroughly enjoyable... with vampires, black magic and occult powers that have lain dormant since the days of Ancient Egypt."—*Vintage Pop Fictions*

Grey Face / Green Eyes of Bâst $15.95
"Sax Rohmer has written a dozen thrilling books, but none of them of greater power or interest than this one."—*The Boston Globe*

The Haunting of Low Fennel / Tales of Secret Egypt $17.95
"...a nice collection of shorts which should entertain those who appreciate old style mysteries based in the post WWI landscape of rural England."—Stuart Dean

She Who Sleeps / Moon of Madness $17.95
"Overall, this sits up there ... as one of the best Rohmers I've read thus far and well worth picking up. Recommended!"—*Side Real Press*

"Although it was Dr. Fu-Manchu who made Rohmer's reputation
it was his entire output that cemented his fame around the world,
and it has barely dimmed over a century later."—Mike Ashley

Available in trade paperback from:
Stark House Press   1315 H Street, Eureka, CA 95501
Starkhousepress.com